PRAISE FOR MINDY KLASKY

"Klasky continues her adorable As You Wish series with this nearly cinematic romantic comedy.... With broadly comic characters, even pacing, and a charming romance, this cozy evening's read will leave readers smiling." – Publishers Weekly

"A lot of books have been written about being a single girl in the big city, but none like this. Klasky provides fun and entertainment while offering a thought-provoking view of relationships. A thinking woman's romance, this one should not be missed!" – RT Book Review

Wish Upon a Star

Book Three of the As You Wish Series

Mindy Klasky

Book View Café
Cedar Crest, New Mexico

Previously published as *To Wish or Not to Wish.*

Book View Café
P.O. Box 1624
Cedar Crest, NM 87008-1624

Book Layout ©2013 BookDesignTemplates.com
Cover by Reece Notley

Ordering Information:
Quantity sales. Special discounts are available on quantity purchases by corporations, associations, and others. For details, contact the "Special Sales Department" at the address above.

Wish Upon a Star/Mindy Klasky – 1st ed.
ISBN 978-1-61138-340-9

Wish Upon a Star

Also By Mindy Klasky

The Jane Madison Series

Girl's Guide to Witchcraft

Sorcery and the Single Girl

Magic and the Modern Girl

The Jane Madison Academy Series

Single Witch's Survival Guide

The As You Wish Series

Act One, Wish One

Wishing in the Wings

Capitol Magic
Fright Court

The Glasswrights Series

The Glasswrights' Apprentice

The Glasswrights' Progress

The Glasswrights' Journeyman

The Glasswrights' Test

The Glasswrights' Master

Season of Sacrifice

The Daddy Dance
The Mogul's Maybe Marriage

To Mark, who discovered Garden Variety Café with me on our honeymoon

Chapter 1

THEY SAY THAT bad things come in threes.

One.

Like every good aspiring actress, I arrived early for my four o'clock audition. I spent the time in the hallway with all the other hopefuls, running through my monologue. Again. For the thousandth time. What was I worried about? I knew my lines cold.

Precisely ten minutes before my time slot, the audition monitor appeared with his clipboard. "Erin Hollister!" he barked, squinting at his computer printout and refusing to look any of us aspiring stars in the eye. I leaped forward with a professional smile, handing him a pristine folder that contained my head shot and résumé. He took it without a word and disappeared into the sanctified privacy of the audition room.

I bowed my head and shook out my hands, trying to relieve the tension that had crept across my shoulders and down my arms. I could do this. I could read for a role in David Mamet's newest Broadway play. I could impress the casting director with my raw power, my vigorous style, my willingness to grapple with thorny texts and thornier social messages.

The door to the audition room opened, and the monitor barked out my name again. Quickly, before he could even notice, I crossed the fingers of both hands and muttered, "Please, just this once." I wasn't quite certain who or what I muttered to, but I'd had the habit of wishing, ever since I was a little girl.

The silly ritual centered me, settled me into place. I pasted a professional smile on my lips before I said, "Thank you," to the monitor. I preceded him into the space, knowing enough not to offer my hand. If he wanted to shake hands, he'd extend his first.

Inside the room, three people sat on chairs, gazing at me with bored expressions. I forced myself to smile as I took two precise steps forward. I knew this audition room well; I'd read for roles here at least a half dozen times before. A half dozen unsuccessful times before.

I hated this room. It was tiny, apparently carved out of the much larger dance studio next door, a sort of architectural afterthought. The wall to my right was covered with mirrors, and a ballet barre bisected my reflected waist. In the past, I'd described this room as the "Check Your Teeth" audition venue—every single person in those chairs would instantly be able to spot a stray fleck of spinach across the cramped space. Or catch a whiff of garlic, for that matter.

I threw back my shoulders. I'd fortified myself with a Wint-O-Green Life Saver in the hallway, for I was wise in the way of auditions. Knowing that I had a total of three minutes to impress the watching trio, I said, "My name is Erin Hollister, and my monologue is from *The End of My So-Called Affair* by Jeanine Thompson

Walker." I took a deep breath, trying to ignore my own reflected image as it loomed in my peripheral vision. I began: "'I can't take it anymore!'"

The casting director waved her hand dismissively. "That's enough. Thanks for coming in."

Thanks for coming in?

Thanks for nothing.

"Thanks for coming in" was the universal kiss of audition death. The supposed politeness meant that they'd sized me up from my head shot, already made a decision before I even walked through the door. I wasn't the "type" they were looking for. There was no room in their show for straight blond hair, for blue eyes, for a fresh, Middle America–wholesome actress. I wasn't worth three minutes of their time.

"Thank you," I said, pasting an automatic smile across my lips. New York might be the largest city in America, but it was still too small to alienate a single casting professional. I didn't wait for them to nod, or to shrug, or to grimace, or to do whatever they would do to prove that they were Much Too Busy to pay further attention to me.

Two. (Remember those bad things, coming in threes?)

I tugged on my light jacket—just right for late May in New York City—as I ducked out of the Equity Audition Center, glancing dispiritedly at my watch. I was late for my Survival Job, the employment that gave me money for food, shelter and general life expenses while I waited for my big break onstage. Or my medium-size break. Or even a little one—who was I to complain?

Concerned Caterers had been a godsend for the three years I'd been trying to break into New York theater. I could schedule my catering gigs around auditions; I would even be able to remove myself from the schedule for a few weeks if I ever landed a real role.

When I landed a real role, I remonstrated with myself firmly.

I slipped into my pavement-eating New York stride, doing my best to ignore a blossoming headache as I dug my cell phone out of my cavernous tote bag. I punched a single button and waited for Sam to pick up.

Ring. Ring. I was going to get his voice mail. Ring.

"Hey, babe," he said, just as I was preparing to leave my sad little message. He sounded rushed.

"Hey."

I heard him suck air between his teeth. He'd obviously parsed my tone. That was the advantage of dating a guy for two years, living with him for nearly ten months. "I'm sorry," he said. "I know how much you wanted that role."

"Yeah—" I said, but he interrupted.

"Can I put you on hold? Opposing counsel's on the other line. I think we're going to settle the Lindstrom case today."

"Go," I said. "I'll see you tonight." He clicked off without saying goodbye, obviously eager not to let his opponent's feet grow cold.

I shoved my phone back into my bag, trying not to take the dismissal personally. Sam had been working on the Lindstrom case forever. Settling that monstrous litigation was a big deal, especially for a guy who was up for partner at the end of the year.

It wasn't like I had tons of time to talk, anyway. I was a block away from the Van Bleeker Mansion, where the Knickerbocker Alliance was holding its annual awards dinner. I glanced at my watch again. Half an hour late. I'd hoped for an earlier audition slot but had taken the only time open for a nonunion actress.

Determined to do a perfect job to make up for my tardiness, I bounded up the mansion steps. With the experience of a trained caterer, I made my way to the service area of the gigantic home. Sure enough, a white-draped card table crouched in the hall outside the kitchen. A swag of fabric was clipped to its front, proudly proclaiming: Concerned Caterers—Your Happiness Is Our Concern. A clipboard was centered precisely on the white square of cloth.

Jack Skellar was managing the event. Jack Skellar, who had disliked me since he joined Concerned as a supervisor, six months before. Jack Skellar, who stood in the kitchen doorway, glaring at his watch. Jack Skellar, whose main purpose in life seemed to be finding catering jobs for every single one of his dozens of cousins. He had already fired at least three friends of mine for minor violations of Concerned's policies, replacing each hardworking actor with a rat-faced relative who was immune from his nit-picking supervision.

Jack pointed at the clipboard and enunciated, "Hol-lis-ter."

Great. He'd be gunning for me all night long.

"I am so sorry," I said, loading all of my acting skill into my apology. "I had an audition—"

"Yeah, yeah," he said. "Hurry up, Hollister. Grab your shirt and get into the dining room—they're still arranging flowers for the centerpieces."

As I scrawled my name on the clipboard, along with the shamed admission of my late check-in time, Jack tugged a cardboard box from beneath the white tablecloth. Inside was a tangle of chartreuse and orange, a color combination so atrocious that my eyes started to cross.

"You have got to be kidding," I said.

Concerned Caterers occupied the elite top tier of Manhattan catering. One of the gimmicks that set us apart from the riffraff was a unique "costume" created for each engagement. I got to keep my costume at the end of every gig—one of the so-called perks of working for the very best.

Alas, Concerned's idea of a costume was the cheapest grade of T-shirt that money could buy. The company scooped them up by the gross (and I *do* mean gross!), dyeing them for each individual job. In theory, the colors matched something about the client, bringing together a variety of unique qualities into a single tasteful statement.

In practice...

Jack plucked one shirt out of the tangle, shaking out wrinkles with a violent flick of his wrists. Shockingly, the fluorescent green and orange wasn't the worst thing about the shirt. A glittery red lion was stamped across the front of the tee, its claws raised up like it belonged on some fancy coat of arms.

My not-so-beloved employer had really outdone itself this time.

"Are you serious?" I asked.

"The chartreuse is from jenever." I must have looked as confused as I felt, because Jack sighed in exasperation. *"Jenever,"* he repeated. "Dutch gin. There's some brand that's packaged with a chartreuse label. We're serving it in the parlor for cocktail hour."

"And orange?" I studied the horrific garment as if it

might somehow come to life.

"William, Prince of." He glared at me as I pondered my scant knowledge of Dutch history. "And before you ask, the lion is part of the Knickerbocker Alliance coat of arms. Let's go, Hollister. We haven't got all night!" Jack thrust the hideous shirt into my unwilling hands.

With a twist of nausea, I saw the size label. Small. I'd been with Concerned for long enough to know that the T-shirt wholesaler gave us deep discounts on size small. And their smalls were *really* small. All of the comfortable shirts designed to fit normal human beings with breasts had been snatched up by my goody-two-shoes coworkers who had arrived early. Or at least on time. Or, to be more accurate, not a full half hour late.

I sighed and took the hint from Jack's imperious finger, heading down the hallway toward the staff restroom. As expected, the shirt was tight enough that my rather ordinary...assets looked like some porn star's inflated balloons. Worse, the sleeves cut into my armpits. I stretched my arms above my head, trying to loosen the damn thing, even a little. My back protested the movement with a sharp twinge that settled into a dull ache, making me wonder if I was coming down with something.

No time for speculation, though. I hurried out to the dining room.

The curious might ask, What flowers go with chartreuse and orange? The answer was...fake ones. Lots and lots of fake, silk chrysanthemums, dyed to match Concerned Catering's unholy version of the Knickerbocker Alliance coat of arms.

Within an hour, the banquet hall was decked out completely. Fake flowers, golden charger plates at every seat (adding to the visual, um, flair), white serving plates, wine glasses, water glasses, an entire battalion of silverware... Before I could admire our collective handiwork, or at least finish blinking away stars from the visual clutter, Jack pounced.

"Coatroom, Hollister," he commanded.

I gritted my teeth as I obeyed. I hated coatroom duty. Far away from the camaraderie of the kitchen crew, the coatroom was lonely. And boring. And cold. Every time the door to the street opened, a blast of unseasonably chilly air gusted across the marble foyer. My thin tie-dyed tee didn't provide a whole lot of protection.

I couldn't believe the number of women who wore fur coats into the mansion. Fur! In May! I wasn't a big fan of wearing dead animals at any time, but the coats seemed completely over the top for a spring night, no matter how unusual the low temperatures. Oh, well. This would likely be the last cold snap of the year for mink owners to impress their friends, at least before the fall show-off season began.

After a long pause in arrivals, when I thought I might be through with my lonely coatroom mission, four women swept through the mahogany door at the same time. They gushed to greet one another with air kisses and exclamations of undying friendship. Or undying gossip. Whatever.

Two wore severe black gowns, as if they were attending a formal funeral. One sported cascades of pearls spilled across far too much décolletage. The fourth was the belle of this fashion-disaster ball. She had obviously received the William Prince Of memo—she wore a shocking orange gown, a shimmering garment that cascaded from her ample bosom to her dyed-to-match slippered toes. As if she feared being overlooked, she had settled a diamond-studded tiara on top of her gray-streaked updo.

Pearl Woman thrust her mink into my hands at the same time that Orange Tiara loaded me down with a silver fox. The coats weighed more than I did. The furs slipped against each other, and I struggled to balance both of them, but the fox slithered down to the ground.

Orange Tiara shrieked as if I'd stabbed her.

Before I could stammer out an apology, Jack glided across the foyer. I realized that he must have been watching me from the hallway, waiting for me to screw up so that yet another Skellar relative could become a proud Concerned Catering employee.

"I am terribly sorry, madam," Jack murmured, scooping up the offended coat in one arm as he offered the enraged matron support with the other. "That clumsy girl should have paid more attention. Please, accept my apologies and send the cleaning bill to Concerned Caterers." He produced a business card out of a breast pocket, all the while muttering more oily platitudes. I stared at the spotless floor in front of me, furious with myself for initiating the debacle, but defensively positive that the fur had not been the slightest bit damaged.

As Orange Tiara finally sailed into the parlor, Jack turned to me and hissed, "Watch it, Hollister."

I swallowed my frustration and turned back to wait for more latecomers. Once Jack was gone, I tried to distract myself from the freezing foyer temperatures by speculating on the menu.

It would be something Dutch, I was sure, in honor of New Amsterdam and the original Knickerbockers.

Maybe the appetizer was rich Gouda cheese, liberated from its red wax wrapper and melted over crusty bread. I wasn't usually a big fan of cheese, but the thought of that creamy goodness, toasty hot from the oven... *That* was comfort food. That could make anyone forget a lousy audition, forget a freezing coatroom. I swallowed hard, suddenly ravenous.

I waited the requisite half hour after the last arrivals, making sure that no other Alliance matrons would need my coat-slinging services. Then, without giving Jack a chance to scold me, I scurried back to the kitchen to help with whatever food remained to be served.

A recycling bin near the door was filled with chartreuse-labeled bottles. Sure enough, that was the jenever. And it looked like the Alliance had made an admirable dent in New York City's supply of the stuff. With that many empties, a healthy number of our society matrons must be totally smashed.

And they hadn't had any melted Gouda appetizers to slow their absorption of alcohol. Apparently, the chef had whipped up some authentic Amsterdam treat. I'm sure it had a fancy Dutch name, but the translation was "fried herring on a stick." Now it was *cold* fried herring on a stick, returned on almost every diner's plate. So, the appetizer hadn't been a grand success.

Jack was in an even worse mood than before. I watched him berate two of his cousins, telling them that they obviously hadn't done their jobs, selling the hors d'oeuvres as delectable Dutch treats. If even Skellar cousins were bearing the brunt of Jack's wrath, the rest of the night was going to be a sheer nightmare.

Eager to look busy, I lifted one of the silver warmers and stared at the plate beneath. Grilled asparagus. Innocent enough. Tiny roasted potatoes carved into roses. They were actually pretty. And stew.

Pungent, gloppy, lumpy stew.

A twist of nausea swirled through my belly and I slammed the warmer lid back onto the plate. As a Skellar cousin started toward the door with a full tray, I asked, "What is that stuff?"

Her pale face looked ghastly against her chartreuse-and-orange shirt. *"Kippenlevertjes met abrikozen."*

I didn't speak Dutch, but I thought I recognized that last word. "Apricots?"

She frowned and nodded. "With chicken livers."

Our Customers' Happiness Was Our Concern? Really? Concerned Caterers might want to consider a new slogan, if it was going to continue in the Dutch line of business.

Before I could say anything, the pastry chef ordered me over to his station. Following instructions, I arranged twelve parfait glasses on a serving tray. With Jack paying eagle-eyed attention from his perch by the double doors, I composed my dozen desserts, following directions from the harried chef. Sorry bites of fruit were spooned out of a hotel tray, rescued from the sweet wine where they'd been allowed to macerate for far too long. Three scoops of ice cream followed—two vanilla, one strawberry. Alas, the frozen confection, um, wasn't. The ice cream was half-melted, so that it settled into a streaky mess at the bottom of each parfait glass. The pastry chef himself topped each deflated little mound with strawberry sauce, the unfortunate crimson streaks looking like a roadmap straight to the emergency room.

"Um, what is this called?" I finally dared to ask.

"Knickerbocker Glory," he growled. "No seconds."

I didn't think that was going to be a problem.

"Great," I said, faking a smile so perfectly that I should have received an instant Tony Award on the spot. Unfortunately, when I had laid out the parfait glasses on my tray, I'd assumed that I would have the full range of motion in my lifting arm. I hadn't counted on my tiny T-shirt cutting off the blood flow at my shoulder. I longed to invent a new catering tray, some type of molded plastic that would fit my shoulder, that would make it impossible for me to spill catered food treasures.

Gritting my teeth and compensating with the ordinary tools of my trade, I barely made it past Jack without disaster. My job wasn't made any easier by the defeated stream of returning caterers, bringing back dozens of untouched plates of *kippenlevertjes.* A few of the *abrikozen* had been pushed around by adventurous diners' forks, but the entrée looked to be a near-complete failure.

At least I carried my desserts across the crowded dining room without incident. I placed the first Glory on the plate of the oldest woman at my table. And the second. And the third. It was my dumb luck that the fourth Glory went to the drunkest woman in the bunch. Orange Tiara.

She may have gotten a late start at the party, but she'd clearly made up for lost time, downing more than her share of the chartreuse jenever. Now, she was declaiming eloquently about her family lineage, some ancient relative, her great-(emphasis with one hand), great-(emphasis with a forearm), great-(emphasis with a lurching torso), great-(emphasis with a nod of her head and a flying diamond tiara)—

And a cascading tray of melted Knickerbocker Glories.

Eight of them. Crashing down on two sedate black formal gowns, one décolletage covered with pearls and a tiaraless orange ensemble.

The dress was definitely not made better by a cascade of melted pink-and-white ice cream.

"To the kitchen, Hollister!" Jack shouted, and I realized that he'd followed me into the dining room. He fluttered around the table, doing his best to extinguish the cries of surprise and outrage. He flung business cards left and right, promised dry cleaning, door-to-door transportation for salvaged clothes, everything short of his nonexistent firstborn child.

Including punishment. Of me.

With one officious glare, he ordered me back to the kitchen to await my fate. I staggered through the doors and huddled miserably in the corner, trying to stay out of the way of the rest of the Skellar family.

Jack didn't keep me in suspense for long. "You're fired!" he snapped, immediately commanding the attention of every person in the bustling room. I would never have believed that a working kitchen could become so quiet, so quickly.

"But—"

"No 'buts'! You showed up late, you ruined a fur coat, you dumped an entire tray of desserts! Are you drunk?"

"No, I—"

"Don't make any excuses to me!"

"But she—"

"Out! Now! Before you destroy anything else!"

"What—"

He whipped a cell phone out of his pocket, sending a flock of business cards flying around the room. "Do I have to call the police to get you out of here?"

He was totally serious.

I looked around the kitchen. Two dozen eyes were locked on me, eyes that shimmered with shock (a couple of the women who had started about the same time I had), with horror (a couple of the guys, who realized that they might just be next in line for Jack's unfair attention), with just a hint of glee at the scandal they were witnessing (the entire horde of Skellar cousins, who were probably already planning a family reunion to welcome whoever was going to take my place.)

My cheeks flamed red, certainly brighter than the glittering lion stretched across my chest. I turned on my heel and fled the kitchen, scarcely taking time to snatch up my bedraggled, fortunately furless coat and my beaten-up leather tote.

As my heels slammed down on the frozen sidewalk outside the Van Bleeker, I tried to accept that I had just lost my job. My Survival Job. The job that preserved my dignity, that let me contribute to the rent, to the groceries, to the life I shared with Sam.

I was going to be sick.

Three. (You didn't forget, did you? I've only told two-thirds of my disaster trifecta.)

I fished out my phone and pressed the first number on my speed dial. Amy. My sister. We'd talked at least once a day, every day, ever since she'd phoned me during my freshman year in college with the staggering news that our parents had been killed in a car crash. In the intervening seven years, Amy and I had become more than sisters. We were best friends.

"Hey," she answered halfway through the first ring. "Are you watching this?"

"Watching what?"

"Food Channel. The history of distilled spirits."

"I don't even want to hear that phrase."

Amy grunted, and I could picture her shifting position on her too-deep sectional couch. "What's going on?"

I told her the whole tragic tale, starting with my audition and ending with my rushing up Fifth Avenue, clutching my coat closed over a chartreuse-and-orange T-shirt, trying to decide if I could blow money on taking a cab home to the Upper East Side refuge that I shared with Sam.

Amy made all of the appropriate noises, clicking her tongue in dismay at the casting director, sighing in exasperation at Jack's family-oriented insanity. When I'd finally run down, she said, "Don't worry. Catering is really outside of your silo."

I gritted my teeth. I hated when Amy lapsed into business-school-speak, an all-too-frequent occurrence, since she'd left her job as a bookkeeper for a law firm and started taking management classes at Rutgers. Unaware of my annoyance, she said, "What about your job at the Mercer? Can you take on more hours in the box office there?"

I sighed. The Mercer Project was a theater down in the Village. Despite their small house, they'd gained a reputation for doing some really innovative shows. For the past three months, I had worked two shifts a week in the box office, selling tickets, enforcing the no-refunds-no-exchange policy and dreaming of the day when I'd be cast in one of their productions. "I can try. I work tomorrow afternoon. I'll talk to them then."

"You know that if you need anything, if you need to borrow any money—"

"Thanks," I said, before she could complete the sentence. Like I was going to borrow money from my sister. She was struggling to make her own ends meet, with her husband over in Germany, serving in the army while Amy stayed stateside to finish her business degree. Every spare penny she had went toward child care for my nephew. Speaking of which... "Where's Justin?"

"I sent him to bed early."

"Another bad night?"

Amy sighed. "Only if you count getting into a fist-fight during recess at school. And refusing to eat his dinner. And using the F-word twice, when I told him that he couldn't watch TV." Justin was not handling his father's deployment well.

"Oh, Ame, I'm sorry," I said. Not that there was anything I could do. Not that there was anything anyone could do, short of getting Derek home.

"The worst part—" Amy groaned "—is that I've got cramps from hell tonight!"

Ah, the joys of sisterly communication. I listened to Amy complain about her body's overly sensitive hormonal wiring. She'd always had a worse time than I, every single month. She was the one who got out of gym class on a regular basis, who stayed home with heating pads and Motrin.

Motrin. I wondered if I had any with me. My back still ached, a low, throbbing pain, and my headache had returned with a vengeance.

Amy had complained of backaches and headaches when she'd been pregnant with Justin. She'd said that Tylenol didn't even start to take the edge off of them. She wouldn't take anything stronger, though. Couldn't, out of concern for her baby, and because of her persistent nausea.

My belly twisted, as it had when I'd seen that hideous liver-and-apricot concoction, spread out on the catering plate.

Back pain. Headache. Nausea. And I'd had a craving for those imaginary Gouda appetizers, too.

I'd read *What to Expect When You're Expecting,* memorized every page so that I could help Amy.

Oh. My. God.

Today was May 21. I counted back. Four weeks. Five. Six.

Oh. My. God.

Sure, I was on the pill. But I'd had strep throat a while back, picked up from Justin when I babysat him one night for Amy. Strep throat, treated with antibiotics. Antibiotics that weakened the pill.

Oh. My. God.

"Hello?" Amy was saying, a slight ring of annoyance behind her voice. "Erin? Did you hear me?"

"Yeah," I said. "Look, I am totally exhausted. I'm going to grab a cab and head home." I'm sure I said something else, something appropriate to end the conversation, but I wasn't really paying attention. And I wasn't looking for a cab, either. Instead, I continued walking uptown. I needed the time to think.

What was Sam going to say? We were both always complaining that we didn't have time to live our lives. We had too many dinners delivered, grabbed too many quick meals out, blew through his lawyer salary because neither one of us had time to cook. We constantly complained about not having clean clothes, because we couldn't manage to do laundry in the few spare minutes we scraped together each week. We waded through piles of magazines and snowdrifts of the *Times* because neither of us had time to straighten up the apartment.

I could change all that. I could manage our home life. I could be the perfect corporate wife—cook for us, clean for us—all while raising our child.

Maybe everything *did* happen for a reason. Maybe I'd lost out on the afternoon audition—the Mamet play, and every other show I'd auditioned for in the past year—because I was meant to start down this new path. Maybe I'd pushed my catering boss beyond forbearance for a reason. Maybe it was time to stop being a child, stop being a starry-eyed little girl who thought that she could ever succeed in the impossible world of the theater. Maybe it was time to be a grown-up. Someone practical. A wife.

A mother.

I was a little astonished at how well I was taking this. I mean, it was a shock and all. I never would have asked for such a sudden change, for such a complete transition in my life. But it was real. It was happening. And it made so much *sense*.

Until I tried to figure out how to tell Sam. Maybe I was wrong. Maybe I wasn't actually pregnant. After all, it had only been six weeks. And I *was* on the pill. I should buy a test at the drugstore before I said anything.

Sam greeted me at the door of our first-floor apartment. (Hmm, the first floor would make it easier to get the baby's stroller out to the street.) He nuzzled my neck as he closed the door behind me. I could smell beer on his breath. "You're home early."

I made some noncommittal noise as I let him lead me over to the living room couch. He'd been watching TV, a Yankees game. Two empty beer bottles sat on the coffee table, glinting next to a nearly full one. Sam nodded toward the collection. "Want a beer?"

I shook my head and shrugged out of my coat. When I collapsed into a corner of the couch, Sam lunged toward the television, howling at the blind ump who wouldn't know a high strike if it knocked him on his ass. I waited for the batter to hit into a double play before I asked, "Did the Lindstrom case settle?"

He swore. "No. Bastard backed out at the last second. Said he couldn't recommend settlement to his client without another ten mil to sweeten the pot." He glanced at me, finally noticing the horror of my chartreuse-and-orange too-small T-shirt. He started to say something, but leered instead. "Well, at least Concerned has one thing going for it."

I crossed my arms over my chest. I should tell him that I'd been fired. Tell him that this was the last "costume" I'd ever have to suffer through.

"What?" he asked, either because he realized I was upset, or because the baseball game had finally flickered to a commercial.

"I think I'm pregnant," I said.

Wow. I really thought that I'd decided to wait. To have medical proof, something more than my wigged-out suspicion. Guess not.

He pulled away as if I'd spilled a tray of melted Knickerbocker Glories in his lap. "You're kidding, right?"

I shook my head. "I don't think so. I'm two weeks late."

"What the—" He jumped off the couch, eyeing me as if I had bubonic plague.

"Come on," I said. "It's not contagious."

"What?" His eyes widened. "You think this is funny? Don't you realize I'm up for partner this year? I don't have time for this!"

Time for this? Like I'd just invited him to a party he didn't want to attend? I forced my voice to stay calm. "Of course I realize you're up for partner. But it's okay. I mean, this might all be happening a little sooner than we'd planned, but—"

"A little sooner?" His voice was hoarse, as if I'd punched him in the gut. "How could you have been so irresponsible?"

That lit a fire under me. I snapped, "Last time I checked, it took two people to make a baby."

"Are you sure it's mine?"

"Sam!" I was so shocked I could barely gasp his name. "I can't believe you said that."

His gaze settled on my belly, on the tight stretch of chartreuse and orange. He could still make everything all right. He could still apologize. We could still talk this out. But then he said, "I can't believe it, either. I can't believe any of this."

He turned on his heel and strode out of the room. I heard him scramble in the foyer, grabbing for a jacket. I heard him turn the locks, fumbling them open as if his life depended on it. I heard him slam the door, as if he were fleeing a horde of raging demons.

And then I heard nothing but perfect silence inside

our perfect brownstone apartment on our perfect block of the perfect Upper East Side.

I collapsed onto the couch and started to cry.

Chapter 2

I KNEW I should be grateful. I should be lighting candles in some church, or writing checks to support orphans in a country I'd never heard of, or knitting bandages for lepers, or something. I was lucky. I really was.

I'd seen the real Sam. Now I knew how he truly felt, without any screen, any filter, any contrived social constraints. Sure, I'd startled him with my announcement, and he'd spoken brashly. But that wasn't really what bothered me.

What bothered me was, he didn't come back. He didn't take a walk around the block to cool off, and then come home to discuss the situation, like a man. Instead, he avoided me, ignored me, treated me as if I were some make-believe monster that would just go away if he squinched his eyes shut and counted to one hundred.

He didn't come home.

The following morning, I called in sick to the Mercer, even though I needed the shift. I needed every penny I could scrounge, now that Concerned Caterers was history.

I left a message with Amy, something mindless and falsely cheery, sneaked into her voice mail when I knew she was at class. No reason to drag her into the spectacular mess I'd made out of my life. She had enough on her mind, with Justin's misbehavior, with Derek overseas, with spring semester classes drawing to a close.

I stared at the phone all day on Thursday, all Thursday night, willing Sam to call.

I'd handled things badly. Poor Sam had had a lousy day—he thought he'd settled the Lindstrom case only to find out that the damn thing was still going to trial. He'd had a couple of beers; he was angry about the baseball game. I hadn't thought out my announcement. I should have cushioned the news for him.

Full of remorse, I finally tried to reach him at his office on Friday. His secretary picked up, and clouds of butterflies swarmed in my belly, worse than any audition jitters I'd ever experienced. "One moment please," she said with a formality that terrified me. "Let me see if he's in his office." I caught my breath, ready to apologize to Sam for dropping such momentous news in his lap without warning, ready to ask him to come home, to talk things through. "I'm sorry," the secretary said a minute later, so smoothly that I knew she was lying. "He's stepped away from his desk."

Stepped away. Yeah, right. Just like he'd stepped away on Wednesday night.

I didn't leave a message.

Friday night, I pictured him hanging out with his friends, drinking beer, playing pool. He was probably crashing on someone's couch, reliving his carefree college days, pretending he was still in Alpha Beta Whatever. Could he really be seven years *older* than I was? I got angrier and angrier as I stared at mindless TV. I couldn't bring myself to climb the stairs to our bedroom. Couldn't imagine sleeping in our rumpled king-size bed.

The thing was, I felt like I'd done all this before. Not the "I'm pregnant" stuff—that was a new one for me. But the "I need to get this guy to pay attention to me" stuff. The "why won't he call me, when I desperately want to talk to him" stuff. The "I'll change my life around, do whatever it takes to make this relationship work" stuff.

That's just who I was. Having a boyfriend was important to me—it made me feel, I don't know, centered. Complete. Balanced. I *always* had a boyfriend. Even if he wasn't the sort of guy that Amy approved of, even if he turned out not to be right for me...

The guys in my life had shaped who I was, starting way back in junior high, when I tried out for the school play because I had a crush on the guy who was a shoo-in for the lead. I never would have discovered my love of acting, if it hadn't been for Corey... Corey... I couldn't remember his last name. But I would never forget that adrenaline-charged rush of excitement when he gave me a lanyard to wear all of eighth grade spring. At least, until he ended up with his own crush, on Alicia Gold. *Her* last name I remembered. Corey had asked for his lanyard back so that he could give it to Alicia.

And I remembered Amy smoothing my hair while I sobbed out my frustration. Amy, telling me that no guy was worth being that upset. Amy, who just didn't understand. Who would never understand. Amy, who had probably *never* lost herself in the crazy, dizzy excitement of a new crush. My sister was far too practical for that. She'd married Derek, her high school sweetheart, and I was pretty sure she couldn't even remember what it was like to be head-over-heels crazy about a new guy.

Saturday morning, I woke up on Sam's couch, curled into a tight knot, tangled in a crocheted afghan. At first, I thought the ache in my belly was from my awkward position. I soon realized, though, that I had an old-fashioned case of cramps. Two weeks late, but cramps all the same. Aunt Flo had returned, and she was a bad-tempered bitch. I must have been late because I'd been so stressed about the Mamet audition. Mamet, and my entire nonexistent future as an actress.

After I showered, I dry-swallowed a couple of Motrin, staring at Sam's masculine clutter in the bathroom. Shaving cream, a dirty razor, a toothbrush that should have been replaced months before. I shuffled into the bedroom and saw his dirty clothes piled in a corner—one scruffy mound for the Laundromat and another for the dry cleaner. I tugged on my rattiest sweatshirt, completing my glamorous outfit with bleach-stained sweatpants.

I shuffled into the kitchen and put on water for tea. As I waited for the kettle to shriek, I looked around the room. Dirty dishes were stacked in the sink. A packet of Pop-Tarts was ripped open, the uneaten pastry left to petrify. A banana was well on its way to turning black.

What was I doing here? What had I possibly been thinking when I spun out my June Cleaver/Donna Reed fantasy of becoming a happy housewife, a loving stay-at-home mom? Why had I been so quick to trade in my future acting career?

Embarrassed by the fantasy I'd spun out the very first second I thought that I was pregnant, I took my time pouring boiling water into a mug. I brewed my Irish Breakfast strong enough to strip the paint from our tiny kitchen's walls and forced myself to think about the past few months with Sam.

When was the last time that we'd really talked to each other? We'd become like a pair of toddlers, playing next to each other in some elaborate gameroom. And, like a toddler, when Sam had felt threatened by my announcement, he'd thrown a tantrum. And, like a toddler, he hadn't apologized. Hadn't even made an effort to apologize. Wasn't, I was now pretty sure, ever *going* to apologize.

And that was the guy I'd been ready to base my entire future life on? When had I lost so much faith in myself? When had I decided that my own happiness was worth so little?

I sipped my tea and was shocked to realize that it had gone stone cold. How long had I been sitting here at the counter, replaying Sam's rejection?

Enough.

I headed back to the bedroom and excavated my suitcase and a duffel bag from the back of the closet. I scooped my things out of the tallboy dresser, tossed in my dresses, a couple of skirts, my blouses. Shoes. Socks and underwear. It took me five minutes to collect my stuff from the bathroom, to circle back to the kitchen for my favorite mug.

That was it.

Did I really have so few possessions? I'd been an idiot to give away my college standbys when I moved in with Sam. I thought I'd been so clever to escape from my blocky futon, my chipped dishes and featherweight silverware, my two-seater kitchen table with the permanently splayed legs.

Well, they were long gone now. And I still had to get a roof over my head. I picked up my phone and punched in Amy's number. "Hey," I said, when she answered. "Want some company?"

* * *

Amy was wonderful about everything. She literally greeted me with open arms. Justin whined that I was turning him out of his bedroom, but Justin whined about everything, so I didn't worry too much.

It had taken me over two hours to get to Amy's place. She lived in New Brunswick, in New Jersey. Unable to face the crosstown hike to the bus terminal, I had splurged on a cab to Port Authority. I just missed a bus, so I had to wait an hour, and then I had a solid twenty-minute walk from the stop to Amy's little house.

By the time I wrestled my suitcase and duffel bag up her front steps, I already doubted my decision to seek refuge there. It was so far from the city. So far from my life.

Sure, Concerned Catering and I had parted ways, but I still had my job at the Mercer. And I was going to attend more auditions—I'd made that vow on the bus. Landing a real role was more important to me than ever. The first thing I'd do when I was near a computer was check out the leads on ShowTalk, a local Web site devoted to all things theatrical in New York. That would ground me. It would remind me that I belonged on Broadway, that I could be more than Sam's (ex-)girlfriend, more than a pitiful failure at every single thing I'd tried since graduation.

But for that Saturday night, New Brunswick was perfect.

Everything was simple in Jersey—I could be Amy's little sister, Justin's relatively tolerant aunt. I feasted on Tater Tots, discovering that I was ravenous after two solid days of moping around. It was Super Soldier Saturday, the time each week when Justin completed a scrapbook page for his father, coloring pictures of what he'd done during the preceding seven days. Justin demanded that I draw Soldierman, a flying superhero who swooped in to help out the good guys whenever they needed an extra hand. I tried not to take it personally when he said that my stick figures looked stupid.

After Justin went to bed back in Amy's room, my sister and I worked our way through the better part of a jug of cheap Chablis. I was well past tipsy when I said, "I just can't believe how easy it was to picture my married life with Sam. It should have been perfect. He's a lawyer. He's rich. Settled. I was totally ready to jump into Instant Motherhood."

"Yeah, right," she said.

"What does that mean?"

"You aren't ready to do *anything* responsible."

"That's a lousy thing to say!" I glared at her.

"It's the truth. You always have a boyfriend, and you always shape your life to match his. But you get really lost in guys. You always have." Having shared that profound thought, Amy sat up on the couch, very straight and very proper. That was the first time I realized how drunk she was. How drunk I was. She held her head very still as she enunciated. "You need to make a plan, if you want to change your life."

I splashed wine over the lip of my goblet, refilling my glass. "What sort of plan?"

"A Master Plan!" she announced. When I stared at her as if she were insane, she repeated, "A Master Plan. Like a business plan, but for your life."

I rolled my eyes, but Amy ignored my skepticism. "You need to think out of the box, Erin. Do a complete drill down, a total cost-benefit analysis of all this relationship stuff." I started to protest—I hated all that business school jargon—but she closed the fingers of her free hand around my wrist. "Erin, you're a strong and independent woman, but you always hide that by latching on to a guy. You don't need Sam back. You don't need anyone."

I blinked away tears, suddenly overwhelmed by sisterly loyalty. Or too much Chablis. I swallowed noisily and said, "Except for you."

"Except for me," Amy agreed, and then she hid a small burp behind her hand.

"But what will a Master Plan do?" I asked. I was pretty sure that slurring my words wouldn't be part of the new regimen.

"It will revitalize your brand."

"Brand?" Even under the influence of way too much alcohol, I took offense at that. "I'm not some new car or something, for you to advertise in a marketing class!"

"You're not anything new at all," Amy said. "But you will be. You'll be you, Erin. Not some guy's idea of what you should be."

I wanted to protest. I wanted to complain. I wanted to say that Amy wasn't being fair, that she was making everything too simple, that she didn't understand.

But she was right about one thing. I really did need a break from the relationship merry-go-round. I needed to figure out why things never, ever worked out, not with any one of the guys I'd dated for way too many years. I sagged into the cushion on the couch and tried not to pout when I asked, "So, what do I do?"

"First!" Amy said, holding up one finger. "You need to get a plant."

"A plant?" I wondered if I was even more drunk than I thought I was. She wasn't making any sense at all.

"A plant. Something small. A houseplant that you can keep in a corner of the kitchen." I nodded as if that was logical, and Amy elaborated. "You're going to develop a core competency in caring for your plant."

I was awed by the responsibility. "Core competency," I said, and I drained my glass. This might be my last chance to get good and drunk, if I were going to be responsible for a plant.

"And then!" Amy announced, holding up a second finger. "One month later, you'll get a fish."

"A fish?" I barely righted the bottle in time to keep from flooding the couch with cheap wine.

"A fish," Amy confirmed. "Nothing fancy. A neon tetra, maybe. Something small. Hard to kill. You're going to leverage your core competency. You're going to grow the relationship."

"Great," I said, but she was already moving on to the next stage.

"And after you keep the fish alive for three months,

then you can get a kitten." Amy cocked her head to one side, as if she were evaluating *me* for potential adoption, and then she said, "Well, maybe a cat. They're less trouble than kittens. You'll really be able to gain traction with a cat."

"I can handle a kitten!" I pulled my sleeve over the heel of my wrist to mop up the wine that I'd just spilled on the coffee table.

"Of course you can," Amy said, with the maddening doubt of an older sister. "And after one year of keeping your cat alive, *then* you can consider dating a guy."

"A year!"

"Twelve months," Amy said, nodding with absolute certainty. "The whole idea is to slow things down. Focus on you—what you want, what you can do. Land more roles, even if they're small ones, like the ones you've already had. You need to forget about men, about what you think they want, what you think they expect of you. It'll take twelve months to transition all the way from cat to man. Trust me. This Master Plan will be game-changing."

Tick. Tick. Tick. My biological clock didn't think I needed to change my game. Or maybe that was just my bladder talking. My kidneys were working overtime. "So let me get this right," I said. "One month for the plant. Plus three months for the goldfish. Plus twelve months for the cat. You're talking about..." I had to stop, to add up the numbers, which proved surprisingly difficult in my inebriated state. "Sixteen! Sixteen months!"

"You dated Sam for longer than that, and where did that get you?" Amy shook her head with all the fierce certainty of an older sister, and a business school student besides. "This is for your own good!

Sixteen months. It couldn't be worse than what I'd just gone through, than the decisions that had left me drunk on my sister's couch, jobless, homeless and manless.

In college, I'd changed my major every quarter, more often than not because I had a new boyfriend and was following him to new and exciting classes. We were talking about less than a year and a half to improve myself under Amy's Master Plan. Certainly I could devote that much time to making myself a better person. A more independent person. A happier person.

I raised my glass. "To the Master Plan!" I exclaimed. Amy clinked my goblet with hers, and we both downed the wine that remained. For good measure, we decided to break into the emergency stash of chocolate in the freezer. By that time, it was three in the morning, and we were both exhausted. I barely stayed awake long enough to wash down a couple of aspirin with a giant glass of water. I fell asleep reciting the steps of my Master Plan.

Justin, of course, was up before dawn, sneaking into his room to retrieve his transport helicopter toy. Despite my dark-of-night aspirin consumption, my head was pounding. I wished that I could invent a fail-proof hangover cure, a perfect pill that would banish aches, nausea and the fuzz on the roof of my mouth. I barely managed to keep from snapping at Justin. After all, it wasn't *his* fault that he had a drunk for an aunt.

I finally gave up on sleep and made the phone call that I'd avoided the entire day before. Of course, Sam didn't answer his cell, but I left him a breezy message, trying to sound glib and carefree when I told him he was off the hook. I asked him to call me, and I hung up with a little laugh, as if I didn't bear him any grudge, as if I were happy with everything in the entire world.

Once again, I wondered why New York's finest directors were never around to witness my acting coups.

Amy stumbled out of her bedroom just as I snapped my cell phone closed. Bleary-eyed herself, she fortified us with strong coffee, stacks of hot buttered toast and more than a few wisecracks about how we were both getting old. Before my body had fully forgiven my alcoholic assault the night before, I stumbled back to the bus stop and into the city.

I spent the ride telling myself that I was starting over. Clean slate. New me. With my Master Plan in place, I would hit every possible audition I could. I would find a new Survival Job. I would turn my life around. I would take charge of my career. I was a free and independent woman who could do whatever I wanted to do, whenever I wanted to do it.

Go, me.

I had plenty of time to perfect my pep talk. Door-to-door took an hour and forty-five minutes. I made a better connection for the bus than I had heading out to Amy's, but I still had to get downtown to the Mercer.

This was never going to work, long-term.

Sunday was always crazy in the box office. There was a matinee at two, and an evening show at eight. Inevitably, patrons left their tickets at home, or they thought they were ticketed for the other show, or they just wanted to check next season's dates against their calendars, so that they could work out exchanges for next December's performance seven months early.

Just to make the day a little more challenging, my

scheduled coworker didn't show up. I supposed that was karmic retribution—after all, I'd called in sick on my last shift. Nevertheless, I felt more and more sorry for myself as the afternoon wore on.

The Mercer's official policy was no refunds, no exchanges, but it was important to keep customers satisfied whenever possible. The line outside my window never ended, and people started asking strange questions that I'd never needed to field before.

Were the theater chairs covered in velvet? Because one woman was allergic to velvet. (The chairs were velvet. I refunded the ticket.)

The sign on the theater door said that this production was simply a reading. One man thought that violated his rights as a season's ticket holder—he wanted a full, staged production, or nothing. (The program had changed at almost the last minute. I refunded the ticket.)

Had anyone onstage eaten peanuts at any time during the previous twenty-four hours? Because one child's allergies might be triggered if she was exposed. (I had no freaking idea, but better safe than sorry. I refunded the ticket.)

And then the school bus arrived. It would have been easy enough to throw a stack of group tickets at some unfortunate group leader, but nothing about my day was destined to be easy. The bus was full of bored, mumbling college freshmen, each of whom had bought a separate ticket that needed to be individually claimed at Will Call.

I glanced at my watch. Twenty minutes until the show started, and the line of people waiting for their tickets still stretched around the corner of the building.

Fifteen minutes. I was getting more frantic.

Ten. I was never going to make it.

"Need some help?"

I barely managed to glance up. "Becca! That would be wonderful!"

Becca Morris was the Mercer's dramaturg. She did background work on every production, researching historic details, doing literary analysis, following through with anything the cast and crew needed to build their onstage reality. Some people said that dramaturgs were in-house critics, helping to sharpen productions, but I'd always thought of them as theatrical psychologists, counseling the show into being the best that it could be.

Whatever Becca's job description was, her additional two hands made a world of difference in the box office. As if by magic, the students started speaking more clearly. Every ticket was suddenly filed in correct alphabetic order. No one came up with any more brainteasers.

The last patron walked away precisely at two o'clock. I collapsed back in my chair.

"Thank God," I said. "I don't know what I would have done if you hadn't shown up!"

Becca shoved her bright red curls behind her ears. "Some days are more challenging than others."

"Tell me about it." I sighed.

"Oh?" she said, her fingers moving automatically to start printing out tickets for the evening performance. "It sounds like there's a story there."

"No story. At least, not one that you want to hear."

"You might be surprised." She grinned.

I didn't know Becca well, but I liked her. I saw her most days when I worked in the box office, and we'd both joined various actor-types over at the Pharm, a bar that the Mercer casts frequented.

Not that I'd be heading over to the Pharm anytime soon. I had to get all the way back to New Brunswick at the end of every evening. I suppressed a shudder, thinking of the late-night denizens of Port Authority. "Well, to start with, I had to take the bus in from Jersey."

She made a rueful face. "I thought you lived on the Upper East Side."

"I did." I gritted my teeth and started to alphabetize the evening tickets by patron's last name. Maybe it was the mindless rhythm of sorting the tickets. Maybe it was the way Becca stayed quiet, making just a few sympathetic noises, but not saying any actual words. Maybe it was my need to sort out what had happened, how and why my life had turned upside down so suddenly. Maybe Becca actually *was* some sort of therapist, some sort of secret psychological counselor who drew out the life stories of those around her.

Whatever the reason, I found myself telling her everything. "Wow," I said, when I was through, long after all the tickets had been readied. "I'm sorry. I didn't mean to go into all that."

"No," she said. "Don't apologize." She reached out with a quick hand, intending to comfort me. We both realized at the same time that she had a large smudge of dirt on her wrist. She laughed. "Whoops! I was gardening this morning, helping my neighbor set out some seedlings."

I nodded, as if I knew the first thing about gardening. Becca was obviously someone who didn't need a Master Plan. I wouldn't know the first thing to do with seedlings.

She took a deep breath, then exhaled slowly. Pinning me with her serious green eyes, she said, "Erin, I've got a favor to ask you."

Great. I didn't feel up to helping anyone with anything. But Becca had pitched in for the matinee and she'd listened to me drone on and on and on. I owed her one. "Sure," I said, forcing a smile. "What is it?"

"I don't know if you've heard, but I'm taking a leave of absence for a year. This is all really sudden—Ryan and I are going to Africa. It's part of a friendship tour thing that the State Department put together."

"Africa!" Ryan's play, the one that was being read that afternoon, was set in Burkina Faso. The show was turning out to be a big hit, even though it was only a reading.

"It's all pretty amazing. There was this whole program already in place, but when they heard about the play, they really wanted to include Ryan. I'm just going to tag along." She blushed, her fair skin turning bright red. "It'll give Ryan and me a lot of time together."

I muttered a few words of congratulations, still utterly mystified about what I could do to help Becca.

She sighed. "This all came up so quickly, though. I haven't had a second to line up a tenant for our place, and we really don't want to leave it empty for the entire year." She flexed her fingers and then met my eyes. "Could I convince you to move into my condo while we're in Africa?"

I'd seen her home just the week before, at the cast party after the first staged reading of Ryan's play. It was stunning—West Village building, river view, gorgeous wall of windows in the living room. She had to be kidding. "What's the catch?"

"There isn't any catch."

"How much is the rent?"

"It's free."

"What!" I thought about looking behind me, to check for hidden cameras. This had to be some practical joke, a bizarre theater hazing ritual that I'd never heard of before.

Becca shrugged. "I know it sounds crazy. I own the place free and clear, though, because someone did me a huge favor a while back, when I was really down on my luck. It sounds like you could use a helping hand now. Having you move in while we're out of the country would sort of...I don't know, restore the balance. Plus, it really would be one less thing I have to worry about before leaving town."

I started to protest. I started to say that her offer was too generous. I started to explain that I didn't know her well enough.

But what had I told myself just the day before? I was starting over. This was a new me. An independent me. A strong me.

"Okay," I said. I tested the thought again. Her apartment really *was* gorgeous. "I mean, thanks. Thanks a lot. I don't know what to say."

"Just say you'll take good care of the place."

"Of course!"

She laughed. "When's your next shift here?"

"Tuesday."

"Great," she said. "I'll leave the keys with Jenn." Her assistant. Becca grabbed a piece of scrap paper and wrote out an address. "You remember how to get there?" I nodded, feeling like I was in shock.

And that was it. I'd gone from homeless to living the high life in the space of about fifteen minutes. I barely remembered to say, "You have no idea how much this means to me."

"You know," Becca said. "I think I do." For just a moment, her gaze grew distant, as if she were remembering something sad. She shook her head, though, and said again, "I really think I do."

When I told Amy I was moving back to the city, she rolled her eyes. I hastened to explain that I wasn't going back to Sam—I still hadn't heard from the guy, despite the friendly message I had left. (His silence, though, was certainly helping me get used to thinking about him in the past tense. It also cemented my intention to activate the Master Plan.)

Instead, I told Amy about Becca's generous offer. Always playing the older sister, she demanded to know what was wrong with the place, what secret charges Becca intended to make, what disaster was waiting just around the corner. That business school brain of hers never turned off.

"I don't know," I finally said. "I don't know why she chose me. But I know that she really means to help." Amy continued to look skeptical. I sighed. "Come on! I'm an actress. I tell made-up stories for a living. I could have told if she was lying to me."

So, I found myself standing in the eighth-floor hallway of the Bentley condo building, my suitcase by my feet. My duffel was still slung over my shoulder. I cradled a parting gift from Amy, a peace lily in a four-inch pot. "It gets really droopy when it needs water," she said. "You can't possibly kill it. At least, not in a month."

My sister always had such high expectations for me. Nevertheless, the Master Plan was under way.

Becca had been true to her word—she'd left a key for me at the Mercer. Slipping into old habits, I crossed my fingers and thought, *Just this once.* I wasn't even sure what I was wishing for, but I took a deep breath before fishing the key out of my pocket and working all three locks. They moved easily, as if someone had recently oiled them.

The door swung open, and I caught my breath. The sun was setting over the river. Sparks flew off the windows of buildings between the water and me, dancing like confetti in the night air. "Hello?" I called, even though I expected the place to be empty. I wasn't disappointed.

I shoved my suitcase over the threshold and stepped inside, closing the door behind me. I fastened the locks automatically, a good little New Yorker. A light switch sat right beside the door, and I soon gazed at my living room—*my* living room!—bathed in the soft light of a floor lamp.

Wow.

I didn't know what Becca's story was, how she came to own this amazing place, but she had to be one of the luckiest people I'd ever met. Most theater people scrimped and saved, renting lousy apartments and sharing rooms with as many companions as sanity permitted. None of us made any money to speak of, and we were all dependent on the whims of casting directors, producers, the general economy and other career disasters.

But Becca had somehow found a perfect home. And now it was mine, all mine, for an entire year. I shook my head, half-afraid that I was going to wake up from a dream.

No dream, though. I picked up my suitcase and carried it into the bedroom. The master bath was bigger than my first apartment in New York. Everything was immaculate—Becca must have spent the past two days scrubbing. Vacuum streaks painted the bedroom carpet, neat triangles that made me feel like I was the first human ever to set foot in the place. I could actually sublet the walk-in closet, if I somehow failed to find another Survival Job.

Bemused, I went to investigate the kitchen. The faucet sparkled, as if I had stepped into some commercial for household cleaners. The cabinets had glass fronts; I could make out enough dishes and glassware to stock an entire Crate & Barrel store.

On the counter sat a cardboard box. The top edges were folded across each other, almost like someone planned on opening the carton soon. I stepped closer and saw that my name was written on one of the flaps, in all capital letters: ERIN. I recognized the printing; it was the same handwriting as on the envelope that Becca had left for me, the one that had held her keys.

Okay.

So, maybe Amy was right. Maybe I *was* about to discover Becca's dirty little secret. Maybe I was about to learn why this amazing place was available and free. Before I could chicken out, I took a deep breath and tugged at the cardboard flaps, yanking them open with one savage pull.

I don't know what I expected to find. A stash of

drugs, maybe. Small unmarked bills, stained with purple dye. A dusty monkey's paw, accusing me from a nest of rotten velvet.

Instead, I found a brass lantern—an old-fashioned oil lamp.

It looked like a prop from a play. At some point in its past, it had probably been shiny, but now it was covered with tarnish. Afraid of leaving fingerprints, I grabbed for the pristine dish towel that hung from a hook on the side of the refrigerator. Cradling the lamp in cotton, I turned it over, looking for a note, for something taped to the bottom, for some explanation of why Becca had left it for me.

Nothing.

I chewed on my lower lip and gathered up a corner of the dish towel to rub against the rounded body. Maybe I could clean the thing, wipe off enough tarnish to figure out what I was supposed to do with it. I started off with tentative pressure, afraid that I would scratch the finish, but that didn't make a dent in the motley stains. I rubbed harder, bearing down on the towel.

I changed the angle of my arm, trying to put some real strength behind my action. My fingers slipped off the towel, and my palm fell flat against the filthy brass. Immediately, an electric shock jolted up my arm. The force was strong enough to make me swear, and I would have dropped the lamp if I hadn't been afraid of breaking the expensive-looking tile on the kitchen floor. My fingers jangling, I barely managed to set the thing on the counter.

My heart pounded so hard that I couldn't take a full breath. What the hell had Becca done? Had she meant to electrocute me? Before I could run out of the kitchen, though, before I could flee from my new home, or think about calling the police or the fire department, or whoever you call when a brass lamp attacks you, I realized that something had changed.

Fog was pouring out of the lamp's spout. Not just any fog, though, not like the steam from a boiling teakettle, or some Halloween haunted-house witch's cauldron.

This fog was made of tiny jewels. Cobalt and emerald, citrine and garnet, the lights poured out. They swirled through the kitchen, caught in their own little storm, spinning like a tornado. Faster and faster they danced, growing, taking up all the space in front of the refrigerator.

I caught my breath and took a step back, afraid of what would happen if the particles touched my skin. I slipped a little on the floor, and I darted my eyes toward the counter, steadying myself against the cool granite.

When I looked back, the fog had disappeared.

In its place was a man. A man, wearing a dark blue police uniform, complete with a tool belt, a nightstick and a gun. His billed cap was pulled down low over his eyes. His jaw looked like it had been carved out of stone, and his dark brown eyes glowed like molten agate. I half expected him to pull a traffic whistle out of his pocket as he raised his right hand in the universal signal of Stop!

But this guy wasn't your average city cop. He had a tattoo, a brilliant etching of flames traced around his wrist. Orange and gold and red, all outlined in black, seared into his skin as if the fire were real, a living, breathing thing. My eyes were somehow drawn to the ink, captured as completely as any robber stopped in the middle of a poorly executed heist.

Before I could say anything, before I could remember how to speak, figure out what to say, the policeman took a small spiral notebook from his breast pocket. He flipped it open like a seasoned pro and produced a ballpoint pen from somewhere. "All right, ma'am," he snapped. "Just the facts. Enumerate your wishes, and we can wrap this up without delay."

Chapter 3

"EXCUSE ME, UM, Officer?" I stammered.

"Teel," he barked.

"Officer Teel?" I said, trying to process what had just happened.

"Just Teel, ma'am."

Okay. That was strange. But what did his name really matter? He couldn't be real, could he? This had to be some sort of joke.

I looked around the kitchen, trying to figure out what was going on. Had Becca rigged her kitchen with some bizarre theatrical tricks, maybe a projector that was creating the image of this hunky cop? But why would she bother to do that? And *how* had she done it?

The brass lamp was on the counter, where I'd dropped it after that massive jolt of electricity. It was tilted on its side, but even at that angle, I could see that all the tarnish had been scrubbed away. The metal gleamed beneath the kitchen lights. Becca couldn't have done *that,* could she?

As I stared at the lamp, the cop, um, *Teel* took a step closer to me. I could smell his aftershave, something sharp and spicy. Whatever else was going on, this guy wasn't any filmed projection. He was flesh and blood. Muscles rippled beneath his uniform, and I could feel the heat of his body across the inches that separated us. He raised his right hand, the one with the tattooed wrist. I could see the curls of hair on the backs of his fingers. No matter how impossible, no matter how bizarre, this guy was real.

He snapped, and a sheaf of papers appeared in his hand, replacing his notepad and pen.

"What the—" I tried to take a step away from him, but the granite counter dug into my back, effectively pinning me in place.

"Your contract, ma'am." He nodded as he handed the documents to me. I glanced at the top page. *Party of the first part... Party of the second part... Do grant freely, for the consideration of time outside of said genie's lamp...*

"Genie?" I croaked.

"Ma'am," he replied with a terse nod. Like that was any help.

"But aren't genies supposed to dress in robes? Flowing pants? A turban?"

"Nine out of ten first-time wishers expect their genie to appear in classic form. Ongoing studies of genie efficiency, however, dictate appearance in the most recent guise, to facilitate prompt wish fulfillment."

This guy and Amy should get together—between her business school jargon and his cop talk, no one could understand either one of them when they really got going. Nevertheless, those last two words caught my attention. "Wish fulfillment?"

He shifted position, anchoring his feet as if he were

at parade rest. "You have the right to four wishes," he proclaimed. "Anything you desire can and will be granted to you, absent any Ethical Interference Quotient, Physical Impact Vector or substantial Time Adjustment Factor violations. You have the right to delay your wishes. If you cannot obtain wish fulfillment in less than twenty-four hours, I am required to inform you of the potential for delay. Do you understand these rights that I have just recited to you?"

"Um, yeah. Sure," I said. Even though I continued to doubt my own sanity, something Becca had said was beginning to make a little more sense. She'd landed her amazing apartment because someone did her a huge favor. This genie must have been the someone. Becca must have received her own four wishes. (Four? I always thought that wishes came in threes. But what did I know?)

But why had Becca passed the lantern on to *me?* "What's the deal?" I asked the cop in front of me. "Why did Becca give me your lamp?"

Recognition flashed deep in those mahogany eyes. "I am not at liberty to discuss Ms. Morris's behavior." But then, my stalwart policeman must have thought better of his own silence. "When did Ms. Morris transfer responsibility for the magical enterprise?"

Magical enterprise? That sounded suspiciously like "criminal enterprise." Nevertheless, I felt obligated to respond. That cop uniform—or the well-muscled form beneath it—was definitely compelling. "Um, today? I mean, I just opened up the box."

"And what was the precise time and date of your intervention?"

"I don't know." I glanced at my watch. "It's what?

Seven o'clock? On, um, May 27."

He sucked in his breath. "And the year?" I told him. "Two weeks!" he exclaimed. His eyes glinted avariciously, and I suddenly wondered if this guy was some sort of dirty cop, if he was on the take.

"Um, sir?" I finally found the courage to ask. "Officer? Is everything okay?"

"Everything is quite satisfactory," he said, snapping back to attention. He seemed more agitated, though. In much more of a hurry. He said, "Time is of the essence, Miss..."

"Hollister," I said.

"Hollister," he repeated. He stabbed a blunt finger toward the sheaf of papers still in my hand. "Are you ready to sign?"

Was I?

I paged through the document, skimming over the section titles. The print was tiny, and the sections were long and confusing. It *looked* like the genie was obligated to grant my wishes, and I didn't owe him anything in return—I'd already done my part by releasing him from his lamp.

What did I have to lose? It wasn't like I had a bank account that he could empty. Or a full-time job that he could fire me from. And it wasn't a *genie* who stole souls, right? That was the devil, I was pretty sure.

The policeman handed me a pen when I reached the end of the monstrous document. Nervously, I licked my lips as he reached across me, flipping back to one of the early pages. "Initial there," he said. "And there." He moved forward a few pages. "And there." Another few pages. "And there."

Maybe I shouldn't be doing this.

He tapped one broad index finger against the signature line on the last page. "And sign there, with today's date."

What the hell. Wishes weren't going to get me into any more trouble than I was already in. And if I was really going to follow through on Amy's crazy Master Plan, it might be useful to have a wish or two up my sleeve. Not that I'd need magic to keep a stupid plant alive. Or a fish. Or a cat.

Really.

He nodded as I dotted the *i*'s in *Erin* and *Hollister* and crossed the *t* in my last name. "Very well." He gathered the pages together and tapped them into one neat stack. Before I could say anything, he turned his tattooed wrist, and the entire bundle disappeared.

"Hey!" I exclaimed. "Don't I get a copy?"

Instead of retrieving the contract from wherever he had stashed it, he gazed at me with those chocolate eyes. "What's your first wish, ma'am?"

My first wish? Already? I swallowed, but my throat had gone bone-dry. I knew that sensation. I experienced it every time I auditioned. My heart started to beat harder, and I had to concentrate to take a deep breath. My fingers tingled just a little.

Wishes. All the power of a genie at my disposal. All sorts of selfish indulgences sprang to mind, but I quickly set them aside. I couldn't be self-centered when there were so many huge problems in the world. Global warming. Habitat destruction. Inner-city poverty.

But then, I thought of Amy. Of Justin. Of both of them waiting for Derek to come home.

"Peace," I said. As soon as the word was out of my mouth, I felt a little silly. My wish sounded idealistic, naive. But, seriously, with a genie at my beck and call? How could I wish for anything less? "World peace," I said. "I want to eradicate war everywhere."

Apparently, that wasn't the right thing to say.

Teel's hands clenched into meaty fists. I could easily picture him bringing down some perp in a back alley. His breath snorted in the back of his throat. When he spoke, he shoved his words over pulverized glass. "That wish will take five hundred twenty-one years, forty-seven days, eleven hours and...forty-two minutes to fulfill."

I was shocked. "That long?"

"What is it with you guys?" he exploded. "You all think we genies can grant Grand Wishes in a heartbeat! Cure disease! Feed the world! Ninety-eight out of a hundred want the hard stuff! And every one of you acts disappointed when I say it takes time to work miracles!"

"Okay," I said, anxious to calm him down.

But he wasn't done with his tirade. "Notify the wishers, they tell me. Explain delays for all wishes taking longer than twenty-four hours to fulfill. Get their understanding in writing."

"It's all right," I said.

"We genies have feelings, too, you know! We worry about the world. We want to make everything nice and safe and beautiful around us."

"Hey!" I said, more sharply than I intended. I had to raise my voice, though; otherwise, he never would have heard me over his own grousing. "Forget about it! Forget about world peace."

He stopped complaining immediately. "Fine," he said, the iron command suggested by his uniform back in his voice. I wondered if he'd just been playing me, trying to get me to give up on the notion of lions lying down with lambs. "Let's try again," he said. "What's your first wish?"

"I don't know!" I was terrified that whatever I suggested would bring on another rant like the one I'd just witnessed. Sure, there were a million things that would help me perfect my single life. A secure Survival Job. Starring in that Mamet play. Permanently plucked eyebrows. (Yeah, even in my excitement about having wishes, I recognized that last one wasn't exactly on equal footing with the others. But think of the lifelong impact, the hours that I could devote to other, more important things!)

I wasn't sure what I truly wanted, what would make me happy. Make me strong. "Can I wait a day or two? Can I have some time to get used to this entire idea?"

He shook his head in disgust. "Yes, you can wait. Summon me as soon as you've made up your mind."

"Summon you?"

Fully restored to cop mode, he nodded tersely. "If you'll take a moment to review your fingers, ma'am."

Review my... I raised my hand, turning it slightly in the kitchen light. I could just make out a faint tattoo on my finger and thumb, rippling flames, like a shadow of the ones on Teel's wrist. When I rotated my hand, the color glistened, changing like oil spread over water. "How did you—?"

"Press your fingers together when you need assistance, ma'am. Saying my name will summon me."

This was insane. If he hadn't been a policeman, if he hadn't spoken with such blunt certainty, I never would have believed him. Before I could protest, though, he raised his fingers to the brim of his cap. "Ma'am," he said, by way of leave-taking.

"Where are you going?" Was I supposed to let him just walk out of here? Were genies allowed to roam around New York City?

"You read the contract, ma'am." Um, not exactly. At most, I'd skimmed the major paragraphs. "I'm entitled to go on patrol between your wishes."

"Oh," I said, trying to sound as if I'd known that all along. "Of course."

"Ma'am," he said again, already striding across the kitchen. At the apartment door, he nodded approvingly at my trio of dead bolts. "Make sure you lock up after I'm gone."

I did, and then I dove for the phone on the kitchen wall. As I punched in Amy's number, I tried to make myself take deep breaths, to keep from hyperventilating. My lips tingled as I waited for her to pick up.

"Hi," she said after the third ring, obviously hassled. "Can I call you back?"

"No!"

I heard the exasperated sigh that she almost managed to cut off. Her tone was tight as she explained, "Justin and I are finishing our *broccoli*. Before he takes a *bath*. So that he gets to *bed* on time."

I glanced at the clock on the stove. Okay, so I was interrupting dinner, a meal obviously made more challenging by my nephew's least favorite vegetable. "I'm sorry," I said. "I know my timing's lousy, but I have *got* to tell you what just happened."

"Justin!" she snapped, ignoring me. "You are going to deliver the goods before you leave this table! Two more bites!" A long pause, my fate resting in the mouth of a five-year-old. I wished that I could invent some flavor-changer, so that vegetables all tasted like candy. Think of the parent-child relationships that one could save...

"One," Amy counted, and then after a long pause, while I imagined my nephew's face contorted into cruciferous agony, "Two. Okay, swallow, and then you can go play for a few minutes." Amy sighed gustily. "Sorry," she said to me. "What's up? Is the apartment a disaster zone?"

"No, no, it's perfect. But you won't believe what I found in the kitchen."

"Roaches the size of Montana?"

"Amy!" Why did she have to be so negative? "I'm serious."

She switched into Concerned Big Sister Mode. "What's going on?"

That was better. "When I got here, I walked into the kitchen, and there was this big box on the counter. It had my name on it, so I opened it up, and there was a brass lamp inside."

"What, like a table lamp?"

"No!" I scooped the thing off the counter, belatedly admiring its graceful curves in the overhead light. "An oil lamp. You know, like the one Aladdin comes out of?"

"I know about Aladdin," Amy said wryly. Justin loved the Disney movie—he could watch that blue-faced genie for hours on end. "So, what was it? A housewarming present?"

"That's what I thought. But when I took it out of the box, it was filthy. I started to polish it, and a—" Suddenly, I couldn't speak. My throat slammed closed, the words trapped inside my lungs. I cleared my throat and tried again. "Sorry. I polished it, and a—"

The same thing happened. This wasn't like getting a frog in my throat. Instead, it felt like my vocal chords simply disappeared. I couldn't speak because my body was no longer capable of making sound.

"What?" Amy said, and then she enunciated with cell-phone exasperation. "I. Can't. Hear. You. You're. Break. Ing. Up."

I stared at my phone. I was on the landline; my cell was buried somewhere deep in my tote bag. "Sorry," I said again, flooded with relief that I could get the word out. I proceeded with caution, testing each word before thinking it, before dropping it into a carefully phrased summary of what had happened. "I...rubbed...the... lamp...and...a—"

That was it. I couldn't say *genie.* Or *fog.* Or *magic.*

I couldn't tell Amy what had happened.

That policeman had more than killer biceps up his sleeves. He was somehow controlling my ability to talk. I sighed and tried to come up with something that would keep Amy from thinking I'd totally lost my mind. "I rubbed the lamp and set it on my bookshelf," I finally finished weakly. "I think Justin will really like it—he can pretend that he's in that movie, flying on a magic carpet."

"That's why you called?" Amy sounded a bit put out.

"Um, yeah." I had to say something else. "I miss you guys. Thanks for letting me stay there the past couple of days."

"Any time. But the next time you're here, *you* get broccoli patrol. Plus you get Justin ready for bed."

"It's a deal," I said, relieved that she'd bought my

dissembling. "Go give him his bath. I'll talk to you tomorrow."

Okay. That had been totally bizarre. Why couldn't I tell Amy about the jeweled lights that had poured out of the lamp, about the policeman genie, about my wishes? I held my hand in front of my eyes, studying the barely visible flames tattooed across my fingertips. What other powers did Teel hold over me?

Before I could seriously consider summoning him back to the kitchen, my stomach growled. Loudly. All of a sudden, I was ravenous. I'd grabbed a bowl of cereal at Amy's in the morning, and a granola bar for a makeshift lunch as I was running to the Mercer box office for my shift.

A quick check of the pantry, the fridge and the freezer proved that Becca had done an excellent job emptying her kitchen for me. Nothing remained, not even the packets of soy sauce and Chinese mustard that filled at least one drawer in every Manhattan apartment I'd ever visited.

Well, it wasn't like I was living in the middle of the Gobi Desert. It was time to learn my way around my new neighborhood.

After a moment's hesitation, I returned the genie lamp to its box and stowed both away in my bedroom closet. By that time, I was actually feeling shaky, I'd become so hungry. I grabbed my coat and my keys, threw my tote bag over my shoulder and quick-walked to the elevator.

Standing on the sidewalk outside my building, I tossed a mental coin. Heads. Turn left.

Halfway to the corner, I was assaulted by the fragrance of baking bread. All of a sudden, I was catapulted back to childhood, to a school field trip to the Mrs. Harton's Bread Factory. I could practically taste the hot-baked bread, pulled fresh from the production line, sliced into steaming hunks and slathered with butter for my elementary school class to savor.

My mouth literally watering, I looked around, trying to find the source of the incredible aroma. A tiny walkway led between two buildings. A neatly printed sign was nailed to the wall: Garden Variety Café. An arrow pointed down the narrow alley.

Like a woman possessed, I followed it. Ivy-covered walls led me to a surprising little courtyard. Four iron tables melted into the shadows, barely reflecting the cheerful gas flame that flickered beside a green-painted wooden door. The alcove was a perfect retreat from the hustle and bustle of the city; it was like I'd stepped into a fairy tale. Any minute now, hobbits were going to stroll over the flagstones, laughing about a fine evening meal of mushrooms.

Hey, in a world with roving, wish-granting, policeman genies, anything is possible, right?

"Still a little cold for eating outside, isn't it?"

I jumped in reflex, biting off a shriek. I hadn't seen the man who stood in the shadows beside the door. As he stepped forward, I saw why I'd missed him. He wore black from head to foot, a long-sleeved work shirt tucked into worn denim jeans. A dark apron was snug around his waist, the long ties wrapped behind him, then brought around to hang in a comfortably loose bow. The guy's hair was as dark as the shadows that had hidden him, unruly waves that clearly defied any barber's control. He looked like he'd forgotten to shave for a day or four.

His left hand was curled around a large stoneware mug. Steam curled above the pottery, and I caught a whiff of bergamot. Earl Grey tea.

He shrugged disarmingly. "Sorry. I didn't mean to startle you."

"No, you didn't," I said automatically, then felt like kicking myself for the transparent lie. "I was just..."

He waited politely, but when I couldn't come up with a story, he nodded toward the green door. "You're here for dinner?" he asked. The smell of baking bread made me nod. He turned the wrought-iron doorknob and gestured for me to precede him inside.

The restaurant was tiny. A kind critic would call it "intimate"—there were half a dozen four-tops scattered across the scrubbed wooden floor. A square of brown butcher paper covered each table. Mismatched dishes sat in front of each chair, flanked by a chaotic tumble of silverware. The entire room could have looked like the back of a Goodwill store, but the effect somehow managed to be one of simple, easy good cheer.

That impression was helped along by the presence of four different groups of diners, all chatting comfortably. One man sat alone at the table nearest the kitchen, though, a traveler's backpack his only companion.

My host waited patiently until I turned my attention back to him. "One?" he asked.

I nodded, and he glided toward the only open table, the one in front of the large stone fireplace. Glancing around the room, I saw that the only decor consisted of simple, framed architectural prints—line drawings of buildings that may never have actually existed. The stark artwork anchored the walls somehow, made them seem more real.

Real. I shivered, consciously forbidding myself from thinking about the flames tattooed on my fingertips, about the markings that my policeman genie had displayed on his wrist.

I wasn't going to ponder my impossible wishes. I was going to eat dinner. Have a normal meal. In a normal restaurant. Like a normal person.

"This is your first time at Garden Variety?" The guy looked attentive, attuned to my response as I pulled my gaze back from the cozy room. I nodded, and he smiled. "We don't have a written menu. I cook what I feel like, based on what's in season. Tonight, we have a cream of asparagus soup or a golden beet salad, to start. I've got a good meat loaf, and roast chicken. Some baked macaroni and cheese."

Everything sounded wonderful, like the comfort food I'd craved without even knowing my own desire. I was a little leery looking around, though. I had no idea how much anything cost.

But I couldn't back out now. Not with the chef himself standing over me like a watchful ninja, waiting for me to make up my mind. Worst case, I'd charge my dinner. And then cut up my credit cards as soon as I got back home, at least until I found a new Survival Job. Throwing caution to the winds, I said, "I'll have the salad. And the macaroni and cheese."

He nodded, as if I'd made the decision he'd expected. "I'll bring you some water, and some bread—it just came out of the oven. Do you want wine? I've got a red that'll be great with the mac and cheese."

In for a penny, in for a pound. "Sounds good," I said, and flashed him my best stage smile, holding the grin until he disappeared into the kitchen.

I looked around the room. Everyone was wearing casual clothes. That was a good sign—if they'd been in suits and silk dresses, I would have been doomed for sure. Backpack Guy even wore a hoodie sweatshirt over torn jeans.

Feeling conspicuously single, I dug in my tote bag, trying to find some reading material. There was my bus ticket from New Brunswick, the one that I'd bought that morning. A receipt from a Starbucks I'd stopped at a few days ago. Not much else.

"Here you go." I looked up with a start as my black-clad benefactor set a basket of bread on the table. The heavenly scent that had initially drawn me to the courtyard curled from beneath a blue gingham napkin. "I thought you might want these," he added, producing a sheaf of magazines from the large pocket in his apron. His other hand deftly balanced a stemmed glass and an oversize bottle of wine. He poured a single sip and then said, "Help yourself to more."

Before I could comment on the unconventional service, Backpack Guy shuffled over, maneuvering between the tables with care. "Thanks, Timothy," he said.

The man in black—*Timothy*—turned to his departing customer and extended a hand, like a panther offering a velvet paw. "Have a good night, Peter. Stay warm out there."

"Thanks," the customer said again. I smiled at him, but he didn't meet my eyes as he hurried out the door.

Timothy turned back to me. "Your salad will be out in a minute or two." He nodded toward the magazines. "Enjoy."

I glanced at the stack of reading material. The current *New Yorker*. That month's *Gourmet*. A home decor magazine, *Circle,* which I'd never heard of before. "Thanks," I said, honestly touched by the thoughtful gesture.

He disappeared into the kitchen, and I thumbed open the *New Yorker.* There was just enough light to read the pages comfortably. I skimmed through the notices of Broadway plays. *Someday,* I thought wistfully. That's what I should wish for, from Teel—a starring role in a career-making play. Something more appropriate for me than the Mamet play had been. As long as world peace wasn't going to happen on my watch...

I reached for the basket Timothy had left and extracted a thick slice of bread. The texture was heavy, rich, and I suspected that I could count at least twelve whole grains if I were willing to invest the time. I dipped my knife into the accompanying pewter cup of warm butter. I wolfed down an entire slice and then forced myself to be more restrained with a second. I couldn't remember the last time I'd had homemade bread. Sam and I definitely had not done any baking on our own.

Sam. Just thinking about him made me angry. There was no excuse for his failing to return my phone call.

Gritting my teeth, I reached for the drop of wine that Timothy had poured for me. It bloomed across the back of my tongue, rich and robust, as if someone had secretly transported me to Tuscany. Shrugging, I filled my glass. If my credit card was going to end up bruised and whimpering at the end of the night, I might as well enjoy the battle.

As if in recognition of my acceptance, Timothy

emerged from the kitchen with my appetizer. The beet salad was formed into a perfect circle, tossed with a fragrant citrus vinaigrette and topped with delicate wisps of fried shallots. *"Bon appetit,"* he said before heading over to clear plates from another table.

My first tentative bite left me scrambling for more. Even as I chewed, though, I told myself that I had to continue on the path to the New Me. I had to land a starring role so that I could live the life I wanted in New York. Alone. Without any lawyer boyfriend to make everything work out fine at the end of a tight fiscal month.

Timothy interrupted that grim meditation by bringing out my main dish, still sizzling from its time in the oven. Goat cheese took a central role in the baked macaroni, playing off cheddar and something mellow—maybe provolone? Buttered bread crumbs on top made the casserole thoroughly decadent, and I fought to keep from licking the generous ramekin clean.

With each bite, though, I forced myself to consider options for my theater career. It was time to seek out another audition, one where I'd get to deliver more than one line of my prepared monologue. Auditions were posted daily at Equity, the actors' union. Tomorrow, I would sign up for the most promising show posted. I'd even make time to go onto the ShowTalk Web site, to gather all the relevant gossip. And if push came to shove, I'd invest a wish in my audition, guarantee myself a dream role.

Problem solved. At least for the rest of the night.

I allowed myself to sit back in my chair, to watch the scene around me. While I'd been eating, a woman had shuffled through the front door, burdened with three gigantic bags. Timothy had helped her transfer the luggage into a back corner, and then he'd seated her at the same table Backpack Guy had occupied. He didn't actually take her order; he just brought out food—soup *and* salad along with a healthy serving of macaroni and cheese, and a steaming quarter of roast chicken balanced on top.

Just as I thought I couldn't eat another bite of my own meal, Timothy paused on one of his prowling circuits around the room. "I've got some great strawberry rhubarb buckle tonight," he said. "And the layer cake is chocolate, with hazelnut buttercream."

I started to decline, but then I realized this might be the last restaurant meal I'd manage for months. "Strawberry rhubarb?"

"You'll love it," he promised.

And he was right. Sweet berries and tangy rhubarb baked on top of a buttery cake, all covered with a caramel streusel topping that made me wish I could take home a gallon of the stuff for breakfast, lunch and dinner the next day. With tremendous reluctance, I finally set my spoon down.

Time to face the music. Too sated to give in to true dread, I closed the *New Yorker* and waited for Timothy to bring me the fiscal bad news.

But first, he cleared away my dishes. He brought a tiny treat from the kitchen, a fragile white patty of crumbly mint candy, like the inside of a York peppermint patty, but with just a quarter moon of dark chocolate ganache kissing the edge. I was surprised as he hooked the chair next to me with his foot, lowering himself onto its seat with a lithe grace. He produced a pencil from that capacious apron pocket and starting writing on the table's butcher paper.

"Let's see. Beet salad. Mac and cheese. Buckle. Wine." He lifted the bottle and tilted it a little, gauging the level against the fire's flicker. "One glass, I think."

One generous glass. One *very* generous glass.

He tallied the column of numbers quickly, underscoring the result with two firm lines. "There you go."

"That can't be right," I protested. He frowned and started to review his arithmetic, but I clarified, "It's not enough."

He laughed, the sound blooming deep in his chest like a purr. "This isn't exactly the Rainbow Room."

"No," I said, smiling as I took out my wallet. "It definitely isn't." I could easily pay in cash, with enough to spare that I didn't have to worry about the rest of the week. I set down the bills, along with a thirty percent tip.

Back to my life reorganization mission. Next up: Replace the Survival Job. I took a deep breath and said, "I have a question for you."

Before I could go on, though, the hungry woman with three bags stepped up to the table. "Mr. Timothy," she said. "I can use the restroom, before I go?"

Okay. That was strange. But Timothy didn't seem the least bit fazed. "Of course, Lena," he said.

As she hunched toward the back of the restaurant, I chickened out. I couldn't ask this guy for a job, not while I was sitting here as a customer. When Timothy looked back at me, I said, "Please! Go ahead. I didn't mean to keep you from your work. Go get her check."

His eyebrows arched for a quick second. "Actually, Lena's a guest."

Involuntarily, I flicked a glance toward the large bags stacked in the corner. It took me a second, but then I realized what was going on. Lena was homeless. Backpack Guy, too. Timothy was running his own luxury soup kitchen, at least at the table closest to the kitchen.

Wow. What would it be like to work in a place like this? Good food, good deeds... I forced myself to meet Timothy's inscrutable gaze. I was surprised to see that his eyes were amber brown, calm and serious. They seemed to belong to an older man than the guy with the scruffy beard sitting beside me. The flesh-and-blood Timothy couldn't be more than thirty years old.

"Any chance you're hiring? I've done a fair amount of catering before."

He stretched and sighed. "I'm afraid not. I'm all set for now."

Disappointment soured the memory of the wine I'd just enjoyed. Of course he didn't have a job. Not for me. No one in their right mind would trust me with customers and gourmet food. Concerned Caterers might as well have stamped a brand on my forehead.

But I could do better than catering, I chastised myself. I was moving on in my life. I was taking charge. Bigger, better, more successful—that was the template for the new Erin Hollister. That was the Master Plan. I even had the peace lily to prove it, back in my apartment.

Obviously unaware of my interior pep talk, Timothy said, "If you leave your name and number, I'll keep you in mind, when I need someone."

I almost said no. I almost told him that I'd been mistaken when I'd asked about the job. I almost explained that I didn't want to wait tables, that I wanted to act, that I wanted to launch my professional career into the stratosphere.

But he didn't care about all that. He was only a restaurateur, although admittedly one who had just fed me the best meal I'd ever eaten in New York. There was no reason to insult him, just because my personal life was in shambles.

I took the pencil that he offered and ripped off a corner of the butcher paper, adding my name and cellphone number with elaborate care. I could always decline the job, if he ever called, after I'd become a huge success.

He glanced at my information before storing the scrap in his apron. "Thank you, Erin," he said seriously, putting just enough emphasis on my name that I knew he was committing it to memory.

I felt myself respond to that personal touch. I started to lean a little closer, to duck my head with just a shadow of flirtation. My hands started to flutter; my fingers thought they wanted to settle on his sleeve.

I stopped myself with a mental jerk. That was the old Erin. That was the Erin who didn't have the faintest idea how to be strong, independent and successful on her own. That was the Erin without a Master Plan.

Instead of flirting, I extended a businesslike hand. "No," I said. "Thank *you,* Timothy." And then, I forced myself to stand, to walk away, to head out into the courtyard, and down the alley, and back to my apartment. Back to the new life I was carving for myself. Alone.

Chapter 4

STANDING IN THE hallway outside the audition room, I forced myself to take deep breaths. I was holding the "sides" for the audition, the actual section of the script that they wanted me to read aloud. Sides were policed like gold; I'd been given the valuable pages precisely twenty minutes before my time slot, not a second more, not a second less. Every detail about auditions had to be scrupulously fair.

I forced myself to take a deep breath and read through the pages once again. I had been walking on air since Wednesday morning, when I'd followed up on my promise to myself, on the vow I'd taken in Garden Variety. Like a good little actress, I'd checked out pending auditions, and I'd been thrilled to find *Menagerie!* on the board. The description practically begged me to try out.

Seeking the Following

Note: all singers should have equal facility acting and performing contemporary musical theater.

LAURA: Eighteen years old. Shy and sensitive woman, too lost in her imaginary world to attend business school.

While Laura limps in her spoken-word scenes, she is a vibrant, showstopper dancer in musical numbers. MUST BE STRONG SINGER.

Okay, so I was twenty-five, not eighteen. But I played young. And I'd performed the role of Laura in a college production of *The Glass Menagerie* to great critical acclaim (in the *Daily Wildcat,* I had to admit, but good ink was good ink.) I understood Laura Wingfield's trials and tribulations, the way that she suffered, the blinders that kept her from comprehending that everyone was afraid when they moved into the real world, when they lived life on their own terms. I had learned to display her perfect vulnerability onstage. Audience members had actually cried when my Laura proved unable to leave her damaged life behind, to go forward as a normal, healthy girl, facing life outside her controlling mother's home.

I shouldn't have been surprised when Amy teased me on opening night. She said that *of course* Laura came easily to me. Laura built fantasies about men, about Gentlemen Callers, the same way that I did, with every guy I'd ever dated. I'd fought back at the time, pointing out that at least I went on dates—something that Laura in the play never managed. Amy had merely smiled her Wise Older Sister Smile and said, "Uh-huh."

Ah, good old sisterly love—always supportive, always considerate.

I didn't care what Amy thought. My Laura Wingfield had brought insight to a classic.

So, when I saw the posting for a musical version of Tennessee Williams's play, I was thrilled. My joy only increased when I read the buzz, over on ShowTalk. Everyone in town was talking about this show. The director was supposed to be phenomenal, and the producers were willing to invest a lot of money. I was over the moon. Musicals were big business in New York—my entire career could be made with a single role. And I was perfect for the lead.

Except for the small fact that I wasn't a showstopper dancer.

And I'd really be pushing things, to say that I was a strong singer.

None of that mattered, though. Fifty percent of a good audition was showing up, looking the part and demonstrating perfect confidence that I was The One the directors needed to cast. Besides, the acting audition was first, before I ever had to worry about singing and dancing. I could ace the acting—it was well inside my comfort zone. Well inside, that was, if I could become absolutely, one hundred percent comfortable with the sides that I was studying. I had ten precious minutes left to master the words, to see how the author of the musical production had modified the language of Williams's classic play.

Ten minutes. Which was why I almost didn't answer my phone when it vibrated in my pocket. Long habit prevailed, though. I barely took my eyes from the precious papers in my hand when I checked the caller ID.

Sam.

I could let the call go to voice mail. I *should* let the call go to voicemail. I'd left him a message *five full days before,* telling him that the pregnancy scare was over. Five entire days, and this was the first chance he'd had to call me back?

But what would ignoring him prove? I'd already staked out the moral high ground, letting him know he was off the paternity hook. I might as well stay up there on my mountain of superiority. Sighing in exasperation, I answered. "I can't talk now."

"Erin!"

"I'm in an audition, and I can't talk."

"Okay." He sounded the slightest bit chastised, if I could judge by that one word. "Come by tonight. I'll be home after eight."

Home. Sam's brownstone wasn't *my* home anymore. Not to mention the fact that Sam didn't have any right to dictate my schedule. "No," I said vehemently. "I don't want to talk there."

So much for my being walked over by every single guy I'd ever known. Amy would be proud of me. Sam hesitated before responding, wasting enough time that I wondered if this was a classic booty call. Did he have any intention of talking to me at all, of trying to work things out? Or was he actually arrogant enough to think that I'd just leap back into his giant bed, roll around a little for old times' sake?

This independence thing was actually starting to feel pretty good. I cut short the suspense of waiting for Sam's reply. "If you really want to talk, then let's meet at a restaurant. Some place down in the Village. I'm living there now."

"The Village?" I heard his incredulity. This conversation wasn't going the way he'd planned.

I hadn't had a lot of time to explore my new neighborhood, but I knew enough to press my advantage. "There's a place called Garden Variety. We can meet there at eight." I gave him the address. He started to negotiate, using all his lawyerly skills at manipulation, but I snapped, "I've got to go, Sam. I'll see you at eight." I hung up before he could say anything else.

Without my conscious permission, my fingers clutched at the fabric stretched across my belly. I'd purposely worn a soft pink sweater set, wanting to connote Laura's old-fashioned vulnerability. The shell was smooth over my flesh, but I could imagine the faintest bump, the evidence that would have existed if I'd truly been pregnant. I tried to return my attention to the crumpled sides in my hand, but I couldn't concentrate on the script.

Dammit! Why had Sam called now? Why hadn't he felt guilty—or horny, or whatever—a day earlier? Or three hours later? Why was he ruining the best theatrical lead I'd had since I'd arrived in New York?

I shouldn't have been so rude to him. I shouldn't have hung up on him. I had *never* hung up on a guy before.

And why was I making such a big deal out of going up to his place? He'd be tired after working all day. I should have agreed to a restaurant that he chose. I hesitated, starting to take out my phone, to call him back, to agree to his simple request that I stop by the home I'd lived in for ten full months.

"Hollister!" The hall monitor barked my name. I jerked my thoughts back from Sam, from the mess I'd made of our relationship, and I forced a perky smile on my face. I'd worn my straight hair in a ponytail, further attempting to look young, shy. Now, my fingers itched to twirl a few strands, to work off my nervous energy. Instead, I crossed my fingers and breathed my personal incantation, "Just this once."

And I stepped into the audition room.

I know that I introduced myself to the three people who held my professional life in the figurative palms of their hands. I know that I read from the sides. I know that the casting director offered up the few lines that belonged to the Gentleman Caller.

Most of the piece was a monologue, though, a chance for me to bring Laura's lovelorn jitters to life.

I said something. I did something. I looked at each of them, the casting director and the artistic director and someone who had some other job related to the show.

The entire time I stood there, I thought, *I need to focus. I need to be here now. I can't think about Sam, about the past. I promised myself. I need to focus.* Around and around, my mind chased itself like a kitten playing with its own tail. I tried to use my tangled emotions, to pour them into the reading, to make my confusion about Sam and the rest of my sorry life inform Laura's dream of her Gentleman Caller, but I wasn't sure if I was brilliant, or only the most pitiful woman in the world.

"Thank you," the casting director said when I was through. And then, impossibly, he added, "Can you come back this afternoon for the chorus call?"

"Yes," I said, surfing to the crest of a sudden wave of adrenaline. I pumped every acting trick I had into the one word, trying to sound like I always made the first cut. While I managed to restrain my enthusiasm as I left the room, I *had* to give a little jump and a yip of surprise after the door closed behind me.

They liked me! At least enough to call me back for a singing audition. Enough to give me a chance to play

Laura as I'd never played her before, with even more conviction than I'd had in college. Despite Sam, despite my distraction, despite my uncertainty, they *liked* me.

Four hours later, though, my enthusiasm had been replaced by pure, unadulterated panic.

I'd returned to the audition hall at noon, even though I knew I'd have to wait. I didn't want to chance getting trapped by a parade, by a street fair, by a roaming band of urban pirates, that would somehow keep me from my afternoon audition slot.

My paranoid promptness nearly cost me my sanity. I waited in the hall outside the audition room, listening as each of the men sang. Every guy was permitted sixteen bars of music—one minute to prove that he was the perfect tenor, the perfect baritone, the ideal Tom Wingfield or Gentleman Caller. More than once, I had to flee to another floor, take a break from the pure musical perfection.

That was bad enough, listening to the men. But then the Amandas started singing—strong altos every one, belting out their snippets as if they wanted the Statue of Liberty to take notice all the way downtown.

I wasn't trying for Amanda, I told myself. I wasn't competing against those women.

And then the first Laura went in. Her voice was rich and clear, so strong that the door to the audition room might as well not exist at all. She was phenomenal. There was no way I could go into that room, not after comparing myself to her. I didn't have a prayer.

I was going to be sick. Fifteen minutes before they called my name—fifteen more minutes of listening to the unbeatable competition. I turned on my heel and fled to the bathroom.

I ran cool water over my wrists and forced myself to take a dozen calming breaths. Toweling off, I stared into the fly-specked mirror. Out of habit, I reached for my necklace, tugged lightly at my pearls. What was I doing wearing pink? It conspired with my blond hair to make me look pale, washed out. I'd been stupid to put myself in front of theatrical decision makers looking anything less than my absolute best. I tugged again, as if I could change the color of my clothes.

As I forced my fingers away from my neck, they glinted in the overhead fluorescent light. Faint golden swirls glimmered against my skin, the vaguest reminder of Teel's promise. I had wishes—four of them. Surely, the tailor-made role of a musical Laura Wingfield was worth a wish. Worth my entire professional future.

I glanced around to make sure that none of the bathroom stalls was occupied, and then I pressed my thumb and forefinger together, bearing down hard. "Teel!" I enunciated.

Immediately, a thick fog coalesced between the sinks and the stalls. Glints of jewel-toned light reflected off the mirrors, the faucets, the metal doors. I caught my breath at the surprising beauty of those swirling bits, and then I blinked. By the time I opened my eyes, a woman stood in front of me.

A woman. Not the policeman that I expected.

I was staring at a woman whose hair was a bottle version of my own, pulled back into a ridiculously high ponytail. Her eyes were green, but I knew she had to be wearing contact lenses to get such a garish color. She wore a red sweater, so tight that I wondered if she could draw a full breath. Her pleated skirt hovered well above her knees, and I was willing to bet my last Concerned Caterers paycheck that she wore a skanky thong. A giant white E was pasted across her chest, and her hands were obscured behind two red-and-white pom-poms. She looked like a horny teenaged boy's dream of a cheerleader, by way of the Playboy Mansion.

As I gaped, I could just make out the glint of flames tattooed around her right wrist.

"Excuse me," I said, half apologizing for staring. "Um, are you a genie?" Okay, stupid question, given how thc woman had just appeared in front of me. But really, how do you start a conversation with an unknown magical creature?

"Hel-*lo,*" she said, chomping on gum as she frowned at herself in the mirror. She transferred her right pom-pom to her left hand, using her free fingers to straighten a ragged outline on her lip gloss. "I'm Teel? We met in your kitchen?"

"Teel!" Now I really couldn't stop staring. "But you—" I started to say, You're a policeman. You're a guy. You're...magic. If Teel was really able to manifest out of thin air—or at least out of a cloud of jewel-colored lights—then why couldn't he, um, *she* change appearance?

Nevertheless, I took a couple of steps away, shuffling back until the sink's porcelain edge returned me to conscious thought. I didn't have a lot of time. Not if I was going to make my audition deadline. If I missed my time slot, my dream of *Menagerie!* would be over forever.

Still, my mind insisted on chasing around one question. "What are you supposed to be? I mean, I understood when you were a policeman, that sort of made sense, with the legal contract and everything. But that?" I gestured toward the sweater, the indecently short skirt. "Who *are* you?"

She clicked her tongue in exasperation and sighed before blinking seven coats of mascara in my general direction. "I'm an actress? Auditioning for a role?"

"In what show?" I asked with a queasy fascination.

"*High School Musical 7?* Senior year of college?" She ruffled her pom-poms beneath my nose. I didn't know where to start, telling her everything that was wrong with that, starting with the fact that there wasn't any such show on the bulletin board downstairs. Instead, I glanced at my watch. Seven minutes before my own audition. Not that I was cutting things close or anything.

I had to accept that my can-do policeman genie was gone. I was stuck with this sexpot—love her or leave her. I swallowed hard and tried to ignore the sickening sweet smell of bubble gum. My voice shook a little when I said, "You told me to call you when I was ready to make a wish."

"Yes?" she said. Immediately, a sharp edge cut beneath the slutty cheerleader parody.

"I need your help for my audition. I need to sing and dance like a star."

An avaricious gleam leaped into Teel's green eyes. "I can do that. What are your other two wishes?"

"Three," I said, immediately wondering if Teel was putting me on. "My other *three* wishes." Was this cheerleader babe really the same genie as my policeman?

She shook her head strenuously enough that her ponytail almost took out an eye. Her pom-poms rustled as they settled on her hips. "One—singing? Two—dancing?" She clicked her tongue in exasperation at my apparently poor math skills. "That leaves two more?"

"Singing and dancing are one wish! They're for the same goal, for getting into the same show."

Teel cracked her gum loudly enough that I jumped. "No way. Singing is totally different from dancing? Think of all those opera singers? Ninety-seven out of one hundred opera singers? They wouldn't know a tap combination if they stumbled into it?"

I was suspicious about my genie keeping accurate statistics about opera. I lashed back. "This isn't opera! It's musical theater! Singing and dancing naturally go together!"

Teel set her hands on her hips, making the letter on her sweater even more, um, prominent than it had been. "Look, who's the genie here? Which one of us knows the rules? I'm telling you, you're asking for two separate wishes." She glared at me when I stayed silent, then huffed an exasperated sigh. "Fine. Are you invoking your arbitration clause?"

Like I had time for arbitration. I glanced frantically at my watch. Four minutes.

"Okay," I said. "Two wishes." What did it really matter? I'd assumed, when I first heard the word *genie,* that I'd be getting three, anyway. So, if I spent two here, I'd still have two left, pretty much like I'd planned it. Or imagined it, in any case—I hadn't *planned* any of this. "Singing and dancing," I prompted as she twirled the end of her ponytail around her finger. "Um, could you hurry up? I've got to be back out there when they call my name."

"All requests? They have to be phrased in the form

of a wish? Nine out of ten wishers? They don't even think about that?" Her annoying uptalk was twisted with just a hint of gloating. She knew that she'd won our argument.

Form of a wish? What sort of idiotic, controlling... I cut off my mental tirade. There were rules all over—rules for serving overpriced catered dinners to wealthy society matrons, rules for breaking up with boyfriends, rules for completing a union audition for a musical that might be the precise ticket I'd been looking for, ever since I arrived in New York.

"Fine," I said. "I wish that I could sing and dance. I mean, sing and dance better than I already can. Well enough to get a role in a Broadway play, well enough to get a role in—"

The cheerleader jutted out her hip and sighed in exasperation, effectively cutting off my explanation. "Are you going to go on all day? You're the one who was complaining—"

I did my own cutting off. "Fine! Go ahead! I only have—"

I started to check my watch, but Teel had already transferred her pom-poms to her left hand. "As you wish," she said, making the words a surprisingly declarative sentence. She raised her right fingers toward her ear, clutched the lobe tightly and pulled twice.

The force of the wish leaped from my genie to me, like a bolt of lightning jumping from a thunderhead to the ground. The jangle of power was every bit as strong as when I'd first freed Teel from her lamp. It knocked the breath out of my lungs and raised the tiny hairs on my arms. I would have staggered back, but the sink was still pressing against the backs of my legs.

As quickly as the power had assaulted me, it was gone.

I swallowed hard, testing my throat for some difference, for some magical musical ability that hadn't existed a heartbeat before. Nothing. I stumbled forward, expecting some arcane grace to guide my feet into a smooth arc. Nothing there, either.

"Teel!" I shouted.

"No time," she said. "You have to get to your audition?" She held up her tattooed wrist, as if a watch face could be seen amid the flames. "You're down to two minutes? No, one minute?"

"Teel—" I started again, furious that there wasn't a dulcet tone of perfect singing ability behind my command. There wasn't a more resonant timbre, a clearer musical note. There wasn't anything.

Ignoring my protest, my slutty cheerleader genie shook her pom-poms. "Ready? Okay! Go, Erin, go," she chanted, shimmying along with her red-and-white plastic puffs. "Fire up tonight! All the way to victory, fight, Erin, fight!"

I grimaced at the absurdity of the cheer and turned on my heel. I didn't have time to fight with her, didn't have a second to spare to argue my case. I'd follow through on—what had she called it? Arbitration?—as soon as I completed what was about to be the most disastrous audition of my life.

Race-walking down the corridor, I prayed that I hadn't wasted too much time. I got back to the audition room just as the monitor called my name. "Here!" I said, filling my voice with mock good cheer. Despair clutched at my belly—my voice sounded the same as always. Good. Solid. But not Broadway-bold. Not at all.

Stepping into the room, I threw my shoulders back and lifted my chin. I quickly crossed my fingers, and muttered my own "Just this once" mantra. I mean, if Teel was going to shortchange me, I had to rely on my own rituals to pull me through.

I forced a confident smile to my lips and crossed the room to the accompanist's upright piano. I handed him my sheet music, waiting for his easy nod before I turned to the trio of directors who waited in their uncomfortable chairs. I tried not to pay attention to the discarded coffee cups by their feet, to the crumpled wrappers from cookies and candy bars. They'd obviously had a long day already, and my audition was only making it longer.

"My name is Erin Hollister," I said, fighting down tears as I confirmed that my voice sounded exactly the way it always had. "I'm singing 'Love Changes Everything' from *Aspects of Love.*"

The accompanist waited for me to take a full breath. He brought his fingers down in a bright chord, then nodded for me to start. "'Love,'" I sang the first word.

And I almost stopped singing.

The sound that flowed out of my throat was like nothing I'd ever heard before. Certainly, it was like nothing I'd ever *produced* before. The note was huge, full-bodied. It filled my chest and soared out of my mouth like a brilliant, perfect bubble. I sang the rest of the line, and each syllable held its own, captivating, drawing the directors forward on their chairs.

The full power of a Wurlitzer organ pumped behind my voice. My breath control was something that opera divas only dreamed of. The lyrics swelled inside me, took on a vibrant life of their own. The accompanist sifted his piano notes beneath my sung ones, keeping pace as the song built, as it became an anthem about the power of hopeless, helpless love.

I knew that I would be cut off after a few lines. *All* actors were cut off after a few lines.

But they let me keep on singing. They let me finish the entire first verse. And the second. I modulated keys perfectly, belted out the dramatic third verse. I hit the highest note, drew out the word *flame* as if my entire soul depended on my ability to embrace the word, to wrap myself inside it, myself, and everyone else in that audition room.

I couldn't believe it. No one ever finished a song in audition. Certainly, I had never finished a song in audition. I'd never sung like that in my life. I wanted to run over to the piano, to beg the accompanist to play something else, anything, so that I could further explore my new voice.

In fact, I barely resisted the urge to press my fingers together, to summon Teel into the room, then and there. I wanted to thank her, to apologize, to tell her that I'd been wrong, that I never should have doubted her, never should have suspected her of shortchanging me on my wish.

Of course, I wasn't going to do that. I wasn't going to give the slightest sign that my performance was anything out of the ordinary. Me? Oh, yes, I sing like that in the shower. Just a little show tune, here and there. Self-taught, I am. Humble, singing me.

"Thank you," one of the women said, her voice warm and sincere. "If you could just head upstairs, Ms. Hollister. The dance auditions are in room 401."

"Thank *you,*" I said, adding a fervent nod and a grin

toward the accompanist.

I almost fainted when I discovered that wish-supported dancing was a hundred times better than wish-supported singing. With singing, I was building on a talent I'd always had, at least a little bit. I'd glimpsed moments of perfect song before, those brief instants when a piece was precisely in my range, when I grabbed hold of the lyrics and belted them out with all the power of Barbra Streisand.

I'd never had that sort of luck with dancing. I'd stumbled through a half dozen professional dance auditions before, but I'd always known that others would be chosen for those roles.

As I took my place with seven other hopefuls, my toes tingled with post-Teel anticipation. The dance captain showed us a tricky combination, one that started out simply enough, but ended with a syncopated shuffle that left half my group shaking their heads in perplexed frustration. As soon as I flexed my knees, though, my body knew precisely what it was supposed to do. I copied the dance captain as if my limbs were tied to his. I matched the exact set of his hands, held my head at the precise angle. My feet executed the steps as if they'd known them forever, as if I just happened to skip through them every single morning on my way out the front door.

The director and producers talked quietly among themselves, then sent three girls home. They had the rest of us work through another combination. Two more of my would-be competitors left. We three who remained danced a third combination. A fourth, and we were all finally excused from the room with a curt, "We'll be in touch."

I knew that I should be gasping for breath—feeling the effects of both physical exertion and anxiety about the audition. My body, though, had been completely transformed by Teel's electric jolt. My genie might have looked like a cheerleader, but she was actually a bioengineer, a scientist, a miracle worker. My heart beat just a fraction faster than normal. My lungs expanded and contracted like they'd done nothing out of the ordinary. Every fiber of my body was ready, all systems were go.

Standing in the hallway, I caught the envious glances of the other dancers, their quick judgment barely masked by ingratiating smiles. We all agreed that the dance captain had been a sadist, that he could have shown the steps more slowly, demonstrated them with greater care.

I took my time straightening my tote bag, pretending that I was searching for my cell phone somewhere in its cavernous depth. In reality, I just wanted the other dancers to go on ahead. I wanted to walk down all four flights of stairs by myself, to race down them. I wanted to feel the metal railing skim beneath my fingertips.

I could still sense the flawless physical knowledge that had possessed my body. I could still feel the matchless swell of music in my chest. With Teel's assistance, my audition had been perfect.

Now I just had to wait for the casting director to call.

Chapter 5

BY EIGHT O'CLOCK, my enthusiasm about the audition had been replaced by a vague feeling of dread. I had spent a ridiculous amount of time in my apartment, trying on every item of clothing that I owned, trying to choose the perfect outfit for my meeting with Sam.

I finally settled on an ice-blue silk blouse that Amy had given me for Christmas the year before. I chose it as a conscious reminder of what my sister would say if she were sitting beside me. In the past week, Amy had become a charter member of the "kick Sam's ass to the curb" club. She was fierce as a tigress when her loved ones were threatened. She'd always been my biggest defender, but her protectiveness had trebled after our parents' death. "He's dead wood," she'd told me more than once during the past week. "You've got to disincentivize him from calling you again. You should have downsized a long time ago."

I loved Amy, but I was looking forward to her graduation from business school. Maybe, then, she'd speak English again.

Glancing out my bedroom window, I could tell that storm clouds were on the horizon—literal ones, not figments of my sometimes overactive imagination. I shrugged on a lightweight rain jacket. Better safe than sorry.

I was halfway to the elevator when I realized that I hadn't watered the peace lily sitting on my kitchen counter. I'd had it for three days. I'd promised to water it twice a week, as I worked through my first milestone of the Master Plan.

Three days. What plant needed water every three days? Besides, Amy had assured me that it would let me know when it needed watering. She'd promised that the leaves would droop just a little bit, that it would clearly indicate when it was thirsty.

I was only looking for an excuse to avoid Sam. I was only trying to delay the inevitable. The plant could wait.

I took a deep breath and headed downstairs, arriving at Garden Variety about five minutes after eight. Stylishly late—that was me. This time, Timothy wasn't waiting in the courtyard. A roll of thunder sounded as I ducked inside the restaurant. I tried not to take that as an omen.

Half of the tables were filled. A homeless woman was huddled at the table in the back, hunched over a full plate of food. Sam was seated at "my" table, right in front of the fireplace.

The sight of him stopped me in my tracks. His hair was rumpled, as if he'd run his hands through it all day long (which I was fairly certain he had.) He had draped a raincoat over the chair closest to the hearth. I recognized the Brooks Brothers garment; he'd bought it in

January, spending part of his generous year-end bonus. At the time, I'd thought it was a silly expense—he rarely needed to wear a raincoat, and there were other things for us to spend money on. Like a new couch for the living room, I'd argued strenuously. One that would be free of beer stains, from one too many enthusiastic viewings of sporting events.

Obviously, I'd lost that battle. I sternly reminded myself that I no longer cared about the battered couch in Sam's apartment. It wasn't nearly as nice as the one in Becca's condo.

I stood a little straighter as I stared at the man I'd thought I would marry. Sam must have had a court appearance that morning; he was wearing a suit. He'd tugged at the knot in his tie so that it hung loose.

I always loved Sam in a suit. I loved the way that he looked like a wayward little boy, like a child who had squirmed away from his mother as soon as he walked into church. I always wanted to reach out to him, to tug his lapels into shape, to tuck his escaping shirttail into his trousers.

But that was absurd. Sam was a thirty-two-year-old man. He should be able to dress like a grown-up, to make it through a workday without looking like a dark-haired Dennis the Menace.

He saw me as soon as I entered, and he flashed me the tightest of smiles. I could still remember how he used to stand when I came into the room, how he used to hold my chair. We were well past such social niceties now. No need to act out polite roles when we'd seen each other at home—flossing our teeth, clipping our toenails, going about the everyday indignities of living.

I took a deep breath and moved farther into the restaurant. Just as I crossed my fingers, ready to utter my wish mantra, Timothy emerged from the kitchen. His black hair was tousled, and he still had a three-day scruff of beard. His caramel eyes glinted as he recognized me, and his baritone "Erin!" raised an answering smile on my lips.

I was inordinately pleased that he remembered my name. It seemed like a good-luck sign, something strong enough to counter the thunderstorm that was grumbling outside. Timothy was part of my freedom-life, my independence down here in the Village. "Table for one?" he asked, glancing around to see which seats were available.

"Actually, I'm meeting a friend," I said, nodding toward Sam.

"Great," Timothy said, but his lips tightened a little. "I'll be over to tell you the menu in just a moment."

I shrugged out of my jacket as I crossed the room. It was warm inside the restaurant, and I felt my cheeks flush. I tried to tell myself that the color would look great against my blue blouse. Sam would get a strong reminder of what he was missing.

Reaching the table, I considered kissing Sam on the cheek, but that felt too friendly for my current state of mind. Shaking hands would have been absurd. I settled for fiddling with my jacket, draping it over the fourth chair with elaborate care. I concentrated on sending the message that I was busy, confident, too occupied to respond to whatever greeting Sam was offering. I was a free woman, strong and independent.

I needn't have bothered with the stage business. Sam was glued to his BlackBerry, thumb-typing some urgent message back to his office. He pressed one final button with grim determination, and then he leaned back in his chair.

"So," he said, eyeing Timothy's back as the chef glided back to the kitchen. "You're already a regular?"

I heard the jealousy larded beneath his words, and I reacted sharply. "What's that supposed to mean?"

"I don't remember your mentioning this place before today."

"I didn't. I didn't know about it until I moved into the—" I stopped short. Suddenly, I realized that I didn't want Sam to know the name of my building. I didn't want him to know any of my business, not while he still had that unattractive sneer on his face. "New apartment," I finally finished.

"About that," Sam said, and there was a nasty edge to his voice. "If you wanted to move out, you didn't have to lie about being knocked up."

"I didn't lie!"

Before Sam could shout back, Timothy appeared at the table, agile as a panther. He settled a basket of bread between us, adding two tumblers of ice water. The effect was to push us into separate corners, to give us a chance to calm down, to press the reset button on our conversation.

Timothy glanced at me, his eyes unreadable, but when he spoke, his voice was a perfect model of calm professionalism. "I've got a green garlic soup tonight, made with chicken stock. And a green salad with sugar snap peas and a white balsamic vinaigrette."

Sam barely glanced at Timothy. "Just leave the menus," he said. "We'll order in a few minutes."

"Um, Sam," I said. "There aren't any menus. Timothy is telling us what's available tonight."

I recognized the flash of annoyance in Sam's eyes. He didn't like other people controlling him, didn't like conforming to the expectations of others. All part of his Peter Pan life. Why hadn't I realized that before? "Well," he said, "if *Timothy* is telling us..."

The man in question refused to rise to the bait. Instead, Timothy held his hands loosely at his sides, as if to show that he wasn't currently a threat. His voice walked a precisely neutral line as he said, "I'll come back in a few minutes. Give you a chance to catch up a little more before you order."

I wanted to tell him that wasn't necessary. I wanted to apologize for Sam's rudeness. I wanted to say that I was starving and I'd start with the soup, and I'd love more bread as soon as Timothy could bring it. But that wouldn't make things any easier for the rest of the conversation I still needed to have with Sam. I settled for a quick smile, and a sunny, "Thanks!"

Where was the Tony Award I so clearly deserved?

Timothy crossed over to talk to the patrons at another table, but I sensed him watching us out of the corner of his eye. Of course he was, I tried to reassure myself. A good waiter monitors when he's needed. A good waiter looks for the slightest sign that a patron is ready to order. A good waiter hopes that his patrons aren't going to draw blood over the bread basket.

Sam muttered, "What kind of restaurant doesn't have menus?"

"Come on, Sam. It's something new. Something different."

"Is that what this is all about? You wanted a change?" I recognized his Lawyer Voice. He was questioning me as if I were on some cosmic witness stand.

I forced my tone to stay even. "Sam, I wasn't looking for a change."

Just the opposite, I thought. I'd tried to settle into something permanent. Something inescapable. Something I was increasingly glad had never come to pass.

Sam glanced around the dining room, taking in the mismatched tables with their eclectic place settings. I saw his gaze linger on the woman at the table by the kitchen, on her collection of bags. I could calculate the precise instant when he figured out that she was homeless. He was quicker at leaping to the truth than I had been. He sounded incredulous as he said, "It looks like you found one, though, didn't you? But I can't begin to figure out why you'd want it."

And that was it. I was completely done with Sam.

As much as it pained me to admit it, Amy was right. At least where Sam was concerned. Maybe where my entire love life was concerned. I had changed myself to be with him. I had adopted his ideas of what was right, what was good. I had fallen into life on the Upper East Side like it was something that I had chosen, something that I preferred.

But I wasn't an Upper East Side kind of girl. At least, not the type that Sam wanted me to be.

Sitting there, in the middle of Garden Variety Café, I could hardly remember the first moment that I'd thought I was pregnant, the first instant that I'd started to dream about my so-called "happy ever after" with Sam. Had I really thought that I'd find complete fulfillment doing our *laundry?* Cooking our dinner while he advanced his career? Giving up my career in the theater to be his wife?

And then, when Sam had called me that afternoon,

just before my audition, I had actually started to slip back into those old ways of thinking. I had slid into habits so well-worn I didn't even need to think about them. I had actually worried about being rude to him, about hanging up on him—when he had refused to take my calls for almost a week. Declined to phone me back, even after I had told him that the immediate threat was past.

Amy was right. I needed the Master Plan—more than I'd ever thought possible. I needed to figure out why it was so easy for me to cave in, to shape myself to what a guy wanted me to be.

Stunned at the truth I was seeing for the first time, I sat back in my chair. "Look," I said. "This obviously isn't working." I waved my hand between us, futilely trying to encompass two years of a relationship gone bad. "*We* aren't working. We probably haven't been for a long time, but we've both been too busy, too wrapped up in our careers, to notice."

"Careers?" He sounded absolutely incredulous. Not snide. Not nasty.

Just completely, one hundred percent certain that I could never achieve my dreams.

I wanted to tell him about the audition I'd had that afternoon. I wanted to tell him about *Menagerie!* About Laura Wingfield. I wanted to tell him that I was going to land the role of a lifetime.

But why bother? Sam had already decided that I could never succeed. He wouldn't—he *couldn't*—understand what the theater meant to me. Sam had never understood anything at all about me.

Now that I thought about it, though, that was only fair. I'd never understood him, either. I'd thought that he was a stand-up guy, the proverbial diamond in the rough. I'd figured that he'd finish playing someday soon, that he'd stop being a frat boy, that he'd be ready to man up sometime this century. I wished that I could invent a compatibility test, something as easy to use as a store-bought pregnancy test. Something to determine whether a couple had what it took to succeed in the long run—before they made the commitment to waste months on each other.

I sighed and said, "Let's just skip the rest, okay? Let's pretend that you've told me exactly what you think about my acting prospects. Let's take it for granted that I cried. You felt bad. We both promised we'd change, and we tried for another week, or a month, or even two. But let's just cut to the end, okay?"

He stared at me, surprise making his eyes go wide. I knew those eyes so well. I'd seen them glint with amusement, at least when we'd first met. I'd seen them laugh as he tugged me into bed. I'd seen them go hard with anger. I'd seen them narrow with shrewd appraisal.

And yet, despite how well I knew his eyes, I realized that I'd never really known Sam. Or at least the Sam I'd known was not the Sam I could stand being with. Not for the rest of my life.

He pushed back from the table. Glancing around the quirky dining room, he let a quizzical look blur his handsome features. He shook his head, started to say something, stopped. He finally settled on, "Do you have anything else you need to get out of my place?"

His place. He'd already accepted the change. He was already moving on. I shook my head. "No."

Of course, I didn't need to tell *him* that there wasn't

any paperwork. He'd never put me on the lease; instead, I'd just paid rent over to him month after wasted month. I guess I should have seen that as a warning sign, his reluctance to make anything between us official. Now, I realized there were lots of things I should have seen as warning signs.

He nodded once. "Goodbye, then. See you around."

Not likely. Not unless he started hanging around the Equity offices. Or I lost my mind and started haunting law firm lobbies. "Goodbye."

As I watched him collect his coat and briefcase, I tried to parse my emotions. I should be feeling anger. Embarrassment. Frustration. A long line of other negative emotions, difficult, dark feelings that I should examine, that I should store away, that I should harvest for future roles onstage. Forget about future roles—I had just enacted some strange liberation scene for *Menagerie!*'s Laura Wingfield, freeing myself from a fantasy version of romance, from a dream that could never exist.

I don't know what Laura would have felt, if she'd ever figured out how to talk to a man. All I knew was that I felt relief.

The door closed behind Sam. I realized that I was holding my breath. When I exhaled, I felt an iron rod of tension melt along my spine. Suddenly, I was ready to stretch out on the broad flagstones in front of the fire. I longed for nothing more than Becca's comfortable couch and a warm blanket, maybe a feather pillow to cradle my head.

"Some soup?" I turned away from the door to see Timothy settle a large bowl in front of me. Steam curled off the surface, carrying the fragrance of fresh garlic sprouts and an elusive hint of hot roasted chicken. I caught a breath of sherry, as well. I blinked and tried to pull myself back to the present. "You look hungry," Timothy said, by way of explanation. He barely acknowledged Sam's absence, taking just a moment to flick his eyes toward the now-empty chair that had held the Brooks Brothers coat.

"I am," I said. Timothy nodded toward the bowl, indicating that I should take a taste. Bright spring garlic melted across my tongue, flavorful without being overwhelming. "This is perfect."

"I've got scallops tonight. And brisket."

I shook my head. "You know? I think I'll just stick with the soup."

He nodded. "Let me know if you need anything else."

"I will," I said.

Timothy turned toward the kitchen, and I started to think about the magazines that he'd had the other night. I wondered whether he'd received the new issue of the *New Yorker*. But before I could ask, everything disappeared.

For just a second, I thought that I must be having some sort of delayed reaction to Sam's departure. I certainly didn't *feel* like my heart was breaking. I didn't *think* that I'd suffer a stroke or an aneurysm or some other dire medical emergency, just because my boyfriend of the past two years had walked out of the room without a backward glance. I'd wanted him to go.

But I couldn't figure out what else was going on. One moment, I was watching Timothy walk back into his kitchen. The next, I was surrounded by nothingness—a vague gray space that stretched as far as my eyes could see. The fireplace, my table, everything about Garden Variety, simply disappeared. I couldn't see my soup, couldn't smell it.

I staggered forward a step, surprised to find that I was standing, when I'd been sitting in the restaurant just a moment before. My feet moved; I could sense my muscles bunching, feel my toes rocking to maintain my balance. When I looked down, I could see my body, but there wasn't anything else. There wasn't anything beneath my feet. My belly swooped in disorientation, and I was grateful that I'd only swallowed a single spoonful of soup.

"Hello?" I called out, hating the fact that my voice quavered. At the same time, though, I was proud that I managed to get out any sound at all. "Help?"

"I do not understand you humans!" I whirled at the voice that came from behind me. "Seven out of ten just look into the distance instead of using their time here to study the Garden!"

"What?" I asked stupidly, absurdly grateful that my eyes had something to focus on. A well-muscled man stood in front of me. His sandy hair was chopped into a brush cut, and his blue eyes were sharp enough to cut wood. He wore a gray T-shirt that was stamped Garden Athletic Department and sweatpants to match. He bounced lightly on his Nike-clad feet, as if he had just finished an invigorating run and was ready to drop and give me twenty.

I wasn't entirely surprised to find a tattoo encircling his wrist. The flames shone particularly brightly in the neutral air around us, kindling with an orange-and-yellow light as if they glowed from within. The black outlines flickered as I stared.

"Teel?" I asked.

"You were expecting someone else?" The efficiency of his tight smile was underscored by the stopwatch that he held in his right hand. I was willing to swear that the thing had appeared from nowhere; surely, I would have seen it when I noticed the flickering flames on his wrist. He nodded as he watched the second hand tick past some noteworthy point, and then he raised his left hand to the pulse point in his neck. After fifteen seconds, he was apparently satisfied with his heart rate, because he nodded and thumbed a button on the stopwatch. "Ready? Get set, go!"

"Go where?" I asked. If I kept my gaze tightly locked on the genie, I could just avoid the queasiness that assaulted me every time I looked at the nothingness around me.

"To the Garden, of course!"

"What are you talking about?"

He bounced on his feet like an overly enthusiastic personal trainer, the kind who should be shot at dawn. "The one right in front of us!" He drilled into me with those thermonuclear eyes. "Let's go, now. You can see it. You can make it real!"

I barely managed not to groan. "Teel, can you just stand still?"

He jogged over to my side. "Okay, now. Take three deep breaths." He settled one broad hand on my chest, watched as my lungs filled, arching his fingers as I exhaled. "There you go. Another. One more, deeper now. Hold it. Hoooold it!" I clamped down on the air in my lungs until I thought I was going to explode. "And exhale! Excellent!"

Again, he fiddled with his stopwatch. I had no idea

what he could possibly be timing. My breathing? I felt like I was confined with some insane paramedic, someone who was measuring the time between my contractions, intent on helping me deliver a healthy baby. Um, if I were actually pregnant. Which we'd all established, cataclysmically, that I was not.

"Okay, now," Teel said, turning away and obviously not noticing—or not caring—that I wasn't bouncing along after him. "Place each hand around an upright here on the fence and stretch—" He started to match action to word, but I merely gaped.

My genie was apparently a master mime. His fingers folded around some sort of post, or a pole, something that was absolutely invisible to me. He leaned into the support, popping out the taut muscles of his calves. He threw his head back and inhaled deeply, as if he were summoning strength from the inner walls of his corpuscles.

"There!" he said after a thunderous exhale. "Your turn. Grab hold of the fence—"

His fingers on mine were warm, hot even. I shook him off with annoyance. "Teel, there isn't any fence!" I pulled away, taking three tottering steps into the void.

"Oh," he said, and he was so crestfallen that I flashed back to the moment when I told my high school soccer coach I was dropping off the team so that I could act in the drama club's production of *Ten Little Indians*. Teel came to a bobbing stop in front of me, still shuddering his arms like a bird practicing to take off, keeping his muscles loose, exuding the very essence of athlete-in-training. "Really?"

"Really." I darted my eyes left and right, refusing to turn my head completely. "I don't even know what you're talking about."

Teel sighed. "Damn. I thought you might be one. A Perceptive. I've never met one, and I'm so close to the end."

"A Perceptive? What are you talking about? And the end of what?"

"My mission. Once I grant all of your wishes, I get to go inside the Garden."

I forced myself to stare into the distance, into the space where Teel quite clearly saw something beautiful, something compelling. All I could make out was a featureless expanse that made my inner ear scream that it was out of balance. I forced myself to concentrate and asked, "But what is it?"

"The most beautiful place in the world." Teel relaxed back on his heels. For the first time in this incarnation, he seemed calm. A smile blossomed across his lips as he spoke. "It's always in full bloom—can't you smell the lilacs? And the honeysuckle?" He didn't wait for my denial. "The stream is just inside—you can hear it. And the birds... They're incredibly loud today. Almost as if they know I'm coming in soon." He closed his eyes, and his rock-hard features softened. "The nightingales...and Jaze."

"Jaze?" I finally interrupted Teel's enraptured recital. "What is Jaze?"

"Who," my personal trainer said, snapping back to my reality. Or at least what passed for reality here in the middle of nowhere. He started bouncing on his toes again, apparently ready to run a 5K.

"Who," I acceded, shrugging.

"Jaze is my soul mate. Or I think he will be, if we ever get into the Garden at the same time. We promised we would wait for each other if...*when* we both get in. She's been there for several months of your human time. I thought it might work out, when you summoned me. Becca passed on the lamp so quickly. She made it possible for you to make your wishes before Jaze leaves."

His voice became more commanding as he spoke, more insistent. Those laser eyes seemed to demand that I make my last two wishes immediately. Trying not to be flustered by Teel's flexible use of pronouns, I asked, "How long will he, um, she... How long will *Jaze* be there?"

Teel glared with a fierce competitiveness. "Time might be up, even now. Ready to make your last two wishes?"

That wasn't fair! He couldn't lure me here and tell me about his mythical Garden, pine away for his girlfriend, um, boyfriend, *whatever,* and then demand that I make my final wishes! A strong jolt of resentment cemented my jaw, and I forced out an answer. "Not yet. I only made the first two today. I have to see how they turn out."

"Eight out of ten wishers complete their wishes in one week." He barked out the statistic with the same conviction legitimate trainers used on their clients.

I'd always rebelled against authority figures. At least, that's what Amy told me, every time she tried to boss me around. I dug in my figurative heels. "I'm afraid I might be one of the outliers."

"But I've waited so long...." Suddenly, there was a wistfulness in Teel's voice that I hadn't heard before, a vulnerability that was distinctly at odds with his current rugged demeanor. He looked over his sculpted shoulder, his eyes swooping upward, so that I was fairly certain he was following the path of an invisible bird.

"I'm sorry," I said firmly. "But you have to understand. I need to make the most of my wishes. I can't just give them away, so that you can go into the Garden."

"But Jaze—"

"Even to meet Jaze," I said, surprised at the sudden iron that I put into my words.

Sam had just given me a new perspective on relationships, and on just how long—or short—a time they might last. I was strong enough to argue for what I needed, independent enough to take care of myself.

Teel apparently heard my newfound determination. He sighed. "But you'll *try* to decide quickly?"

"As soon as I know what to ask for," I said, nodding firmly. I shouldn't have been so assertive, though. The motion of moving my head up and down was enough to send my stomach reeling again. "Um, Teel? Can you get me out of here now? I really don't feel well."

He glanced down at his stopwatch and nodded, as if we had finally met some preordained time limit. "Promise me you won't delay, though."

"I promise," I said. Truth be told, I was starting to feel sick enough that if Teel had offered to trade one wish for getting me out of that disorienting whirl of nothingness, I just might take him up on it. Fortunately for me, though, my genie reached up to his tanned earlobe and tugged hard, twice.

All of a sudden, I was back in Garden Variety. I could feel the chair beneath me. I could hear the crackle of the fire, the murmur of conversation at a couple of nearby tables. I could see the homeless woman at the back gathering up her bags, checking their belts and buckles, readying herself to return to the May night outside. I could smell the still-steaming green garlic soup in front of me.

The hint of sherry in the bowl was too much for my uneasy stomach. I pushed the soup away and forced myself to take a trio of deep breaths.

Only then did I dare look around. Had anyone noticed my disappearance? Had anyone seen me blink out of existence, and then back in again?

Apparently, no one had. Not one person in the restaurant was gazing in my direction. I'd somehow managed to go to Teel's Garden and return without raising a single suspicious eyebrow.

I forced myself to take a piece of bread from the basket Timothy had brought, hoping that some ballast would steady my stomach. I tore off a bite, relishing the crisp crust. I made myself chew a dozen times before I swallowed, telling myself that my belly would settle down once it had something inside it. I gulped a little water to reinforce the message.

After a few minutes, Timothy circled back. He frowned when he saw the bowl of soup pushed away. The expression looked fierce against his unshaved cheeks, but his voice was gentle. "Rough night?"

I found a wry smile somewhere inside my confusion. "You could say that."

"Can I get you something else?"

I shook my head. "Let me just settle up on this."

He picked up the bowl. "It's on the house."

"That's not fair!"

His eyes darted toward the door, tracing the path that Sam had taken as he left. "Fair enough, I think.

Are you okay to get home?"

For just a second, I imagined him walking me back to the Bentley. I pictured him standing in my doorway after I'd worked the triple locks. I imagined him resting a hand on my arm, raising his fingers to trace my cheekbone. I felt his lips on mine, warm and growing hotter as he teased a willing response from me.

Blushing, I forced away the fantasy.

I was through with men. I was strong and independent, and I wasn't going to cash in those hard-won chips for the first guy who was nice to me at the end of a long day. I had a Master Plan, and I wasn't about to throw it out the window.

"I'm fine," I said.

He nodded. "Don't be a stranger."

I found myself snared by the serious expression on his face, by the grave simplicity of his words. "I won't be," I said.

I pushed back my chair and reached for my jacket, but Timothy took it from my hands. He held it behind me, finding the perfect angle so that my arms slid easily into the sleeves. His fingertips twitched the collar into place, and I was aware of the fleeting ghost of his palms against my shoulders, brushing the coat against my frame.

Independent women could let men help them into their coats, couldn't they?

"Thanks," I said.

"Have a good evening." For just a moment, I thought that he was going to say something else, but we both saw the flicker of a raised hand from a table against the far wall, the gesture of a contented diner calling for his check. Timothy smiled wryly and said,

"Don't get wet out there."

I twitched my hood into place and stepped into the courtyard. It had obviously rained hard while I'd been in the restaurant. In fact, a few stray raindrops still splashed onto the flagstones in the courtyard, but I'd missed the worst of the weather.

I was hurrying toward the Bentley when my cell phone rang. Who'd be calling after nine? It wasn't Amy—I had a ring tone set for her. Sam, either. He had his own tone, one that it was time to delete. I fished out the phone and stared at the screen. A 212 number, unknown to me.

A 212 number. Here in New York. In New York, the theater capital of the world.

My heart started pounding as I remembered the casting director in the dance studio—was it only that afternoon? "We'll be in touch," she'd said. And I had walked out of the audition hall, certain that I had the role.

My fingers tingled as I pressed the glowing green button and answered the call. If I wasn't cast as Laura Wingfield in *Menagerie!* there was no justice in all of New York City.

Chapter 6

THERE WAS NO justice in New York City.

The casting director was kind enough. She told me that I had amazed the director. I had wowed the choreographer. I had made the lyricist recognize new potential for the songs that he had written for the show's world premiere.

But the producers had decided to go with Martina Block, that actress who had become so famous a few years ago, on that reality TV show. She had the big name, the marquee appeal. She could fill a Broadway house, sell tickets for months and months on end.

Nevertheless, they wanted me to be Martina's understudy. The casting director hastened to assure me that my job as understudy would be so important, so vital, that it was practically a full role in itself. Serving as understudy was so demanding that I wouldn't even be able to perform in the chorus. It would be fantastic experience.

The only catch was, I wouldn't go onstage. Not unless something terrible happened to Martina.

I was so disappointed that I wanted to cry. I wanted

to collapse onto one of Timothy's metal chairs. I wanted to grind my cell phone underfoot. I wanted to throw my head back and howl at the beclouded moon, mourning cold, cruel fate.

Instead, I thanked the casting director for her consideration and said that I'd show up for the first read-through, a week away.

What else could I say? I needed the job. I needed the exposure. I needed the pittance of a paycheck, the fraction of what I would have earned if I'd landed the star role. At least it was more than I'd been getting at Concerned Catering. By a dollar or two.

And I could stretch the truth a little, tell everyone that I had a role in a new musical. In the battle to win the new me, I could claim a victory. It was just a smaller victory than I'd anticipated. A much smaller victory.

The more I thought about that, the more I realized that I was furious with Teel. My genie had promised me. We had a contract. In fact, when I thought back to my panic in the audition hall bathroom, I had been specifying the details of my wish, I had been clarifying that I wanted to use my singing and dancing skills to get the lead in *Menagerie!* when Teel had cut me off.

She was bound to grant my wishes, wasn't she? To make my dreams come true! She had to make this right. She had to make my wishes work the way that I'd intended.

I forced myself to wait until I was back in my apartment before I pressed my tattooed fingertips together and called her name.

There was the electric jangle I'd come to expect. The fog was becoming old hat, but this time it cleared up much faster than before. I barely blinked, and then I was face to face with Fred Flintstone.

Okay. It wasn't really the cartoon character. Instead, it was a fat slob of a guy. His belly hung over his dirty blue jeans. His Yankees T-shirt was at least one size too small, and he really should have considered adding suspenders to the belt that wasn't doing its job. A monster-size bag of nacho cheese Doritos filled one hand and a beer occupied the other. Tattooed flames glinted dully against the aluminum can.

I was so astonished that I sat down on my couch. "Where's the trainer?" I asked.

He belched in response, long and low. When he rubbed the back of one forearm across his mouth, he left behind a sprinkling of fake orange cheese. "A lot o' good that did me. No need fer a trainer, if I'm stuck outside the Garden. It's not like Jaze is ever gonna see me." His beady eyes narrowed as he studied me. "Unless y' changed yer mind. Ready t' make Wish Three?"

I shook my head, a little overwhelmed that Teel's appearance could have changed so completely in such a short time. I shouldn't have been surprised, though. I mean, there was nothing that the personal trainer had in common with the skanky cheerleader, or the cop. But this guy, this mass of morose flesh... I found myself seeking out the tracery of his tattoos once again, just to reassure myself that he was really Teel.

He scooped up a huge fistful of Doritos and shoved them into his maw. Around the crumbs, he said, "Well, not t' put too fine a point on it, but what d' y' want from me? Why'd y' call me here?" He chugged down half a can of beer as he waited for my reply.

"My wishes," I said. "The first two. You didn't do what you said you would."

He craned his neck to either side, as if he'd spent too many hours watching TV and had just figured out how to haul his carcass out of his recliner. When his spine had completed its concerto of audible pops, he shook his head vigorously. Only then did he point at me, sparing the index finger that had been curled around the beer can. "Can y' sing better 'n before y' made yer wish?"

"Well, yes," I said, "but—"

"And can y' dance better?"

"Yes, but—"

"Two wishes granted, then. I done my part."

"But I was supposed to get a role in *Menagerie!*"

"Did y' wish fer a role in, what d' y' call it, *Menagerie!*"

"I told you why I wanted to sing and dance. I told you that I wanted the lead."

"But did y' wish fer it? It's all about the wishes, is'n it?"

"You didn't let me! You didn't let me get a word in edgewise!"

"I don' recall anyone shovin' a gag down yer throat. Y' did well enough, askin' me fer what y' got." As if to punctuate that circular logic, he tilted the bag of Doritos up to his lips, pouring a fluorescent orange stream of crumbs into his mouth. He chewed loudly and then said, "Y' wanna make another wish? Wish fer the lead?"

"No!" I answered immediately, out of frustration, but also with a sense of outrage. "I already spent two wishes on the show! I want you to do what you should have done in the first place!"

"Y' want me t' pull yer contract? 'Cause it says right there in black 'n' white that y' got t' make yer wishes clear. If y' did'n say y' wanted t' be in that play, then I did'n have any obligation t' put y' in that play. But yer free t' make another wish now."

He was doing this to drive me crazy. He wanted to make me use up a third wish, to get him that much closer to his precious Jaze, even though I couldn't imagine anyone—male, female, genie or human—who would want to spend thirty seconds with this carb-stuffed, beer-soaked slob.

I dug in my heels. "Fine," I said. "Go back to whatever you were doing."

"Yer not gonna make a wish? Y' got two left, y' know."

"I know. I'm not wishing right now. Have a good evening." I glared at my fingertips. I'd give just about anything to invent some sort of summoning magic in reverse—something that would let me send Teel back to where he'd come from. I settled for a pointed sigh, and then I said, "Good *night*."

Teel raised his stained fingers to his earlobe and pulled twice. I distinctly heard him belch before he faded away.

I tried not to feel sorry for myself while I sat in rehearsal, but it wasn't easy.

The director, Ken Durbin, gathered all of us in one room. We were seated at tables that were shaped into a circle, so that everyone could see everyone else. One wall was covered in mirrors, which made the sound echo a little. As we entered, we completed "Hello, My Name Is" name tags; I resisted the urge to draw a frowning face above the *i* in *Erin.* That wouldn't be the most professional way to meet my fellow cast members.

The show only had four acting roles: Laura (the role

that should have been mine), Amanda (Laura's dreamy, out-of-touch, faded Southern belle mother), Tom (Laura's brother, who longs to escape the cesspit of family interactions) and Jim (the Gentleman Caller, Tom's coworker and Laura's completely impossible crush.)

The musical version added a dozen singers and dancers to Tennessee Williams's original play. They would perform a variety of roles, acting out neighbors who gossiped about the batty Amanda and Laura, and playing Tom's factory coworkers, along with a cavalcade of dream-suitors whom Laura imagined might carry her off to eternal married bliss. None of them had lines—they told their story entirely in song and dance.

It took me about twenty-seven seconds to realize that there were three tiers in *Menagerie!* society. First came the name stars, the four leads who would literally see their names in lights. A substantial distance behind came the singers and dancers, the ensemble who would make this musical version of a classic soar above other plays. And at the very back, sweeping up after the entire fiesta of lights and glory and fame, like the circus workers who followed along behind the elephants on parade, were the understudies. Me, sitting in as not-Laura.

At least I found a kindred spirit in Shawn Goldberg, the understudy for the Gentlemen Caller. I'd met him a couple of years back, when I'd first moved to New York. We'd attended a casting seminar together, both listening to a presentation from some long-forgotten casting director, then trying to impress the guy with our respective pitches. I know that I never got a job out of the deal; I didn't think Shawn had, either. In the intervening years, we'd run into each other at a handful of parties.

Shawn seemed overjoyed to see me. We both took seats at the foot of the table, as far away from Ken Durbin and Martina Block as it was possible to be. Shawn insisted on kissing me on both cheeks, and he exclaimed that I didn't look a *day* older than when we'd met. He just *loved* what I was doing with my hair, and he would positively *die* if I didn't share his black-and-white cookie with him.

At least the cookie left a sweet taste in my mouth, to counteract the self-pitying acid of introducing myself to everyone as Martina's understudy.

After we'd gone around the circle, Ken leaped to his feet. He was a short man, lithe, with a dancer's body despite his having reached middle age. He seemed unable to keep still; even when he was standing behind his chair, he bounced up and down on the balls of his feet. When he spoke, his voice was higher than I expected; the tone made his words seem even more urgent, more important. His wiry gray hair moved with every toss of his head, and his dark brown eyes darted around the room, including everyone in their survey.

Ken wowed us for almost an hour, telling us about the power that he saw in our American classic. He talked about the archetypal strength of the characters, the ways that they had persisted through the decades, how they had become hallmarks of American culture. He waxed eloquent about the raw creativity of the American musical, an art form born on the hallowed streets of Broadway. He delivered a paean to the artistic spirit, to the songwriters and choreographers and designers who would forge our production into a thing of everlasting beauty.

I would have been inspired, if I'd felt like I belonged.

When Ken finished his eloquent introduction, he announced a short break before we settled down to the excitement of reading through the text for the very first time. Even those of us who knew Tennessee Williams's play inside and out, he said, were bound to be surprised by the energy!—and the vibrancy! and the excitement!—of the book for the musical.

The dancers led the stampede for the door; they'd been kept from their cigarettes for too long. Familiar with the scene from every other play I'd ever worked on, I could picture the entire gaggle of them, hovering by the door to the rehearsal hall, sucking down as much nicotine as they could squeeze into their bloodstreams before they were required to return. I was consistently amazed that dancers could meet the physical demands of their roles, given the nicotine abuse of their bodies. (I'm sure there were some dancers who didn't smoke, but not any of my acquaintance.)

Shawn raised a single imperious eyebrow at our colleagues' behavior, then returned his attention to the lead actors. He leaned close to whisper, "*Someone* should tell Martina that bikini undies are *so* last year. She really should get herself a decent pair of boyshorts."

I followed his pointed glance. Martina was leaning in close to Ken Durbin, twisting in her chair so that her black gabardine slacks were stretched tight, subjecting her to the scourge of Visible Panty Line. Shawn's expression was so scandalized that I couldn't help but laugh. I whispered back, "Is there No Hope For The Future?"

I drew out the last five words, making them as dramatic as I dared in a room where I might be overheard. Martina had risen to fame by competing on a reality television show for a role in a big-budget musical produced by a certain major entertainment corporation that had a certain strong business tie to a certain big-four television network.

Martina's reality show competition had ranged from gross-out eating contests to big-glitz song-and-dance numbers. She had cemented her win in the final round, where each contestant was required to deliver a speech to the judges. Martina's had been entitled "No Hope for the Future." She had written about the horror of industrial farming, decrying the plight of cattle fattened on corn, destined for slaughter. Much to the glee of entertainment columnists everywhere, she had begun her speech with the now-immortal phrase, "I am a cow!"

At least it got her noticed.

Shawn shook his head. "So, what do you think it'll take to off the leads? Some arsenic in their tea? Colonel Mustard with the candlestick in the conservatory?" He twirled an invisible dastardly mustache.

I laughed. "I wouldn't put anything past you!"

"Just you wait, my dear. Just you wait!"

I pretended to look shocked, but I was actually quite amused. Shawn had always been good for a laugh, and now that we were engaged in an "us against them" struggle, it felt good to know he had my back.

Of course, I still had Teel up my proverbial sleeve. I *could* have summoned my genie, used a wish and been released from this entire depressing ordeal. Teel would have been thrilled. After talking to his obnoxious Yankees fan incarnation, I was just about positive that he'd railroaded me into making my singing and dancing wishes precisely because he knew I wouldn't get the role that I desired. He knew that I'd come back to him, speeding through my wishes as if they were tissue, and I had the head cold of the century.

A tiny voice, though, whispered that I was being paranoid. My genie could grant wishes, but he couldn't read the future. He'd had no way of knowing that Martina Block was going to audition for the role of Laura. He certainly couldn't have guessed that Martina would be cast instead of me.

Nope. I'd told the truth when I spoke to Teel's fat-slob persona. I'd spent two wishes getting where I was, and I wasn't going to invest another. Besides, if I applied a third wish to land the lead, I'd have to arrange for Shawn to star, as well. Otherwise, I'd have to watch every bite of food I ingested, for the entire run of the show. Or at least make sure there weren't any candlesticks on the set.

As Shawn cast a shrewd eye toward the industrial-size coffeemaker, I nudged him with my elbow. "Don't even think about it!" I warned. "We'd be the very first suspects."

He shrugged. "There'd be two others, at least. The understudies for Tom and Amanda."

"I don't like those odds."

"Just you wait," he said. "A few weeks into rehearsal, and you might be ready for anything."

A tingle of apprehension rippled down my spine. I didn't know whether I was afraid that Shawn was right...or that he was wrong. What if I ended up hating *Menagerie!* What if the show was terrible, and I was stuck in it for months?

Yeah. Like being stuck in a Broadway show was a bad thing.

In the end, the second half of rehearsal went like clockwork. The cast read through the script. An accompanist played the musical pieces on a piano while the songwriter spoke-sang the words. Ken assured everyone that the show was in a state of flux, that we'd discover more about our characters as we worked together. We'd find the unique shape of our production, pitching in to create a stunning new version of Williams's play.

I was exhausted by the time we filed out of the rehearsal hall. Listening to Martina's take on lines that I believed should be mine was more wearisome than I'd expected. I felt drained, enervated, as if I'd spent the entire day locked up with a difficult friend who bemoaned her perfectly satisfactory love life while I had none of my own.

It was only late afternoon, but I barely stifled a yawn. "I could go to sleep right now and not wake up until tomorrow morning."

Shawn laughed. "Not me!" He preened a little as he bounced down the sidewalk. "Patrick and I are going to a party tonight."

"It's Monday!"

"Cole Porter's birthday is only celebrated once a year," Shawn said with a sly wink. "I've been working on my medley for weeks."

I grinned, despite my fatigue. "How de-lovely," I said. Shawn blew me an air kiss and sashayed off into the afternoon light.

Shaking my head, I made my way downtown. It felt good to walk. The air was warm, hot even, but the typical summer humidity hadn't settled in yet. The pedestrian gods favored me, and I made every single light. A distant church bell was tolling four o'clock as I turned onto my street.

Somehow, in the past two weeks, everything had become automatic about living in the Bentley. I said hello to George, the doorman. I dug out my keys as I crossed the lobby. I hit the correct button in the elevator without thinking. I moved down the hallway, already imagining the cost-effective ramen noodles I was going to eat for dinner—I had my choice of chicken, beef or spicy shrimp.

But this time, there was something different about my new home. This time, neighbors stood in the hallway.

I hadn't met any other Bentley residents yet; if not for the cluster of mailboxes in the lobby, I could have believed that I was the only person living in the entire building. Now, though, a woman stood in her doorway, directly opposite mine, talking to a man in the hall. I slowed my footsteps as I approached, reluctant to call attention to myself, not wanting to interrupt a conversation between strangers.

But the man in the hallway wasn't a stranger.

"Timothy!" I exclaimed, so surprised that I almost dropped my keys. I flashed on the picture I'd painted in my mind just before I'd left Garden Variety a couple of weeks before—the image of Timothy standing in my doorway, kissing me good-night. I shoved away the thought; it wasn't worthy of me. Not the new me. The one with the Master Plan.

"Erin," Timothy said, smiling in easy recognition. He looked comfortable in his sleek black jeans, in his matching soft work shirt and his capacious apron.

"What are you doing here?" I managed to choke out. It was absurd for me to be blushing. He couldn't have read my mind when we'd last seen each other. He had no way of knowing that I'd been thinking of him that way.

But what *was* he doing there? Was it possible that Garden Variety made deliveries? I glanced at my neighbor, but her hands were empty. In fact, *Timothy* held a pair of paper grocery bags. A forest of greens cascaded over one edge.

The bright leaves reminded me of my Master Plan peace lily, languishing on my counter. I really had to water it, as soon as I got inside. It was high past time for Amy to ask about how the plant was doing. My sister knew me too well to accept a lie.

Obviously unaware of my inner lily-based guilt, Timothy gestured with his shopping bag. "Just picking up some produce from Dani. I assume you've already met?"

"Um, no," I said, really looking at my neighbor for the first time. She could have been a poster child for some senior citizen "green" movement. Her work shirt looked every bit as soft as Timothy's, but hers was faded denim, embroidered with intricate designs—flowers and leaves and rainbows all picked out in brightly colored thread. Her too-long jeans were nearly white from wear. She'd rolled up the cuffs to show off a pair of Birkenstock sandals that might have been the first ones off the company's production line. She complemented the open shoes with brilliant turquoise socks.

By way of greeting, she laughed. "I've knocked on your door a couple of times, but you've always been out." Her voice was soft, comfortable, as if she'd spent her years consciously rubbing away any hint of rough edges from her words. "You're subletting from my son and his fiancée. I'm Dani Thompson." I found myself smiling when I met her earth-colored eyes. Her face was weathered, deep wrinkles telling stories about long days spent beneath the sun. Her hair was woven into a long braid, hanks of gray twining through dark chestnut.

"Pleased to meet you," I said, extending a hand. I felt calluses on her palm when we shook.

"Likewise," she said warmly. "And I'd love to chat now, but I'm late getting a blog post up. Guerilla gardening waits for no woman!" She glanced at her watch, a huge, blocky Timex that looked as if it had taken a licking more times than anyone could remember. Before closing her door, though, she raised one hand to cup Timothy's cheek. "You'll let me know if there's anything I can do?"

"Of course," he said. He smiled reflexively at her touch, but the expression faded as soon as she stepped back.

Dani glanced at me. "Perhaps we can share a cup of tea soon?"

I nodded, liking the idea, even though I didn't know much about the woman. She tsked and looked at her watch again, then said goodbye and darted back inside her apartment.

I stared at Timothy as Dani's door snicked closed. When the silence ripened into something tangible, I said, "Um, this is a strange coincidence."

He shrugged. "Dani has a way of bringing people together."

"But here? I mean, what are the chances?"

"When you basically sublet from one of the city's key guerilla gardeners? And I run a restaurant specifically designed to make use of guerilla produce?"

I stared suspiciously at the greens in his bag. "What *is* guerilla gardening?"

He nodded toward Dani's closed door. "Dani leads the Gray Guerillas. They're a group of senior citizens determined to reclaim city land. They plant wherever they can, trying to make the city a more beautiful place to live. They sell their produce to people like me." His lips twisted into a self-mocking smile. "People who want to make a difference."

I remembered the smudge of dirt on Becca's wrist, when she'd helped me in the box office. She must be a guerilla gardener, too. Come to think of it, I'd read an article in the newspaper about the new environmental movement. The mayor had even held some sort of press conference, a month or two before.

I hadn't realized that Timothy had such a social agenda with his restaurant, but I wasn't actually surprised. Anyone who made a point of feeding homeless people and calculating prices on slips of butcher paper...

I glanced at his bags of produce and realized that I should invite him into my apartment. Offer him a cup of tea. Something to eat.

Remembering my earlier vision of him standing on my threshold, though, I blushed. There was really no way for me to follow through on the invitation. I didn't have the first idea of what to serve a real chef. Yeah. That was the problem. My lack of cooking ability.

I glanced at Timothy's face, trying to figure out if

he thought it was weird, my keeping him standing in the hallway. I wished that I could invent a mood thermometer, a simple device to tell me a person's emotions. I didn't need to read minds—I wasn't greedy. I just wanted to know if the people around me were amused. Puzzled. Whatever.

Timothy's face was inscrutable, though. His beard was scruffy, as always. His hair still looked like it had never been introduced to a brush. Funny. The rough-and-tumble image didn't seem immature on him. It didn't make me think of a spoiled little boy. Timothy, unlike Sam, looked like he was destined to be rumpled, rough-edged in a nonthreatening manner. An adult who was making his way in a less-than-perfect world.

Upon closer examination, though, I saw something more. There were creases beside his eyes, weary lines that made me think he was exhausted. I thought about the maternal tenderness Dani had shown, just before she ducked back inside her apartment. "Hey," I said, as if I had a right to know. "Is everything okay?"

He sighed. "It's that obvious, huh?" Shrugging, he set his grocery bags on the floor, nudging one with his toe when it started to fall over. He clenched his hands into fists and then loosened them, like a cat contemplating the best path to trapping some elusive prey. "I think I'm going to lose Garden Variety."

"Lose it! Why?" I didn't waste time wondering at the jagged shape his words cut into my heart. Sure, I was new to the neighborhood. Of course, I'd only eaten at Garden Variety a couple of times. Yeah, this was only the third time I'd talked to Timothy. But I already loved the restaurant, adored Timothy's concept, and I respected what he was doing, feeding the homeless for free even as he ladled up incredible meals for us paying customers.

He ran a hand over his face, like a man pushing away the lingering tendrils of a nightmare. His fingers were long, wiry, and I could only imagine the work he accomplished with them, day in, day out, in his kitchen. A disobedient part of my imagination strayed toward what else he could accomplish with strong hands like that, but I bit the inside of my cheek, reminding myself that I was through with men.

At least until I had my personal life under control. Until I'd achieved my own personal goals. Until the Master Plan said that I could take an interest in anyone male. A little more than fifteen months from now.

Damn. I really had to remember to water that peace lily.

Timothy said, "My lease is up in seven weeks, and my landlord is making it impossible for me to stay."

"Why? What's he doing?"

He shrugged, letting the lithe movement siphon off some of his obvious frustration. "He's tripling my rent."

"That's crazy!"

"He's allowed to—it says so in my lease. But I'll never make enough on the restaurant to meet his demands."

"Does he have someone waiting to move into the space?"

"I don't think so." Timothy shook his head.

"But why would he do that? It doesn't make any sense!" Outrage boiled beneath my words.

"He doesn't really care if he gets someone who can pay what he's asking from me. He just wants me out."

"But why?" My shock made the words sharp. I couldn't imagine what Timothy had done to offend his landlord. He was soft-spoken, perceptive, a shrewd businessman. Sure, his restaurant model was a bit unusual, but in the crowded field of food purveyors in New York City, that should be a virtue, not a vice. Certainly not a vice to warrant a tripling of rent, a virtual death sentence for his business.

"According to the letter I got this morning, I'm encouraging vagrancy. I'm bringing an undesirable element into the neighborhood."

"Undesirable—" I spluttered.

"Let's face it," he interrupted, and then he sighed. "The homeless folks I serve aren't exactly the most popular people on the block."

I thought about the look that had crossed Sam's face when he realized what was going on at that back table. But then, I remembered the quiet submissiveness as Lena asked for Timothy's permission to use the restroom. Garden Variety's homeless customers weren't hurting anyone—except for, maybe, Timothy. And then, only if you measured the bottom line, which I somehow suspected he rarely did.

"What are you going to do?"

His face was grim, his eyes hardened into agate pools. "Close up shop. Unless I can figure out a way to pay three times the rent without driving away every single paying customer I have. And without abandoning the people who rely on me, like Dani." He nodded toward my neighbor's closed door. "She needs to sell her produce to keep the Gray Guerillas up and running, so I can't just shop somewhere cheaper."

Before I could offer any brainstorms—or at least

some heartfelt condolences—my phone jangled with Amy's ring tone. I glanced at my watch. Five o'clock. A strange time for her to call; she was usually fixing Justin's dinner just about now. "Excuse me," I said. "I should take this." Timothy gestured broadly as I snapped open my phone. "Hey," I said. "What's up?"

"Erin!" The urgency in her voice slammed a knife between my ribs.

"What's wrong?" Fear jolted my heart into overdrive. Timothy leaned forward, obvious concern stretched across his shoulders, written on his features. I could only shake my head, though, unable to answer his silent question, unable to explain.

"You have to get out here!"

"Where? Amy, where are you?"

"New Brunswick Memorial." Her voice was shaking so badly I barely made out the words.

"What happened? Are you okay?" And then a sliver of ice shot through my brain. "Is Justin?"

"He tied a towel around his neck for a cape. He said he was Soldierman. I only went inside the house for a minute. The phone was ringing, and I told him to stay in the front yard." She started sobbing—harsh, racking cries that broke my heart.

"Amy, what happened? What happened to Justin?"

"He climbed up on the roof. He climbed up, and he jumped off, like he thought he could fly." I caught my breath, picturing the rose trellis that Justin must have used as a ladder, the gutter he must have balanced against before he leaped. "Erin," Amy said, "he won't wake up. My baby won't wake up!"

Chapter 7

"I'VE GOT TO go," I said to Timothy. Any thought of solving his restaurant woes had boiled off in the panic of my sister's frantic voice.

He snatched up his grocery bags, keeping pace with me as I raced to the elevator. "What's wrong?"

"My nephew. He—" The words caught in my throat. He fell off the roof. He's unconscious. What was Amy not telling me? Had Justin broken his neck? His back? Was he in a coma? My hands began to shake as I punched the down button.

"Where is he?" Timothy asked, holding open the elevator door as soon as the car arrived. I started to pound the G for the ground floor, knowing that beating up on the elevator wouldn't make it move any faster but feeling like I had to do something. My fingers had turned to ice.

"N-New Brunswick Memorial," I stammered, trying to focus. The elevator took centuries to move down eight flights, its idiotically perky bell marking off each passed floor. I used the time to dig for my wallet, fishing out cab fare to the bus terminal.

Four dollars. Four crumpled bills, shoved deep into their slot, as if they were embarrassed to be seen with me. I swore as the elevator door finally opened on the ground floor. "Where's the nearest ATM?"

"Here," Timothy said, putting down one of his grocery bags to dig into his apron. He pulled out three perfect twenties.

"I can't take that!" I was embarrassed that I was so ill-prepared, ashamed that I didn't take better care of my finances.

He shoved the bills into my hand. "I know you're good for it." When I still hesitated, he reached out to extricate my forlorn wallet from my trembling fingers. He snapped the clasp closed over my scant hoard and returned it to my purse. The gesture was personal enough that it made me catch my breath, and I realized that my heart was galloping so fast my chest ached.

Despite my panic—*because* of it—I closed my eyes and took a long, steadying breath. When I looked at Timothy again, my heart lurched back to something approximating its normal rhythm. "No wonder you've got landlord problems. You're a lousy businessman, Mr.—" I cut myself off, suddenly realizing that I had no idea what Timothy's last name was.

"Brennan," he said with a wry grin. He pulled a business card from that deep apron pocket, adding it to the money in my fist. "Timothy Brennan."

"Pleased to meet you," I said, trying to joke my way past the terror that was already rushing back into my throat.

"Come on," he said. "It's easier to hail a cab at the corner."

He shifted both grocery bags to his right hand and

pushed open the Bentley's heavy glass door with his left. He settled in beside me as we race-walked down the street, his fingers hovering by my elbow. As we passed the alley that led to Garden Variety, he said, "Are you all right to get there on your own? Let me just put a sign on the door, and I'll come with you."

"That'll take too long," I said automatically, even as part of my brain chimed that it would love Timothy's company. I glanced at my watch. "There's a bus that leaves in twenty minutes. I think I can catch that one."

"Here," he said, and this time he reached into one of the grocery bags. He produced a plastic clamshell of black raspberries, the perfect little fruits nestled together like a jewel hoard.

"What—" I started to ask.

"You're going to be starving by the time you get to Jersey."

Reflexively, I stashed the fruit in my tote bag. I couldn't imagine eating ever again, but I wasn't going to waste time arguing with him.

We'd reached the street corner, the one that fed onto busy Eighth Avenue. Timothy stepped off the curb, raising his free left hand with such authority that a cab skidded to an immediate stop. My knight in soft black clothing opened the door, swinging his grocery bags out of the way so that I could climb into the back. As I maneuvered around him, he settled his fingers on my arm. I looked up, surprised, and he leaned in for a quick kiss, a brush of his warm lips against the ice of mine. I caught a hint of mint on his breath before he stepped back.

I stared at him, astonished. "Go," he said, nodding toward my tote, toward the wallet that held his business card. "Call me when you know what's going on."

I could have asked him what that kiss meant. I could have told him that I wasn't getting involved with anyone, that I was living my life separate, alone, without a man to complicate things. I could have explained about the Master Plan. I could have said that I really was able to take care of myself, even if I didn't have enough cash, even if I didn't carry snacks, even if it regularly took me fifteen minutes to hail a cab, on a good day.

Instead, I let him hand me into the taxi. I was strangely aware of his palm against the small of my back, of the way he folded his other hand above the door, so that I couldn't hit my head. I listened as he told the cab driver to take me to Port Authority. I sat back in astonishment as he closed my door, as he slapped the roof of the cab twice, sending me on my way with the competent flat of his hand.

I sank into my New Jersey Transit bus seat with seconds to spare.

Grabbing another cab on the far end of the trip, I soon found myself attempting to navigate the sterile hell of a hospital emergency room. My first stop was the triage station. As I wasn't spurting blood or screaming in agonized pain, I was referred to a different desk. The nurse there checked her records, and calmly told me that no Justin Carlson had been admitted. I insisted that she was wrong, and after another consultation on her computer, she referred me to a third desk. Which passed me on to a fourth. And then a fifth.

I was a little astonished that so many petty bureaucrats worked so late in the day.

At last, I circled back to the first desk, the one that

was right off of the emergency room. A different nurse was staffing the station, and she pulled up Justin's record immediately. I wanted to curse, to rant, to rave about the vagaries of computer files, but I settled for asking how Justin was doing. The nurse stared at me with reptilian eyes and stated that she could not provide any information about the status of a minor. I insisted that I was his aunt, but that blood relationship apparently wasn't enough to vanquish the hospital's privacy rules.

Recognizing a stone wall when I saw one, I retreated to the waiting room and collapsed into a gray leatherette chair, determined to figure out a different solution. This entire nightmare felt horrifically familiar. Amy and I had gone to the hospital after our parents' car crash. We had been shuffled from one room to another, forced to check in with nurses and candy stripers and a million other people who supposedly had our best interests in mind. We'd run up against administrative brick wall after administrative brick wall until a weary chaplain had finally ushered us into a small private room, to give us the news that changed our lives as siblings, as daughters.

I hated hospitals.

I dug out my cell phone and punched in Amy's number, but she didn't pick up. I left her a message, then sent a text for good measure. She'd know that I was at the hospital, at least, stranded in the waiting room, trapped, for all my good intentions.

An hour passed as I fumed, frantic and alone. I left my fingers crossed. I muttered, "Please, just this once," as if it were a mantra powerful enough to change the universe.

I couldn't say what made me finally look up at the precise instant that I did. I couldn't say what cosmic force drew my eyes to the swinging door on the far side of the room, to the porthole window that barely let me glimpse into the hospital corridor beyond. I couldn't say why I happened to see Amy frozen there, her face streaked with tears, her hair tangled as if she'd been riding roller coasters all night long.

I sprang to my feet and dashed for the door. "Excuse me, miss!" Stone Wall planted herself in front of me, immovable as a defensive end. "Only emergency personnel back there."

"I can see my sister!"

"If you take a seat, she'll be out soon enough."

"I've been trying to find her for hours!"

"If you'll just take a seat—" I could hear the force of repetition behind her words, the oaken certainty that she controlled the doorway. I turned on my heel and walked back to my chair. Stone Wall harrumphed her way back to her desk.

Poised on the edge of the cushion, I craned my neck so that I could keep Amy in sight. She was arguing with a doctor. I could see that she was getting more and more upset. She ran her fingers through her hair. Tears tracked down her cheeks. The tendons in her neck stood out, and she clutched at the doctor's white jacket.

Made desperate by Amy's own panic, I did the only thing I could think of. I raised my right hand in front of me, tilting it so that my tattooed flames glimmered under the fluorescent lights, a ghost of a pattern barely visible in the harsh, clinical setting.

I pressed my thumb and forefinger together firmly

and said, "Teel!"

The mist was thicker than it had been in my apartment or in the bathroom at the audition hall. Motes danced in the air, red as blood, green as the cross emblazoned on a canister of oxygen behind the nurse's station. Silver glints swirled in, echoing the stainless steel around us, and the blue cross from paperwork on Stone Wall's desk was splintered into sapphire shards.

The fog swirled around me, luring me into its dance, pulling me into its circular force. Everyone else, though, every*thing* else remained anchored, steady, stable. Stone Wall was frozen in her chair, frowning in midtap as she organized a stack of papers. A man whose face was creased into a worried frown lowered himself into his chair, his hands already on the armrests, his legs bent in midair. A trio of high school kids gathered around a single cell phone, pointing at the screen and opening their mouths to shriek at something they clearly found hysterically amusing.

And yet, I was able to move. I could turn my head. I could gasp in shock and surprise as the sparkling fog coalesced into a human form, settled into a human body: a party boy of a type I suspected only my fellow actor Shawn could love. Teel wore leopard-skin pants made out of some clingy fabric that emphasized every taut line of his anatomy. His chest was barely covered by a black leather...*thing,* a garment that swooped down from his shoulders, framing the astonishingly erect nipples on his waxed chest. His hair was bleached platinum blond and spiked to stand straight up. His tattoo flared at his wrist, writhing in a complex dance of flames. It drew my eyes immediately, compelling me to take a step closer even as I tried hard to swallow my surprise.

"Time to join the par-tay?" he crowed.

Before I could respond, though, he looked around the room, took in the authoritative letters that said Emergency, the nurse, a cadre of frozen doctors barely visible around the corner. "Oh!" he said. "Even better!" He thrust out one leopard-spotted hip and raised long, pointed fingernails to his earlobe. Tugging twice, he made Leather Leopard Boy disappear.

In his place stood a dreamy doctor.

He wore a white coat over blue scrubs. A stethoscope draped around his neck like a tamed snake. Pens poked out of his pocket, and a BlackBerry hung at his waist. He was tall—tall enough that I needed to look up at his face. His cheekbones were chiseled into the perfection of a male model. He had a strong jaw and a cleft chin and compassionate blue eyes that danced behind the longest eyelashes I'd ever seen on anyone, male or female. His hair was black, silvered at the temples with just enough gray that I instinctively believed this was a man to be trusted. This was a man to be believed.

Except for the fact that he was a genie.

"Just sit back," he crooned, "and tell me where it hurts." His voice was low, rumbling with masculine reassurance. Something inside me unwound a little at his cool competence—this was a man who could get me past any swinging door, any junkyard-dog nurse.

"I have to see Amy," I said, nodding toward my sister. She was just as frozen as the others around us, just as locked into place by the magic that had brought Teel to me.

"We'll take care of that," Dr. Teel said. "Right now, though, I want to make sure that you're all right."

I almost melted at the concern that coated his words. The tears that pricked my eyes made me realize just how tense I'd become during my mad rush around the hospital, during my endless wait. I recognized the rocks that had replaced the muscles beside my spine. I realized that my jaw was set into a grim cliff of defiance. Teel's tone unlocked all of that tension, let me take a deep breath, let me relax back to my normal, neurotic self.

Nodding, he produced some sort of scope, turning on the brilliant white light and holding it at an angle that made it clear he was ready to study my eyes, ears, nose, throat and possibly the inside of my brain. "Three out of ten wishers fail to recognize their own compromised health, when they're intent on completing their wish cycles. Open your mouth and say, 'Ah.'"

"There's nothing wrong with me, Teel!" I pushed his hand away. "I just need to get to Amy! They won't let me through that door. I have to find out what's going on with Justin."

Teel nodded and clicked off his blinding scope. "Let's see what we can do about that, then." He produced a pen from his pocket and summoned a medical chart from midair. He took three steps toward the swinging door and then turned back to me. "Coming?"

"Wait," I said, even as I closed the distance between us. "Aren't you going to make me use a wish?"

His smile was patient. "Erin, it's not always about the wishes."

"It isn't?" I said doubtfully. I was worried about Justin, but I was totally thrown by this Teel. My genie had become a creature totally foreign to me; his central *cause d'etre* had evaporated. His concern for my well-being was welcome, but I felt as if a magic carpet had been swept from beneath my feet.

Again, he gave me that soothing grin. "We'll worry about wishes when we know what's going on here." His voice was calm and reassuring, as if he were providing professional medical assistance to a madwoman. When I still hesitated he added, "With any luck, you'll need your last two wishes to straighten everything out here."

There we go. So much for my genie's kinder, gentler side.

"Ready?" he asked, and I nodded. Before I could brace myself, Teel tugged twice at his earlobe.

The world around us sprang back to life. Stone Wall finished tapping her papers into order. The exhausted man sank into his chair. The high school students screamed with laughter at whatever they were viewing on their screen. Teel clicked his tongue, as if he had arrived at some firm diagnosis, and then he strode across the waiting room. I scrambled beside him like an eager puppy.

Stone Wall glared at me. "I've told you, miss. No one—"

"This woman is with me, Nurse," Teel said, modulating his voice into the time-honored placating tones that had served medical professionals from Marcus Welby to McDreamy.

"Oh, I see, Doctor," the nurse replied. "I'm sorry. I was just—"

"Doing your job." Teel completed her sentence with a firmness that brooked no argument. "Thank you." He held the door for me with a suave professionalism. The actor in me wanted to step back to admire a job well done. The sister in me dashed forward, before the opportunity could disappear.

"Amy!"

She turned before the second syllable was out of my mouth. All of a sudden, my arms were full of frantic sobbing sister. She smelled of sweat and dust and something that might have been terror. "Erin! You came!"

"Of course," I said, hugging her close. Just like I had when we learned the truth about our parents.

Teel stepped up to the doctor Amy had been talking to. He inclined his head and muttered a question. I couldn't make out precisely what either man said, but I could tell they were using words that belonged in the *Guinness Book of World Records* for "most syllables in an English-language noun."

I clung to my sister until she loosened her death grip, just a little. "What happened, Amy? How's Justin?"

She shook her head. "It was only a minute! I only left him for a minute! They say I need to talk to social services, and I haven't been able to reach Derek, and I can't get anyone on the base to return my calls. It was only a minute, Erin!"

I reassured her as best I could, catching her biceps between my hands. I ordered her to take a deep breath, another, another. I started asking her specific questions—what had Justin been doing in the front yard? What time had she received the ill-fated phone call that pulled her inside? What did she see when she came back out to the yard?

Gradually, I pieced together the story. Justin had broken his arm, and he might have sprained an ankle. His cape had dug into the flesh of his neck, leaving a nasty laceration. But the major problem was that he had hit his head when he landed. The doctors had done an MRI; they'd identified a huge subdural hematoma. Justin was in emergency surgery; the doctor at Amy's side had been finishing a complete medical history while one of his colleagues worked to save my nephew's life.

By the time Amy finished her scattered recitation, Teel was wrapping up talking to the doctor, nodding and murmuring in subdued tones, looking every bit the expert surgeon called in for a consultation. Finding strength in the cool sapphire glance he shot my way, I settled my hand on Amy's elbow and pulled her forward. "Doctor," I said, nodding toward the man who had been talking to Amy before my arrival. "What do we do now?"

"Have a seat in the waiting room. Dr. Finley will be out as soon as he's through with the surgery."

And so we sat. And waited. And waited some more. I wanted to invent a time machine, a remote-control box that I could use to fast-forward through the stultifying bits of my own life.

Teel held true to his new identity. It wouldn't make sense for a real doctor to sit with two random family members in the waiting room—even I could see that. Instead, he went about his work, as if he were legitimately on staff at New Brunswick Memorial. I watched him stop by the triage station, browsing through charts that had accumulated on a corner of the desk. An orderly looked up, clearly ready to ask who he was, but Teel merely shot his cuff, pointedly glancing at his watch. The action revealed his flame tattoo—orange-and-black figures that sparkled across the room.

That tattoo was like a Get Out of Jail Free card.

Even I felt myself drawn forward, even though I was fully aware of the magic embedded there. Teel must be using it to blur perception, to change the way that everyone treated him. The orderly nodded respectfully and stepped back. A passing nurse offered Teel a clipboard, waiting patiently for him to initial a few pages. Teel glanced at each sheet before he signed, as if he truly understood whatever medical mumbo jumbo was printed there.

As he passed back the papers, he looked up at me. His gaze was intense, like cobalt lasers focused all the way across the waiting room. Something about his expression made me catch my breath, and then I realized that I'd stopped staring at his eyes, that I was back to studying his tattoo.

I almost followed him as he headed toward a door marked Surgery. I could feel the pull of those flames, sense them more strongly than I had in any of Teel's other guises. I forced myself to sit back in my chair. Teel was only playing a role, I reminded myself. Everything about him was just for show. He wasn't actually a doctor; he only played one to meet my needs.

I turned my attention back to my sister.

At first, I didn't have to say a word. I just listened to Amy repeating herself, telling me that it had all been an accident, that she couldn't believe what had happened. Then, I tried to distract her, recounting the day's rehearsal, my interrupted conversation with Timothy in the hallway outside my apartment. She still wasn't really listening, but then I had a brainstorm, remembering the raspberries that Timothy had given me.

I extracted the fruit from my tote bag. It was none the worse for wear; each berry glistened as if it had a light within. When I offered up the tart-sweet jewels to Amy, she ate the first one reluctantly, but I saw the instant her taste buds locked in on the delicate flavor. She bolted down a half dozen without stopping. "Timothy?" she finally said, licking her lips. "Didn't you mention him the other day?"

"Yeah," I said.

Funny. The entire trip to New Brunswick, I'd pictured his warm brown eyes. I'd replayed how he'd calmly taken command as I stood in the hallway, unable to organize my thoughts after receiving Amy's call. I thought about his kiss—quick and casual and strangely...inevitable.

But now, I found my thoughts drifting back to Dr. Teel. His eyes were completely different from Timothy's warm cappuccino. Teel's gaze was precise. Commanding. Shiver-inducing.

Teel was a *genie*. What the hell was wrong with me?

"Is there something going on between you two?" Amy asked.

"Of course not! We just met an hour ago!"

"What?" Amy asked.

"What?" I countered, brilliantly.

"I was talking about your restaurant guy," she said. "Timothy."

I could feel my cheeks heating up. "Sorry," I said. "I'm just distracted, I guess." I shook my head. "I don't think there's anything there. His life is pretty complicated. He's probably going to have to close down his restaurant—his landlord is about to triple his rent."

"Doesn't he have a lease?"

"It's up in six weeks. The whole thing is a mess." I told her about his giving me bus fare for my emergency trip.

Amy wrinkled her nose. "Erin, hard stop that right there," she said. I supposed that I should be grateful she was relaxing enough to slip back into business school jargon. "You just broke up with Sam. You need to evolve that situation—that's why you agreed to the Master Plan. You *promised.* You can't just jump into something new."

"I'm not jumping anywhere!" I protested.

"Erin!"

"Amy!" I matched her, tone for tone.

"How is that peace lily doing, anyway?" She loaded the question with a lifetime of suspicion.

"It's fine," I lied. "It has three new flowers."

Well, it might. I hadn't looked at it in a week.

Amy harrumphed. Even though it annoyed me that she was questioning my fitness for the Master Plan, I was grateful for the distraction, for the break from her fear over Justin. What did it matter, if I had to put up with Amy-the-big-sister, Amy-the-business-manager? Anything, to ease her fear about her only child.

An hour went by, and another. My eyes became grainy. Even though it was approaching midnight, I was ready to track down a vending machine, buy some caffeine, hot or cold, whatever I could find. Fishing for my wallet, I dragged myself to my feet. "Hey, Ame," I said. "Do you want—"

Before I could complete the sentence, my sister clutched my forearm. Her fingers were iron talons, gripping to the bone. I glanced over my shoulder, and I saw what she had seen. A doctor, shuffling toward us, fatigue carved deep on his face. A surgical mask hung from one side of his face, drooping beside gray-tinged lips.

I shook my head. I didn't want this doctor. I wanted another one. I wanted someone who was youthful and spry. Someone who walked like he didn't have a care in the world. Someone who was young and confident and handsome.

Teel. I'd take Teel. I'd be happy to have Teel walking toward me...right...now.

"Mrs. Carlson," the surgeon said, looking at Amy with basset-hound eyes.

"No," she said, digging even deeper into my arm. She started to shake her head, her hair flinging from left to right.

"I'm sorry. Justin had a very serious injury—"

"No!" Amy screamed.

The blood drained out of my head. A wave of ice crashed over me, as if I were a coach drenched in a Gatorade shower. But this was no victory celebration. This was no success. This was the worst news I'd ever received.

I was going to be sick. I was going to cry. I was going to raise my voice in a keening wail, match my sister note for note.

But I did none of those things. Instead, I tugged my arm free from Amy's death grip. I pinched together my thumb and my forefinger. I raised my chin, looked at the defeated surgeon and I clearly pronounced, "Teel."

Once again, the world froze around me. I suppose there was a jangle of electricity, a wash of energy, but my body was too numb to feel its effect. I blinked hard, trying to close myself off from Amy's raging grief, from Dr. Finley's stolid explanation.

And when I opened my eyes, Teel was standing in front of me.

"This isn't right," I said, without preamble. I was certain that he knew what had happened. His eyes looked darker than they had before, heavier. Shadowed.

"I'm sorry." The silver in his hair glinted as he inclined his head. I wondered if real doctors took classes in medical school—bedside manner for the delivery of bad news.

"You have to change this," I said. "You have to save Justin."

An eager gleam flashed across his face. "Is that a wish?"

"Yes!" I shouted. "It's a wish! You're that much closer to your goddamned Garden!"

He nodded, as if I were a distraught patient agreeing to some highly unpleasant medical procedure. "Go ahead, then."

I met his eyes belligerently. I was determined to get this one right, to say exactly what I wanted, without any possible room for misunderstanding. This wasn't about an audition, a Broadway role. This was about a little boy.

"I wish that Justin was fully recovered from his fall. That he had no head injury or broken arm or sprained ankle, or anything else wrong with him. I wish that he was as healthy as he was before he decided to play up there on the roof."

Teel blinked those impossible eyelashes, pulling me into his gaze. Looking at him, I knew that he could do precisely as I asked, he could rearrange the past, he could guide us through the future.

He raised his hand to ear. His fingernails were very short, perfectly trimmed. His hands were hard, strong, as if he practiced Swedish massage when he wasn't saving lives in the emergency room. He captured his earlobe and said, "As you wish."

Two pulls. An electric shock that made me wonder why hospitals bothered with resuscitation paddles—they should just keep genies on hand to do all the dirty work.

I gasped and lurched forward, moving as much from the pain as from the sudden sensation that the world around me was functioning again. Amy was sobbing next to me, clutching my arm, but this time she was only trying to steady herself, to catch her balance. She wasn't trying to rip out the bitter roots of grief.

Dr. Finley was shaking his head, running a hand over his balding head. "I have to say, Mrs. Carlson, I've never seen anything like it. We rechecked the MRI three times—that initial reading had to be some sort of mistake. I cannot tell you how sorry I am to have put you through that sort of fear."

"But Justin's okay?" Amy said.

"He's fine," the surgeon said. "We'll keep him overnight just to be certain, but he's already telling the floor nurse that you always let him have ice cream for a midnight snack." Amy's laughter was mixed with a relieved sob. The surgeon graced her with an avuncular smile. "He'll probably be a bit sore tomorrow—you'll want to give him some children's Tylenol. But he's a very lucky young man."

Amy thanked the surgeon, pumping his hand up and down, hanging on as if she were afraid the good news would disappear if she let go. Dr. Finley patted her on the arm understandingly and muttered more reassuring things.

I looked at Teel. *Thank you,* I mouthed, my back turned to my sister. He nodded with the perfect aplomb of a doctor who saved lives every day.

Amy's hysterical laughter was interrupted by the ring of her cell phone. She dug it out of her pocket awkwardly, still reluctant to let go of poor Dr. Finley. "Derek!" she exclaimed as soon as she glanced at the screen. She spun around, dropping the surgeon's arm in her haste to reassure her husband, halfway around the world.

I added my own thanks, and then the bemused doctor went on his way. Amy edged across the waiting room, putting her finger in her free ear to block out ambient noise. Her voice had dropped, and I knew she was sharing her terror with Derek, letting him know that all was well, absorbing all the reassurance that a loving husband could offer from such a distance.

I took the chance to talk to Teel. "You're amazing."

"Ten out of ten wishers say that. Ready to make your fourth one?"

I shook my head. "No, seriously."

"I *am* serious," he said. "Completely serious." Once again, he pinned me with those blue eyes. He grinned like a shark swimming through crystal waters, looking for an easy dinner. I began to understand why there were so many television shows featuring smart, sexy doctors.

"I can't, Teel. I need to decide what to wish for."

"And ten out of ten wishers say *that,*" he said. He raised a hand to rub at the back of his neck. Suddenly, I was reminded just how long the day had been, how many hours had passed since I had first stumbled into rehearsal. I saw the glint of light from Teel's tattoo, a shimmer of flames that caught my vision and tossed it back at me. I shook my head, a little dazzled by my genie's stunning good looks.

Or his magic.

Or my fatigue.

Something.

"I'm sorry," I said, and further embarrassed myself by barely catching a yawn against the back of my teeth. I thought of the short-lived avatar of Leather Leopard Boy. "You probably have some place to be, don't you? There's got to be a party somewhere back in the city. Something to entertain you, while you're waiting for me to make that last wish."

He took a step closer to me, and his voice dropped to a private rumble. "Suddenly, I find myself pretty entertained, standing right here."

Before I could think of an appropriate response, he leaned in and kissed me.

Chapter 8

IT WAS A really great kiss.

It was the sort of kiss that you see onstage after hours of rehearsal, where the actors move perfectly, where there's no awkwardness of bumped noses or clicking teeth, where both people manage to breathe, even as the kiss lingers and deepens and heats....

Maybe my legs started to tremble because I was tired. Maybe I felt dizzy because it had been hours since I'd last eaten a meal. Maybe I felt hot, then cold, then hot again because it was June and the waiting room was over-air-conditioned.

All I knew was that by the time Teel pulled back, I needed to reach out to him. I needed his steadying hand on my hip. I needed the length of his body against mine. All so that I could continue standing.

A smile lit his deep blue eyes, glowing from within like a beacon on a cold, dark night. "Easy there," he said, as calm and controlled as if he were pointing out obscure medical details from an X-ray on a lighted screen. His fingertips cupped my elbow, and once again I found myself staring at the flame tattoo that peeked out from his starched white cuff.

"I'm sorry," I said, because I had to say something. Because I was confused. Because nothing else sounded right, as I tried to regain my balance.

"No reason to be." His gaze continued to scorch me, and I could not help but wonder what statistics he had up his proverbial sleeve. How many wishers kissed their genies in the middle of hospital waiting rooms? How many wishers contemplated doing a whole lot more than kissing? How many followed through?

Before I could act on the tendrils uncurling inside my belly—or quite a bit lower, to be one hundred percent truthful—Amy bounced back to us. Her face shone as if she were a little kid, just awakened on Christmas morning. When she saw Teel's hand on my hip, a little cloud scudded across her features, but she blinked away her sisterly concern in a smiling heartbeat. "Derek got called away, but I was able to give him the 411 before he had to go. I'm going to find Justin now. I need to get some full optics on what's going on, and they said they're moving him into a regular room for the rest of the night."

"Great," I said, because it was my turn to say something. It was hard to force out the word in anything approaching a normal tone.

"Are you coming?" she asked, already turning toward the nursing station.

I shook my head before I'd given any conscious thought to a reply. I didn't want to trail after my sister. I didn't want to leave Teel's side. "Um, no. You go ahead. It'll be easier to settle Justin down to sleep if I'm not around."

"You aren't going back to the city, are you?" She

sounded shocked. "He'll want to see you in the morning!"

"No, no," I reassured her, and waved at the bank of gray leatherette chairs. "I'll just grab a nap here."

"Those don't look very comfortable." A frown returned to Amy's face, settling into a crease between her eyebrows.

"Amy, don't worry about me. I'll be fine." I made my voice as strong as I dared. I didn't want her to think anything was amiss. Even so, my overprotective big sister cast a doubtful glance at Teel. Before she could voice concerns I really didn't want to hear, I prompted her. "Go on, Ame. Justin is probably wondering where you are this very minute."

It probably wasn't fair for me to prey on her maternal solicitude. But with Teel beside me, I didn't feel like playing fairly at all. Amy turned on her heel and started to walk away, but she only got a half dozen steps before she whirled back.

"Do you have any more raspberries?"

Raspberries. What raspberries? Oh, the raspberries that Timothy had given me.

Right before he had kissed me, on Eighth Avenue. Not ten hours ago.

So there I was, kissed by two different men, when I had sworn off guys forever. When I'd vowed to live my life, strong and independent, under the rigors of my Master Plan for well over a year. Another fifteen months without the complication of any Y chromosomes.

"Um, no," I said to Amy, trying to hide my confusion. "That's all Timothy gave me."

My perceptive big sister frowned at me, and I could

just imagine the difficult questions she was getting ready to ask. I preempted her by glancing toward the elevators. "Go," I said. "You have to let Justin know what Derek said. He's waiting for you."

At last, Amy focused on the maternal task at hand, hurrying off to my nephew's hospital room. I waited until the elevator doors had closed behind her before I returned my attention to the genie at my side.

"What was that all about?" I asked, forcing myself to keep my voice even. It took the better part of my actor's training to drown the breathiness in my tone as I looked at his leading-man-handsome face.

Teel sounded eminently reasonable as he said, "Justin is probably hungry. He's up way past his bedtime, and the raspberries would have helped him settle down."

"I wasn't talking about fruit."

"I know." That smirk would have been infuriating on most faces. On this incarnation of Teel, though, it made me want to raise a finger to the cleft in his chin. It made me want to test the wiriness of his hair. It made me want to measure my hands against his, to feel the strength of his muscles and bones as his fingers closed around my wrists.

I sighed and forced myself back to sanity. I was exhausted. That had to be why I was thinking such irresponsible thoughts about my *genie*. "Amy was right," I said, determined to deal with the ordinary details of life in the real world. The nonmagical world. The world that I had lived in, every day, for twenty-five years. Without a genie at my side. I cleared my throat and went on. "Those chairs *do* look uncomfortable."

"Who said you have to spend the rest of the night in

a chair?" He arched an eyebrow, and there was no mistaking the sly invitation behind his words.

I'd always wanted to be able to arch a single eyebrow. A skill like that would have served me well on any stage in the country. Instead of responding with clinical curiosity, though, I felt a red-hot flush kindle in my cheeks. "Teel, stop it. This is all happening so fast."

"Nothing has to happen that you don't want to happen." There was that doctor tone, again, that calm, logical timbre that made me melt just a little more. "I'm only suggesting that we go someplace else for the few hours left tonight."

"Go where?"

"As a senior resident, I have dibs on the sixth floor on-call room."

"Senior resident?" Despite the tension sparking between us, I grinned. When my genie took on a role, he didn't do things by half measures.

He shrugged and dosed me with another one of those flawless smiles. "I thought someone might get suspicious if I became the chief of staff."

I couldn't help it. I laughed.

I also let Teel guide me toward the elevator. He must have scouted out the on-call room after he'd made his rounds, during the long hours when Amy and I had waited for Dr. Finley to report on Justin's surgery. I tried not to think about what Teel's research meant, tried not to focus on who else he'd considered inviting to join him in his sexy-doctor bachelor pad.

I assumed he was a bachelor.

I stopped breathing and cast a quick glance at his hand. No wedding ring in sight. No pale shadow of a band recently removed. At least, not by this incarnation.

By the time Teel marched me down the darkened hall of patients' rooms, my body had begun to remind me that it was almost three in the morning. My head seemed reluctant to keep up with the rest of me; I felt like I was floating a couple of inches above the black-and-white tile floor. I took a deep breath, thinking that would clear my thoughts, but the increased oxygen only made my fingers tingle.

Tingle, and not in a good way. Not in the way that Teel had evoked with his devilish grin and his not-so-subtle suggestions. And that kiss.

Tingled, instead, like I was going to collapse right there, in the corridor.

I caught my lower lip between my teeth, exasperated with my body's shortcomings. Annoyed. But also—if I was going to be totally honest with myself—a little bit relieved.

I was finding it all too easy to slip into my old boyfriend-collecting ways. All too easy to let myself become fascinated with Dr. Teel, pulled into the orbit of his magnetism, just as I had been with every single guy I'd ever dated. This was why Amy had invented the Master Plan. This was exactly the type of situation I was supposed to avoid as I got over Sam. As I figured out whatever was next in my dating life.

As Teel quietly shut the door of the on-call room behind us, I made a valiant—but ultimately unsuccessful effort—to keep from yawning. "I'm sorry," I said, embarrassed, only to lose myself in another mammoth yawn.

He shrugged. "I have that effect on women." His

eyes sparkled in the overhead fluorescent lights.

"No—"

He shook his head, cutting short my protest. Sitting on the bed, he patted the mattress firmly. I joined him, but I suddenly felt as awkward as a high school freshman on her first date. Um, more so, given that most high school freshmen weren't in a bedroom on said first date.

"I—" I started to explain, started to justify, started to protest my own confused feelings.

"Hush," he said, leaning over to pull off my shoes. "Lay down." He stretched toward the foot of the bed, then shook out an institutional blue blanket. "Relax," he whispered, and he reached across me to flip off the light switch.

In the sudden dark, he curled up beside me. I felt the length of his body, warm and comforting and somehow familiar. I was almost asleep when his arm settled around my waist. My eyes were closed as he breathed into my ear, "Now, what about that fourth wish?"

I stiffened immediately.

Was that what this was all about? Was Teel only interested in me so that I would make my fourth wish? Had he staged this entire seduction scene so that I'd do his bidding?

"Get out of here!" I said.

"But—" he protested. I felt him shift by my side, and I realized he was going to switch on the overhead light. All of a sudden, I imagined his tattoo glimmering in the fluorescent gleam. Those flames had pulled me, twisted me, turned me into something I didn't want to be. They'd almost made me forget the value of the Master

Plan.

"No!" I said. "Don't turn on the light!"

"Erin," Teel said, and his voice rumbled with deep concern. Fake concern. Concern manufactured completely for his own benefit.

"Please," I said, sifting some of my true exhaustion into the words, adding a note of real pleading. "Just let me go to sleep. We can talk about it in the morning."

I could feel the tension in his body, still stretched out beside mine. I knew that he wanted to say something else, that he wanted to protest. I was certain that if we talked, he would wear down my resolve, smooth it away. "Please," I said again, forcing every last ounce of will into my voice.

And he took pity on me. Or else I fell asleep before he could turn on the light, before he could lure me back into his sphere of influence with the flames around his wrist. Somehow, I had escaped my genie's concerted effort at seduction and, at long last, I slept.

* * *

By morning, he was gone.

I lay on the strange mattress, staring up at a ceiling that I could barely make out in the crack of light that peeped beneath the door. What had happened the night before? Had Teel stolen every vestige of my free will with his tattoo?

I rolled my head on the flat pillow. It wasn't that simple.

Sure, Teel had done something with his magic. He had heightened thoughts that I already had, increased the confused emotions that churned just beneath my heart. But I had been attracted to him in his doctor guise, separate and apart from the compulsion of his ink. I'd been drawn to him well before he shot his cuff, before he snared me with those tongues of red and gold, with the shimmering black outline around the flames. That was just the way I was. The way I thought. The way I felt around attractive, available guys.

I'd told myself the night before that I had to back off, had to stay away. I really did believe in the promise that I'd made to Amy. I really did think that the Plan would make me happier, in the long run, and I was prepared to see it through—plant, fish and cat.

But now? In the light of day? After a few hours of much-needed sleep?

It was pretty clear to me that Teel stood outside the parameters of the Master Plan. I had enjoyed kissing him. I might even have enjoyed more, if he hadn't ruined the mood by pushing for my fourth wish.

I should be allowed to play with Teel, to have a little fun. He wasn't a guy that was bad for me, like so many of my past boyfriends. I wasn't changing my entire life to be like him, rearranging what was important to me to stay with him forever.

I *knew* that Teel was going to leave me behind as soon as I made my fourth and final wish. I was absolutely certain that we couldn't have anything permanent.

Our strange relationship made him *safe.* A whole lot safer than any human man I might find myself attracted to. A little fling with Teel could fortify me to get through the remaining months of the Master Plan. My genie could sort of be like methadone, a treatment for the dangerous heroin addiction of my disastrous love life, while I perfected the Master Plan of leaving my habit behind forever.

Sighing, I climbed out of the bed. I remonstrated with myself when I started to pick up the pillow that Teel had used. There was no reason to hold it close. No reason to breathe deeply, to see if I could catch a hint of his scent on the cotton. What would it prove if I could? What did it matter? Neither Teel nor I was serious about a relationship.

I tugged the sheets up to the top of the mattress and plumped both pillows. I didn't know what the proper drill was—did doctors change the linens when they left the on-call room? I shrugged. I'd only used the bed for a few hours. No one was going to die if they came in contact with my sheets.

No one was going to die....

The casual phrase flung my thoughts toward Justin, toward his brush with disaster. Barely taking time to make sure the hallway was clear before I ducked outside, I hurried downstairs to the hospital's main visitor desk. In short order, I was directed to a room on the pediatric floor.

I heard Amy laughing before I walked through the door. I could tell that she was forcing herself into Mommy mode, pushing herself to set the limits that she believed were proper. "Justin, that is enough playing around. I want to see you eat every bite of those pancakes—I got that extra syrup just for you. You can tell Dr. Teel more about Soldierman after you finish eating."

Dr. Teel. My heart started pounding so hard that I was grateful I was in a hospital. They could revive me if I collapsed on the floor, couldn't they?

But that was absurd. Teel didn't mean anything to

me. I wasn't emotionally wrapped up in him.

I pasted a beauty-pageant smile across my lips and sailed over the threshold. "Justin!" I cried, leaning in for a sticky maple kiss.

"Aunt Erin!" My nephew seemed none the worse for his hospital wear. The arm that had been broken twelve hours before was busy pushing pancakes around on a plate, avoiding raising a forkful to his lips. His once-sprained ankle peeked out from beneath a skimpy hospital gown, pink and slender and unbruised. Justin beamed at me as if he sat on top of an island, surrounded by an ocean of playthings—plastic toys, an entire box of crayons, a snowbank of papers covered with drawings.

Teel had been as good as his word.

My genie was leaning against the railing on the far side of Justin's bed. He looked as suavely handsome as he had the night before—ravishing blue eyes, impossibly long lashes, wiry salt-and-pepper hair. A smile crooked his lips, as if he were daring me to say something, but I couldn't quite figure out which words to string together, here, in front of my eagle-eyed older sister. Not when I wasn't sure if I wanted to throttle him or throw myself at him. Not when I was furious at how he'd tried to seduce me, and at the same time grateful that he'd saved Justin. Not when I was still working out the details of how the Master Plan applied to Teel. Or didn't, as the case very well might be.

Amy said, "Erin, where have you been? I was getting worried!"

Relieved to be spared an immediate comment to the stunning doctor across from me, I made a face at my sister. "You worry too much. I fell asleep in the waiting room." I saw skepticism blossom on Amy's face, so I added, "Outside the Dermatology wing. They've got a couple of couches there, and the room was totally deserted last night."

I was a little surprised—and grateful—to find how easily the lie came to my lips. Even if I had told Amy that Teel had found me a quiet room, I was sure she would hear something in my voice, some trace of the internal balancing I'd been working on since I'd woken up alone that morning. Now wasn't the time to fight about the Master Plan, about who was—and wasn't—included in it. Not here, with Justin bouncing in his eagerness to be freed from his hospital bed, with Teel looking on in bemusement.

Amy reached out a hand to smooth my nephew's cowlick. "Sit still," she admonished her son. "No jumping in bed." And then she said to me, "Dr. Teel stopped by to see how Justin was doing."

My genie spared an easy smile for all of us. "Actually," he said, "just Teel is fine."

"Teel," I said, nodding as if I were processing that information for the first time. Keeping up the charade, I asked him, "How is Justin this morning?"

"Fine," my genie said, raising his own hand to ruffle Justin's hair, undoing any maternal grooming that Amy might have accomplished. "His energy level is obviously quite high. His vitals are all strong."

My sister beamed. "And when can we get out of here?"

Teel shook his head with a professional frown. "We want to keep Justin under observation for a little while longer. Of course, we're pleased any time a patient turns around as rapidly as this young man has done, but the neurologists will want another scan this afternoon. Just to make sure everything is going as well as it obviously seems to be."

A frustrated frown darkened Amy's face, painting circles beneath her eyes. I realized that she was exhausted. I might have stolen a few hours of sleep curled up next to an exploitative medical-genius Adonis, but my sister had spent the entire night beside her son's bed, riding a wave of exhilaration at his recovery, even as her adrenaline chewed up more and more of her already-stretched reserves. "Amy," I said. "He's fine. It's just a precaution."

Her lips trembled a little as she sparked a smile for Justin's benefit. "Of course," she managed.

Teel gave us both a searching glance. "Why don't you two get something to eat? The hospital cafeteria doesn't have the best food, but you look like you could use something."

Amy answered with a mother's immediate concern. "Oh, no, I couldn't leave Justin."

Teel smiled easily. "I'll stay here. Justin and I can talk to each other. You know. Man talk. And he can finish his breakfast." Justin had perked up at the notion of private time with Dr. Teel, but he ended up frowning at his syrupy plate.

Amy glanced at me, as if she were asking my opinion. I was still a little upset with my genie for attempting to manipulate me into making my fourth wish, but my concerns didn't have anything to do with Justin. My nephew would be perfectly safe with Teel. And my genie just might get him to eat a few bites of pancakes. Besides, Amy looked like she might crumple into a pile of sweaty clothes at my feet if she didn't get some sustenance into herself soon. "Come on, Ame. They'll be fine."

She made one last attempt to divert Teel. "Don't you have somewhere you need to be? Rounds or something?"

Again, he graced us with that all-encompassing smile. "No one's going to come looking for me," Teel said.

Well, that was for sure. No one official even knew that Teel existed. I waited for Amy to fret another minute, and then she admonished Justin to be good before we finally headed toward the cafeteria.

I hadn't realized how much my sister needed to talk. She needed to tell someone about how frightened she had been. She needed to say how much she hated hospitals—had, ever since our parents died. How she couldn't stand being solely responsible for Justin's welfare. How she despised Derek's hitch in the army, even if it meant so much to him, even if he was a hero. How she couldn't wait for her husband to get home, so that Justin wouldn't feel the need to test quite so much, to explore quite as much as he did. How she couldn't believe that Justin had survived his fall—from the roof of the house!—without even a scratch. How she'd been so frightened...

I smiled and nodded and agreed with every single circular word that she said. I didn't even try to keep her from loading up her cafeteria tray with enough food to feed Derek's entire platoon. If she thought that she wanted milk and coffee and juice and cereal and oatmeal and a banana and yogurt and a granola bar, well, that was fine. I'd help with some of it.

"I should have known that he'd try that flying thing.

I should have prethought the situation."

"That's ridiculous," I chided, and I wasn't only commenting on her jargon. "How were you supposed to read the future?" She stared at her coffee, her eyes welling up with tears. "Ame? What's going on? How were you supposed to know?"

"Erin, he told me he was going to jump!"

"What? When? Before you went to answer the phone?" I stared at my sister in shock. I'd been listening to her self-condemnation for hours; it had never occurred to me that she might have a real reason to take responsibility for Justin's youthful exuberance.

"No, not yesterday. But a dozen times before. He says that Derek flies all the time, and he always says he's going to do it, too."

"Derek flies in *planes!*"

"That's what I tell him. And he always nods. And he always agrees. But I should have realized that he was just waiting. Just testing me."

There was something about the way she said it, something about the way her voice broke on the last word that finally clued me in to the fact that something else was going on here, something major. "Amy? How else has Justin been testing you?"

She wouldn't meet my eyes when she said, "He was kicked out of the public pool last week."

I was shocked. "Why?"

"For dunking a little girl." She became fascinated with her spoon. "After three warnings."

"Amy!"

Now the floodgates were open. "And he purposely spills his milk every night at dinner. He took the picture of Derek and me, the one above the fireplace, and he scribbled through Derek's face. And he's wetting his bed every night."

Cold fingers clutched around my heart. "Why didn't you tell me any of this? Amy, why didn't you say anything?"

"What was I supposed to say? That I can't be a good mother to my son? That I can't be the parent he needs me to be?"

"Amy, that's not true! You can't be the *father* he needs you to be. Justin is angry, and he's scared. He's acting out. You aren't supposed to handle all of this on your own. You have to ask for help!"

Her lips trembled. "I'd have help, if I had just agreed to go with Derek. I'd have help if I let us live on base. As it is, I'm just drawing lines in the sand, working toward a degree that I may not even get."

I heard the self-condemnation, miles deep beneath her words. All I could do was reach out to pat her hand, to shake my head in violent disagreement. "You *will* get your degree. And you can get help here, now. You'll join up with Derek as soon as you finish school. It's just one more year."

She shook her head. "I'm being selfish."

"You're being *foolish,*" I contradicted. "When you get home, I want you to call the base. Ask them to recommend some programs, a counselor or something. Get some help, for both of you."

"Okay."

"Promise!"

"Erin—"

"You made me agree to your stupid Master Plan! Making a phone call for the health of yourself and your son is the least you can do in return." She looked ashamed, which only made me press my advantage. "Okay? Amy?"

She sighed. "Okay. I promise." She reached for the granola bar, breaking it into four pieces and shoving two of them in front of me. "Speaking of the Master Plan..." she said, the note in her voice clearly informing me that the earlier topic of conversation was closed. "What's going on with you and Dr. Teel?"

I choked on honey and oats. "What?"

"I guess you decided to throw out the entire Master Plan."

"What do you mean?"

"I mean that you've obviously decided to skip over plant, fish and cat, and go directly to man. I saw Dr. Teel's hands on you last night, and the look you gave him. You were batting your eyelashes like Scarlett O'Hara."

I felt my cheeks turn the color of Amy's tomato juice. "I wasn't batting my eyelashes!"

She didn't say anything, just looked at me with that big-sister certainty that I hated. "Okay!" I finally exclaimed, as if she'd placed me on the rack and was about to take out the red-hot pokers.

"Okay, what?" she asked, primly peeling the banana.

"Okay, so I was flirting with him. Just a little. But there isn't anything there, really. He isn't a threat to the Plan." I couldn't actually explain why, though. I couldn't tell her about Teel's genie identity, about the single ungranted wish that was keeping us together for the short-term. I couldn't let her know that Teel didn't count, that he was never going to be true boyfriend material, that he was—at most—a harmless substitute for the real thing.

I scrambled for something I could say, anything to wipe off the knowing smirk on Amy's face. "Really. It's no big deal. We just slept together."

"*What?*" People at all the tables around us turned to gawk, apparently unable to believe that a human being could actually produce a squawk at the volume Amy had just broadcast.

"Hush!" I grabbed her glass of ice water and pressed the plastic cup against the burning pulse points in my wrists. "Not *slept* together, slept together. We just fell asleep. Don't look at me like that! Nothing happened!"

"I *knew* you didn't find some stupid couch in Dermatology!" Foolish me. I thought I'd tricked my sister. Amy nodded shrewdly. "You're a fast worker."

"I wasn't working!" I protested. Then, because that made me sound like a hooker, I grimaced and tried to change the subject. "Will you get me a cup of coffee? A large?" I shoved my wallet into Amy's hands, intent on making her do something, *anything,* so that she'd stop staring at me in that infuriating, know-it-all way.

Obviously amused, she unfastened the clasp and fished out a couple of crumpled dollar bills. When she pulled them out, a bright white rectangle drifted onto the table. With a gasp of foreboding, I reached for it, but Amy got there first.

"What's this?"

"Nothing." I snatched at the business card.

"'Nothing' doesn't make you blush. What is it?" She glanced at the card. "Timothy Brennan? Is that Timothy, the raspberry guy? You carry his *card* with you?"

I squirmed. "I told you. We were talking about his landlord problems when you called last night. I was frantic, so he gave me his card. He wanted me to let him know what happened with Justin."

"Erin!" Amy turned my name into a two-act drama of disappointment, disillusionment and family tragedy.

"What?"

"I thought we had an agreement. You told me that you were totally on board with the Master Plan. I conceptualized a whole new future for you!"

"I *am* on board! Just because I talk to a friendly neighbor doesn't mean he's my boyfriend!" I heard the shrill note of protest in my voice, and I fought to keep from flashing on the memory of Timothy's lips on mine, of his gentle hand at the small of my back as he helped me into the taxi. "I'm allowed to talk to a guy, Amy! The Master Plan isn't the same thing as entering a convent!"

"Fine," she said, but I knew that look in her eye. I'd seen it for years—whenever she thought that she was gaining the upper hand, that she was right, that she was in charge. In control. She shoved the business card across the table. "Call him."

"What?"

"If there's nothing going on between the two of you, then call him. Right now." And then she warned, "I'll know if you're lying!"

I rolled my eyes in exasperation as I glanced at the huge clock on the far wall of the cafeteria. It was ten in the morning. What was the chance that Timothy would even answer his phone? He had to keep late hours, didn't he? Closing up the restaurant after all his customers had left? His phone had to be safely shut off this early in the morning.

Forcing myself not to flinch under Amy's watchful gaze, I whipped out my cell and punched in Timothy's number. I wanted to invent an automatic messaging machine for callers to use, so that they could avoid anyone picking up on the other end of the line.

He answered on the first ring. "Brennan."

Just my luck.

"Timothy," I said, trying to mask my surprise. "This is Erin. Hollister. From the restaurant. And the Bentley."

"You're the only Erin I know," he said, and I could picture his easy, feline grin spreading across his unshaven face. "How's your nephew?"

"He's fine," I said. "Better than fine, actually. It's like nothing ever happened."

"That's great!" He sounded truly happy for me, almost like he'd stayed up late, worrying about my family drama. Stayed up late, as I had with Teel.

My lungs suddenly seemed too small to breathe for my body. My palms started sweating, and I flashed again on the feeling of Timothy's lips against mine. His kiss had been so different from Teel's. He hadn't sparked passion, hadn't set off a chain reaction of desire, of frustration, of Master Plan justification. Instead, his lips had seemed familiar, comfortable, comforting. Now, his voice on the phone was warm as he said, "I know how worried you were."

Before I was aware that Amy had moved, she snatched the phone out of my hand. I bit off a shriek of protest, but she merely gave me a superior smile as she tapped the device against the table before settling it beside her ear. "Whoops," she said. "My sister just dropped her phone—sorry about that. Who is this?"

"Amy!" I grabbed for the cell, but my sister leaned back in her chair, effectively keeping it out of reach.

She'd won every game of keep-away we'd ever played as kids. I hated the gloating smile that spread across her face—I knew it well, from the days when all my favorite Barbie dolls had been imperiled.

Master Plan, Amy mouthed at me, before she exclaimed, "Timothy! Erin has told me so much about you!"

"Ame," I warned. I hated my big sister. I hated the way she ruined everything for me. I hated her stupid Master Plan, and I hated—

"I would *love* to see your restaurant." Amy smiled the entire time she was talking. "Maybe this weekend? Saturday night? That would be wonderful! Oh, no, I'll bring Justin along. He's great. No, there must have been some misunderstanding, or he's some sort of medical miracle, or—"

"Amy!" I said through gritted teeth as I finally succeeded in prying my phone out of her hand. She was laughing at me as I said to Timothy, "I am so sorry! It's me again. My sister is insane." I glared at Amy, who merely widened her eyes into perfect circles of innocence.

He laughed. "It sounds like she's just blowing off some steam. You both must be exhausted."

I flashed on the bed in the on-call room, on the feeling of Teel curled up around me. The memory felt like a betrayal, like I was lying to Timothy even as I continued our conversation under my sister's highly amused gaze.

But that was absurd. I didn't owe Timothy anything. I wasn't involved with him—with him or anyone else. That was the whole beauty of the Plan, wasn't it? It kept things simple?

I didn't know what to say, how to answer. I must have stammered out something remotely appropriate, though, because Timothy said, "I'll let you go. Bring Justin and Amy in on Saturday. I look forward to meeting them."

"Sure," I said helplessly. "We'll be there."

"Take care," Timothy said, and something about the way the words resonated made it sound like he was serious, like he meant more than just a platitude.

"You, too," I said, flashing one last time on the chivalrous way he'd handed me into my cab. Not that I'd needed him to. Not that I'd asked for any man to come rescuing me. I was committed to the Master Plan—a simple fact that I would prove to my doubting, conniving, evil, manipulative sister.

I snapped my phone closed. "You bitch!" I said to Amy.

She laughed. "Come on. It'll be fun."

"You're not really going to come, are you?"

"I've run out of ideas for Super Soldier Saturdays. Taking a field trip to the city will be just the thing for Justin."

"But you're the one who made me commit to the Master Plan! You're the one who told me I need to take things slowly!"

"Exactly. And now I'm going to check up on you. Make sure that everything's on the up-and-up."

I recognized Amy's tone of voice. That was the military wife and mother who had decided to go to business school instead of meekly moving to her husband's base. That was the big sister who knew precisely how hard to yank my chain. Desperate, I reached for the only weapon I could think of. "Aren't you worried that it might be too much for Justin? I mean, after this whole hospital stay and everything?"

Of course she saw right through me. She always could. "It's four days away. By Saturday, Justin will be ready to compete in the Olympics."

Despite myself, I smiled. Amy might be a suspicious, double-crossing shrew of an older sister, but it was much better to see her laughing than to watch the utter despair I'd witnessed the night before. "We should get back up there," I said. "He's going to think we've abandoned him."

Amy nodded her agreement, and she led the way back to Justin's room. We arrived to find my nephew sitting up in bed, pointing at a sheet of paper and ordering Teel, "No! Draw it the right way! Make Soldierman's cape fly out behind him!" His breakfast tray sat on the nightstand, every bite of pancakes eaten. His orange juice and milk had both been finished, as well.

Teel twisted his handsome features into a grimace as my nephew pounded on the paper. "Justin, I'm a doctor, not an artist!"

Justin giggled. "You can draw it! Draw Soldierman right!"

Amy reached over and ruffled her son's hair. "What's the magic word?"

"Please?" Justin whined, spreading the single syllable over his best angelic smile.

Teel rolled his eyes in fake exasperation and started to sketch a flying soldier. Amy nodded at the handiwork. "That's great, Dr. Teel," she said. "It'll be perfect to put into our notebook on Super Soldier Saturday."

Suddenly, I knew what she was going to say next. I

could hear the words spinning through her thoughts before she could voice them. I opened my mouth to protest, ready to explain that Amy was wrong, that Amy was nuts, that Amy was absolutely not to be trusted under any circumstances.

But she spoke before I could. Looking at Teel with perfect mock innocence, she said, "Dr. Teel? Maybe you'll join us on Saturday. We're all getting together for dinner at a restaurant in New York, one of Erin's favorite places."

Justin's face lit from within. "Really? We get to visit Aunt Erin in New York City?"

"Really," Amy said with a broad smile. I barely resisted the urge to glare at her, smothering my annoyance only because Justin would never understand. And Teel might understand too much.

Justin clutched at my genie's sleeve. "Oh, please? Will you come to New York with us? Please, Dr. Teel? Please?"

Teel laughed at my nephew's enthusiasm, shaking his coat free as if Justin were an overly exuberant puppy with a chewing problem. The motion made his tattoo flash, but I seemed to be the only person in the room who was aware of the orange-and-black ink. Teel looked from Justin to Amy before settling his gaze on me.

I wasn't sure what he saw on my face. I didn't think that he could actually read my mind. I was pretty confident that I'd have to say something out loud if I wanted to derail the looming disaster of his joining us at Garden Variety. I'd have to tell him flat-out "no" in front of Justin, in front of Amy.

And I just wasn't up for the fight. Not with my sister looking on, measuring me closely to see if I truly was committed to the Master Plan. Not with Justin pleading for a trip that had more subtext than his prepubescent brain could ever imagine.

Teel clearly interpreted my silence as permission. He turned to Justin and said gravely, "Sure, Justin. I'll come to New York."

I gave Amy a saccharine-sweet smile. "I can't wait," I said.

Her beaming response nearly blinded all of us. "You'll see, Erin. This is going to be a classic win-win. We're all going to have a wonderful time!"

She waited until Teel bent back over Justin's drawing before she mouthed a secret message at me: *The Master Plan! You'll be fine!*

Chapter 9

THREE HOURS LATER, I stumbled into rehearsal, feeling completely hungover. It wasn't just because of my scant sleep the night before. It wasn't just that I had eaten a bunch of hospital food for breakfast. It wasn't even the thought that my sister was doing her best to test my commitment to the life reorganization plan I'd voluntarily agreed to implement, even though it went against every fiber of my character.

It was the combination of all those things, steeped in the low-grade, recurrent misery of knowing that I should be the person standing front and center at rehearsal. I should be performing the role of Laura Wingfield, using my new-wished skills of singing and dancing to evoke all of the passion, all of the drama, that *Menagerie!* could bring to satisfied Broadway audiences.

Instead, I was stuck at the back of the rehearsal room, my feet up on the seats in front of me, my script tucked in by my side as I leaned over and exchanged snarky comments with Shawn.

A week into rehearsal, Martina Block still hadn't

caught on to the key concept of our show. She continued to insist that Laura should be Big! And Dramatic! And Exciting! Every Single Moment She Was Onstage! Martina refused to accept that the brilliance behind Ken Durbin's concept was the *transition,* the way that Laura changed from a shy little mouse in the spoken-word scenes into a fully realized, completely emotionally mature woman in the show's musical numbers.

Martina's self-centered reading consistently failed to capture the meaning behind a single line of the classic script that Tennessee Williams had crafted. She utterly ignored the traditional Laura, the retiring young woman who was so incapacitated by her anxiety that she could not work in a traditional office. Instead, over and over again, Martina burst into scenes with all the energy and confidence of a reality TV star.

Which, truth be told, she was.

"There we go," Shawn whispered to me after Martina had growled spiky defiance at her mother throughout her first two scenes. "I think she's ready for her close-up."

I choked back a laugh, recognizing the allusion to *Sunset Boulevard.* Shawn had captured the problem with Martina Block in a nutshell. She pictured herself as a big-time Movie Star; she bulldozed her way through scenes, set on one single emotion, as if close-up cameras were waiting to capture her perfectly composed, oh-so-fake facial expressions: Suffering! Angst! Drama!

Shawn started to goad me into another laugh, but I whispered, "Hush!" I barely made my rebuke audible. We were exposed there, in the back of the room. It wasn't like we could hide in a darkened theater. Not yet. The show wouldn't move from rehearsal space to the stage for another two weeks.

Fortunately, Ken hadn't heard Shawn's snarking or my strangled reaction. Our director paced across the front of the room, the picture of unbridled enthusiasm. His every step bounced, as if he were a barely tethered balloon tumbling in a cross breeze. "Okay, Martina," he said, his voice surging with excitement. "Let's go back to the beginning of the scene. I want you to focus on the *atmosphere,* on the mood. Tom is out on the landing, sneaking in late. He's washed in moonlight. You appear, like a Civil War ghost, pale in your nightgown—"

Martina snapped her script closed, as if she had just won an argument. "About that nightgown," she said, tossing back the curtain of her luxuriant blue-black hair. "Don't you think it would work better if Laura wore something short? A baby doll? With maybe some fur along the bottom hem? You know, to make her...what's the word? Vulnerable?"

Ken barely let Martina finish before he shook his head. "This isn't the *musical* scene," he clarified. "This is still the straight dialog." He sounded like a man explaining basic addition to a first-grader.

But Martina wasn't six years old. And Ken had already told her precisely the same thing four other times that afternoon.

"I *know* that." Martina's voice turned icy. I sat up a little straighter in my chair, waving my hand to silence yet another snide remark that Shawn was about to whisper. This confrontation was going to be good. Martina went on: "I am *suggesting* that we take some *risks* in the straight play. That we lay some *ground-*

work for the changes that come out in the musical *numbers*."

Shawn hissed, "She's *suggesting* that she flash the audience at the top of the show. Hit them with her best shot."

Martina couldn't have heard the specific words; Shawn had barely mouthed them. Nevertheless, the sibilance of his whisper must have distracted her—she shielded her eyes and peered toward the back of the room. The gesture immediately annoyed me. The rehearsal room wasn't that large, and Martina wasn't that far away.

"Have you authorized press in here?" she complained to Ken. "My contract specifically states that I get to review all questions from the press before any interview."

Ken stopped his bouncing long enough to shake his head. He pitched his voice to a soothing tone, one that I never could have managed under the circumstances. "Those are just the understudies, Martina."

Just the understudies. Great. Like my ego really needed more of a beating.

Ken cast a pointed glance at the stage manager, who chimed in with a perky, "All quiet in the back of the room, please."

Shawn rolled his eyes and sank lower in his seat. Martina waited for a painfully long moment, as if she expected to hear us rustling and rattling and otherwise ruining her artistic concentration. When she chose to continue, she looped back to the earlier discussion. "My contract specifically states that I have consultation on all costumes."

Once again, Ken managed to temper his voice to the

perfect pitch of reason. The guy really should consider teaching seminars on dealing with the insane. "And you will, Martina. As soon as the designs are finalized, you'll be consulted. For now, though, let's continue with the read-through."

Martina pouted and ruffled through her script. At first, I thought that she was going to refuse to recite her lines. She fooled me, though. She launched into the scene with a soaring passion, with an enthusiasm that bordered on religious zeal. She chewed every word with ferocious energy, chiding her brother for his late-night arrival as if he were a little boy and she an old-time matron.

After Ken recovered from his shock, he interrupted. "Let's try something a bit more...demure, Martina. Show us Laura's vulnerability. Her tentativeness. Her, um, fear."

Martina glared at the director. I wondered if I would ever have that much confidence, that absolute certainty that I was right, even when the director had explicitly defined his vision, when the playwright had clearly telegraphed a different direction, when the plain words of the script indicated a reading completely different from the one that I wanted to make.

Martina sighed dramatically, but she tried to provide Ken with the approach he'd requested. I didn't need a camera close-up, though, to know that her jaw was set in stubborn defiance. Her teeth grated across each syllable.

After a single sentence, Ken sighed. "Martina, let's try—"

"I'm sorry," she said, and all of a sudden, she was the very model of contrition. She collapsed into her chair, reaching a tragic hand toward the actor playing Tom. The very picture of grace, Martina murmured an apology to her fellow professional. Then, she looked up at Ken through her lashes, stopping just short of hooking her finger into her lower lip in a perfect illustration of little-girl submission to authority. "I am *so* sorry. I would be able to concentrate better if someone had set up proper craft services."

Shawn snorted so loudly that he received another glare from the stage manager. I tugged at his arm and once again said, "Hush!"

"Craft services?" he whispered in disbelief, barely remembering to keep his shock inaudible to the front of the room. "What does she think this is? A movie set?"

I tried to sound sympathetic, even though I was every bit as incredulous as my fellow just-an-understudy. "It's what she's used to."

"Poor baby," Shawn sneered.

Ken, though, was offering more sincere sympathy. Or at least something that sounded like it. "We'll look into setting something up."

"I'm not asking for full-scale catering," Martina said, her voice the perfect mimic of reason. "Just a table. Some snacks. You don't even have to make it available to non-Equity."

Shawn looked like he was going to fly across the chairs, to strangle Martina in one dramatic gesture. That would have been fine with me—her precious Hollywood expectations annoyed me, as well. Besides, if Shawn killed her, I'd land the role I coveted.

I allowed myself a moment to contemplate the sheer pleasure of that little development.

Reluctantly, I tugged at Shawn's sleeve. "Sit down," I whispered. "Shawn!" He finally relaxed back into his chair, but he didn't look any more forgiving. "Come on," I cajoled. "What are you complaining about? You're a union member."

"But I don't lord it over people who aren't," he pouted, loudly enough to warrant yet another stage-managerial glare.

I bent over my script and tried to appear studious. Ken exploited Martina's contrition, asking her to go back to the beginning of the scene. With Tom, she plodded through the dialog, providing a barely serviceable imitation of a meek young woman confronting her more worldly brother.

At last, they arrived at "Fly Free," the first big ballad of the show. The piano accompanist played the introductory few bars, setting the mood for the piece, which had yet to be fully orchestrated. Martina rose from her chair, as if the music moved her so completely that she couldn't be confined, couldn't be restrained to one place. She counted out ten bars, nodding her head, and then, when she should have launched into the soaring lyrics, she spoke the words: "'No one understands me—'"

I choked. Audibly.

I knew that Shawn and I were on thin ice, lurking in the back of the room. I knew that we had to mind our manners or we'd be tossed out altogether. I knew that we were supposed to sit there, meek and mild and eternally grateful for the opportunity to observe the master at her work.

But Martina was being absolutely ridiculous.

As if she needed to justify herself to me, her angry

voice projected to the very last row of chairs. "My contract provides—"

"Yes, yes," Ken soothed. "Of course, your contract provides that you can speak your songs for the first three weeks of rehearsal, so that you can protect your voice." He sighed deeply, and I was suddenly certain that *he* would never have agreed to that contractual term, if he'd been consulted by the producers. That term, or pretty much any of the others. He shook his head, momentarily deflated by the battle. "Let's take a break, shall we?"

"Fifteen minutes," called the stage manager, biting off each syllable. Martina clearly managed to annoy everyone with her precious demands, even the normally unflappable professional crew. Of course, I had to admit that she'd had her picture on the cover of half a dozen magazines the week before, all blaring her success at being cast in *Menagerie!* The producers couldn't buy that sort of publicity. However annoying Martina might be, her pop-star appeal was going to cement our show's success.

"Her contract, my ass," Shawn muttered, as Martina struck up another lament for the lack of craft services.

"I can't believe that Ken lets her get away with this crap," I said, once I was sure there was enough ambient noise to cover my annoyance. Even as I complained, though, I tried to nurture my inner Pollyanna. "He probably just wants to help her ease into the show. That must be it. It'll get better as we go along. It has to." I heard the doubt in my voice, though. I was pretty sure that nothing about Martina Block was going to get better with the passage of time.

Shawn pursed his lips. "Sure it will. And we can put

a show on in my effing barn. I'll make the goddamn costumes!" He sighed in disgust. "Come on," he said. "I'll treat for coffee. You look exhausted."

"Thanks a lot," I said, trying to sound offended by his assessment of my appearance, but secretly grateful for the offer of caffeine.

As Shawn held the door for me, he said, "I hope that he was worth it."

My cheeks flamed as I strode down the sidewalk. Of course Shawn matched my pace, step for embarrassed step. "There isn't any 'he'! " I protested.

"Of course not, Little Miss Innocent."

"I wasn't—"

"Oh, no. You just happen to own an entire wardrobe of identical outfits." I glanced down. "You wore that blouse yesterday, sweetie."

I sighed and filled him in on my evening. Somehow, it all came rushing out—kissing Timothy, kissing Teel, Amy's maniacal plan that had us all dining together on Saturday night. I stopped just short of confessing my commitment to restructuring my life. I knew that if I told him *that,* I'd never hear the end of it.

Shawn handed me my coffee, saluting me with his own blue-and-white paper cup. "If only you weren't stuck as an understudy in *Menagerie!*" He rested a wrist against his forehead, as if the unfairness of the situation made him grow faint. "You could turn this whole thing into a wildly successful sitcom. Just picture it! Your name in lights! And then you'd have your own coffee on set, fresh and hot, from craft services. Your show would be the comedy hit of the season—I can see the ads now, maybe even the cover of *People.* Man Number One? Or Man Number Two? Will She or

Won't She? Watch Erin Decide in This Week's Episode of *Erin's Two Boyfriends!*"

"That's not funny!"

He laughed at my indignation as he dumped half of Hawaii's annual pure cane sugar export into his own cup. "Actually, sweetie, it is."

All the way back to the theater, I tried to convince Shawn that I had sworn off men for life. He wasn't buying a word of it.

So much for my acting career. And it wasn't like I was going to learn any great stage tips, watching Martina butcher the role that should have been mine. My caffeine buzz wore off well before my deserved exasperation.

* * *

Suffice to say, the rest of my week didn't get any better.

Martina continued to misconstrue the role of Laura Wingfield in every possible way. Ken voted down her suggestion that Laura wear fluorescent dresses (to emphasize her being different), that Laura be followed by a spotlight every instant that she was onstage (ditto), that Laura be the focus of two new scenes and four new songs (ditto, again) and that the entire production be renamed *Laura!* (Um, ditto.) Perhaps needless to say, Martina argued that her contract gave her the right to make every one of her absurd proposed changes.

Shawn continued to tease me about the tangle of my love life, despite my increasingly shrill protests that I didn't have a love life, didn't want a love life and would never, ever tell him about any love life I might choose to pursue in the future.

Amy continued to check in every afternoon, more

often than not leaving a message when my phone was turned off during rehearsal. Justin had recovered completely, without even a bruise to remind him of the folly of playing Soldierman. Every time Amy called, she put Justin on the line—he was more and more excited about Super Soldier Saturday and his trip into the city. When I heard my nephew's shrill enthusiasm, I could almost forgive Amy for placing me in an untenable position vis-à-vis Timothy and Teel.

Almost. But not quite.

On Saturday afternoon, our rehearsal was cut short by more of Martina's diva machinations. "I'm sorry," she said, collapsing into a chair after reblocking the play's tricky first scene for the sixth time. Martina kept insisting that Laura was being "marginalized," so Ken changed where all the actors stood. By now, Amanda and Tom were delivering most of their lines from shadowy corners, all so that Martina's ego remained well fed. Her ego, alas, seemed to be the only thing about her that was receiving ample nourishment. "I just can't concentrate anymore," she whined. "My blood sugar's too low."

Even from the back of the room, I caught the stage manager rolling his eyes. He reached for his backpack and started digging around; we had all learned that he kept a stash of granola bars for just such an emergency.

Martina draped the back of her hand across her brow, as if the lights in the rehearsal room were just too bright for her poor, exhausted eyes to handle. "Please," she said. "Not another granola bar. All that sugar... I need something *healthy*. Fresh fruit. Broth."

Broth? What world did she live in, where purveyors of consommé lurked in the wings?

She sighed again. "Craft services would understand."

Ken started to say something, but swallowed his words before he could risk annoying his star. He sounded defeated as he announced, "Let's call it a day, everyone. I've got a meeting with the costume designer in half an hour, anyway."

"Costume designer!" Martina said, sitting up straight. "I have some ideas I want to share with you!"

I left, before I said anything I might regret. Fortunately, Shawn wasn't around; together, we might have killed the woman on the spot.

Walking home, I tried to tell myself that Martina had given me a present. I could have been cooped up inside the theater. Instead, I was outside, enjoying a fresh breeze, basking in the surprisingly bright sunshine. Clouds floated overhead, as if they were trying to illustrate a children's book called *Erin and the Sunny Summer Day*. I had plenty of time before I had to meet Amy and Justin at Garden Variety, before I had to juggle the inevitable chaos as I introduced Timothy to my family. To Teel.

I rounded a corner, turning south to head down to the Village, and I found myself in the middle of one of New York City's street fairs. The celebrations roamed from neighborhood to neighborhood all summer long. Typically, they lasted for an entire afternoon, stopping traffic for a couple of city blocks, forcing grumpy drivers to pursue detours while pedestrians commandeered the streets.

I wandered past dozens of booths offering everything from used books to new spices to practically anything cooked on a stick. One stand boasted dozens of

American flags, ranging in size from tiny plastic rectangles to massive, intricately stitched masterpieces perfect for displaying on the skyscraper of your choice. "Happy Flag Day!" the cigar-chomping vendor shouted at anyone who would listen. "Get your flags here! Happy Flag Day!" To bolster his patriotic message, he was blasting Sousa marches from an iPod through speakers the size of the Empire State Building.

I shook my head, trying to clear my ears, and I hurried past. The next booth, though, snagged my attention. The vendor had set up bowling pins, each painted a different shade of khaki or olive green. One pin in the middle stood out; it was painted a brilliant crimson. The vendor held matching rings, which he tossed from hand to hand as he delivered his patter. "Step right up, ladies and gentlemen! Take your chances! Toss a ring around a pin and take home a prize! Step right up!" As if to punctuate his speech, he threw three rings in quick succession, lassoing a pin with each round.

I glanced at the prizes that were strung across the top of the booth. Centered above the bowling pins, leaning forward as if he wanted to leap into my arms, was Justin's Soldierman.

Okay. The vendor had no way of knowing that he had Soldierman at his beck and call. But the plush figure could have been sculpted with Justin specifically in mind. The thing was at least four feet tall, and he wore desert fatigues. His face was all but hidden behind sewn-on plastic sunglasses, and his hands were covered by leather gloves, as if he'd just marched in from some tricky desert maneuver.

And, impossibly, he wore a red cape. Red, to match the solo bowling pin in the center of the booth. The S might look suspiciously like one worn by Clark Kent on superhero duty, but I didn't think Justin would mind the copyright infringement.

The hawker caught me staring. "Ready to try your luck, little lady?"

Little lady? What, had I stepped back in time, to a 1950s carnival? I had to shout, to make myself heard above the Sousa marches from the booth next door. "How much for the soldier?"

"One lucky toss, little lady. He's the grand prize—ring the red one, and he's yours. Three dollars a ring, or five for ten."

I shook my head. I had about as much chance of snaring that bright red pin as I did of bowling a perfect 300. I started to turn away, but a breeze chose that unfortunate moment to spring to life. Soldierman's cape caught on the warm air, soaring behind the rugged figure's shoulders.

Justin would love him.

I fished into my wallet for two crumpled five-dollar bills. "I'll take five," I said.

The hawker made a big deal out of counting out my rings. He gave me two khaki, two olive and one that was painted the same bright red as the grand prize pin. "Okay, little lady," he said. "Take your time now. Choose your target and make your toss."

Both khaki rings flew wide of the gleaming red pin. The first olive ring fell far short. I overcompensated with the next one, hitting the plastic sheeting at the back of the booth. That left the red ring. The red ring for the red pin. The red ring to get Justin the best present I'd ever given him.

I closed my eyes and crossed my fingers, muttering a

quick, "Just this once." Then, before I could spend too much time calculating, too much time growing tense, too much time overthinking the way I did with everything in my life, I tossed the red ring in a high, looping arc.

It landed squarely around the neck of a bowling pin.

A sand-colored pin four to the right of the red one. "Congratulations!" The carny shouted, raising his voice above marching bands and crowd noise.

"I won?" I asked, a little dazed by my throwing expertise.

"Absolutely, little lady! One first-place prize, just for you."

But he didn't reach for Soldierman. He didn't stretch for the carabiner that anchored Justin's hero to the line across the front of the booth. Instead, he produced a plastic bag from somewhere behind his table. A plastic bag that held about two inches of water. A plastic bag that held two inches of water and a goldfish.

"I want Soldierman!" I said, sounding only slightly less mature than my five-year-old nephew.

The vendor barely glanced at the giant plush figure. "He's the grand prize. You won a first prize."

"I don't want a fish! I want the soldier!"

The hawker's eyes grew hard. "Three for one, five for ten."

"But—"

"Three for one." He spat out the words. "Five for ten." He started to put the fish back beneath the table.

"Fine!" I said, feeling unfairly manipulated. After all, how many people nailed *any* of the bowling pins? I had a sneaking suspicion that I could toss rings for the rest of the day and never come close to snagging the red one. Weren't all these carny games rigged somehow? Didn't all these guys cheat?

Before I could be tempted to throw away the last change in my wallet, I grabbed the goldfish and stalked off. The Sousa marches followed me down the street, as if they were congratulating me on my sorry win. I held up the fish, staring at its bulging eyes. There wasn't a lot of water in there. It was a good thing I was rescuing the little guy. Saving him from the street fair. Saving him from the hawker, who obviously didn't care about his prizes, about his contestants, beyond finding the next fool willing to part with three for one, five for ten.

I wasn't an idiot, I told myself. I recognized coincidence when it stared me in the face. The Master Plan required that I get a fish. I'd had my peace lily for almost three weeks. Time to move on to the next stage.

As I hurried through the rest of the festival, the lingering strains of patriotic music made me think of a song from *Menagerie!*—the big number that opened the second act. The piece started with a flourish of brass, designed to shock an audience that had just returned from drinks and snacks and bathroom breaks. Coming on the heels of Amanda and Tom's big fight at the end of Act One, "Perfect World" allowed Laura to express everything she ever wanted in life. The music was a classic Broadway showstopper; it had a driving beat and the type of rousing chorus that audiences sing in the street after a show. With my Teel-enhanced singing, I could belt out the lyrics like an improbably delicate Ethel Merman, even while managing the complicated dance combination for the chorus of the song.

Alas, Martina had only walked through the piece a few times. Her contract said that she didn't need to start actual dancing until we transferred from the rehearsal room to the theater—ten more days. I was beginning to question why we were bothering with rehearsals at all, at least until Martina was contractually bound to participate.

I wondered who her agent was. Martina had certainly received more contractual exemptions than any actor I'd ever encountered. If only she'd asked for some guaranteed nights off, once the show started to run... Then, I'd know that I would actually get onstage at some point. I'd be certain that it was worth my time, worth my emotional investment, to attend every single rehearsal. I'd feel like I had chosen well when I invested half of my magical capital—two of my four wishes—on my career....

By the time I got back to the Bentley, I was beginning to worry that my fish was actually dead. Wouldn't that just be perfect—I'd be scuttling the second stage of the Master Plan before I ever began it. I couldn't tell if the poor goldfish was fluttering its fins in the water, or if it was merely rocked by my motion. I rushed past George, scarcely taking time to say hello to the doorman. I worked the three locks on my apartment door in record time, practically holding my own breath.

In the kitchen, I scrambled for the largest container in the cupboards, a stainless-steel mixing bowl that Becca had left behind. I shoved it under the faucet and turned on the water. As I waited for the bowl to fill, I glanced toward the peace lily that Amy had given me.

The poor plant was splayed across the counter. Its jaunty stalks had deflated, as if someone had let the air out of their once-bright green stems. The leaves looked dusty and frayed, where they weren't outright brown from drought. The single bloom had curled into a tight fist, turned from bright white to a pathetic, parched yellow.

One. (Remember me? The girl who learned the hard way that bad things come in threes? Well, I couldn't imagine anything much worse than killing my lily, than destroying the very firsts step of my life-transformation plan. This was just great. How could I tell my big sister that the score was now Master Plan: 1, Erin: 0?)

Water started to flow out of the stainless-steel bowl, cascading into the sink. I slammed off the faucet.

I wanted to invent an alarm, a beeping reminder that would tell me when to water a stupid plant. So what if I hadn't kept that peace lily alive? It had probably been dry when Amy gave it to me. The damned thing might have gotten...spider mite. Didn't that kill things, totally unprovoked? Wasn't it a brutal destroyer of perfectly healthy houseplants? I couldn't be held accountable for an invasion of spider mite. Spider mite meant that the first stage of the Master Plan didn't really count. I shoved the lily into the corner, telling myself that I'd deal with it later.

Back at the sink, I sloshed a little water out of the stainless-steel bowl and moved it to the counter. It took me a full minute to pick open the knot in the goldfish's plastic bag. Finally, I was able to turn the bag upside down, to release my piscine pet into his shiny new home.

"There you go," I said as he sank to the bottom of the mixing bowl. I bit my lip and waited to see if he would recover. "Come on," I urged him. "Come on!" He sat on the bottom of the bowl while I stole a dozen breaths for both of us, and then, slowly, he began to swim around the bowl. "Yes!" I shouted. I glared at the wimpy plant that had unceremoniously given up the ghost. "Take that, Master Plan!"

I had a fish. I'd moved on to the second stage of my plan—more than a week early, but there couldn't be any true harm in that.

I narrowed my eyes as I looked at my new companion. I couldn't call it an "it" forever. It needed a name. That was part of caring for a fish. That was part of protecting a living creature.

"Tennessee," I decided. It was perfect, to name him after the playwright who was going to be my key to fame and fortune. Somehow. If I could just get Martina Block out of the way. "Welcome to the Bentley, Tennessee."

The fish took a half-spirited lap around his bowl. I drew a deep breath, unwilling to admit—even to myself—how pleased I was to see his recovery. And when I exhaled, I found that I'd been whisked from my apartment to nowhere.

Chapter 10

OKAY, NOT NOWHERE. To the Garden.

This time, I knew enough to look around for Teel. He was standing right behind me, dressed as the doctor I knew and loved. Well, not quite loved. Lusted after. In a completely safe, Master Plan–approved way.

"Fourth wish?" he asked, as soon as he caught my eye.

The demand got my back up. No "hello." No "how are you?" No "I'm looking forward to seeing you at dinner tonight." Maybe Teel *wasn't* going to be a work-around for the Master Plan. I was sick and tired of hearing about my last wish. "Take me back," I said, locking my eyes on him to avoid becoming queasy.

"I thought that if I gave you a little time, you'd figure out what to wish for." His voice was calm, reasoning. I heard everything I'd fallen for back in the hospital—the man who had been worried about *me,* about my mental health, my physical well-being, even as everything around me was spinning out of control. "Don't be angry with me."

"You used your tattoo to control me."

He favored me with a beatific smile. "I use my tattoo to control everyone."

I snorted. "Like that's supposed to make me feel better!" I started to turn away, but there wasn't anywhere for me to go. The emptiness of the Garden space made my belly tremble, and I quickly whirled back to confront my genie once again. "Why did you bring me back here, anyway? It's not like I can see what you can. Your Garden isn't real."

"It is to me." He sighed and stretched out his hands, gesturing toward something that had to be the Garden's invisible fence. The motion made the cuff of his sleeve ride up, baring part of his flame tattoo. I refused to let my eyes follow the ink. "Jaze is still in there," he said, so softly that I had to lean forward to catch the last word.

"How do you know that?"

"I can *feel* him." Teel clenched his fists around the fence I couldn't see. His tattoo flickered with more life; the flames rose and fell in fascinating patterns. "Erin," he whispered. "Make your fourth wish."

There were a million things I could ask for. I could become the most famous actress the world had ever known, recognized by hordes around the world. I could make myself a billionaire, use my fabulous wealth to fund productions, to create drama schools, to distribute scholarships for deserving actors. I could build a string of theaters, of play festivals, of anything I wanted across America, across the *world*.

My mind reeled as I spun from wish to wish, from possibility to possibility. I could do anything. I could *have* anything. I could use my fourth wish however I wanted.

My fourth wish.

My last wish.

Forever.

Gasping, I staggered away from Teel. What if I had thrown away my wishes before Justin had fallen? What if I needed Teel's magic again, to save someone close to me? How could I squander my last gift, now, without knowing my future, without knowing what I would truly need?

Besides that, what right did Teel have to manipulate my mind? To control what I was thinking? What I was doing?

"No!" I spat. "Leave me alone!"

Teel looked astonished that I had broken free. He glanced from his wrist to me, and back again. His fingers tightened around the unseen fence, clutching so tightly that I thought he might break one of the small bones in his hands.

And then he forced himself to take a step back. He drew a deep breath. Another. A third. His hands—clenched into fists at his sides—relaxed. His cuffs slipped back into place, covering the mesmerizing orange and gold and black tattoo.

I blinked and looked around, suddenly freed from the heady sensation of power. Teel shrugged and offered a lopsided grin. "You can't blame a guy for trying."

Before I could answer, he raised his hand to his ear. One tug. Two. And I was back in my kitchen, no genie in sight.

My breath shuddered in my lungs as I forced myself to take a few steps forward. I'd come so close to doing what Teel wanted me to do. I'd almost made that last wish. Almost given in to his desire.

But I hadn't. I'd found the will to resist. I'd found the will, and I'd maintained the power.

I clutched the edge of the granite counter. *I had maintained the power.*

I had never had power in any relationship with a guy. Sure, I'd bargained over my virginity, back in college. But I'd ultimately decided to give that gift away. And ever since, I'd been struggling to figure out who I was, what was important to me, what *mattered* when I was with a guy.

I'm sure a psychiatrist would have a field day with all the reasons I acted the way I did. I was the last-born in my family, and I was used to giving in to my pushy older sister's demands. I was orphaned at a relatively young age, and I didn't get to study my parents' successful marriage, never got to pattern my own serious dating after their solid relationship. I made my career as an actress, as a person who made her real personality as transparent as possible, as insubstantial as I could, so that I could assume the colorful roles I performed onstage.

Or maybe I was just a scaredy-cat wimp, afraid to trust my instincts with men.

With *men.* But not with a genie.

I'd taken a stand with Teel. I'd withheld my fourth wish. I'd done it, in the never-world of the Garden, in a place where I could barely stand on my own two feet without being overwhelmed by dizziness. I'd stood up for what I believed, for what I wanted, what I needed. And *damn,* it felt good!

And that was what I would gain by seeing the Master Plan through to the end. I would discover that sort of power in all of my relationships, with all men. I'd be strong. Powerful. In control.

I glanced at the bedraggled peace lily in the corner. It wouldn't be a great witness to my being such a strong person. But Tennessee would speak up on my behalf, wouldn't he?

Er, if fish could speak.

I tapped the side of the stainless-steel bowl, making the water ripple. Tennessee deserved a better home. Something with a view of more than the ceiling. I'd track down a goldfish bowl for him after dinner.

Dinner. I'd have to hurry, or I'd be late to meet Amy and Justin. And Teel.

Sure enough, Justin launched himself across the flagstones of the Garden Variety courtyard as soon as I made my appearance. He flung his thin arms around my neck, crying, "Aunt Erin!"

I returned his hug. "Don't you look all handsome, in your big-boy shirt and your khaki slacks!" For just a flash, the khaki of his pants reminded me of the bowling pin, of the near miss in my battle for Soldierman. Oh, well. Justin couldn't have any idea of the treasure that had nearly been his. He didn't know what he was missing.

And I sure wasn't going to tell him. I had no intention of mentioning Tennessee to anyone that night. Least of all, my sister, who would be fast to accuse me of violating the Master Plan because I'd skipped ahead a week.

"Mommy said we were going to meet lots of your friends tonight. I have to be extra-special good, because you might be in a bad mood."

"Is that what Mommy said?" I asked, rolling my eyes

at Amy. She smiled innocently.

"Are you in a bad mood, Aunt Erin?"

"Not yet," I said. But the butterflies that attacked my stomach from the inside hinted at a different story. I reminded myself that I had just gained the upper hand in the Garden. Dinner was going to be fine. Just fine.

I hoped and prayed.

In any case, Justin's smile was as bright as Teel's lamp had been, post-genie-release. He pointed to the bright geraniums that blazed in puddles at the edge of the courtyard. "Mommy said that I shouldn't mention the flower she gave you. The special lily." As soon as the words were out of his mouth, his eyes grew to the size of baseballs.

I forced a smile onto my lips. "Don't worry, Justin. I don't mind your mentioning the flower."

Amy eyed me with suspicion. "Do you still have it?"

"Of course!" Well, that wasn't a lie. It was still on the counter, dust, desiccated leaves and all. That was still "having" it, wasn't it? Maybe I could crumble the leaves and feed them to Tennessee. Cover up the evidence of my failure while sustaining the next step in my personal evolution. I'd look into the suitability of peace lilies as fish food the first chance I got.

Justin reached up and tugged at my hand. "What type of restaurant is this, Aunt Erin? Can I get pizza?"

"I don't know," I confessed. "This restaurant serves a different type of food every day. They probably don't have pizza. But you'll like something else they have."

"I don't like a lot of food," Justin said, wrinkling his nose in anticipation.

"That's because you haven't eaten at Garden Variety." Rebellion was sparking in my nephew's eyes, and I suspected that my simplistic response wasn't going to take us very far. Instead of trying to find another conversational path, I looked at Amy. "Ready?" I asked.

"I was just going to ask you the same thing," she said. I saw the amusement in her face, the certainty that I wasn't up to keeping the Master Plan. I was ready to show her, though. I was ready to prove that I could handle anything. I opened the restaurant door, waiting for the two of them to precede me inside.

Timothy was waiting for us. "Erin," he said, darting a private smile just for me before he reached out to shake my sister's hand. I quickly made introductions, forbidding myself from thinking about what Timothy's quick glance had meant, about what he might be thinking. While we'd spoken the morning after Justin's hospital stay, I hadn't seen him for the rest of the week. I'd purposely kept my distance, determined not to fall off the man-free wagon.

That was all part of the Master Plan.

Timothy gained innumerable coolness points by offering his hand to Justin. My nephew shook gravely, his eyes going wide. Before we could make small talk, though, the door opened again. I turned, bracing myself to see Teel, to make the stilted introductions that would no doubt amuse my sister to no end.

Instead, I bit off a string of curse words that would have taught Justin more than he'd ever heard from his father. Or his father's platoon. Or division. Or however swearing soldiers were organized.

"Shawn!" I ladled years of onstage experience into the frosty greeting for my fellow actor. "What are you doing here?"

"Erin!" He matched my brittle greeting with an expansive shrug, leaning in to kiss me on both cheeks. "Darling, I'm here for moral support."

I darted a glance at Timothy, who looked a little confused. He had no idea why I might need support, moral, immoral or otherwise.

Sure, I'd told Shawn about dinner. I'd wanted some sympathy. I'd wanted someone to remind me that I could juggle the evening with perfect aplomb, that I could stay sparkling and witty while my all my romantic worlds collided.

But I hadn't expected an audience.

"I don't need any moral support," I said through gritted teeth.

Shawn wasn't at all perturbed. "Then I'm here to celebrate Flag Day. Three cheers for the red, white and blue!"

Justin tugged at Amy's hand and asked in a stage whisper, "Mommy, is that one of Aunt Erin's friends? Is he the one who's going to give her a bad mood?"

I barely kept from snapping at my nephew. Instead, I took my frustration out on Shawn. "Where did you leave Patrick?" I asked nastily.

"Patrick?" Shawn contrived to look utterly confused.

"Patrick Ferguson?" I demanded, planting my hands on my hips. "Your boyfriend? Let me guess. His Uncle Sam costume hasn't come back from the cleaners."

Shawn's laugh was a sharp bark. "Uncle Sam is strictly amateur night, sweetie. You should see what he really wears to show his patriotism!"

Justin whispered loudly, "Mommy, what's amateur night?"

Timothy swooped in to the rescue. "Table for four, then?"

I slanted a glance at Amy. I could see her giving Shawn the once-over, completely approving of his outrageous sense of humor, even if she immediately recognized that he would never be a challenge to the Master Plan. To the wreck of my love life. It was going to be a long, long night.

"Five," I said through set teeth. "There will be five of us."

Timothy shrugged. "No problem. Let me just slide that table over." He matched actions to words, along the way producing a packet of crayons for Justin. He settled us in our chairs with an easy grace. "Wine, while you're waiting?" he asked, already gliding toward glassware. Timothy poured generous amounts of Chianti into goblets and promised a glass of milk for Justin before disappearing into the kitchen.

Shawn watched him leave, cocking his head to one side to take a more appraising view of Timothy's jean-clad backside. "Oh, sweetie, I think I'm going to like *this* restaurant."

I glared at him before rolling my eyes in the general direction of my innocent nephew. "Don't even get started," I warned.

Before Shawn could reply, Justin shouted, "Dr. Teel!"

"Inside voice," Amy said automatically, as we all turned toward the door. I barely heard her, though, because the temperature in the room shot up a thousand degrees. I staggered to my feet, as if I were a hostess greeting a treasured guest at a dinner party.

Teel strode across the room, comfortable, commanding. He wore a white dress shirt and charcoal slacks; he looked like he'd just come from a photo shoot at GQ. The smile that he flashed at me was so smooth, we might never have had our little confrontation in the Garden.

In fact, he looked so stunning, I found myself reconsidering the logic behind withholding my fourth wish. I'd been thinking about punishing him, about paying him back for trying to manipulate me. Maybe I should go with a different motivation instead. By holding on to my fourth wish, I could keep Teel close to me. Bind him to me forever in his sexy doctor guise...

As if he could read my thoughts, Teel walked directly to me. He kissed me hello as if he had every right to do so, not hesitating to settle his blunt fingers on my arms. Our kiss wasn't as passionate as the one we'd shared at the hospital, but it felt more intimate, here in public, where I knew people were staring at us. I felt the corners of his lips curl against mine; he was smirking, even as he made my knees grow weak.

One tiny corner of my mind said that it was all right for me to respond to him that way. It was perfectly acceptable. He was a genie, not a man. He was wholly outside the boundaries of my Master Plan. I was going to explain that to Amy, use this dinner to illustrate the exception that proved the rule, the progress I was making with reforming my love life.

A throat cleared behind me, and I leaped away as if I'd been burned.

Of course, Timothy stood there, holding Justin's milk. A jaunty Mickey Mouse straw sprouted from the lidded cup, the squeaky-voiced little rodent waving a cheerful hello to anyone willing to pay attention.

Which, at that moment, was precisely no one.

"Aunt Erin," Justin said, "why are your cheeks all red?"

Surprising salvation came in the form of Shawn, who rose and offered Teel his hand. "Shawn Goldberg," he said, and I could tell from the roughness of his voice that he, too, was smitten by my genie. Poor Patrick—he might end up regretting his decision not to honor the Stars and Stripes with the rest of us. "Pleased to meet you."

"And this is Timothy," Amy said, gesturing to our host. "Timothy, this is Dr. Teel. A long-time friend of my sister's." She didn't bother to disguise the amusement in her voice. I wondered what made her immune to Teel's charms. She seemed to be the only person in the room not throwing herself at my genie's feet.

Amy, that was, and Timothy. Timothy Brennan definitely did not warm to the genie in our midst.

He wasn't rude. He couldn't afford that, in his own restaurant. Instead, he became excruciatingly polite. Without asking, he poured a glass of wine for Teel as we all took our seats. He offered the Chianti with a steady gaze that would equal throwing down a gauntlet in some corners of the world. Or niches of history. Whatever.

If Teel recognized that he was being challenged, he didn't say anything. He took up his goblet with a nod, half saluting with the glass. Timothy's lips froze partway between a smile and a snarl, and the two men continued to take the measure of each other.

Once again, Justin broke the tension. "I'm hungry, Mommy. What are we going to eat?"

My laugh was an octave higher than I wanted it to

be. I tore my gaze away from the Neanderthals in front of me and gave Justin an impossibly bright smile. "That's just what Mr. Brennan was just going to tell us!"

Timothy shrugged back on his role of host. "In honor of Flag Day, I've got a fruit salad with strawberries, white peaches and blueberries. Or, if you'd prefer, there's a green salad with cherry tomatoes, white radishes and a blueberry vinaigrette. For main dishes, I have molasses braised short ribs and firecracker shrimp."

Justin wrinkled his nose. "What's firecracker shrimp?"

Timothy addressed him directly, as if a five-year-old could be the most important food critic in his universe. "They're shrimp, cooked in a spicy sauce. They still have their shells on, and you can see their eyes."

"Cool!" Justin said with excitement. I didn't know if he'd ever tried to eat crustaceans, but the notion of food staring back at him obviously had substantial appeal.

In the end, we ordered two plates of short ribs and three of shrimp, with fruit salad to go around. As the food came out of the kitchen, I forced myself to relax. I covered my most awkward moments with a clever application of fresh, hot bread, spread thick with creamery butter. What were a few extra calories, when I had my sanity to maintain?

Shawn and Teel devoted themselves to entertaining Justin, telling stories to make him laugh. They took turns drawing Soldierman on the table's butcher paper, and each of them spun out a story about the superhero's adventures.

Once again, I regretted not winning the giant plush doll for my nephew. For all I knew, though, Justin was continuing to misbehave at home, continuing to drive Amy nuts with his disobedience. I certainly didn't want to do anything to encourage my nephew to resume his flying career, or to do anything else to upset the balance in Amy's challenging life.

Amy might drive me nuts with the games she played, but she was still my sister, after all. The only one I was ever going to have. And at the end of the road, she was always there for me—even if she made me crazy along the way. This whole insane test with Teel and Timothy was just another chapter in our lives as sisters, just another joke she was playing on me. We'd laugh about it soon enough. When we were staying up too late, drinking cheap wine and raiding the emergency chocolate stash.

As my sister watched her son soak up all the male attention, a wistfulness grew on her face. She might have orchestrated this dinner as a way to test me, but she'd been drawn to Teel herself. Oh, Amy didn't want one of Teel's knockout kisses for herself; I knew that she was one hundred percent faithful to Derek. It was just that there was something...satisfying about watching a man talk, watching a man entertain a worshipful little boy. It didn't hurt, of course, that Amy thought Teel was a doctor at least partially responsible for Justin's miracle recovery. She could never know precisely *how* involved Teel had been.

Once, when Justin earnestly announced that Soldierman wanted to be with his family but had to stay away and fight a war, I saw tears glisten in Amy's eyes. She dashed them away before Justin could spot them.

We adults saw them, though. Shawn leaned forward and seized three crayons at once, drawing a massive Humvee for Soldierman to drive. In short order, Justin had him add helicopter rotors and a giant drag parachute. Shawn complied, providing sound effects to bolster the vehicular embellishments.

Amy laughed and clapped her hands, earnestly thanking both Teel and Shawn for their handiwork. Shawn leaned in and kissed her on the cheek, while Teel merely gave her a solemn nod.

Soon enough, Soldierman and his incredible vehicle were lost in a riot of rib bones and shrimp carapaces. It was impossible to eat the Flag Day dinner with anything approaching grace or delicacy. Timothy acknowledged as much, carting out extra napkins and bringing us all finger bowls with slices of lemon. (Justin was enamored with the bowls, and he made Amy promise that they could use some at home for their next meal.)

When we got to the end of dinner, Justin's glass of milk remained untouched. Amy nodded toward it and said, "Come on, Justin. Finish up."

He took out the fancy Mickey Mouse straw and spun it around on his finger. "I'm not thirsty," he said.

"Justin," Amy warned.

My nephew stared directly at his mother. As if he were an automaton, he reached out, curling his fingers around the side of the cup. "Justin!" Amy said again, her voice cutting through the amusement of our little party.

Slowly, steadily, Justin started to tilt his wrist. The milk sloshed to the edge of the cup, teetering on the brink of pouring over.

I wanted to tell him to stop. I wanted to say something to Amy, to break the ferocity of her embarrassed glare. I wanted to explain to Justin that spilling milk was not a way to bring his father home, was not a way to make Derek love him from afar. I wanted to invent a cup that could never spill, never break, never ruin a surprisingly perfect meal out with family and friends.

Before I could figure out anything to do, though, Shawn reached out an easy hand, settling his fingers on Justin's forearm. "Hey, dude," he said. "Drink it, then clink it."

Justin's destructive concentration was broken. "What?" he asked.

"Drink it," Shawn said, draining his own water glass. "Then clink it." He set his glass down with finality, flicking his fingernail against the rim to make a faint belling noise.

Justin laughed. "Drink it!" he said, draining his milk in one long gulp. "Then clink it!" He flicked his own glass.

"Exactly," Shawn said. "That's the way Soldierman does it, right?"

Shawn winked at Amy and me, accepting my silently mouthed, *Thank you.* It took Amy a little longer to relax, to sit back in her chair, but she finally managed, with the help of her glass of Chianti. I knew that she was grateful to Shawn, but I suspected she was also a little jealous, frustrated that her little boy responded so much better to a man's guidance.

Throughout the entire meal, Timothy remained on the edge of our increasingly louder little party. He spirited away empty plates like a ghost. He refilled water glasses. He replaced empty wine bottles.

I wanted to ask him to pull up a chair, to join us for a few minutes, but there were other tables to serve, other patrons to provide for. Once, I watched him usher an ancient homeless man to the small two-top by the kitchen; the mammoth plate of ribs that he served his guest threatened to upend the table. Another time, I caught him looking at me, his caramel eyes dark, shadowed by a dozen conversations we might have had. Should have had. Especially when he shifted his gaze to Teel, and the corners of his mouth turned down with a hundred unasked questions.

At last, Timothy emerged from the kitchen bearing desserts for all—generous portions of strawberry shortcake piled high with fresh whipped cream. He balanced a plate of star-shaped cookies, as well, each one covered in blue and red and white frosting. A bottle of Southern Comfort nestled in the center of the tray, presiding over tumblers full of ice.

Glancing around the room to make sure that the few remaining patrons were taken care of, Timothy hooked a chair with one foot, pulling it up to our table. He finally sat down beside me, relaxing as if the furniture had been made for him. His ease seemed like an extension of his flowing grace, light-years away from the exhaustion of a man run ragged from serving up perfect dinners for dozens of customers.

As he started to pour the liqueur, everyone complimented him on the food.

Everyone but Teel, that was. My genie merely accepted a glass, then sat back in his chair, watching. His cobalt eyes were hooded, as if he were thinking, calculating. As if he were trying to figure out a way to use Timothy to get what he wanted. To trick me into making my fourth wish.

I smiled at Teel sweetly and was rewarded by his quirking a single eyebrow. I suspected that both of us were suddenly thinking of the kisses we'd shared, the two electrical storms we'd ridden out together.

I was, in any case. And my water glass was empty, just when I needed it most. I blushed when Timothy passed me his own.

Shawn sipped his Southern Comfort and shuddered with all the excitement of a lapdog. "This has been wonderful," he drawled. And then, he sat upright, as if he'd been struck by lightning. Or by a brainstorm—something possibly much more dangerous.

"Timothy!" he exclaimed. "Have I got a business deal for you!"

The restaurateur eyed him with a panther's cool amusement at a frolicking cub. Shawn glanced at me, bouncing up and down in his seat, as if he'd become possessed by the spirit of our hyperactive theatrical director. "Erin! This is going to be perfect!" He turned back to Timothy before I could begin to figure out what he was going to say. "Come work craft services for *Menagerie!*" Shawn exclaimed. "For the show that Erin and I are in."

Amy barely had the decency to cut off a snort of amusement. "Inside voice," I muttered, glaring at her. She should have been proud of me. Supportive. I'd proven to her, all night long, that I was sticking with the Plan, that everything was perfect. Well, almost perfect. I felt Teel stiffen beside me, and he shot his cuff at Shawn's invitation to Timothy, as if he needed to check the time.

I turned to face Timothy head-on. Part of the motion was so that I wouldn't be snared by Teel's tattoo. But part was truly because I wanted to hear what Timothy would say.

"Isn't craft services more of a movie thing? Catering on a set?" Timothy sounded polite, but perplexed.

Shawn guffawed, his enthusiasm enhanced by the sweet peaches-and-whiskey liqueur in his glass. "Exactly. We've got a movie star in the cast. A true diva." He explained about Martina. "After the trick she pulled today, the director is desperate. You could name your price, if you could just get Martina to shut up."

Timothy whirled on me, his eyes narrowed. For the first time since I'd met him, I felt a little frightened by the power he kept under control, intimidated by the energy he kept under wraps. "Did you tell him?" he asked, nodding toward Shawn with an intensity that seemed completely disproportionate to our lighthearted conversation.

"Tell him?" I managed to ask, astonished by the force of Timothy's question.

"About my deadline." Timothy's eyes drilled into me. His nicked pride shimmered around him like an aura. "About the lease."

"No! I didn't say a word!" Amy was nodding, though, clicking her fingernails against the table in that way she had when she was speculating on a good business deal. Okay, maybe I had shared a few details, but only with my sister. She didn't count.

Shawn saved the day with his perfect look of confusion. "Erin didn't tell me anything. But your food certainly did. If you can turn out this sort of stuff for a minor patriotic holiday, I can't wait to see what you could do for us on a regular basis."

And that was when it struck me: Timothy was an artist. Just like I was, like Shawn. He created something out of practically nothing, manufactured a party out of raw ingredients.

Everything that had happened that evening should have thrown Timothy for a loop. Shawn's outrageous interference. Teel's possessive attention toward me. Justin's restlessness at a table full of grown-ups. Amy's moodiness, her occasional tearfulness as she contemplated her uncertain future.

But Timothy had risen to the occasion. He'd presented a dinner that would make any chef proud, as casually and as gracefully as if he were boiling a couple of eggs for breakfast. He made everyone—even me, as I struggled to prove that my Master Plan was in full force and effect—feel comfortable.

Timothy's restaurant business was like my acting—it was part of him. It was his power, his soul. I understood that in a rush of intuition, the same way that I'd understood his sorrow and frustration when he'd told me that he might need to shut down Garden Variety.

And Shawn had just presented a way for Timothy to hold on to that power, to have a fighting chance to keep his dream intact. Shawn pushed. "Will you do it? I can give you the stage manager's number tonight."

Timothy directed his mocha gaze at me. "Erin?"

There were layers of questions embedded in those two syllables. Did I mind if he catered for the show? Would it matter, for whatever fledgling thing might be growing between us? What exactly *was* that unshaped thing? And did Teel have any rights to smother it, to smash it? What did I want? And why hadn't I been in touch for the entire week since I'd seen Timothy in the hallway outside my new apartment?

Dammit.

I had a plan. A Master Plan. A Master Plan that I'd advanced that very afternoon, by acquiring Tennessee, by following through on this entire dinner.

Women with Master Plans didn't blush, did they, just because a man they had kissed one time might be working beside them? They certainly didn't look at *another* man they'd kissed—twice—as if seeking permission, did they? They didn't have to fight for breath, struggling against an attack of nervous butterflies that threatened to do all sorts of extremely unfortunate things to their very full stomachs. Right?

Teel's sapphire gaze was bemused. Timothy's expression was expectant.

For good measure, I glanced at Amy, who had actually raised a hand to her mouth, waiting to see what I would do. Shawn was staring at me, too, shooting me with little daggers of impatience, of disbelief that I wasn't immediately leaping on the bandwagon for his perfect solution to our rehearsal woes.

I swallowed hard. "Please, Timothy. Your catering is exactly what we need. We'd be lucky, if you chose to do it."

Shawn whooped. Amy sighed. Justin demanded that someone draw him a Soldierman, this one eating a star-shaped cookie.

But Timothy only nodded, like a lion assessing some new domain.

And Teel took the opportunity to plant his hands on the table, to let his sleeve ride up just enough to reveal the whorls of his tattoo. For one chilled second, I wondered if he would use Timothy against me, if he would find some way to force my fourth wish through Timothy's catering.

I avoided looking at the ink. Whatever happened from this day forward was going to be a result of my own thinking. My own decisions. My own desires. That was what I'd learned that afternoon in the Garden. That's what it meant to be free. Alone. Independent. Strong.

A woman with a Plan.

Wasn't it?

I nodded again and made myself smile with more certainty than I felt. "We can't wait to have you join us," I said.

Chapter 11

TWO. THOSE PESKY bad things again, marching on toward their nearly inevitable *three.* If only I knew then what I know all too well now....

Tennessee the Flag Day fish didn't live to see the Fourth of July. I woke up one Thursday morning to find my poor little goldfish belly-up in his specially purchased glass bowl.

I was devastated. I had done everything in my power to keep him safe from harm, to help him live a happy and healthy life. I had changed his water every third day, rapidly becoming an expert at using my little white net to catch him, to scoop him into a holding bowl (okay, a water-filled Pyrex measuring cup, but I didn't use the cup for anything else), then transfer him back to his meticulously scrubbed home, newly filled with fresh tap water.

The past week, though, he had worried me. Tennessee had lost the brilliant orange gleam he'd had when I carried him home from the street fair. His scales had taken on a dull coat of slime, and he seemed to hover at the top of his bowl too much, bobbing up and down.

Hoping to avert what I feared was his increasingly imminent demise, I'd increased the frequency of our bowl-cleaning regimen, upping the water changes to every other day, then every day.

And now, all that effort was for naught. Farewell, Tennessee. I hardly knew ye.

As I scooped him out of the bowl for the last time, I felt a twinge of guilt. He'd been a good fish. A loyal fish. He'd made so few demands on me—a few flakes of food, a quart or two of fresh water. I sniffed back tears as I deposited him in the toilet bowl, wondering if a regimen of crumbled peace lily leaves would have made the difference. I'd never gotten around to trying.

Okay. Maybe I wasn't all that upset about losing a *fish*. But I was pretty bummed that I'd officially failed at the second phase of my Master Plan.

I had just returned to the kitchen after flushing Tennessee when my cell phone rang. I swallowed hard and cleared my throat, but I still sounded weepy when I answered. "Hey, Ame," I said, pulling her name from the caller ID.

"What's wrong?" Her sisterly radar zeroed in on my tears immediately.

"Nothing," I lied.

"Nothing, my a—um, foot," she said. Justin must have been within earshot.

I unsuccessfully tried to swallow a sob. "Tennessee died!"

"Tennessee? As in the state?"

I sniffed. "As in the playwright. As in my goldfish."

"Goldfish! You didn't tell me that you got a goldfish! The Master Plan is working!"

I choked out a protest. "No, it isn't! Not with Tennessee gone!"

"What did you do to him?"

"I didn't do anything! I fed him every day, just like it said on the fish food, only a few flakes at a time! I changed his water every third day, then every day, toward the end!"

"Jeez," she said. "Did you buy stock in Arm & Hammer?"

I rubbed at my eyes, wiping away my tears. "What do you mean?"

"Baking soda. Arm & Hammer baking soda."

"Why would I buy baking soda for a fish?"

"Not for the fish. For the water. Everyone knows that New York City water is soft. The pH is all wrong for goldfish. You need to add a little baking soda when you change the water, to keep the fish from getting slimy. From going belly-up."

Oh.

"Don't get upset by this little setback, though," Amy said. "I'm really proud of you for proceduralizing the Master Plan. If you got the fish, that must mean the plant is doing really well, right? How many flowers does it have now?"

I glanced at the dead peace lily on the counter. I'd kept it there as a sort of penance. As a denial that I was violating the central tenets of the Plan, moving forward before I'd perfected the past. I tried to figure out how many blooms it would have, if it had lived.

"Erin?" Amy asked when my silence stretched out a bit too long. "You do still have the plant, don't you?"

"Yes!" That wasn't a lie.

"And it's alive?"

"Um, not exactly."

"I do not *believe* you!" So much for sisterly pride. "This isn't like putting socks on an octopus! You had one simple plan, and you couldn't even stick with it for, what, six weeks?" She was really angry. "I *knew* you were cheating, when you kissed Dr. Teel! Dr. Teel doesn't count, you said, and stupid me, I went along with that. But keeping a peace lily alive? Is that such a big deal? And a goldfish! Even Justin can keep a goldfish alive!"

"Thanks, Amy," I said in a tiny voice. "You're really making me feel better."

She started to say something else but stopped herself before a new world war actually melted our telephones. Instead, after a very long pause, she opted for, "So? How was rehearsal yesterday? Did Martina ever get that dance combination down?"

I made an agonized noise halfway between a scream and a sob. "I thought that she'd be *better* once we got into the theater, but she's actually worse! You know, she has to sing now, and she has to work through the dance steps. Yesterday, she was driving me nuts—her voice is all warbly, that sort of reality-show sound, and no one else even seems to realize it! She doesn't have an ounce of breath control, and she can*not* sing and dance at the same time. By the end of rehearsal, I thought I was attending a meeting of the Four-Pack-a-Day Society, the way she coughs and sings and trips and shouts all at the same time."

"Wow," Amy said when I finally ran down. "It went that well, huh?"

I winced. "I guess I still have a few issues with Martina," I said primly.

"I'm really sorry," Amy said, and she sounded sincere. For all her berating me about the Plan, she really was on my side. She always had been.

I glanced at the clock on the oven. "I've got to go. We're trying to rework a major number in the second act. For the twelfth time. Just kill me now."

"At least you've got Timothy's food, for comfort."

Every day, I'd been reporting on the classy fare that Timothy brought to rehearsal. Shawn had been right, of course—Ken Durbin had jumped at the opportunity to have real catering on our set. Whatever the theater was paying Timothy wasn't enough—Martina's complaints about starvation had actually been reduced to no more than one per rehearsal.

I had to admit, though, my personal satisfaction with Timothy's catering had little to do with Martina finally shutting up. Sure, his food was good; often, it was the only real sustenance I got in a day. But the real advantage of having Timothy at the theater was that I got to see him—at least in the mornings, before he hurried back to Garden Variety to serve lunch, and then again for a couple of hours in the afternoon. Timothy was being run ragged; all of his usual prep time was being spent at the theater. But I had to assume that the producers were making it worth his while. Broadway pockets were notoriously deep where finicky stars were concerned.

I loved watching Timothy work. I loved his feline energy, his scarcely controlled power as he moved behind his table, setting out treats, talking easily to everyone in the cast and crew.

Talking easily, that was, to everyone but me. Each time I had a conversation with Timothy, I found myself more tongue-tied than the time before. Despite his easy smile, despite his welcoming shrug, I had trouble putting two words together. My mind did strange things, throwing up images of Dr. Teel's sharp gaze, countering them with memories of Timothy's easy grace that night in Garden Variety, when we'd all gotten together for dinner. I kept thinking about kissing Teel in front of Timothy, about how guilty I'd felt when I turned around, caught in the act.

I wasn't an idiot. I knew myself well enough to recognize the signs of a crush. But I absolutely could not have a crush on Timothy. I couldn't have a crush on any man. Not until I'd completed the Master Plan. As stupid as I'd thought Amy's plan might be when she first proposed it, I had come to believe that I truly needed it. I needed to carve out a new life for myself, free from the sort of idiotic sacrifices I'd made for Sam, and for all the other guys before him. Following it was the only way that I'd ever stop imitating the life of Laura Wingfield, wishing for the perfect man, afraid of living my actual life.

Amy interrupted my daydreaming. "Speaking of Timothy, can you do me a favor?"

"Um, sure," I said, instantly wary.

"Can you tell him I can't interface until four o'clock this afternoon? Dr. Teel can't get here until two."

"What?" There were so many things wrong with her request, starting with the totally obnoxious verb *interface,* that I didn't know where to begin asking questions. "You're meeting with Timothy?"

"Didn't I tell you? I needed a class project, creating a business plan for a company in the service sector. I asked Timothy if I could do one for Garden Variety."

"When did that happen?" Amy and I talked every

single day. I couldn't believe she hadn't mentioned it before.

"About a week ago? Maybe two? A couple of days after we all had dinner at the restaurant."

"Amy, you were keeping it a secret!"

"Sort of like you, not telling me about your poor, departed peace lily?"

Touché.

I had no choice but to go back on the defensive. "And what do you mean, 'Dr. Teel can't get here until two'? Why is he coming over there at all?" My genie had absolutely no reason to be hanging around my sister.

"He's just going to keep an eye on Justin while I go meet with Timothy."

"He can't!" I practically shouted. Teel was a genie! He was absolutely irresponsible! He couldn't be trusted with my *nephew!*

Of course, I couldn't say any of that out loud. As far as Amy was concerned, Teel was a brilliant medical doctor who had not only served a key role in saving Justin's life but was now instrumental in bringing my nephew's behavioral problems under control. "Seriously," I said, struggling to muster my arguments. "Doesn't he have to be on call or something?"

"He said he could handle it. Justin loves having him around. I think it's good for him to spend time with a man. You know, until Derek gets back."

I couldn't believe it. I didn't trust my genie, not as a babysitter. I'd seen him dressed up as a buxom cheerleader, as a leather-bound party boy—not exactly ideal models for child-care providers. Besides, I didn't want Justin to get too dependent on him. At some point, I was going to make my fourth wish, and Teel would be off to his Garden. Justin would be left high and dry, victim of yet another man who disappeared from his life.

Of course, I knew what Teel would say if I challenged him. He'd tell me that he needed to do *something* to fill the time between my wishes. A genie had to keep himself busy somehow....

And I knew what Amy would say, if I challenged *her.* She'd accuse me of getting emotionally involved with Dr. Teel. Of putting way too much importance on what he did in his spare time.

Well, the guy *could* kiss like no one I'd ever met. But that wasn't my problem with him as a babysitter. That wasn't why I thought he was dangerous.

I knew better than to protest more, though. Amy was my big sister. She'd never listen to my complaints, especially when I couldn't back them up with cold, hard facts. I sighed and grabbed my purse, snagging my keys so that I could rush out the door. "Look, I'd love to fight with you about this, but I really do have to get to rehearsal."

"Fine. You'll tell Timothy, though?"

"Yeah," I said. "I'll tell him." We said our goodbyes, and I dumped my phone into my tote bag. I was still annoyed when I tugged open my apartment door. My mood was definitely not helped when I almost tripped over a cat.

"What the—" I exclaimed.

Three. I'm telling you right now, my life would end with the tagline "happily ever after" if I could just stop those bad things from tripling up on me.

The universe was laughing, and I was the butt of the

joke. Have you heard the one about the woman whose Master Plan involved a plant, a goldfish and a cat?

The animal on my doorstep wove herself between my ankles. She was purring so loudly, I could hear her without bending down. She was a tiny calico, mostly white, with patches of orange and black on her face and chest. As I stared, she arched her butt high into the air, shaking her tail back and forth and yowling as if all the demons in hell were chasing her.

Dani Thompson's door flew open across the hall. "Tabitha!" she scolded. "How did you get out here?"

The cat looked up at her and shook her hindquarters again. This time, her howl sounded like she was being skinned alive.

"What's wrong with her?" I asked, trying to step away from the poor thing. Tabitha merely flowed between my ankles again, rubbing hard against my legs.

"She's in heat," Dani said grimly.

"Oh!" Tabitha confirmed the news with another unearthly cry. "Where did you get her? I've never, um, heard her before."

"We found her on a guerilla raid last week, over by the Jefferson Market library. She must have sneaked out of my place just now, when I was carrying in my groceries." Dani clicked her tongue and picked up the animal. Tabitha immediately started to butt her head against Dani's chin, making my neighbor laugh. "The poor thing was soaking wet, and she was hungry enough to chew on my handbag. I brought her home with me because Lorraine Feingold is allergic to cats, and no one else lives in a building where they can have pets." She shook her head and sighed. "I was hoping I could get her through this heat before bringing her down to the shelter."

As if Tabitha could understand every word that Dani said, the animal let out another incredible shout. I shook my head a little, trying to clear the ringing in my ears. "Shelter? Won't she quiet down after she's through being in heat?"

Dani grimaced. "I don't have to give her up because of the noise. She was quiet as a mouse, the first couple of days. No, it's the guerilla supplies. I can't trust her near the compost box for a minute, and she's already chewed up half my fall seedlings. I'm worried she'll get into something that's poisonous for her."

"Poor thing," I said. "She doesn't know any better." Without thinking, I reached out to take her from Dani. She melted into my arms, flowing across my chest like a living blanket. If possible, her purring ratcheted even louder.

Dani pounced on the opportunity. "Will you take her?"

"I can't!" I protested automatically.

"Why not?"

"I killed my peace lily," I confessed, as if those words would make perfect sense to an outsider. "And my goldfish died this morning. I know that sounds strange—it's just that I have this Master Plan."

"I'm sure you do," Dani agreed soothingly. "And part of it should involve keeping Tabitha out of the shelter. If those places get too crowded, you know, they have to put pets down."

I would have resented Dani's pulling my heart-strings more if Tabitha hadn't chosen that moment to bat playfully at my nose. She kept her claws tucked neatly away—she really *was* a sweet cat. And I *had* planned on getting one sometime soon. And Dani really *did* need someone to help her out, now. Weakening, I said, "I don't have any cat food. And I'll need to buy a litter box."

"I've got all of that. I'll bring it over, right now."

And that was it. I couldn't fight Dani's simple determination, her absolute confidence that I was going to do the right thing, that I was going to step up and save poor Tabitha. I couldn't argue against the purring furball that insinuated itself around my neck. I never got a chance to explain that I needed more time, that I needed to step back to the plant stage before I could even think of taking in a living, breathing *mammal.* Before I really understood what was happening, Dani had transported all of Tabitha's worldly possessions into my apartment.

We put the litter box in the bathroom, and we set out food and water in the kitchen. Tabitha seemed to like the apartment; she immediately found the brightest patch of sunlight on the living room floor and stretched out her meager frame until she seemed to be six feet long. She looked up at Dani and me and yowled again, a haunting cry that made the hair rise on the back of my neck.

"How long is that going to last?" I asked Dani.

"It should only be a few more days. I'll pay for her to be fixed, when it's over." I started to protest—surely, the Master Plan required me to be responsible for my cat's medical care—but Dani shook her head. "She's my responsibility, financially at least. I'm the one who brought her here."

I thought about the packages of ramen that still made up the better part of my kitchen supplies. A little financial help from Dani would be more than welcome. "All right," I said, reluctantly. "We'll talk about it more when she's ready." I scritched Tabitha on the head one last time, and then let Dani and myself out of the apartment.

Listening to the cat's yowl turned out to be good preparation for that day's rehearsal. By the time I arrived at the theater, Martina was in full cry. She was working through a supposedly delicate scene in the second act, when the Gentleman Caller comes to visit. In Williams's original play, the encounter is heartrending; the audience learns along with Laura that she will never gain the strength to break free from her mother, from her dreams, from her past.

In *Menagerie!* the scene was transformed into something infinitely more powerful. After delivering her painful, stilted lines in the spoken play, Laura was supposed to sing a haunting ballad, belting out a powerful paean to individuality and strength and the cost of making one's own decisions. The number should have been a blockbuster, ending with a final chorus sung after a vigorous dance interlude. The score provided a pause for enthusiastic audience applause, then launched into an immediate reprise, sung half an octave higher.

And therein lay the problem.

Martina insisted on turning the song into a punk anthem. She opened the first verse with a banshee shriek that was nowhere in the score. She shouted out her words, punching up the rhythm, doing her level best to torture a beautiful ballad into an angry, rebellious screed.

She could pull it off for two verses and a chorus—if

you liked that sort of thing. (Could anyone, anywhere, anytime, truly like that sort of thing? I wanted to invent a Human Invisible Fence, a dog collar that I could strap on Martina, so that it would zap her with a bolt of electricity every time she howled. Still, someone *must* appreciate that Queen of Punk introduction, because Ken never ordered her not to do it.)

The entire venture fell apart, though, after the dance section. Martina was winded by the time she got to the end; she panted like a racehorse during the gap for audience reaction. Then, she insisted on launching the reprise with the same violent shout that she used to lead off the number. The problem was, she couldn't sustain anything approaching a lyrical sound—not after the demanding verses and certainly not after the dance interlude. Every single time she tried, her voice cracked. Try after try, the first line of the reprise was lost in a scratchy, painful croak.

After every single attempt, Shawn leaned closer to me, digging an elbow into my side, clutching my knee as if he were a drowning man, pretending to scream in agony at the monstrosity that Martina was bringing to life onstage. Every line of his mugging face argued that I was the better performer, that I should be onstage.

All of the understudies had my back. They all told me that I was a better performer than Martina, every time Ken had us run through scenes. But that and four bucks would buy me a Starbucks latte. Martina's name continued to draw attention from the press; just the other day, the *Times* had run an article about reality TV show stars, and what they were doing now. More free publicity for *Menagerie!*—another strike against my ever going onstage.

Nevertheless, every time we understudies rehearsed, every time we ran through scenes, I spun out a fantasy where Ken changed his mind. Even at this late date, he accepted that he'd made a terrible mistake, that he never should have given in to the producers. Over and over, I delivered one hundred percent—through every spoken scene, every song and dance number. The rest of the cast noticed, and Ken did, too.

But even if Ken *wanted* to fire Martina and hire me to take her place, he couldn't. Not without alienating the producers, the guys with the money who were eagerly counting on sold-out houses for weeks.

As a company, we had tried everything to help Martina. The composer had rewritten the piece, transposing it to a different key. The choreographer had modified the dancing, not once, not twice, but three separate times, fighting to build a level of energy that would satisfy the audience, while still matching Martina's fitness. Or lack thereof.

We were down to the worst possible option—adding dialog between the two parts of the song, meaningless lines delivered by Amanda and Tom solely to pad out the scene, to give Martina a chance to recover. Then, once she had her breath back, she could belt out the reprise, preferably without her ear-piercing rebel yell.

That modification was fraught with peril, too, though. No matter how many times Ken came up with new words for the other actors, they sounded harsh compared to Tennessee Williams's original poetry. The additions were fake and flabby and forlorn. They were utterly unnecessary.

And even *that* wasn't the biggest problem.

No, the biggest problem was that the audience

wasn't going to understand. They'd applaud like crazy at the end of the song, and then they'd quiet down to hear the important, plot-driving lines that Amanda and Tom had to say. Everyone would be disappointed when they realized that Amanda and Tom weren't actually saying anything crucial, anything to advance the actual story. Then, when Martina's song broke out again, the audience would have no idea whether they should sit back for new, multiple verses or whether they should just enjoy a brief, now meaningless, reprise. They might clap, but the most we could hope for would be polite applause. The audience would be confused. They'd be lost. And losing audiences was the very last thing we wanted to do, especially three-quarters of the way through the second act.

After one particularly off-key yowl from Martina, Ken interrupted the accompanist with a shout of disgust. "Stop!" he called. "Stop, stop, stop! Let's take a break."

Martina, apparently blissfully unaware that she was the source of the entire company's angst, made a beeline for the wings. I turned to Shawn. "Are you getting anything to eat?"

He grimaced. "I'll wait until the path is clear."

I smiled tightly. None of us ever wanted to get between Martina and the craft services table. Nevertheless, my stomach growled. I was really hungry. Not to mention, I was looking forward to seeing Timothy.

I was a big girl. I could face Martina. After all, avoiding her wasn't going to make her go away.

Miraculously, she was nowhere in sight when I got backstage. Timothy stood alone at the table, refilling one of the platters of food, his attention completely snagged by the delicacies he was setting out. It was warm in the wings, and he'd shed his long-sleeved work shirt in favor of a black tee. The cotton garment accentuated his muscles; his biceps rippled as he reached across the table. The motion drew my gaze to his waist, to the pair of black denim jeans that looked as if they'd been designed solely with him in mind.

I wasn't only captivated by his body. Sure, that was part of it. But even more striking was his economy of motion, the controlled way that he completed his work without using any more energy than necessary, without wasting a single movement, a solitary action.

Watching him was peaceful. Soothing. He was a man who knew what he wanted to do and had built a world where he could do it. He was a man in control.

Except for that little detail about his rent.

What would happen to Timothy if he lost Garden Variety? I couldn't imagine him working in someone else's kitchen. I couldn't see him manning the grill at some chain restaurant, churning out mundane menu offerings, the same happy-happy products day after day after day. He'd be beaten down by the commonplace details, destroyed by the boring humdrum inanity of it all.

I cleared my throat. Timothy looked up slowly, the motion controlled, as if it were part of some ballet. "Erin," he said, and his voice was as warm as his caramel gaze. His lips curled into a hint of a smile. As always, he had that scruffy beard, that rebellious three-day growth.

Damn. I'd forgotten the English language. Again.

Timothy, unaware of my stupid inability to speak, said, "Could you help me for a moment? Just hold these, while I get the serving fork?"

Grateful for the distraction, for the bit of stage business, I took the stack of plates that he handed me. Somehow, the familiar action freed me up to use my words. "Um, Amy called. She asked if she can move your meeting to four."

"That's fine," he said. "Thanks for being the go-between." He put one serving fork onto the tray in front of me, then turned back to rescue another from a box behind him.

Before I could scrape together another conversational gambit, Martina Block interrupted. "I hope that you have some *protein* there," she announced in a voice capable of scraping paint off the theater's back wall. She plucked the top plate from the stack that I held, scrutinizing it as if she expected it to be dirty.

Martina had obviously used the break to freshen up backstage. She moved in a cloud of perfume that made my eyes water. She had renewed her makeup, too—the outlined edges of her lips were sharp enough to cut paper. She wore more eyeliner than a club full of Goths.

Timothy's shoulders stiffened as he turned to face her. "Of course," he said, his voice the frozen model of politeness that I had first heard him use with Sam.

"What's that?" Martina brayed. My attempt at conversation with Timothy was forgotten as he described the puff pastries—havarti and prosciutto, fig with blue cheese, chocolate pistachio cream. He was the consummate professional chef, speaking to a particularly demanding customer.

And if he could be polite to her, then I could, too. After all, Martina and I didn't have to be enemies—no matter what Shawn might say. We were both professionals. We were both working toward a common goal—the success of our show.

I took a fortifying breath and moved into the cloud of her perfume. Mentally testing my voice, I strived for deference. For friendship. For a companionable sharing of theatrical frustrations. I cleared my throat and said, "That last dance combination is really difficult."

Martina turned to stare at me as if I were some insect mounted in a cotton-swathed display case. She narrowed her eyes and jutted her chin forward as if she couldn't quite make out my features. And then she said with a chill usually reserved for known terrorists or torturers of defenseless animals, "I'm sorry. Have we met before?"

I would have been embarrassed under any circumstances. I would have been mortified at the thought that I had worked with a woman for over a month but had remained so insignificant, so undistinguished, so unworthy of notice, that she couldn't even remember *seeing* me before.

But the shame was a hundred times worse because Timothy was watching. He was there, to hear me stammer a reply. He saw me utterly at a loss to defend myself, to take a stand, to act like the adult I supposedly was. Before I could figure out some way to tell Martina that we *had* met—that we had worked together every day for nearly a month—she managed to make it all even worse. She peered down her nose at me and said, "I'm not accustomed to discussing dance combinations with a caterer. Now, could you hurry up and fetch me a regular coffee?"

Outraged, I said, "I am *not* a caterer."

I snapped the words without thinking. I didn't mean

to imply that there was anything wrong with caterers. I didn't mean to say that I was better than anyone who *was* a caterer. I simply meant to say that I was an actor, that I was a theater professional, just like she was. I was entitled to as much respect as Martina got.

Before I could clarify my intention, though, Timothy turned away from the table. His shoulders were rock-hard as he collected a cup of coffee for Martina. His face was unreadable as he passed her the caffeine.

And then, before I could figure out a way to make everything all right, to explain that I hadn't meant to denigrate him or what he did for us, the stage manager called us all back to our places. Martina huffed and left her coffee cup on the table, scarcely touched. Panicked at the thought of actually talking to Timothy after my faux pas, I scrambled to get back to my seat in the house.

I told myself that I needed to get settled before the action could start onstage. I needed to make myself invisible, like a good understudy.

As soon as I sat next to Shawn, I thought of all the things I could have said, should have said. I could have laughed off Martina's rudeness. I could have told Martina she was an idiot, a drama queen, a pretentious Hollywood star who couldn't begin to carry a Broadway musical. I could have adopted a professorial tone, instructing her on how to perform her role, how to play the part of Laura without ruining the show.

But I didn't do any of those things. Instead, I'd let the role of Laura control me. I'd let myself become a tongue-tied child, a girl afraid of the world around her.

All of that was bad. But worst of all was that I'd forgotten about Timothy. I'd forgotten that *he* had been cut by Martina's snobbery as badly as I had, probably even worse. I should have stuck up for him immediately, without hesitation. My tongue-tied intimidation around Martina had led me to insult a guy I really liked.

The more I thought about it, the worse I felt.

I leaned over and whispered to Shawn, "I've got a terrible headache."

He waited for Martina to finish her rebel yell. "No wonder."

"I'm getting out of here," I said. He glanced toward the stage manager, and I shook my head. "I don't want to interrupt. Rehearsal should be over in an hour, anyway."

Shawn grimaced. "I'll cover for you, sweetie."

"You're my hero," I joked. I kissed him on the cheek and squeezed his arm in thanks before I slipped out the back of the theater.

There. Why was it so easy to talk to Shawn? Why was it so simple to kiss him on the cheek, to close my fingers around his arm? Why was it so comfortable, gossiping with him, when I couldn't bring myself to say two complete sentences to Timothy?

The Master Plan, that was why. Shawn was never going to figure into my Master Plan. I could grow an entire forest of peace lilies, monitor aquariums full of fish. I could keep dozens of cats in my apartment. But not one of those endeavors was going to lead to the day when I tried to seduce Shawn Goldberg. He was my friend, my good friend, but he was never, ever going to be anything more.

But Timothy? The more I thought about him, the more I was sure that I wanted Timothy to stick around.

He was a prime candidate for stage four of the Plan. The primest candidate I'd seen since I'd let Amy talk me into the whole thing.

I'd be lucky, though, if Timothy would even spare me the time of day, after the idiot I'd made of myself that afternoon. He must think that I was as stuck-up as Martina, that I was as superior and snotty and self-centered....

I squinted into the bright sunlight as I pounded my heels into the sidewalk. Heat radiated off the streets, blasting me with a reminder of why I hated the city in summer. A fetid whiff rose from the storm sewer as I crossed Seventh Avenue.

I tried not to think about the iron set of Timothy's shoulders. I tried not to worry about what a disaster *Menagerie!* was shaping up to be. I tried not to dwell on how I couldn't even put "understudy" on my résumé if the production tanked on the first night, if I never walked onstage. I tried not to focus on how different the show would be if I'd been cast, if I'd been placed in the starring role. I tried not to tell myself all the things I could have said to Martina, all the advice I could have given her, all the ways I could have stood up to her imperious rudeness, if only I'd had two wits to rub together back there at Timothy's table.

I was practically frothing at the mouth by the time I got back to the apartment. I slammed my key into the top lock.

I should have told Martina exactly what I thought, exactly how I *knew* she should perform the piece. I should have spoken to her, actress to actress.

I twisted the key, opened the lock, jammed the key into the middle one.

I should have spoken to Timothy, assured him that I valued his career, that I appreciated everything he did for us.

I threw open the middle lock, then shoved my key into the third one.

I should have told them both that I was a free and independent woman, that I had a Master Plan. That I was stronger than either of them imagined I could be. That I could be infinitely better than either imagined.

Beyond angry with myself, I kicked the door open.

A white streak shot past me.

"Dammit!" I cried, lunging for Tabitha, the cat, but I didn't have a prayer of catching her. She flew toward the stairwell at the end of the hall with a guttural yowl that shook the corridor walls. She shot down the internal steps that led to the ground floor, the lobby and the great outdoors.

"Tabitha!" I cried. But I shouldn't have bothered saying anything at all. My cat was long gone.

Chapter 12

THE WORST PART was, I'd have to tell Dani what happened. I thought about just scribbling out the bad news in a note and taping it to her door. I couldn't do that, though. I had to confess in person.

Later. I just couldn't face her right then. I couldn't face anyone.

Instead, I closed my apartment door, kicked off my shoes and collapsed onto my couch. Even with the Bentley's ample air-conditioning, I thought that I just might melt into a puddle. It didn't help that I started to get angry all over again, every single time I replayed my idiotic conversation with Martina. Why hadn't I stood up to her? Why hadn't I stood up for *Timothy?*

I closed my eyes and forced myself to take a dozen deep breaths.

I was exhausted. I don't know if it was my anger at Martina, or the walk from the theater in the high summer heat, or the frustration of losing Tabitha, but I could barely keep my eyes open. What did it matter if I took a nap, anyway? It wasn't like I had anyone actually waiting for me. Counting on me. Planning on enjoying my companionship and witty conversation.

Somewhere between self-recrimination and self-pity, I actually fell asleep. I dreamed that I was stranded in a massive industrial kitchen, facing a stainless-steel conveyor belt that carried mile after mile of chilled puff pastry. My job was to complete an endless supply of turnovers. Each filling, though, was more disgusting than the last. I begged to be released from my obligation, but orders kept coming in, broadcast over a loudspeaker. I could hear endless braying laughter as I fell further and further behind—all the nightmare of an old *I Love Lucy* routine, with none of the humor.

Suffice to say, I did not have a restful night.

As the early summer dawn leaked through my living room windows, I stumbled into the kitchen to get a glass of water. It was Independence Day, the Friday of what would be a long weekend for almost everyone else in Manhattan. We *Menagerie!* actors, though, had a rehearsal scheduled. We were slipping further and further behind; the constant blocking and reblocking was taking its toll. The entire cast had grumbled when Ken announced the change, but we were committed to spending the day in the theater.

I was feeling sorry for myself, still running the tap to get something approaching a cool stream when the faucet disappeared in front of me. The faucet, the sink, the granite counter—all were gone.

"Teel!" I exclaimed through gritted teeth. The last thing I needed now was to be dragged off to the Garden.

"Special delivery!" said a crisp alto voice. Teel stood to my right, dressed as a mail carrier—summer uniform of shorts and a light blue shirt, snappy eagle logo over her breast pocket. Her mouse-brown hair was pulled back in a braid, and years of walking from door to door in all weather had left deep lines beside her muddy hazel eyes. Her skin was dark with a natural tan, and freckles accented her forearms. Her tattoo stood out against her wrist, the golden flames complementing her bronzed flesh. A large leather satchel slumped at her feet, letters cascading over the side.

"I'm not expecting any special delivery," I said, biting off my words. I had absolutely no desire to stand in front of the invisible Garden with my genie. I wanted to get back to my apartment, to my glass of water, to my day-long rehearsal.

"But I am," Teel said, apparently unconcerned about anything I might desire.

Ranting wasn't going to get me anywhere. Raving, either. I dug my toe into the ground that I couldn't see and asked with false patience, "What delivery are you expecting?"

"I'm so glad you asked! I'm expecting to be delivered into the Garden. Today. To see Jaze."

"I'm not ready to make my fourth wish yet," I said automatically.

"You should wish today. Rates might be going up tomorrow."

"Rates? What are you talking about?"

She shrugged and admitted, "I don't know. Isn't that just something the postal service says? Aren't rates always going up?"

I wasn't in the mood for witty banter, for genie fun and games. "Teel, if you don't mind, I was in the middle of something back home."

"Really?" She kicked the bag at her feet, sending envelopes flying. I realized that they were all blank. Empty. Meaningless. "What could possibly be more important than helping your genie achieve her life's goal?"

"Life's goal? You go into the Garden and that's it? That's the end of the magical road for you?"

She looked uncomfortable. "Well, *love's* goal, then. I go to the Garden and then I come out refreshed. Better able to help motivated wishers. Like you used to be."

I sighed at the criticism. "I promise, Teel. When I figure out what I want for my fourth wish, you'll be the very first to know."

"Some people are dedicated to their tasks," she chided. "'Neither snow, nor rain, nor heat, nor gloom of night, stays these couriers from the swift completion of their appointed rounds.'"

"Yeah," I said. "I've seen that on the post office across from Penn Station."

"It's true, you know. We genies strive to complete our appointed rounds quickly. *When you humans help out.*"

I refused to rise to the bait. "It's not like you're just sitting here all the time, waiting for me. I understand that you took care of Justin yesterday."

"So?" She sounded defensive.

"So, I'm not sure I like you hanging out with my nephew. You're not exactly a good influence, you know."

"What better influence could there be than a public servant, delivering mail, bringing messages of good cheer to all and sundry?"

"You aren't taking care of him in the form of a

mailman," I pointed out. "Teel, you *know* that Justin can be wild. What would happen if something went wrong? What if he fell off the roof again? If he really hurt himself?"

She pinned me with those hazel eyes. "Then I'd pull you in. You could make your fourth wish and everyone would be happy."

It wasn't a threat. Not exactly. I was the one who'd brought up the topic, who'd even initiated the thought of Justin being injured. Nevertheless, goose bumps rose on my arms. I rubbed hard and said, "Don't even think about it, Teel. You can't put a little boy's safety at risk, just so you can get inside your stupid Garden."

She snorted. "We mail carriers are experts at the fine print, even if you aren't."

"The fine print?"

"Section thirty-seven of your contract?" I wasn't about to admit that I hadn't read that section in detail. Or any other, for that matter. She scoffed, "Come on—it's nowhere near as complicated as calculating international postage. As your genie, I'm contractually bound not to injure you or anyone in your immediate family. And yes, Justin counts as immediate," she clarified before I could ask. "I promise—he's perfectly safe with me. Besides, he does everything I tell him to do. I taught him how to ride his bike yesterday afternoon."

"He's been doing that for two years."

"Not without training wheels."

Wow. That *was* something. Amy had tried to teach Justin so that they could surprise Derek with a video, but my nephew just couldn't get the hang of it. He got nervous when he went too fast, and he scuffed the toes of his shoes along the ground. Amy had given up after replacing two pairs of hole-worn Keds.

"I'm impressed," I said grudgingly.

"Impressed enough to make a wish?" Teel glanced back at the bag of mail, as if to remind me of the meaning of responsibility. Of obligation. When that action didn't draw an immediate response, she looked back at the Garden. "Can you believe it?" she asked wistfully. "The freesia never blooms this close to the fence." She closed her eyes and inhaled deeply.

"Nice try," I said. For all I knew, there weren't freesias anywhere near us. In any case, I wasn't going to make my fourth wish, just because my genie thought the air smelled nice.

Now, Teel-the-doctor had a much more intriguing pitch. He was easy on the eyes. Easy on the lips.

I thought about telling Mail Carrier Teel that I wouldn't talk to her if she didn't switch over to her doctor form. A tug on her earlobe, and she could do it. I could even make her kiss me, if I wanted to do that. Dr. Teel had been eager enough, in the hospital. In Garden Variety. Eager enough, and totally disconnected from the emotional turmoil of my Master Plan.

I shook my head. What was I thinking? What sort of person would I be, if I made my genie do my bidding, solely for my physical gratification? Especially when I had absolutely no intention of giving up my fourth wish. Not yet.

Especially when I was giving so much thought to bringing Timothy into the Master Plan—at least, when I got to the "man" stage. In a year or so, that was, if I considered myself to have completed plant, fish and acquisition of cat, despite my rather obvious failures on all three fronts.

I made my voice as hard as I knew how, applying every acting trick in my arsenal. "Teel, send me home now." When she hesitated, I pushed. "*Now.* Or I will never make that fourth wish."

With an alacrity I'd never seen her exercise before, Teel raised her fingers to her earlobe. Two sharp tugs, and I was back in my living room, facing the sunrise alone.

Shaking my head, I dragged myself into the bathroom. Waiting for the water to heat up for my shower, I looked at Tabitha's litter box. I really felt bad about letting the cat escape. I couldn't imagine what I was going to say to Dani. And there was absolutely no way that I could tell Amy what had happened. It was one thing for me to lose a plant and a goldfish—that could happen to anyone, Master Plan or not. But to lose a cat, as well?

I shampooed my hair twice, as if lathering, rinsing and repeating would be enough to turn my entire life around. I knew myself well enough to recognize that I was working hard to delay something, to avoid an obligation. I towel-dried my hair, pinning it off my neck in an attempt to survive the summer heat. I slipped on a cotton sundress, hoping that its cool mint plaid would be comforting in the fifth, or sixth, or seventh hour of rehearsal. I decided to skip makeup. It was far too hot for makeup.

And then, I'd run out of excuses. It was time to deal with the mess I'd created yesterday. It was time to deal with Timothy.

I collected my tote, double-checking to make sure that I had my keys before I flung open the front door. And I almost tripped over the cat lying in the hallway.

"Tabitha?" I asked, as the calico leaped to her feet. She chirped a friendly greeting and began to weave herself between my ankles. "What are you doing here?"

Of course she didn't answer. I looked up and down the hallway, but I couldn't see any sign of human intervention. Tabitha must have finished her walkabout, only to realize that life was a whole lot better with reliable food, fresh water and a nice, soft bed.

I glanced at Dani's door. Now I was grateful that I hadn't followed through on my first impulse the night before, that I hadn't left a note explaining how irresponsible I had been. Dani never needed to know that I'd let Tabitha out, that our cat had been wandering the busy streets of Greenwich Village on her own.

I shooed the calico into my kitchen and opened up a can of cat food—the smelly stuff that looked like shredded high-end tuna. Tabitha was purring up a storm by the time I put her bowl onto the floor. She started to push it around with her nose like a pro.

I could have watched her for hours. When she was through eating, we could play with a real fur mousie, one of the toys Dani had provided. Or I could brush her! Any cat deserved to be brushed after a traumatizing walk around town!

There was more of that avoidance behavior. Like it or not, I had to track down Timothy. I wasn't an idiot.

Leaving Tabitha's face still buried in Tuna Supreme, I marched myself down to Garden Variety. The street outside the Bentley was deserted; all of New York City had evacuated for the long Independence Day weekend, lured to beaches and mountain cabins. All of New York City, that was, except for us hardworking actor types.

Timothy's courtyard was as deserted as the street. When I turned the doorknob to enter the restaurant, it was locked.

Well, I'd tried. That was good enough. It wasn't like I was obligated to break down the door, to force my way inside. If Timothy had wanted company, if he'd planned on being open for the holiday, he certainly would have left the door open. No need for me to stand around, waiting to have one of the most awkward conversations of my life. No need for me to apologize, after all.

But that was ridiculous. It was barely nine in the morning. Timothy had no reason to open the restaurant this early in the day. He was probably in the back, cooking up whatever treats he planned on bringing to our midmorning rehearsal. I forced myself to knock against the glass windowpane. I was surprised by how loud my rapping sounded, echoing off the flagstones.

Nothing.

He wasn't there. He was probably at his home, wherever *that* was. He was sleeping in on this holiday morning. He might even skip catering for our rehearsal; who knew what arrangements he'd made with Ken?

Almost convincing myself that I'd done all I could, I started to turn away. And that was when I heard the lock turn. I whirled back, excuses and apologies on my lips.

"You look terrible!" I gasped. I was so surprised by Timothy's appearance that I forgot to be nervous. I forgot to be shy. I forgot to have a mindless, Master Plan–unapproved crush.

"And good morning to you," he said wryly.

He opened the door far enough for me to enter, and

I slid past him, silently kicking myself for my exclamation. All of the lights were off in the dining room. The tables looked ghostly, huddling beneath their shrouds of butcher paper. The mismatched plates and silverware seemed drab, almost dusty in the dark.

"I was working in the kitchen," Timothy said, extending a hand by way of invitation. I followed, without saying a word.

I felt like I was being allowed backstage in a theater. Stainless-steel refrigerators and freezers lined one wall. I was facing a huge, deep sink. A deep fryer sat beside a massive ten-burner stove.

A center island occupied the middle of the room. Its surface was covered with papers, a snowbank of pages littered with tiny black writing. "What's all this?" I asked.

"A business plan from your sister. And supporting documentation." I picked up a random page. It was a blueprint, a proposed redesign for the front room. I saw immediately that the massive fireplace was gone, that a half dozen more tables were crammed into the space. Timothy studied the expression on my face before he said, "She has a lot of ideas."

"She always has," I said.

"She included financials. And architects' drawings. And all the statutes and regulations about running a restaurant in New York City. It took me all night to read through this stuff."

Well, that explained the pallor of his cheeks, his bloodshot eyes. Now I understood the hopeless set to his shoulders and the subdued way that he set his words between us. Hell, Amy's advice had been stressful for *me* over the years, and I was used to her bossiness. She'd never backed up her sisterly recommendations with a library's worth of documentation, though.

Timothy huddled on his high stool, staring at the tumble of papers as if every page might sprout wings and take flight. He barely managed to hide a sudden yawn behind his fist.

Poor guy. At least exhaustion was something I could fix. Or camouflage, anyway. I crossed the kitchen to the triple-pot coffeemaker and went through the motions of brewing up some fresh, hot caffeine. Timothy started to protest. "That thing's tricky—"

"Yeah, the switch is hidden at the back," I said. At his curious glance, I shrugged. "I used to work catering, remember? I've handled my share of tricky coffeemakers."

Within seconds, the rich aroma of coffee filled the kitchen. I reached for two mismatched mugs and asked, "Cream? Sugar?"

"Isn't that supposed to be my line?" he asked ruefully.

"Not this time," I said. It felt good to be doing something for him, after all the times he'd waited on me. And it kept me from needing to talk, from needing to apologize about rehearsal, as I'd originally planned on doing. Instead, I made a much bigger production of the coffee than was strictly necessary, measuring out sugar into my cup, pouring a precise amount of heavy cream from a pitcher that I found in the refrigerator.

Timothy took his black, which didn't really surprise me. Gave me less to do, but didn't surprise me.

He took his first swallow, and I watched a little color return to his cheeks. Caffeine wasn't going to implement Amy's plans. It wouldn't solve his landlord problems. But I no longer worried that he was going to collapse on the kitchen floor in front of me. "Okay," I said, when I thought that he could handle more conversation. "What's Amy's verdict?"

He cleared his throat, looking as uncomfortable as if I'd asked him to share his sexual fantasies. He became fascinated with the handle on his coffee cup. He reached out for a stack of papers, tapping them into a single neat pile, then turning them on edge and tapping them again.

"What?" I finally said. "What did she tell you?"

He finally braved my gaze. "Look, I don't want to drag you into the middle of this."

"You're not dragging me. I'm already here."

He sighed. "Amy's not right for this job. She doesn't understand what I'm trying to do here. And I don't think she ever will."

Ouch. Amy was my sister. I had to stick up for her. "Amy is very good at what she does!" Timothy shook his head, and I couldn't tell if he was contradicting me, or merely trying to interrupt. "She *is!*" I insisted. "She's one of the top ten in her class! And that's with juggling a lot of other stuff, with Justin—"

"Erin," Timothy said. My name on his lips sounded strange, almost like it hurt him. He shook his head again. "I wasn't criticizing her. It's just that what she's learning, what she's being taught to do, none of it matches who I am. What Garden Variety is all about."

Okay. I could understand that. Sisterly loyalty or no, I had to admit that Amy didn't always understand. She certainly didn't get what I was doing with *my* life. She thought that acting could be managed like any other business, like any other career. Now that I was no longer so intent on defending her, I could think about the million times I'd tried to explain to her, tried to communicate the artistry of my chosen profession.

"Give me an example," I said.

Timothy waved a frustrated hand toward the wall of refrigerators. "I tried to explain what I'm doing with local foods, but she keeps telling me that I should buy from traditional vendors. If I just work with the regular guys, I could get my produce for half the cost." He shook his head. "She's right, of course. I could. But it wouldn't be organic. And it wouldn't support the farmers I already buy from. It wouldn't help Dani and the Gray Guerillas."

"Well, maybe Amy just doesn't understand that piece of it. She's been trying to make Derek's tiny paycheck stretch a really long way for a long time. She has to cover tuition, and child care for Justin, and still have enough to buy groceries at the end of the week. It's hard to value organic when you aren't certain you can fit *anything* into your budget."

"I know," Timothy said. "I'm not trying to work a revolution overnight. She's got every right to believe what she believes—that's the way most Americans have bought groceries for decades. I just need her to see that I do things differently. That there's a reason for what I do."

I didn't think they were at a permanent impasse. But something else was bothering Timothy. I could tell from the frown that ironed a crease between his eyebrows. "What else?" I asked.

"She wants me to set menus. To cook more of the same things for multiple nights, for a month at a time. She says that I can be more efficient, not only with my purchasing, but also with the time I spend cooking. And she says that very few—probably none—of my customers come in often enough that they'll even realize."

I could see exactly what Amy was thinking. She was used to managing meals for two, planning menus for the nights when she could barely see straight from exhaustion. She knew that most of the restaurants around her served the same fare, night after night, week after week, boring month after boring month after boring month. From a business perspective, her suggestion would make everything run more smoothly. I tried to explain her point of view. "Just the predictability would make things easier...."

"I don't want predictability!" Timothy slammed his fist down on the center island, making me jump. He must have realized that he'd startled me, because he lowered his voice and said, "I don't want to do the same things, day in, day out. That's why I started Garden Variety in the first place. If I wanted predictability, I could have worked at McDonald's."

He glanced at the papers in despair. Okay. Amy had said that he should buy conventional produce, that he should work from a conventional menu. Neither of those suggestions was enough to justify the emotional stress I was seeing. Neither was enough to keep a man awake, worried and frustrated, all night long. I pitched my voice low, as if I were trying to comfort some feral animal. "What else did Amy say? What other suggestions did she make?"

He swallowed hard and glanced at the door that led to the dining room. "She told me to get rid of the table by the kitchen. Or, more precisely, to transform it into a four-top. For paying customers. Try to turn it three times on a busy night."

I closed my eyes. Once again, Amy's advice made perfect business sense. Earning income from twelve diners would be much more profitable than giving away food to two or three.

But there wasn't a chance that Timothy would give in on that. There wasn't a possibility that he'd lose that anchor to his ideals. The table for the homeless folks was the key to what he was doing with Garden Variety. It was the root of his fight with his landlord. It was the core of his beliefs—how he cooked, how he served, how he worked in the professional culinary world.

And Amy had missed all that. She'd been blinded by textbooks, by professorial lectures. She'd been constrained by course deadlines and family obligations.

I'd been an idiot to think her counseling Timothy could ever work out. "I'm sorry," I said. "Amy shouldn't have called you. She shouldn't have talked you into being her class project. Garden Variety and B-school are a lousy match."

"She thought that she could help." He was trying to sound gracious. He even came close to succeeding.

I shook my head, though. This was just another version of the arguments that Amy and I had tossed back and forth for years. My sister understood dollars and cents. She had, ever since that law firm bookkeeping job, the one that had convinced her to go to business school in the first place. She was born understanding business plans and return on investment.

She'd never, though, ever, in all the years I'd been struggling in New York, comprehended why I put myself out there in auditions, why anyone would dump so much time and effort and money into something so unlikely to pay off.

I reached out and touched Timothy's arm. It was important that he hear me. Important that he understand. "Timothy, she's wrong. Just because Amy quotes some business school case study, that doesn't mean she knows what she's talking about. Her class assignment was to develop a business plan for a restaurant. But she had no right to take *your* restaurant and turn it into a carbon copy of every other one that's out there. She should have listened to you. Respected you. Built on what you're already doing and found ways to make it better."

"I don't want to cause trouble for you."

The look of concern on his face made my belly swoop. For just a moment, I was back to being tongue-tied Laura Wingfield; I couldn't think of the next words to say, the right way to respond. But then I looked around the kitchen, at the seasoned pots and pans, at the well-scrubbed stove and sink. Honest, straightforward tools. Pointing toward an honest, straightforward conversation. "Just tell her that she's wrong. That's what she needs to learn, if she's going to succeed in her class. In her career. And it's what you need to say to your landlord, too, if you're going to make this place work."

For the first time that morning, a smile flirted with his lips. "And how, exactly, did you become so wise?"

I grinned back. "I've had a lifetime of telling Amy that she's wrong." And that, finally, left me with the perfect opening for the conversation that had brought me there in the first place. "Speaking of which," I forced myself to say. "I was wrong yesterday."

"When?" He looked mystified.

"When Martina went off on caterers. When she tried to insult me, and you got caught in the backlash."

"Martina is a spoiled bitch who cares more about her designer shoes and her reality-show credentials than she does about any human being around her. Besides that, she can't act her way out of a paper bag."

My lips twitched. Of course, I couldn't agree more. "Still. I should have called her on it."

"You were in a tough position. You don't want her complaining about her understudy showing her up."

I gritted my teeth. "She doesn't even know that I *am* her understudy."

"That's her problem. Not yours. Seriously. I've watched enough of those rehearsals to know. Everyone says the same thing, whenever you run through a scene. You're better than Martina, and it's a crime that you weren't cast in the role."

It felt wonderful to hear someone else say that. Wonderful to know that it wasn't just my spite, my selfish anger with Martina, coloring my perspective. "Thank you," I said.

"There's no reason to thank me," he said, his voice filled with a new determination. "It's the truth." He pushed himself back from the center island and began stacking Amy's recommendations into one neat, orderly pile. "Shouldn't you be getting over there?"

I glanced at my watch. "Yeah. I guess. Are you joining us today?"

Timothy shook his head. "Ken said not to bother. He figured everyone would rather work straight through and get out early enough to see fireworks."

"Great," I said. No one had asked me. I'd rather get

free food than see fireworks, any day of the week. Get free food, and visit with Timothy, that was.

He laughed. "Don't sound so excited."

"I can't imagine how Martina is going to react."

He rolled his eyes as he led me back through the shadowed dining room. "Think good thoughts," he said as he unlocked the door to let me leave. "Martina just might surprise you, after all."

* * *

Martina surprised me, all right.

She surprised me by coming up with entirely new ways to drive me insane. It started while we were collecting our bags, giving up on rehearsal after six hours. Six hours, and we only got through two scenes. At one point, Ken sent all the lead actors backstage, told them to look over their lines while we understudies took a pass at the action. Thinking about what Timothy had told me that morning, I let myself believe that Ken was running us understudies so that he could get a break, get some perspective on what the play was *supposed* to look like.

Of course, my time onstage was miniscule, compared to the main cast's. By the end of the day, my mind was muddled by a combination of starvation and disgust. I couldn't believe that Martina had presented so many questions about staging, so many arguments about blocking, so many ideas about how Laura's character should evolve. We'd been through all of this a thousand times before. Didn't she realize that we were rapidly running out of time? We had one month until opening night, one month left to pull together our entire masterpiece—costumes, full orchestra and every single scene in the entire musical.

The final straw was Martina announcing to Ken that she'd like to receive her Lucky Red Dragon early.

"Lucky Red Dragon?" Ken had asked.

"It's in my—"

"Contract," Shawn had completed in a drawn-out whisper, digging his elbow into my side.

Somehow, Ken managed to keep a civil tongue in his head, questioning Martina with an appropriate level of concern to determine that Lucky Red Dragon was a brand of Chinese soda, flavored with ginseng and a dozen other herbs and secret spices. Ken was contractually bound to provide a case of Lucky Red Dragon by opening night, and an additional case every week for as long as the play ran with Martina in the lead. Our fearless diva insisted that the carbonated beverage was the only thing that gave her the power to appear onstage, to sing her heart out for the masses.

"If it's so important to her," Shawn groused as we collected our belongings at the back of the theater, "you'd think that she'd keep her own stock permanently on hand."

"And give up a chance to send us all scurrying around on her behalf?" I asked. I would have said more, but Ken was walking down the aisle. I didn't want him to overhear and think that I was bitter or anything. I pasted on a smile and asked Shawn, "Are you going to see fireworks tonight?"

He made a face. "What? Try to find a spot on the river? Patrick and I are making our *own* fireworks, sweetie!" He growled playfully and air-kissed my cheek before hurrying out the theater's double doors.

Before I could follow him, I heard Ken exclaim, "Timothy! Am I glad to see you!"

I looked up to see Timothy standing in the back row of the theater. I couldn't be certain how long he'd been there; his black clothes made him disappear in the shadows. I ran a quick mental movie of how I'd acted during the last endless hours of rehearsal. If he'd been sitting behind me, then he'd had ample time to observe Shawn's snide comments, to monitor my laughing attempts to shush my partner in understudy-crime.

Timothy shook Ken's hand. "What's the problem?"

"Have you ever heard of Lucky Red Dragon? It's a soda or something. Chinese."

"Sorry," Timothy said, shaking his head.

"Could you try to track some down? Martina needs it."

Timothy's face tightened visibly, but he kept his voice neutral as he asked, "A bottle?"

"A case. Each week."

Timothy shrugged. "I'll see what I can do."

Ken barely managed to mutter a few pleasantries before he stumbled out the door. I was left alone in the theater with Timothy. "I thought you weren't coming over here today. Did you leave something backstage?"

He shook his head. "I came to see you."

Wow. So much for hoping he hadn't noticed me, hadn't been paying attention. Timothy was direct. Not witty and flirty and beating around the bush. He just made a straightforward statement of what he wanted. Just like I'd told him to do that very morning—to Amy, to his landlord.

I hadn't planned on his applying that technique to me, though.

As I tried to remember enough words in the English language to reply, he asked, "What are *your* plans to see the fireworks?"

I wrinkled my nose. "I love watching them, but I hate fighting the crowds. I'll probably just go home and turn on the TV."

"I've got a better idea," he said.

"Serving up dinner at the restaurant?" I wondered if he could possibly be taking me up on my long-ago request for work.

He shook his head. "I closed the restaurant tonight. One of the perks of owning the place." I looked a question toward him, utterly mystified about what he might have planned. He said, "Trust me."

And I did. I trusted him. I'd trusted him every time I'd set foot inside Garden Variety. I'd trusted him when I'd seen him in the hallway of my apartment building. I'd trusted him whenever I'd taken a break from the play that Martina was ruining, whenever I let some delectable catered treat bring me back from the edge of insanity.

We left the theater and made our way through the hot city streets. Heat shimmered off the asphalt, radiating off the sea of pedestrians that flooded the sidewalks. Sometimes, the summer turned city crowds crazy. Tonight, though, there was just a jangling hum of expectation, of excitement. Everyone was flowing toward the river, toward the traditional Macy's display of fireworks.

But Timothy led us upstream. He seemed to have some special skill for finding paths through the crowd. He eased between people like a shadow flickering beneath a jungle canopy. I stumbled once, missing a gap that he had found effortlessly, and he reached back for my hand, folding his fingers around mine as if he'd intended to touch me the entire time.

Before I could question where we were going, before I could ask what Timothy had planned, we were entering one of the huge hotels near Times Square. Timothy guided me across the cool lobby, slipping across the marble floor like a predator heading into its lair. He led us to a hidden hallway, to a service corridor that looked like a hundred other service corridors I had haunted during my catering days. A staff elevator waited there, its doors opening as soon as Timothy pressed the call button.

"Where—" I started to ask, but the amused twist of his lips silenced me. He pressed the button labeled R.

R. For Rooftop.

The elevator opened onto a tiny lobby, a grimy greenhouse that crouched on the roof. The flyspecked glass would have made the room unbearably hot, but someone had blocked the door open. A sultry breeze wafted through.

As we stepped onto the building's roof, a dozen white-aproned maids looked up from their gossiping clusters of three and four. A couple of bellhops stood apart, talking to each other with the slouched shoulders and easy camaraderie of hard-working men on a break. A clutch of uniformed busboys broke off their conversation in Spanish, calling out greetings to Timothy. He answered them with an easy wave and a smile.

"Who are these people?" I asked.

"They work here," he said quite reasonably. He still held my hand, and he was drawing me away from the others, toward the far edge of the roof.

"But what are *we* doing here?"

"Getting the best view of the fireworks in all of

Manhattan." He gave in to my confusion. "I know the head chef of the restaurant. Jean-Louis and I go way back."

I could have asked a dozen more questions, but there wasn't really any need. Timothy knew people. In the same way that he knew the homeless people who ate in his restaurant, in the way he'd come to know our cast and crew. It was easy, *effortless,* for Timothy to slide between worlds. And tonight, he'd brought me with him.

A black railing marked the edge of the roof. Timothy staked out a place for us on the very corner, far from the laughing hotel staff. I caught my breath as I looked out. We could see all the way across to the river; not a building hampered the view.

Something about that open expanse made me reluctant to edge all the way up to the rail. I knew that it would protect me. It would keep me safe. Nevertheless, I couldn't help but think about how many hundreds of feet I could fall. I wanted to invent an invisible safety net, a massive, unseen hook that I could fasten to my sundress, to keep me safe and secure.

As if he sensed my fear, Timothy moved to stand behind me. His chest was warm against my back, solid. Comforting. I edged a little closer to the corner. A warm breeze billowed up below us, startling me, and I jumped away from the edge. Timothy laughed, a chortle that sounded almost like a growl. He stepped even closer, settling his arms on either side of me, catching me in the corner between his body and the railing.

With anyone else, I might have felt restricted. I might have felt confined. With Timothy, though, it seemed like I was supported, protected. Even though I knew the hotel staff was talking behind us, even though I knew we were two people surrounded by millions of other New Yorkers, I felt as if we were miles away from anyone else.

I let myself lean back against his chest. I gave myself permission to melt into the solid heat of his body.

When the first burst of fireworks went off, his arms tightened around me, holding me close when I jumped with the inevitable surprise.

I had always thought that fireworks were beautiful—full of mystery, full of light. The dull concussion as the shells launched, the sharp crack of the explosion. The flaming stars, the weeping cascade of sparks. Pure white, red, green, the occasional shock of other colors, painting the clouding canvas of the night sky.

I had always thought that fireworks were beautiful, but I had never seen them like I did that night. They seemed close enough that I could lean out over the abyss, that I could soar between them, lost forever in their stars. The explosions were so loud that they made me catch my breath. I had to laugh when multiple stages caught, popped, burst into colored flame. I had never known that I could watch, forever, feeling my heartbeat slow to match another person's, feeling my breathing synchronize until the full power and glory of the finale could blind me and deafen me and make me eternally grateful for the cage of flesh and bone that kept me safe.

I don't know how long we stood there, after the fireworks were over. I closed my eyes, resting my head on Timothy's collarbone, thinking nothing, saying nothing. A lifetime passed and then I felt his broad hands on my waist, holding me safe and secure. Turning me to face him.

"That was amazing," I said.

"It was."

There were entire conversations buried in those five words. I knew that he was telling me stories, about his life, about all the things he knew and thought and believed. I knew that he was asking me questions. And I understood all the answers that I wanted to give him. I understood that I wanted to lead him to the ghostly staff elevator at this magical hotel. I wanted to guide him back to the Bentley, to my apartment, to the king-size bed where we could watch my bedroom grow rosy with the light of dawn.

The streets were surprisingly empty by the time we left the rooftop. Timothy and I walked, hand in hand, as if we were the only two people on the sidewalks, the only two people in all of New York City.

He nodded to the doorman when we got to the Bentley. He stood close to me in the elevator. He radiated heat against my back as I opened the three locks that led into my apartment. He closed the door behind us, taking care to see that it latched.

It was the most natural thing in the world to sit next to him on the couch. Every moment that we'd known each other had siphoned into this funnel. He was supposed to cup a hand behind my head. I was destined to pull him close, to hook my fingers under his black leather belt. We were meant to fall back onto the wintergreen throw pillows, to laugh against each other's lips, to lose ourselves in a tangle of hands and hair and twisted, crumpled clothing.

I barely felt the impact as Tabitha jumped onto the arm of the couch. I might not have realized she was there at all, if Timothy hadn't looked up, hadn't grinned at her and lightly eased her back to the floor.

But that interruption was enough. Tabitha's intrusion was like a lightning message from my superego, a reminder transmitted in thousand-point type.

I had the Master Plan.

I couldn't let myself be distracted by Timothy's touch. I had promised myself, promised Amy. I'd never made anything stick, never kept a single vow I'd ever made before, not where men were concerned. I had never chosen to place *my* feelings, *my* needs above those of some broken relationship with a guy, some desperate thing that I thought was a panacea.

Plants, fish, cat. The words spun through my head like a mantra. Plants. Fish. Cat.

Man.

Given my track record with the first three, I had little hope that anything would ever work out with Timothy, not in the long run.

But Tabitha had come home, right? Just one day after running away?

Maybe my luck was turning. Maybe I was becoming more responsible. Maybe I could set aside the Master Plan and do what I wanted to do, when I wanted to do it. Maybe bad things only came in twos this time, not the threes that had ruined my life before.

Yeah. Right. A cat decided, by the inscrutable workings of her own feline mind, to come home to me, and I was turning that into a demonstration of my responsibility, my fitness, for taking on obligations in the adult world? I had a Master Plan precisely so that I wouldn't let myself get into this trouble, wouldn't let myself make the same mistakes I'd made over and over and over again.

"What?" Timothy asked, pulling back.

"I—" I started to say, and I was embarrassed to find that I needed to clear my throat. "I'm sorry," I whispered.

For just a moment, he collapsed against me. His neck sagged, and his head brushed against my shoulder. He exhaled, long and slow, and his breath seared my arm.

I stiffened with remorse. "Timothy, I'm sorry. I—I can't..."

He levered off of me, planting his hands on either side of my trembling body. Now that I'd interrupted us, I was completely confused. I knew what I *wanted* to do; I knew that I wanted to pull him back to me, drag both of us into my bedroom, once and for all. But I also knew that I couldn't. I needed to prove to myself that I wouldn't.

My frustration boiled over into hot tears—frustration with myself, with Amy, with Sam and all the other guys who had made me doubt my ability to ever have a sane, balanced relationship. I hated my stupid, confused, Laura Wingfield life, with more passion than I'd ever hated anything before.

"Hush," Timothy said, smoothing his hand down my back.

"I—" I gulped. I didn't have the faintest idea how I was going to finish that sentence.

"Hush," he said again.

It took a moment for me to swallow hard. To smother the tears. To take a deep, shuddering breath. Another.

"Timothy," I started to say.

"It's all right." He rose to his feet, the motion so smooth, so even, that I could imagine he'd planned it all evening. "I shouldn't have come here."

"No," I said, but I didn't have any more words to add.

He shook his head, looking down at me. He reached out one finger and touched it to my lips, like the chastest of kisses, like a promise. And then he glided around the couch, stalking to the door with a panther's grace. The silence echoed long after he had left.

Chapter 13

I WAITED UNTIL morning before I called Amy.

"I hate you," I said, the instant she picked up.

"Good morning to you, too," she said. "Happy Super Soldier Saturday."

"I'm through with the Master Plan. It was a stupid idea. I don't know why I let you talk me into it."

"Let me guess. Dr. Teel dumped you."

"No!" I almost threw my phone across the room. I could picture her gloating as she ate her breakfast of fat-free lemon yogurt over one sliced peach, skin removed. I knew my sister way too well. "Why would you even say that?"

"So it was Timothy, then. You two got together. Are you moving in with him? Or is he moving in with you?"

For a moment, all I could do was splutter. Of all the obnoxious, superior, controlling, manipulative things for my sister to say... "You make me sound like a total slut! Amy, I don't move in with every single guy I meet."

"Stop me if I'm driving beyond my headlights here. Let's review the whole reason you agreed to do the

Master Plan."

"Amy!"

"You like Timothy, right?"

"Well—"

"And you *know* that he's a better catch than Sam ever was, right?"

"Anyone—"

"And you were all set on marrying Sam, right, before he dumped you cold?"

"But—"

"Erin, you might as well eat the reality sandwich." She sounded like a lawyer making a closing argument in court. "You've been out of circulation for, what, six weeks now? When was the last time you didn't have a boyfriend for six weeks? No wonder you got itchy. No wonder you're all ready to drop the Plan."

"Don't be ridiculous!"

More courtroom drama. "When was the last time you went six weeks without a guy in your life?"

"Amy!"

"When?"

I rolled my eyes and counted backward. "Ninth grade, all right? The entire spring semester."

"And when was the last time you made decisions based on what *you* wanted to do, instead of worrying about what some guy wanted, what some guy might think? When was the last time you walked away from some candy-apple crush because it made you act stupid? Erin, we have been over this again and again. You have to learn how to incentivize your own choices!"

I hated her. I hated her stupid business school jargon. I hated her absolute certainty that she was right. I hated the fact that she actually *was* right.

Oh, I wasn't ready to move in with Timothy. But I was definitely more attracted to him every time I saw him. And the only reason I *had* sent him walking the night before was because of Amy's stupid Master Plan. The Master Plan, and the way it was supposed to free me from making idiotic crush-based decisions.

There was also, in the light of day, the minor snag that I didn't actually know that much about Timothy. Oh, I knew a lot of meaningless details about him. I was pretty much an expert on his philosophy of restaurant management. I knew that he was kind. I knew that he was amazingly competent in the kitchen.

But I didn't know the first thing about the real guy. I didn't know anything about his family. About his past. About any friends he had. Hell, I didn't even know where he lived.

"Erin?" Amy asked. I realized that I'd been quiet for a long time.

"Yeah, I'm here. But I've got to go now. And I really do hate you."

"Are you dumping the Master Plan?"

"No." I shook my head to emphasize my decision, even though she couldn't see me. "I'm not ready to do that. I still need it, to keep me from doing something stupid."

"See?" Amy sounded immensely proud. "Am I a wise and wonderful sister, or what?"

"Not so wise," I argued. "And don't push it for wonderful. And I just have to say, you are totally wrong about me and Dr. Teel."

"Yeah, right. I've seen the way he looks at you. And that lip-lock at Garden Variety wasn't exactly platonic."

"Let's just say that there's more to Dr. Teel than meets the eye."

"Oooh!" She clearly sounded intrigued. "Do tell!"

"Nope," I said. "I'm not the type of girl to kiss and tell."

She started to push for more details, but I asked the only question I was certain would deflect her. "How's Justin? Have things gotten any easier at all?"

"Yeah," she said, and I could hear the surprise in her voice. "They have. He is so proud about riding his bike, he made me take a dozen photos to send to Derek. And he's finally stopped with the spilling-the-milk thing. I'm a little tired of clinking my glass every meal, but Shawn was on to something there."

I was glad to hear that *something* positive had come out of that awkward dinner at Garden Variety. Actually, I was truly happy that Amy was catching a real break with her unruly son. She really did deserve one.

"Wait a second!" Amy said. "You're not going to distract me that easily! Tell me what you know about Dr. Teel!"

So much for diversion. Nevertheless, I was still the younger sister. I hadn't completely forgotten how to hone my reputation for brattiness. I smiled broadly and said, "Whoops! Gotta run! Talk to you later!"

I didn't answer when Amy called me back.

* * *

I was *good* at avoiding my sister when I didn't want to talk to her.

I became *expert* at avoiding Timothy.

I wanted to talk to him. I really did. I had to do something, say something, to smooth over the new awkwardness between us. I had to get past my embarrassment, move beyond the horrible tangle of emotions that nauseated me every single time I remembered freezing on my couch, every time I relived shutting him down like I was some sort of virgin schoolgirl tease.

We could get past that. I could hold true to the Master Plan and still have casual conversations with a guy. In fact, I'd be even *better* at working the Plan if Timothy and I became friends, really got to know each other. I worked out elaborate dialogs, careful conversations that were designed to elicit data about Timothy's background and family and friends.

But something always kept me from delivering my lines. Okay, on Saturday and Sunday, it was my fault. I avoided the catering table altogether, telling myself that I wasn't hungry, that I had to cut back on the high-calorie snacks. I just couldn't face the patient smile I was certain I would find on Timothy's face. I was too embarrassed. Too regretful that I'd changed my mind when I'd had him, literally, in my grasp.

By Monday, I decided to face the music, to grab the proverbial bull by the horns. Shawn, though, was particularly despondent over our second-class status that day—those rehearsals focused on scenes with the Gentleman Caller. I had to stay close to my fellow understudy, to snark with him about the terrible job the leads were doing.

On Tuesday, Martina sucked all the air out of the room, cross-examining Timothy on the ingredients for the petit fours that he served.

On Wednesday, I ducked out of rehearsal the instant that Ken called a break, racing down to the Mercer box office for the one shift a week I still worked with them.

On Thursday, Timothy set up trays of food, but he left them unattended. The stage manager said she thought he had some sort of meeting, but she didn't know the details.

On Friday, Ken Durbin kept me working during all of our breaks; he wanted to make sure I had mastered the blocking, in case I ever actually needed to go on-stage instead of Martina.

On Saturday, I was all ready to say something, anything, but I became completely overwhelmed when I realized it had been one solid week since Timothy and I had talked. One solid week since we had tangled on my sofa. One solid week since he had closed my front door behind him.

I chickened out.

I simply couldn't trust my judgment. Not where men were concerned. I'd spent all of high school and college developing bad habits, habits that I'd polished to a high sheen with Sam. No, I'd made the Master Plan for a reason, and I had to stick with it. And if that meant avoiding small talk with a guy I wasn't going to do anything else with for nearly a year, then fine.

Of course, even when I successfully stayed away from the catering table in the wings, I kept hearing about Timothy. Martina had traded in her whining about craft services so that she could devote all of her energy to demanding her Lucky Red Dragon soda. She insisted that she could not manage opening night without the beverage, that it was the key to her success. She had drunk a bottle every night that she'd performed on that awful reality TV show, and she wasn't about to do less for our production.

Ken reassured her—and anyone else within earshot—that Timothy was searching for the drink nonstop. So far, though, it was nowhere to be found. Everyone Timothy talked to said that they were familiar with the name, that they used to be able to order it, that they'd heard it had been taken off the market. Timothy had even gone so far as to comb through the back streets of Chinatown, relying on a hand-drawn label and the carefully written Chinese characters for *lucky* and *red* and *dragon.*

Martina whined and moaned, but it looked as if we were going to open *Menagerie!* without ginseng tonic. Definitely without the additional twelve secret herbs and spices.

I had to give Ken a lot of credit. Despite Martina's prima donna behavior, despite our being weeks behind in rehearsals, despite the ever-growing array of artistic questions and issues and problems, he continued to channel his boundless energy into building an incredible show. As with any new musical, we were always shooting at a moving target. Every rehearsal, we changed dance numbers, tweaked songs, reworked spoken dialog, striving tirelessly for perfection.

Ken continued to fold us understudies into rehearsals, making sure that we learned all the lines, all the songs, all the blocking for each and every scene. He included us in the vocal and motion warm-ups every day (usually the best part of every rehearsal for me, because I got admiring looks from the other performers. All the other performers but Martina, that was.) Ken always had us walk through each scene in place of the leads at least once, so that we knew the blocking, understood the structure. In theory, we could go onstage at a moment's notice—and for that I was eternally grateful.

In practice, of course, we understudies were nowhere near as integrated into the show as Ken made it seem. I was constantly jockeying for position so that I could get a sight line for new dance combinations. I had to remind the stage manager three times before I got a copy of the lyrics for a last-minute new song, a number that Ken added to the second act when he concluded that no one understood Tom's motivation for bringing the Gentleman Caller home to visit.

Being an understudy was a constant education in humility, a never-ending reminder that I hadn't been good enough to land the lead. In my case, the struggle was even more stressful, because I truly believed that I *had* been good enough. I just hadn't been famous enough. And I hadn't tailored my magical wishes specifically enough.

And that was another source of stress in the weeks after the Fourth of July—Teel. My genie was growing desperate. He pulled me to the Garden constantly, not worrying about whether he was interrupting rehearsal, dragging me away from Amy and Justin on Super Soldier Saturday, blasting me out of deep, desperately needed sleep.

Teel claimed that he didn't know how long Jaze would be in the Garden. He claimed that his soul mate could be heading back into the real world (or whatever passed for real, to a genie) at any instant. He claimed that their love would be split asunder forever, if I didn't make my last wish immediately.

I felt for him. I really did. And yet, I was certain that *Teel* wouldn't push himself to make his fourth and final wish if our roles had been reversed. He'd be selfish and self-centered, just as he'd been when he manipulated me into spending two wishes for dancing and singing skills that I would likely never share with an audience.

And so, I grew accustomed to seeing Teel as a bank manager (pinstripe suit, even in the middle of the July heat), as a grocery store cashier (uniform apron), as a swimming instructor (indecently tight Speedo.) Male, female, young, old—Teel played more roles than I had ever dreamed of performing.

And every once in a while, he came back as the doctor. Much to Shawn's amusement, he even showed up at the theater a couple of times, making suggestive jokes about house calls, spiriting me away for a quick cup of coffee during breaks. He thought that he was seducing me. He thought that he was bringing me around, drawing me closer to making my last wish. He thought that he was winning me over by reminding me of some of the hottest kisses I'd ever experienced.

And those kisses had been good, I had to admit, especially now that I was deep in my Master Plan–induced drought.

But every time I saw Dr. Teel, I thought about Justin. My nephew talked about Teel constantly. He'd drawn the doctor on several pages of his Super Soldier Saturday scrapbook. He'd even sketched in a superhero cape once, turning Teel into the amazing, incredible Soldierman. I knew that Teel only helped out with Justin because of boredom, because I wouldn't make my fourth and final wish. Nevertheless, I was secretly proud that I was assisting Amy. Justin's improved behavior was the best reason for me to delay making my fourth wish.

Over and over, I reassured myself that my delay didn't really matter, that my keeping Teel from meeting Jaze in the Garden was harmless. Expected, even. Lots of genies must end up in the Garden while the loves of their magical lives worked in the outside world. Even if Teel missed Jaze completely in the Garden, they'd have ample opportunity to interact out here in the real world, in my world, once they were both back on the regular wish-granting rota. At least, that's the way I *thought* it would work.

It was absolutely exhausting, keeping all of those justifications flowing through my thoughts at the same time.

Every night, I got home from rehearsal too tired to do anything but take a shower and climb into bed. Tabitha had taken to sleeping next to me, stretched out longer than seemed possible for her scrawny little frame. She had become the world's most affectionate cat. Dani continued to visit her regularly, bringing by canned cat food a couple of times a week, keeping up the financial end of our bargain. Nevertheless, I found myself supplementing more often than not, feeding Tabitha nearly double what we'd originally planned. At least her poor wastrel frame was starting to fill out a little.

Alas, the morning came when Tabitha was set to discover what a traitor I was. Dani knocked on my door, holding a cat carrier. "Ready?" she asked.

"Ready as I'll ever be," I said. "Tabitha drove me nuts all night, meowing and walking into the kitchen, like I forgot to feed her."

"Poor baby," Dani said. "She doesn't understand what 'nothing by mouth after midnight' means. She'll be fine after the surgery, though."

Dani picked up our jointly owned cat adeptly. Dani

backed her into the cat carrier. Dani maneuvered the little cage door closed. In fact, Dani had done everything to set up this entire excursion, tracking down a vet, making an appointment for the spay, even rounding up the cat carrier.

I'd explained that the timing was bad for me, that we were down to one week before *Menagerie!* previews opened. Dani listened, but she ignored me, brushing aside my concerns with a single reminder that Tabitha could go back into heat at any time. Neither of us wanted to hear *those* yowls again. Dani would keep an eye on Tabitha during her recovery. I didn't have to worry about a thing.

It was easier to give in than to fight.

As we walked through the city streets to the vet, Tabitha expressed her constant displeasure, complaining from the carrier as if we were torturing her. Some people looked at us with amusement on their faces, but most folks who noticed our screaming banshee frowned as if we were horrifyingly bad parents. Fortunately, we only had to wait a few minutes in the vet's waiting area, and then we were escorted into an examining room.

"Let's see," Dr. Ricker said, turning the carrier upside down to extract the suddenly shy Tabitha. "What a beauty you are!" she said encouragingly, as if she didn't see a dozen cats every morning.

Once Tabitha was safely on the examining table, the vet stroked her with confident hands. "Let's just see how your ears are," she said, producing a medical tool so quickly that Tabitha didn't have a chance to protest. "And your eyes look fine." The vet ran her hands along Tabitha's spine, and then she started to feel her belly.

"Hmm," Dr. Ricker said, her eyebrows knitting.

Dani stepped closer to the table. "Is that a good 'hmm' or a bad 'hmm?'"

For answer, the veterinarian merely stroked Tabitha, coaxing her onto her side. That angle exposed two rows of bright pink nubs rising from the spotless white fur of her belly. "Have her nipples always been this prominent?"

I looked at Dani. She looked at me. We both shrugged. "I don't know," Dani said. "I don't think either of us has really paid attention."

Dr. Ricker nodded. "Has she been in heat recently?"

"About three weeks ago," Dani answered.

"And how long was she outside?"

"Before I found her?" Dani sounded perplexed. "I don't know. I mean, she was a stray—"

"No. When she was in heat," Dr. Ricker clarified.

Dani protested, "We didn't let her go outside. We didn't want her breeding."

I had to say something. Even though I felt like I was admitting some horrible social crime, like I was standing up in front of a room of doctors and saying that I regularly practiced unsafe sex, like I was labeling *myself* the most promiscuous female in all five boroughs, I had to say, "Well, actually..."

The other women turned and stared at me. I reached down to stroke Tabitha's head, seeking as much comfort as I was giving. "Tabitha *did* get out. Just for one night. I tried to catch her, but she was gone before I had a chance...."

Dr. Ricker nodded. Dani just stared at me as she said, "You let our cat go outside while she was in heat, and you didn't tell me?"

Three. There. The last of the bad things had come

home to roost, until I started on another perfect triad of disaster.

I'd killed my lily plant. I'd killed my goldfish. And now, I'd let my cat get pregnant. I was single-handedly dismantling the Master Plan with the efficiency of a colony of carpenter ants. I was never going to date another man for as long as I lived. I didn't deserve to.

"I'm sorry," I said to Dani. "I wanted to tell you, but I didn't think it mattered. She came back so quickly! And she's been so good—she's eating, using her box. I thought she was fine."

Dr. Ricker looked from me to Dani. "She *is* fine. She's just pregnant."

Dani sighed. "We might as well take her home for now. We'll reschedule...after."

This time, Tabitha was eager to get into her carrier. Dani and Dr. Ricker said a few more things to each other; the vet decided to waive her fees, even though we'd taken up plenty of her time. Hands were shaken. Tabitha yowled. I felt like I was a child, hanging my head after a particularly disappointing parent/teacher school conference.

As Dani and I headed out the door, I wrestled with the carrier. We'd walked three entire blocks before I finally said, "I am so sorry."

Dani continued another ten paces before she answered. "I know you didn't mean to do anything wrong."

"I ruin everything I touch!"

Dani stopped and stared at me. "That seems a bit dramatic, doesn't it?"

I shook my head. "You don't understand! I have this Plan! My sister and I agreed on it!"

"And your Plan doesn't include taking care of a litter of kittens?"

"It doesn't include any of this." Without really intending to, I found myself babbling about the entire stupid arrangement, the idiotic goals that I'd agreed to, just because Amy had said I should. Dani stood there beside me, on a quiet street in Greenwich Village. She listened to every word I blurted out, and she didn't speak, she didn't interrupt, she didn't tell me that the morning was hot and getting hotter and she definitely had better things to do than advise some overwrought underperforming actress on her practically nonexistent love life.

"Wow," I said when I was finished. And that's when I realized what my confession sounded like. It reminded me of all the times I'd unburdened myself, talking to my mother. All the times I'd told her about having a crush on a cute boy at school, on some guy who didn't know I was alive. All the times I'd told her about trying out for a school play, about hoping, wishing, dreaming of a role that I knew would be so perfect that I'd be happy forever.

That was the worst thing about Mom and Dad being gone, the worst thing, by far. I could never talk to them like this. Never again.

Dani eyed me steadily, her expression somehow telling me that she knew what I'd been thinking, that she could hear the little whispers that still rattled around inside my head. She said, "It sounds like you needed to share that with someone."

"I guess so. I'm just sorry, for your sake, that it was you."

"I'm not." She grinned and picked up the cat carrier, which I'd deposited on the sidewalk somewhere in the middle of my tirade. "I only had a son. I've always wondered what it would be like to listen to a daughter, to hear her version of why the world is an unfair and terrible place."

I fell in beside her as we continued back to the Bentley. "Thanks. I think."

"You're welcome." Dani clicked her tongue. "Well, we can always hope that Tabitha will have a small litter. The Guerillas aren't going to be much use, taking kittens."

"I'm sure I can find some people at the theater," I said. If nothing else, I could foist a couple off on Amy. I could always convince her that Justin needed to learn how to be responsible for a pet. In fact, *two* kittens would entertain each other; they'd be much easier to care for than one, living alone. I could already hear my crafty arguments, the words running together like lines in a play.

After all, I owed Amy, for the Master Plan, if for nothing else. Two kittens would be a perfect down payment on that debt.

* * *

My conversation with Dani nagged at me, though. When I told her about the Master Plan, I'd ranted about the plant, the fish, the cat. I'd sort of skipped over the "man" part, avoiding any details. Especially any details about one man in particular. Dani hadn't pushed for specifics, and I hadn't volunteered any.

Somewhere along the way, I was going to have to fill in the gaps. I couldn't just hang out with Tabitha for a year, prove that I could handle a cat, then magically expect to find Mr. Perfect waiting for me on my doorstep. I had an obligation to *build* a perfect relationship, to pave the way for future steps of the Plan.

I'd run out of excuses. It was time to talk to Timothy. And Dani could help me with that.

The next morning, I peeked outside to confirm that she'd already picked up her morning paper before I knocked on her door. "Good morning," I said, when she answered. I tried to make it sound like we greeted each other every morning.

"Good...morning." She waited patiently. I thought about bailing on my mission. I could just ask her if I could borrow a cup of sugar. An egg. A stick of butter. I could give her a status report on Tabitha, tell her about the cute way our cat had curled up beside me while I slept the night before.

But she already knew about the Plan. She wasn't an idiot. She could help me navigate from Step C to Step D, from Cat to Man, but only if I let her. I took a deep breath. "Dani-I-know-this-is-really-strange-but-I-was-wondering-if-you-have-Timothy's-address-I-need-to-see-him-before-our-next-rehearsal-and-he-may-not-be-at-the-restaurant-this-early-in-the-morning."

"Timothy?" she asked, and I was pretty certain she was laughing at me. "Timothy Brennan?"

"Yes," I said. My heart was pounding so hard that I wasn't sure I'd be able to hear her when she answered me.

"I've got it with my Gray Guerilla papers," she said. "Come on in."

Still half-convinced that I should turn tail and run away, I stepped over the threshold. Dani's apartment was much smaller than mine. It was darker, too. Her living room window looked out onto another building, instead of the river view that I enjoyed. A large work-table hulked against the wall to my right; I could make out a jumble of seed packets, a bag of potting soil and a tangle of gardening tools.

"I know you must think this is really strange," I said.

Dani's smile lit her face as she picked up a three-ring binder from her coffee table. "No," she said, shaking her head. "I don't really think it's strange at all."

"I mean, I'd feel weird if you gave out *my* address to anyone." What was I trying to do? Talk her out of this, when it had already taken my entire store of willpower to come over here in the first place?

"If you had evil, nefarious purposes in mind, you could track Timothy down at the restaurant," Dani said reasonably. "Or at rehearsal."

Of course she knew that he was cooking for the show. She'd been selling him produce all along. She took an index card from her notebook and wrote out an address. I was surprised to see that it was only a few blocks away. "Thank you," I said, and I left before I could change my mind.

Outside the Bentley, I swung by Garden Variety. Sure, it was a Sunday morning, but he might be there. I wouldn't want to go invading his private space, only to find that he was cooking away in the restaurant kitchen.

No such luck.

The courtyard was empty, the tables and chairs stacked and chained in the corner. I knocked sharply on the door, but there was no reply. I even walked farther down the alley, found the service door to the kitchen, knocked on it. Still no answer.

I took Dani's index card from my pocket. No time like the present.

A block from Timothy's building, I ducked into a little bakery. Cup of Gold, said the sign over the door. I'd walked by it a dozen times before, but I'd never set foot inside. Three people stood in line in front of me. Three people, giving me time to think. Time to change my mind.

I set my teeth and stepped up to the counter. Two red velvet cupcakes. Two cups of coffee—one black, one fortified with sugar and cream. Two napkins. A box, complete with a bow.

Timothy's building didn't have a doorman. Someone was leaving just as I arrived. I smiled breezily, as if I belonged there. I waited for the elevator, taking care not to look in the mirror that hung beside the mailboxes in the lobby. The last thing I wanted to do was stare at myself.

Fourth floor. To the right. Third door.

Knock.

"Erin!"

He opened the door on a chain. In the spare seconds it took for him to close it, to slide the chain, to open it again, I tried to parse his tone of voice. Was he pleased to see me? Or was that pure shock in his voice? Certainly, it couldn't be anger?

"Erin," he said again, when the door was open. "Are you okay?"

Of course. He must have thought that something terrible had happened, after my avoiding him for three weeks. "No," I said, and then I shook my head. "I mean, I'm fine." Wonderful. I was getting this conversation off on a great foot.

After a long pause, he said, "Come in."

The place was small, but light streamed in from two large windows. A tiny kitchenette gleamed to my right. We were standing in the living room. A door to the left showed a bedroom, and I could just glimpse a rumpled navy comforter sprawled across the mattress.

Fighting an involuntary blush, I extended my peace offering of food and drink. "Coals to Newcastle, I guess."

"Coals are always welcome," he said, but his voice was wary.

A newspaper draped across the small dinette table in the corner. "Please," he said, gesturing me toward one of the two ladder-back chairs. "Have a seat."

I was glad that there was someplace to sit, other than the couch. I didn't think that I would trust myself to go on with this, otherwise. Not after the last time we'd sat on a couch together. Timothy swept away the newspaper. He collected two plates from his kitchen. He looked a question toward me, and I nodded, to indicate that he should open the box. "Red velvet," he said. "My favorite."

"Wonderful!" I said, but my voice sounded fake to me. Staged. As if I were reading a bad script. I reminded myself that I'd come here because I wanted to know more about him. My plan was working perfectly so far.

I looked around the room. Everything was crisp. Clean. The furniture was tailored, the colors subdued. Bookshelves lined the opposite wall. A blue-and-white abstract print was framed above the table where we sat. I looked at it closer, recognizing the signature in the bottom right corner.

Timothy Brennan.

"It's a blueprint!" I said, honest surprise breaking the brittle varnish in my throat.

He shrugged. "It was my thesis project. To get my architecture degree."

"You're an architect!"

"Was," he said. "Or I thought I would be, anyway." He leaned back in his chair, stretching his legs in front of him with a predator's restlessness. "What's this all about, Erin?"

I blushed.

Everything had made perfect sense inside my head. I'd come over here. We'd eat breakfast together. I'd get to know him better. I'd fill in some of the blanks, get answers to all the questions that swirled inside my head. I'd lay the groundwork for some future friendship with him. For something more, possibly. Probably. Hopefully. Down the line.

I'd forgotten one little thing, though. He had no idea what I was planning. From his point of view, I'd avoided him for three weeks. I'd brought him to my home, then thrown him out, and then ignored him for nearly a month.

Did he think that I was trying to seduce him now? Did he think that I'd changed my mind about our Fourth of July fireworks? That I was determined to pick up what we'd left off?

Well, was I?

Oh. I had to say something.

"I don't know you," I said. When he frowned, I hurried to add, "I mean, I like what I *do* know about you, but that's all professional. That's all work. I don't know where you grew up. I don't know if you have any brothers or sisters. If you had any pets when you were a kid. What your favorite color is. I don't know you. And I want to. Um, know you."

It sounded a little stupid when I phrased it like that, but Timothy relaxed a little in his chair. His voice was deceptively mild as he asked, "And then, what? You'll compare all that to Teel's life? You'll add up the totals, and then you'll get back to me with a final decision?"

"Teel!" My genie's name shocked me.

"Isn't that what's going on here?" Timothy's voice was steady, but there was a jagged edge beneath his words. "I saw the two of you, that night you all came into the restaurant, with Amy and Justin and Shawn."

"That night—" I cut short my protest.

"And he comes by the theater often enough. Takes you out on breaks. You talk to him, all the time."

"There's nothing going on between Teel and me." I wanted to look away. I wanted to chew my lip. I wanted to cross my fingers and make some idiotic schoolgirl wish—"Just this once"—to make things easy and comfortable and familiar.

"Right. I guess the coffee down at the corner is just better than what I provide?"

I blushed and scrambled for an explanation. "He's a friend. It's hard to keep in touch with friends when a show is going on."

Timothy sighed. "I might have believed you, a while back. I might have believed you when you stopped by the restaurant after I stayed up all night reviewing Amy's plan. When we went up on the roof together. When you brought me back to your place." He had to stop, to clear his throat. "But Erin, *three weeks*. You've avoided talking to me for three weeks. I'm not going to compete in some beauty contest with Teel. I'm not going to beg for your attention. That's not a game I'm comfortable playing."

"There's nothing going on with me and Teel!" I said. I couldn't believe that my wonderful get-to-know-you conversation was snagged here. I looked Timothy in the eye and said, "This isn't about Teel. None of this has ever been about Teel."

He held my gaze. I could hear him breathing. I sensed that he was measuring me, testing me, and I had no idea what else I was supposed to say. "Timothy, you have to believe me. Teel isn't my boyfriend. He never has been. He's my—"

Genie. I wanted to say genie. I wanted to say it; the word was right there, the two syllables hovering on the tip of my tongue.

But I couldn't. Just like I hadn't been able to tell Amy about the magic lamp, all those months ago, when I stood in Becca's kitchen.

Frustrated, my eyes filled with tears. Timothy noticed, just as he had that night in my apartment. Just as he had in the shadows, as we lay on my couch. This time, though, something inside him hardened. His face turned to stone. "Right," he said. "Whatever."

He stood and walked to the door, opened it. The hallway outside was empty. "Thank you," he said, making the two syllables sound impossibly formal. "Thank you for stopping by."

I didn't know what else I could say. I didn't know what else I could do. I took my cup of lukewarm coffee and walked out into the hall.

Three days later, I made my way to the theater. At the drugstore next to the theater, I stopped and splurged on junk food—a bottle of full-test Coca-Cola and a sleeve of four Reese's peanut butter cups. The snack food of champions, I told myself.

I wasn't going near the catering table. I couldn't imagine talking to Timothy ever again. Not after that disaster in his apartment.

I needed sustenance, though. We were about to undergo our final dress rehearsal. We were running *Menagerie!* from start to finish, making every possible effort not to stop. We were using all of the lights. All of the sound cues. All of the costumes. Our entire orchestra was going to be there, for as long as we needed them, even though their union demanded overtime pay after three hours. All the understudies were going to watch, silent, from the back of the theater. Ken wasn't going to use us; this was the last chance for all of the stars to master their roles.

Final dress rehearsal.

Previews would start the following night, would run for two weeks, while we tested the show in front of live audiences. Critics would be out there, judging our creation. And then, the show would open officially, and *Menagerie!* would climb into the stratosphere, ride Martina's television fame to join the ranks of the world's most successful musicals. I could only dream that we would run as long as *Cats,* as *Phantom of the Opera,* as *Les Misérables.* If we ran for twenty years, Martina *had* to move on to something else, didn't she? I *had* to have a chance to perform onstage, at least once. Didn't I?

Shawn was waiting for me in the back of the theater. He'd brought three bottles of VitaminWater, the pink kind, and a bag of red licorice twists large enough to feed the entire population of Canada.

"Going for the hard stuff, I see," he said, nodding toward my own snacks.

"It's going to be a long day," I answered.

Ken interrupted before I could say anything more, summoning everyone to the stage, cast and crew. When we were all assembled, all eagerly awaiting words of wisdom from our fearless leader, Ken called into the wings, "Timothy? Can you join us for a moment?

I tried not to stare as Timothy stepped onto the stage. I hadn't seen him since Sunday. He didn't look toward me at all, but I couldn't tell if that was coincidence or calculation.

Ken bounced over to Timothy and clapped a hand on his shoulder. "You are a god among men."

Timothy shrugged, obviously uncomfortable with being the focus of everyone's attention. "I should have done it sooner. I don't know why I didn't think of reaching out to the west coast importers. They have more direct lines than anyone here in the east."

"No," Shawn said beside me, finally realizing what they were talking about. "He couldn't have..."

Ken overheard and contradicted. "He did. Ladies and gentlemen, our own Timothy Brennan has laid in a month's supply of Lucky Red Dragon! Let's all give him a hand."

Everyone cheered. Martina, who was holding court at the front of the stage, raised an iridescent green bottle. A bright crimson dragon was splayed across the label, thin as a worm. Chinese lettering blazed across the bottle, picked out in gleaming gold.

Ken reached out to shake Timothy's hand. "Thank you," he said.

Timothy headed back into the wings, and Ken returned his attention to all of us. He reminded us that he had faith in us. He told us that he knew we could bring *Menagerie!* to life. He told us that he didn't believe in those old theater maxims, that a terrible rehearsal meant a great opening night. He said that we were going to have an amazing rehearsal, and tomorrow would be a fantastic first night of previews.

"Okay, folks," he wrapped up his pep talk. "Let's take it from the top, in half an hour. Full costumes, full makeup. Make it perfect!" Ken was bouncing on the balls of his feet as he finished. I wondered if he'd had springs installed on the soles of his shoes. He had more energy than any five other people I knew. It was a good thing. This show would have drained a lesser man.

The cast exploded into a flurry of chatter. As Shawn and I began our retreat to the back of the house, we passed Martina. She had struck a pose by the footlights, showing off her emerald soda bottle to a group of admirers.

Okay. I didn't think that anyone on the show still admired Martina. Some of the dancers, though, clearly thought that she could get them a shot at Hollywood, at one of those dance competition shows. Either that, or they just enjoyed passing time with someone who was so clearly inferior to their own professional skills.

In any case, Martina had an eager community of listeners as she expounded on the drink in her hand. "It was an energy drink before there were energy drinks. It has ginseng *and* twelve secret herbs and spices."

Great. She could read the seven English language words on the bottle. Ten, if you counted the drink's name.

Martina's braying laugh grated on my nerves, and then I heard her shout, "Well, we wouldn't be cutting things so close if that caterer had done his job. Idiot! It's not like I was asking for anything difficult."

I stopped in my tracks.

I knew that I should just shrug off her words. I knew that there was nothing I could say that would change her, that would turn her into a different person, into a kinder woman, a gentler soul. She had insulted Timothy before, though, and I *still* felt guilty for saying nothing that time. If I stayed silent now, I was agreeing with her.

And I did not agree with Martina Block. I did not agree with Martina Block about anything.

I pivoted on my heel and faced her directly, even though I was outside the privileged circle of her onstage fan club. "His name is Timothy Brennan."

"What?" she asked. As she had in the past, she stuck her neck forward as she addressed me. She narrowed her eyes until she looked like a myopic stork.

"The caterer's name is Timothy Brennan. And you *did* ask for something difficult. You asked for something almost impossible."

Martina glanced at the bottle in her hand, shrugging as if it were a common Mountain Dew. "And who are *you,* to tell me what's difficult and what's not?"

Blood rushed in my ears, so loudly that I couldn't hear the titter of the crowd's reaction. I blinked, but I couldn't see anyone around us, any of the cast and crew. I only saw red, a wall of fury, of hopeless, helpless rage. A tiny corner of my brain remembered that I should walk away. I should stay silent. I should let Martina wallow in her conceited ignorance.

But I couldn't. I couldn't back down again.

"I am Erin Hollister," I said, and each word was steady, even, razor-sharp. "I am your understudy. Just like I was when you didn't know me last week. Or the week before. Or eight weeks ago, when we started working on this show." I thrust out my hand and repeated, "Erin Hollister. Pleased to meet you."

Martina recoiled as if my palm were diseased. Her right arm flew back, and for just a moment, I thought that she was going to throw the bottle of Red Lucky Dragon at me. But then, I realized what was really happening. I saw the truth.

Martina had lost her balance, on the very edge of the stage. Her prima donna recoil from my extended hand had sent her teetering on the lip of the platform. Lacking any instinctive control of her body, any notion of a dancer's balance, she flailed for stability.

I leaped toward her, trying to grasp her free hand. The rest of her circle moved, too, some closing in, others backing away, all of us flowing in painfully impossible slow motion.

Martina opened her mouth to scream, but gravity claimed her before she could make a noise. Helpless, I watched her fall into the orchestra pit.

Chapter 14

WITHIN SECONDS, A half dozen people had grabbed their cell phones, had punched in 911. Ken dashed backstage and appeared in the orchestra pit almost instantly; he must have taken the stairs three steps at a time. We actors crowded the edge of the stage, peering down, trying to make sense of the chaos below us.

Martina was fully conscious. She was screaming, howling with more volume than she had ever put into her songs onstage. Ken had his hands full trying to keep her from moving. Even from my vantage point, though, I could see that her leg was twisted in a terrible way. I could handle the sight of blood without any problem; I could mop up Justin's ordinary cuts without a flinch. But the angle of Martina's knee wasn't natural. It wasn't normal.

I staggered upstage.

There was no way that Martina Block was going to open *Menagerie!* I was going onstage.

Eight weeks before, I would have been thrilled. Eight *hours* before, I would have been certain that the universe was functioning properly for once, that I was getting precisely what I deserved.

Now, though, I was overwhelmed with guilt. Had I made Martina fall? Had I planned for her to stand on the edge of the stage, for her to tumble into the pit? I *knew* what a drama queen she could be; I'd been rolling my eyes about her for months. I had to have anticipated some grand reaction to my question. I had to have realized that she was in danger. That she was going to tumble over the edge.

"I didn't—" I said to no one in particular.

"Of course," Shawn said, materializing at my side. The words were right, but his eyes were narrow.

"She just—"

"She just fell down, all by herself." Shawn nearly spat the words. I couldn't tell if he truly thought I'd done this on purpose, or if he was just furious with himself for not taking his own extreme action.

And he didn't even know the full truth. He didn't know that I could have called on Teel at any time. I could have made my genie move me into the lead role. I could have made my final wish, and everything would have happened cleanly, safely, without Martina getting hurt.

But I hadn't done that. I'd been too selfish to call on Teel; I'd wanted to save my magic for a rainy day. And now, Martina was the one to suffer.

The doors to the lobby crashed open, and a team of paramedics stormed in. They rolled a gurney between them, maneuvering it down the theater aisle with a calming competence. The stage manager rushed to meet them, to show them how to get down to the pit.

I couldn't watch. I couldn't stand there and observe as they evaluated Martina's physical state, as they discussed the best way to shift her over to the gurney, as they ran through the patter of their professional reassurance. I walked away from Shawn—from angry, jealous Shawn—and I stared at the set around me. The walls of the Wingfield apartment felt as if they were closing in around me, trapping me in their dingy embrace.

Finally, a lifetime later, the paramedics were rolling the gurney out the door. I forced myself to turn around. I watched them assure Ken that they'd take Martina to St. Vincent's. He looked torn for a moment, then dispatched the assistant stage manager to accompany his star to the hospital.

By the time Ken turned back to us actors, his face was composed. He was calm, confident, the fearless director who could lead us through any disaster—even the loss of our star during our final rehearsal. The only sign that he was utterly, completely panicked was that he stood stock-still. Not a single bounce on the balls of his feet. Not a solitary twist of his neck as he worked out nonexistent kinks. Not the tiniest twitch on his lips.

And he was staring at me. Ken's gaze was locked on me, as if I were the answer to his prayers, as if I could provide the perfect resolution to this crisis. And that's when I realized that everyone in the entire room was looking at me, as well.

Panic started to ride my heart. I tried to breathe, tried to reason past my terror.

I could do this. I was a professional actress. I had trained for this role; I had sat through countless hours of rehearsal, of staging, of blocking and reblocking. *This* was the reason that I hadn't been cast in the chorus; *this* was the reason that I'd staked my career on the distant, offhand chance that I would succeed, that I would actually appear onstage. The distance had closed. The offhand had come to pass.

I was going to play Laura Wingfield in *Menagerie!*

"Let's go," Ken said. "We'll start the show from the top. Places in fifteen minutes, people."

The cast exploded into chatter, noisier than a cloud of cicadas. Ken crossed the stage to me. "The costume mistress will have to take in a few seams for the spoken-scene costumes. We'll take care of that after the run-through. You can wear street clothes for now. The dance costumes should be fine. The dressers will have them ready for you in the wings."

He didn't give me a chance to say anything, which was probably just as well. What words could possibly assure him that I was ready for the role? Could possibly assure myself?

The rehearsal was a disaster.

Okay. Not a complete disaster. My genie-inspired singing and dancing skills carried the musical numbers. But the straight play? The lines that Tennessee Williams had written? The words that had originally drawn me to this production, seduced me into the show, because I had played a flawless Laura in college, because I knew Laura's heart and soul as well as I knew my own?

I stumbled over every single word. I couldn't remember the blocking. I stepped on other actors' lines, repeatedly cutting them off or—worse—forgetting to come in when I was supposed to.

Every time I made a mistake, the entire cast *tightened,* ratcheted to a new level of tension. Stress radiated off of Ken—he was back to his constant movement, to his restless twitching. He paced up and down the theater aisles, and even with the theatrical lights blinding me, I could see him tugging at his hair, making his wiry gray curls stand on end.

With all the time we'd lost to Martina's accident, we didn't break for lunch. Instead, we kept right on rehearsing, moving immediately from the blockbuster, bring-down-the-house scene at the end of Act One directly into the song-and-dance extravaganza that kicked off Act Two. Everyone was tired, thirsty, hungry. Timothy's catering tables looked as if they'd been swarmed by Mongol hordes. Not that I went anywhere near the tables. I couldn't imagine dealing with Timothy, on top of everything else.

By the time we finished, all of us actors looked like the survivors of some natural disaster. Makeup streaked our collars. Our costumes were twisted; a few were torn. My lungs ached, and I realized that I'd been close to hyperventilating for the entire afternoon.

Ken gave us fifteen minutes to change into street clothes, and then he delivered his notes. He had detailed instructions for the conductor, dozens of references to late entrances, to lingering tremolos. He had specific comments on the singing, individual lines that he wanted to crisp up, to punch out, so that the audience could not miss their import. He reminded the dancers to focus on their arms, on keeping the visual lines of the show clean, crisp. He worked through every scene of the spoken play, giving countless recommendations to the actors playing Tom and Amanda, to Shawn's enemy playing the Gentleman Caller.

But he never said a word to me.

I felt like I'd become invisible, like I was only imagining that I was in the show. I knew that I'd been bad, but so bad that Ken wouldn't even *talk* to me? I sank deeper into my chair, wishing I could disappear.

Wishing... In the back of my mind, every time I'd flubbed a line, every time I'd made a mistake, I'd heard a little voice urging me to summon Teel. Press my fingers together, say his name, that's all I had to do and my genie would get me out of this mess.

I couldn't do that, though. I didn't want to succeed solely because of magic. It was one thing to hone my singing and dancing; I'd never claimed to be a musical theater star, before auditioning for *Menagerie!*

At heart, though, I *was* an actor. I was supposed to know how to deliver lines. If I spent my final wish perfecting my acting skills, then I'd be admitting failure to myself. I'd be admitting that I had fooled myself all along, every single time I'd ever dreamed of a successful theater career. If I summoned Teel, I might win the battle of *Menagerie!* but I would lose the war of my independent, self-respecting acting life.

I couldn't do it. No matter how disastrous the afternoon had been, I couldn't admit utter failure by making my fourth wish.

At last, Ken dismissed the rehearsal, reminding everyone to arrive half an hour early the next night, for our first preview performance. Everyone rushed away, chattering like squirrels, making plans to go out for drinks, promising to run lines just one more time. Ken stood at center stage, staring at the elaborate walls of the Wingfield apartment, the perfect recreation of their cluttered, stultifying home.

I finally excavated the courage to croak out two words: "I'm sorry."

Ken shook his head. "It's not your fault. It would have been impossible for anyone to step in this late."

"Maybe we can delay the premiere? Cancel the first week of previews and brush up on things?" I sounded like I was haggling for a trinket, bargaining at a flea market.

"Not a chance. The *Times* is coming tomorrow night. And the *Washington Post* is sending someone up—they've asked to take a backstage tour. They're doing a whole article on late-summer can't-miss getaways."

Can't miss.

I swallowed hard and forced myself to meet Ken's spaniel eyes. "I don't know what to say."

"Say that you'll go over the lines tonight. Say that you'll do your best tomorrow. That's all we can ask for."

I should have appreciated his support. I should have thanked him for his calm acceptance. But something inside me knew that he was speaking out of resignation, not confidence in my ability. I nodded and stalked toward the theater doors. I barely managed to wait until I was outside before I phoned Amy.

"What's wrong?" she asked, immediately picking up on my despair.

"I'm playing the lead in *Menagerie!* Starting with tomorrow's preview performance."

I thought that I could hear her raucous war whoop, all the way from New Jersey. "That's amazing! What did you do? Poison Martina?"

"Pushed her off the stage," I muttered.

"What? Just a second." Amy covered her phone, and I heard her shouting to some riot in the background.

"Quiet down! I'm on the phone with Aunt Erin." She returned her attention to me. "I could swear that you just said you pushed her off the stage."

"Okay, I didn't push her. But she fell. And I think it was my fault."

More muffled noise as Amy tried to quiet the troops. "What happened?" she finally asked.

I started to explain, started to describe the freak accident, but I only got partway through the story when I realized Amy couldn't hear a word that I was saying. "*What* is going on there?" I asked.

"Dr. Teel is here. He and Justin just cooked steaks on the grill, and Justin is setting the table so that we can eat before I head out to my Services Marketing seminar."

"*Justin* is setting the table?" I wondered if Amy was worried that aliens might have taken over her son's body.

My sister laughed—the first carefree belly laugh I'd heard from her in months. "You wouldn't believe it! He actually made his bed this morning without my asking—because Dr. Teel was coming over today!"

Amy babbled on for a couple more minutes. I could hear the joy in her voice, the release from stress. It wasn't the same lighthearted chatter that we had shared before Derek went overseas, but it was close enough. "Oh!" she finally cut herself off. "They've got everything on the table. I've got to run." Then, almost as an afterthought, she added, "Are you going to be okay?"

"I'll be fine," I said, trying to sound reassuring. I didn't need to worry much about acting. Amy wasn't really listening.

I shook my head as I terminated the call. Even if I'd considered using Teel to get out of my theatrical mess, even if I justified forfeiting my pride, the entire foundation of my acting career, I couldn't do that to Amy. Not now. Not with Justin showing so much improvement. Not with him behaving for the first time in two years. I couldn't let Teel escape to the Garden just yet.

I was a big girl. I could take care of myself. I just needed to get home, to read through my script, to study my notes. I had a whole night ahead of me—more than enough time to perfect the role of Laura Wingfield.

I was halfway through the first act, reciting my lines like a madwoman, when the apartment disappeared.

"Teel!" I bellowed, more exasperated than I'd ever been before. "I do not have time for this!"

He was wrapped in his doctor guise—wickedly glinting blue eyes, perfect hair more pepper than salt, a pure-white dress shirt slicing into perfect charcoal trousers. I couldn't believe that he'd actually spent the evening standing over a hot Weber grill; he looked completely unruffled, more ready for a night at the opera than an evening of child care.

Speaking of which... "Aren't you supposed to be taking care of Justin?"

"He'll never miss me. My time with you will only be a heartbeat for him. Unless...."

"Unless what?" I snapped. "Unless I make my fourth wish, and free you to go into your Garden, and you abandon him just when he's happy for the first time in months?"

"Well," Teel said, shrugging eloquently. "When you put it that way..."

"What other way *is* there to put it?" I was practically shouting. I didn't have time for this rigmarole. I had to get back to my apartment, back to my script. Fewer than twenty-four hours remained before I was making my Broadway debut, and I wasn't going to let my genie screw up anything. I glared at him. "How do you even know about what's going on with the show?"

"Amy told me, right after she got off the phone with you. She was really worried—she said you sounded completely overwrought. She almost skipped class, to come spend the night with you."

Great. My floundering theater career was going to make my sister fail out of business school, as well. I let my concern for her boil over into anger. "She had no right to tell you what's going on with me. I'm supposed to have some privacy, you know? I'm supposed to have a way of living my life, without your constant magical interference! I'm supposed—"

Teel took a step back, raising his perfectly muscled hands in front of him, pushing back at the invisible nothingness between us. "Erin, you really need to calm down. This sort of hysteria isn't going to help anything at all." He twisted his wrist and produced a prescription pad out of thin air. I thought that he was going to offer me some sort of pharmaceutical assistance, but instead he said, "Make that last wish, and everything will work out just fine. Doctor's orders."

I heard the seductive note in his voice. I'd felt the rumble of this incarnation's laugh, deep in his throat, as he held me close. I'd swooned beneath the attention of those lips....

Without thinking, I took a step closer to the unseen Garden. Another. Another.

And then I shook my head, throwing off the vestiges of control that my genie had cast over me. "Teel, stop it. I can't. I can't make my fourth wish now." I offered up the most selfless of the tangled reasons behind my thinking. "I can't leave Amy stranded. She needs you to help out with Justin."

As soon as I saw the scowl on Teel's handsome brow, I regretted saying the words. I'd tipped my hand. Like some sort of idiot child playing Go Fish, I'd announced exactly what I was looking for. "*That's* what's keeping you from wishing?" Teel said incredulously. "Because Amy needs me to babysit Justin?"

There was no way to unsay the words. I was left trying to explain. "It's not just the babysitting. It's the way he acts around you. You get him to help out around the house. He remembers what's right and what's wrong. He's a good kid, with you around."

"I do all that?" Teel asked, and his cultured doctor's voice was astonished. It sounded as if he'd never considered the possibility before. But then, he rapidly came down to earth. "Well, you don't need to worry about that anymore. I'm through with babysitting. Effective immediately."

"You can't do that!" I heard the sheer panic in my voice. He couldn't leave here, leave the Garden, and never go back to Amy's home. He couldn't leave Justin alone, unattended. Even if I sprinted to the bus station the instant that Teel freed me from the Garden, it would take me almost two hours to get to my nephew. Two hours when he could go climbing on the roof, playing out in traffic, running away from home, whatever other life-risking disasters his young mind could think of.

Teel shot his cuffs, as if he'd wrapped up some particularly difficult patient consultation. I caught the glint of his tattoo, but I refused to look at it. Instead, I stared into his cobalt eyes. "So help me, Teel. If you abandon Justin tonight, I will *never* make my fourth wish. I'll keep you waiting until the day I die."

He stared at me. "You wouldn't dare."

"Test. Me."

That steel was born of more than fear for Justin. I was tired of being manipulated. I was tired of being powerless. Tired of being buffeted by fate, by coincidence, by the power of a genie intent on seeing his Garden-bound lover sooner, rather than later.

I was tired of Teel interfering with my love life. With my family.

His kisses weren't real. They weren't true. I had exempted them from the Master Plan because they had nothing to do with my real life. And I was ready to take control again over that real life. I was ready to make my own decisions.

I raised my chin, and I said, "I won't do it, Teel. I'll hold on to my wish, until long after Jaze has left the Garden. He'll go on to grant a hundred more wishes, a thousand more, whatever total your genie rules require. He'll go *back* to the Garden again, three times, four, and you will never set foot inside there. Do not threaten me. Do not threaten Justin. And keep away from the theater. Keep away from Timothy."

Something inside Teel collapsed. I couldn't define what it was—he still had the broad shoulders of a medical Adonis. He still had the perfect hair, the flawless eyes, the sculpted lips that beckoned to me.

But something crumpled inside him. Some perfect

certainty, some absolute knowledge that he was right, that he could manipulate me, that he could get his way in this, as in all other things.

"All right," he said, and he used the same tone of voice that the other surgeon had used back at the hospital, the doctor who had come to Amy and me in defeat to say that Justin was lost forever. "You win."

"Really?" I couldn't help but question his submission.

"I won't drag Justin into this." His eyes were pulled back to the unseen fence, to the invisible Garden beyond. "Justin is safe tonight. You know I'd never hurt him. But after tonight, I'm through. After Amy gets home from class, I won't see him again."

"That's not fair!" I protested. "He won't understand!"

"You'll find a way to explain it. Tell him that I had a job to do. Like his father."

"Teel—"

"I won't give you this power over me. I won't give you that reason to hold back your wish."

I wanted to protest. I wanted to tell him that he wasn't being fair, that he was using a little boy to get what he wanted.

But I heard the hypocrisy before I even formed the words in my mind. I had just been willing to use Justin for *my* own cause. I could hardly blame Teel for doing the same. Both of us made me sick.

"And Timothy?" I asked, because I had to say something.

Teel looked surprised. "I don't care about Timothy. Your love life is your own responsibility."

"You're the one who kissed me!"

"If I recall, you kissed me back."

And he was right, of course. I *had* kissed him back. I'd told myself that it didn't matter, that it was outside the Plan, that it was separate and apart from my actual life. But nothing was separate. Everything was all entwined—Amy and Justin, Teel and Timothy. My life was a knot of family and friends, and I was the only one responsible for unraveling the tangle I'd created.

I should just let Teel go. I should wait until Amy got home, then use my last wish to guarantee a perfect performance. That's what I'd wanted, from the very beginning. That was how I'd intended to shape my career.

But I couldn't. I still needed to prove to myself that I could make *Menagerie!* work. Under my own power.

"Fine," I said to Teel, heaving a huge, exhausted sigh. "Just take me back, for now. I have a lot of work to do, and it all has to be done tonight."

Silently, Teel raised his fingers to his earlobe. His face was carved with a fatigue I'd never seen there before, and I realized that our emotional skirmish had exhausted him. He tugged twice, and electricity shot across every last one of my nerve endings as I was catapulted back to my own living room.

* * *

Four hours later, I was seriously considering leaving a ransom note, faking my own kidnapping and disappearing from New York City forever.

I had started through the script five separate times, muttering my lines in an auctioneer's patter. If I flubbed the words three times in any one scene, I forced myself back to the beginning. The rule made sense—I needed to know the lines so thoroughly that I didn't have to think about them. They needed to be a part of me, ingrained so deeply that I could concentrate on the songs, on the dance, on everything that made *Menagerie!* magical.

The biggest problem was that Ken had changed a lot of the original Tennessee Williams dialog. I could no longer put my finger on when he'd made all of the modifications—it wasn't like he'd started out to write a better play than the master. No, the changes had happened because Martina had wanted a larger part, more central staging, more time onstage. Try as I might, my memory kept lapsing into the original, into the finely crafted show that I'd memorized years before, on the college stage.

In a perfect world, we could have transformed it back. Without Martina around to complain, we could have returned to Tennessee Williams's pure, lyrical scenes, we could have deleted all of the accumulated garbage that had piled up in rehearsals.

But it was too late for that. The other actors had memorized their new lines; they knew their entrances and exits based on the new script. There was no way to go back; I could only forge ahead.

Somewhere along the way, I started pacing. I moved from table to couch to chair, back and forth, across the row of floor-to-ceiling windows. For the first ten rounds, Tabitha shadowed me, weaving between my ankles in death-defying feats of feline attention-getting. When I showed no sign of stopping, however, she commandeered one of the throw pillows on the couch and began the meticulous grooming of her paws. I forced myself not to pay attention to her as I started round one thousand four hundred twenty-seven of line recitation.

All the while, one part of my brain was vaguely aware that the late-summer sunlight was slipping away. Lights twinkled on in the buildings between the Bentley and the river. The sky turned indigo, then violet, then black.

I was running out of time.

Still, I paced. I wrestled with the script. I tried to pour the disjointed words into my skull, connect them to my tongue, wire them to my arms and legs as if I could invent a robot Laura, a guaranteed creature that would never fail the show, fail the cast, fail Ken. Fail my dream of who I wanted to be.

I was so intent on muttering lines that I almost missed the knock at the door. I froze, certain that I was imagining things. I glanced at my watch and was astonished to see that it was after ten o'clock. Tabitha was curled into a tight ball on the couch, one of her paws covering her nose and eyes, as if she could not bear my presence any longer.

Before I could convince myself that my panic was bringing on auditory hallucinations, there was another tap at my door. I peered through the peephole and was astonished to see Timothy. I threw open the door. "What are *you* doing here?"

He flashed a tight panther smile. "I figured you'd be frantic about now."

I started to react indignantly, but gave up the emotion halfway through making the face. "Come on in."

He stepped inside. Neither of us looked toward the couch. I ran my hands down my sides, trying to shove my fingers into my trouser pockets. My sweatpants didn't have any pockets. I had to fill the silence that was gumming up the air between us. "I guess Lucky

Red Dragon wasn't so lucky, was it?"

Timothy shrugged. "The stuff is probably toxic. She's better off not drinking it."

A month ago, I would have laughed. Now, my face felt like it would break if I reacted to anything he said. "Look, Timothy. About Teel—"

"I was wrong. I shouldn't have pushed."

"No—"

"I told you I wasn't going to compete against the guy, though. I lied."

"What?" I had heard all the words, but I couldn't figure out what they meant.

"I said I wasn't going to compete. But then I thought about him keeping you company tonight. I thought about him telling you that everything was going to be all right. I thought about him being the one to hold you, to help you. And I knew that I wasn't going to let him do that without a fight."

He pinned me with the hypnotic gaze of a cat tracking prey. The muscles in my legs went slack; I honestly thought that I would fall, if I didn't reach out for the back of the sofa.

"So," Timothy said. "Is he here?"

I shook my head. Timothy looked past me, into the kitchen. He glanced to his left, toward the shadowed bedroom.

"He was," I said, my voice so soft that I wondered if Timothy could hear me. "He was, but we fought."

Timothy had heard me. He'd stiffened at my first words. I almost didn't recognize him when he asked, "About what?"

"You," I whispered. "And Justin. And how Teel thought he could control me."

"Thought?" Timothy moved closer, barely breathing the word.

I nodded. "It's over." I chose my words carefully, plucking each one from the silence between us. "I know you won't believe me. I can't really explain, but the thing I had with Teel was never real. It was never...true. It was a stupid game that I played because I could." I shrugged. Without being able to divulge Teel's actual identity, that was the best that I could do. "It's over," I repeated.

Timothy closed the distance between us. His hands framed my face, and heat radiated from his fingers into my flesh. His lips on mine were hot, hard, but they gentled as I responded. His arms shifted, folding around me, pulling me close, and I let myself melt into the iron support of his body.

This wasn't the pure, electric bliss of kissing a genie. It wasn't an ecstatic impossible union with magic. Instead, it was the earthy support of a true, human man, the constancy and certainty of a man who knew what he wanted, who was willing to fight for what he got.

I wanted to lace my fingers between his. I wanted to guide him to my bedroom. I wanted to collapse onto my bed with him, to finish the conversation that we'd begun months before, in the courtyard outside his restaurant.

But I couldn't. I still had lines to learn. I still had a show to prepare for, a cast that was counting on me, against all odds.

"I can't," I whispered against the raspy growth of his beard. "I have to go through the script again."

He sighed, and his arms loosened just a fraction.

"How is it going?"

Hating the answer I had to give, I clutched him closer, stealing back the space he'd made between us. "I can't get through the scenes. I can't hold on to the lines. I know that I know them, but I just can't keep them straight."

Impossibly, he laughed. When I pulled away in indignation, he settled his arms around my waist, keeping me close. "What did you eat for dinner?"

What did I eat for *dinner?* What sort of question was that? I hadn't had *time* to eat dinner! I had lines to memorize. I had blocking to review. I had an emergency to survive.

He stepped away from me and nodded. "That's what I thought." He glided past me, into the kitchen.

I stared as he pulled open the refrigerator door. A bottle of water glinted on the top shelf. An apple rolled around in one of the bins. A bottle of ketchup leaned against a jar of mayonnaise in the door. "You're kidding," he asked. "Right?"

"I don't eat at home a lot," I said, blushing as he slid over to the pantry. Even I was a little embarrassed by the confession there: an empty box of granola bars and the soy sauce packets from some long-ago Chinese takeout. At least there were a dozen cans of cat food. Tabitha didn't go hungry, even if I couldn't put together a meal fit for an anorexic supermodel.

"No wonder all of you actors attack the catering table," he said. "This is crazy."

"There hasn't been time," I said. "With the show opening..." I trailed off, afraid to say the word *tomorrow.*

He shook his head. "This is like a bad TV competition. Even I can't put anything together with this." He glanced at the glass-clad cabinets, at the full complement of dishes and bowls and glasses that had been left behind by Becca. He took a quick look at the clock on the stove, and he said, "Wait here."

Before I could protest, he let himself out the front door. The nearest grocery was the bodega over on Eighth. It would take him at least twenty minutes to get there and back. That would give me a chance to run through the first scene again.

Only five minutes passed, though, before there was another knock at the door.

"Where—" I started to ask as Timothy edged past me. He had a carton of eggs under one arm and a brick of cheddar cheese in the other. A cloth grocery bag was slung over his arm, and I could just make out fronds of fresh herbs at the top.

"Dani," he said.

"You woke her?"

He grinned. "Wednesday nights are the regular Guerilla Gathering. I was going to take a chance that she'd still be awake, but I could hear them all talking before I knocked. They're planning their autumn attacks, and things are getting a little heated."

I followed Timothy into the kitchen. Tabitha deigned to take an interest in our late-night activity; she started butting her head against Timothy's leg, weaving between his feet in an effort to get him to drop some cheese onto the floor. He made a cooing noise in the back of his throat, but he didn't waste any time setting to work. As if by magic, he extracted a frying pan from a drawer. The smell of melting butter soon had my mouth watering.

"Towson, Maryland," he said, as he rotated the cookware, coating the surface evenly.

"What?"

"That's where I grew up. Wasn't that the question you asked me on Sunday?"

I winced, thinking of that abortive conversation. "I shouldn't have come over there. I had no right to interfere in your home like that."

He caught my gaze and held it steadily. "I'm glad you did. Even if I didn't do a great job of telling you so."

"No, I mean, I should have figured out some other way of talking to you. I should have figured out a way to explain during those three weeks. To tell you about the Plan."

"The Plan?" He glanced at the frying pan. The butter was dark, nearly brown. He moved it off the burner and turned off the flame. "What Plan?"

"It was a stupid idea that Amy had. To help me get over Sam."

"Sam?" Timothy looked totally lost.

"Brooks Brother lawyer? Joined me for dinner at Garden Variety one night?"

Timothy nodded. "And didn't like ordering without a menu. Hated the idea that I had a table for my private guests."

"That's the one." I shook my head. It seemed like Sam and I had broken up a century ago.

"So? What's the Plan?"

"Amy says I rush into things. She says I need to prove that I'm responsible. She's my older sister, and she's always been more organized than I am. She's always been right, so I went ahead and agreed. I promised."

Timothy leaned back against the counter and folded his arms across his chest. The action showed off the muscles in his arms, and I had to swallow hard. "I'm not going to like this very much, am I?"

I took a deep breath. "I have to keep a plant alive for a month. And then I can get a fish. When I keep the fish alive for three months, I can get a cat. After a year with the cat, I can date a man."

Timothy laughed.

"I'm serious," I shouted.

"And that's supposed to be your plant." He gestured to the corner of the counter. The dead peace lily looked even worse, now that it was coated with dust. I nodded. "And your fish." He pointed at the empty bowl. "And you got yourself a cat."

Tabitha obliged by jumping onto the counter. I picked her up and returned her to the floor. "She was in heat," I confessed. "I let her get pregnant."

"So that night that we came back here..."

I had to look away. It all sounded so stupid, now that we were talking in the kitchen. But then, when we were face-to-face, on my couch... "I felt like I was lying to Amy. Lying to myself. I mean, I'd made a promise!" I sighed. "But it's more than that. It's more than a stupid game. I feel like I ruin everything I touch. I've never succeeded on my own. I've never shown that I can make it here in New York, make it onstage. Before *Menagerie!* I had more catering gigs than I did actual acting jobs. I needed the Plan, to prove that I could stick with something. Anything."

I sensed him move, more than I saw him. His thumb and forefinger were gentle on my chin as he made me look at him. "'Needed', you said. And now?" he asked.

He was standing too close to me. He was looking at me too steadily. My heart was thundering in my throat. I wanted to step away; I wanted to step toward him. "I'm not much good at working the Plan," I whispered.

"I think I'm glad about that," he said.

He brushed another kiss across my lips with matter-of-fact certainty—no fireworks, no impossible flare of unimaginable pleasure. Just reality. Long, lasting reality.

He turned around and replaced the frying pan on the burner. "One brother," he said, as he cracked eggs into a bowl, talking as if we hadn't taken a break to discuss my crazy, mixed-up Plan. "No sisters. Mom and Dad still live in Towson—it's a house in the suburbs near Baltimore, just like every other house in the suburbs. Public school, ran cross-country. I had a dog."

"A dog?" I asked, as he whipped half a dozen eggs into a saffron-colored froth.

"I grew up with a lab mix. Fred. Mom and Dad have a corgi now." He shook his head slightly. "And what was your other question? Favorite color? Blue. Dark blue, though. Not anything pastel."

I leaned back against the counter. "Like the lines in a blueprint?"

He glanced at me quickly. "I went to University of Maryland. I was going to be an architect—I took five years of classes for it. But somewhere along the way, I realized that it took too long."

"The classes?"

He flexed his fingers before he found my saltshaker. "The job. Projects stretch out, year after year. I could spend three and a half years creating the perfect stairway banister, and I'd never get any closer to really helping people. Really having an effect on their lives."

"So you became a chef."

He shrugged and ground some fresh pepper into the bowl. "Everybody eats. Every day. It seemed like a more direct way to do things."

As I absorbed that, he quirked a questioning eyebrow. "Plates?" he asked, as if that were the most natural next thing to talk about.

I took them out of the cabinet. Trying to hold up my end of the bargain, I also collected silverware from a drawer. I poured tall glasses of water for both of us. Timothy worked some magic with the skillet and a spatula, and he carried both plates out to the dining room table, avoiding the slinky land mine that was Tabitha.

I took my first bite, and all thoughts melted from my head. "This is amazing," I said.

He grinned, like a cat lapping up cream. "So? Are we going to run lines from the show?"

"Run lines?"

"Isn't that what you were doing when I got here?" He nodded toward my script, toward the scrunched pages where I'd dropped them on the couch. "Go on," he said. "Tom's first line is, 'Laura, you don't know how difficult it is out there.'"

I stared at him. "How do you know that?"

"I've spent enough time over at rehearsal, haven't I?" And then he repeated, "'Laura, you don't know how difficult it is out there.'"

He was quoting from my first scene, the most difficult, because it wove together new lines and old like a patched Depression-era quilt. "'Tom,'" I said, dredging up the response. "'Was work hard today?'"

"'Hard,'" Timothy recited, spearing another bite of eggs. "'They don't understand what a man can do.'"

The next line rose without my thinking about it, and the one after that. I recited the text as easily as if I were reading it in front of me. Timothy grinned and crossed the room to retrieve my script. There was a limit to what he could memorize, after all. He was a chef, not an actor. He settled the pages on the table between us, flipping to the right place with a minimum of effort.

And so we fed each other, tossing lines back and forth over the omelet. When our plates were empty, Timothy returned to the kitchen. He produced a peach from the bottom of the bag, and a melon that was not much larger than his fist. I watched in amazement as he reduced them to a summer fruit salad, adding slivers of fresh basil and a splash of something that turned out to be white balsamic vinegar.

We moved on to the second act, not pausing as Timothy found my teakettle, as he dug out a spray of mint leaves that rapidly became an aromatic tisane. We plowed through the play's climax, the shattering of the glass animals that gave the show its name, the final scenes of pure, high emotion that wove together new lines and old, the staid and the experimental.

"And that leads into the reprise of 'My World, My Dream,'" I said, after reciting my last line.

"Perfect." Timothy leaned back in his chair. Tabitha had climbed onto his lap sometime during our recitation. Her shed white hairs stood out against his black T-shirt, but he didn't seem to mind.

"I can't believe that you knew those opening lines."

"So do you," he pointed out. "And the entire rest of the script. And you can do the song and dance numbers, as well."

I grinned, but the action turned to a yawn. "Excuse me," I said, embarrassed. I looked at the teacups on the table between us. "Thank you," I said, and I caught the next yawn in my throat. "I don't mean to be rude, but I need to go through all of that again, and I don't want to bore you to tears."

"You could never bore me to tears," he said. And suddenly, we weren't talking about the play. We weren't talking about the rescue package of a late-night dinner, of a dessert, of completely unexpected companionship on the night that I truly had believed my entire professional life was falling apart.

We were talking about that kiss that we had shared. We were talking about the potential that had hummed on our lips.

His eyes looked black in the dim light. His gaze was so intense that I wanted to look away, wanted to bury my face in my hands, wanted to do something—anything—to escape the ferocity of that expression.

"Timothy—" I said, but I had no idea how I was going to finish that sentence.

"Go lie down." He nodded toward the bedroom. My eyes widened, but he shook his head. A smile chased his lips. "You're exhausted. Rest for a few minutes while I clean up out here, and then we'll run the lines again."

My intended protest was foiled by another yawn. "Just run water in them," I said. "I'll clean up later."

"Fine," he said, but I could tell that he was lying; he was going to wash all the dishes.

Tabitha padded after me as I crossed to the bedroom. I kicked off my shoes and lay down on top of my comforter. I heard the water running in the kitchen, soft and soothing. I closed my eyes. Tabitha jumped onto the bed and stretched out along my side. Her purring was loud, so loud that I could barely make out the sound of Timothy in the kitchen. I took a deep breath, exhaling as I heard Timothy's amused voice reciting Tom's first line.

I was asleep before I could deliver Laura's reply.

Chapter 15

SUNSHINE WAS STREAMING through my bedroom windows when I woke up.

That wasn't the light of dawn, creeping around my shades. It wasn't the tentative light of early morning, luring me back to wakefulness. No, I was facing the full blast of summer, the sun high in the sky.

I started swearing even before I looked at my clock.

11:55.

I had slept away half the day. Half the day, when I should have been reading through my script, when I should have been practicing my lines, my dance moves, my solo songs.

And Timothy had let me do it. More than that, I realized, Timothy had *helped* me to do it. He'd come in sometime during the night, settling a fleece throw over my shoulders. He must have removed my shoes from their haphazard scramble at the foot of the bed also—they were lined up neatly by my closet door, presumably so that I wouldn't break my neck when I got out of bed.

I hadn't heard him at all, hadn't been aware that

he'd been anywhere near me. I guess I'd been more exhausted than I'd thought. A lot more exhausted.

"Hello?" I called as I scrambled to my feet. "Timothy?"

Silence.

I ran my fingers through my hair, rejecting the idea of taking a shower. The guy had seen me at my strung-out worst the night before; he could hardly be put off by bed-head. On second thought, I did run a quick toothbrush around my mouth, splashed water on my face, scrubbed my cheeks to pink brightness with a towel. Some sights were just too terrifying to contemplate, for anyone.

"Timothy?" I called again, as I ventured out of my bedroom.

But Timothy was nowhere to be seen. I realized that I'd been expecting to find him stretched out on the couch, his black jeans contrasting with the light upholstery. I'd expected to see him waiting for me with a lazy smile, with an apology for letting me sleep, for letting me waste the last day before my Broadway debut.

Instead, all I found was Tabitha, stretched out in the longest square of sunlight she could find. She twisted lazily as I entered the room, putting her ears back and yawning as if she were possessed. When I failed to be impressed by her curled tongue and her mighty incisors, she devoted her attention to grooming her side.

So, one spoiled house cat, holding place of pride in the living room sunlight. No restaurateur anywhere in sight.

If I had to be honest with myself, I'd admit that I was disappointed.

I stumbled into the kitchen. On the counter, next to

the stove, was a shining thermos. One of my mugs sat beside it, the handle beckoning to my hand. As I stepped closer, I saw a loaf of bread wrapped in a white napkin. A small pewter pot of butter was buried deep in the linen folds—just like at Garden Variety. Timothy must have raided the restaurant to set out the treat for me.

I burrowed beneath the linen and touched the bread. It still had a hint of warmth, just a whispered reminder of the oven. All of a sudden, the rich, yeasty aroma made my stomach clench. Sure, Timothy's midnight omelet had been an unexpected treat, but that had been hours ago. A lifetime ago.

I tore into the bread like a starving woman. I bolted the first hunk without butter, relishing the crunch of the crust between my teeth. I forced myself to slow down, to chew, to swallow. As I slathered butter onto the second chunk of bread, I saw that Timothy had left me a note.

"Erin—Thought you could use the rest. Enjoy tea and breakfast, then take a long bath (check the fridge)."

He'd signed it with a capital T—the initial dashed off like an afterthought.

Check the fridge.

I opened the KitchenAid door with a little apprehension, only to find that my empty refrigerator had turned into an herbal garden. Safe from Tabitha's feline interest, sheaves of lavender rested on the top shelf. The fragrant flowers were bright in the well-lit interior. A small jar nestled between the stalks. I unscrewed the lid and dipped a finger inside. A salt rub, apparently made with some high-end oil. I sniffed. A touch of eucalyptus, by the smell of things.

Tears sprang to my eyes.

Maybe I was so emotional because I wasn't fully awake, after my unplanned sleepathon. Maybe I felt like sobbing because I was nervous about the night to come, about my Broadway debut. Maybe that tiny ache pounded in my temples because I was hungry, because I hadn't bolstered my body's defenses with all of the bread that Timothy had left, with any protein, with anything approaching a balanced diet.

Or maybe I was just touched that someone—no, that *Timothy*—had reached out to me. That he had done all of this for me. That he had realized how panicked I was the night before, that he had fed me, that he had recognized how much I needed to sleep... That he had even understood how starving I'd be upon awakening... That he had cared so much about me.

My tote bag was lying on the kitchen counter. I dug around in it until I found my phone, then punched in his number before I could convince myself not to. Four rings, then voice mail. I didn't leave a message. I couldn't sort out my words; everything sounded too dramatic, too *deep and meaningful,* too desperate.

I swallowed hard and snapped the phone closed, tossing it onto the counter as if I were afraid it might bite me. It skittered across the granite, coming to rest against my desiccated lily. The phone was reflected in the clear glass of Tennessee's fishbowl.

Okay, so, I'd failed at the Master Plan—failed and left all the evidence in plain sight, as a constant reminder of how much I had to learn, of how much I needed to accomplish, before I'd be fit for a real relationship, for an adult give-and-take with a man worth my time. Like a mantra, I repeated to myself that I'd killed my plant, killed my fish, let my cat get pregnant.

I knew that I was supposed to start at the beginning. I was supposed to build up to a real relationship with a live, breathing man. I was supposed to take baby steps, to prove to myself and to Amy and to all the world that I could handle things. That I was an adult. That I was mature.

To hell with the Master Plan.

It was all a ridiculous game, anyway. Who was to say that a peace lily was the right type of plant? Why was a goldfish more important than a neon tetra? Why was Tabitha the cat I was supposed to care for—couldn't I have waited until I found a cat on my own, adopted a kitten from the shelter, chosen another feline companion, one that wasn't in heat when she arrived on my doorstep?

All of it—the plants, the animals—they were just a way to avoid making a commitment. To avoid taking responsibility for who I was. Who I wanted to be.

The Master Plan was a way for me to isolate myself, to cut myself off from the real world, from responsibility. The Master Plan built a wall around me as effectively as any wall that Laura Wingfield had ever erected, with her precious, fragile spun-glass animals.

I was stronger than that, though. I was strong enough to run my life without the Master Plan.

As soon as I reached Timothy, I would tell him exactly how I felt. I would kiss him and not draw back out because of some stupid sense of obligation, some idiotic belief that I owed myself, that I owed Amy, that I owed some unattainable, textbook ideal that had seemed like a really great concept when I'd just lost the boyfriend of my dreams. Lost the boyfriend of my nightmares, as things turned out. In the end, Sam had not been worth one split second of emotional agony.

From this day forward, I was going to do what I wanted to do, not what was dictated to me. That's what I should have done a long time before.

Better late than never.

I pulled my trash can out from beneath my sink. Refusing to make a ceremony of my action, refusing to give the stupid Master Plan any more power over me than I'd already given it for the past three months, I dumped the dried-out peace lily into the white plastic liner. A small cloud of dust puffed up as it hit the bottom, a reminder of just how long I'd delayed taking charge of my life. I steeled myself against feeling guilty and tossed the fishbowl after.

Literally and figuratively dusting the past from my palms, I poured a mug of tea from the thermos Timothy had left behind. The scent of Earl Grey rose from the steam, a perfect complement to the armful of lavender that I excavated from the refrigerator. I carried the herbs into the bathroom and turned on the water in the tub. While it filled, I headed back to the kitchen, grabbing another generous hunk of bread and spreading it with warm, soft butter before I picked up my mug.

I made the bathwater as hot as I could stand it. The lavender floated on the surface, tiny petals spreading as they soaked up the water, as they yielded their fragrance. I stripped out of the clothes that I'd worn to rehearsal the day before—a lifetime ago—and I took the opportunity to roll my neck around, to work out the worst kinks of tension that had settled deep inside my muscles, inside my bones. Grabbing a couple of extra towels, I rolled one into a pillow, positioning it to cradle my head against the tub's hard rim.

Making sure that my tea and the salt scrub were within reach, I eased myself into the water. The heat melted my bones, soothed my muscles. The scent wafted over me, enveloped me. When I closed my eyes, I drifted away—I could have been anywhere, anytime.

I couldn't say how long I soaked in that luxurious bath. At some point, I used the salt scrub, rubbing it into my elbows, into my knees, working it between my toes. For long minutes, I leaned back against my towel pillow, closing my eyes and thinking that the finest spa on earth could never be more luxurious than this.

As the water started to cool, I decided to run through my lines. Each and every word perched on the tip of my tongue, ready to tumble out. All of my hesitation from the night before, all of my uncertainty, had been washed away during the night. I couldn't say if the lines came easier because I'd successfully run them with Timothy the night before, or whether they'd fallen into place because I'd slept on them, or if they'd become accessible because I was so perfectly relaxed. Whatever the reason, I did not stumble over a single word. As I spoke, I could picture where I was supposed to stand, what I was supposed to do. The entire show was laid out before me, like a movie that I could pause on a DVD, a recording that I could break down frame by frame, second by second.

At last, it was time to emerge from the perfection of my bath. I wrapped myself in a gigantic bath sheet, luxuriating in another towel to gather up the dripping ends of my hair.

I took my time getting dressed. I dawdled over choosing slacks. Ultimately, I went with the always-appropriate-for-Manhattan black, sleek trousers that hugged my body just enough to show they cared about my making my best impression. I added a wintergreen peasant blouse, pleased with the way the fabric complemented my skin tone. My cheeks still glowed pink from the heat of my bath.

I towel-dried my hair. The costume mistress would tuck it under a wig for my role as Laura. That way my spoken-word character's mousy brown mess could be traded for lustrous locks in the end-of-show dance extravaganza.

Similarly, I didn't bother with makeup. I'd get a full palette of the stuff once I arrived at the theater. We were well past the years when actors wore orange pancake makeup, but the experts would load me up with a much thicker foundation that I typically used on my own. They'd go light on the blush, and my lips would stay relatively natural in tone, but my eyes would get a heavy dose of mascara and eyeliner. They would sparkle from the last row in the theater.

I slipped on some strappy sandals. I loved the way they made me feel, as if I were queen of some private domain. The heels clicked on the tile floor in the kitchen as I headed out to finish off the loaf of bread. I supplemented the creamy butter with the last of the cheddar cheese, which Timothy had left in the fridge. There were a few bites of fruit salad, as well, not as sparkling, not as bright, as it had been for my surprise midnight meal, but welcome all the same.

I could get used to having food in my kitchen.

Tabitha came to investigate as I swallowed the last

of my late lunch. Or early dinner. Whatever—the theater forced us actors to keep strange hours. I bent down and scritched the cat's head, eliciting immediate purrs of approval. Feeling festive, I gave her a full can of fresh food. She was eating for an entire litter of kittens, after all.

That thought reminded me that I still had to coerce my sister into taking at least two of the kittens. I had been totally scattered when I'd talked to Amy the day before. I glanced at my watch. She must be in class at this hour. Oh, well. I could leave her a message.

"Hey, Ame, it's me. I should have said this yesterday, but I was a little nuts. I'm leaving tickets for you at the box office—they'll be under your name."

I knew that she'd make it. No matter what she had on her calendar, no matter what classes or study group, my only sister wouldn't miss my Broadway debut. As I savored that phrase—*my Broadway debut*—I thought about the breezy message I'd just left for her. Stars of shows always left tickets at the box office.

I was the star. I could do whatever I wanted to do. The theater staff would cooperate. They always did. Besides, there was no way that I'd be asking for more than Martina had demanded.

I wrinkled my nose at the thought of our dearly departed diva, and I collected my script and my tote. I looked around the kitchen one last time before trying to call Timothy again. Another four rings. Another pickup from his voice mail. This time, I did stammer out a message: "Hi. It's me. Um, Erin. Um, thanks, um, for everything. I mean, um, the bread was amazing. And, um, the lavender. Um. I'm heading over to the theater. Um, I'll leave a ticket for you at the, um, will-call window. Um, thanks."

There. That had been brilliant. Why hadn't I done that before, when I'd first gotten his voice mail? I grimaced and wished that I could invent a device that would let me delete stupid messages I'd left on other people's cell phones. Oh, well. There was nothing to be done for it now.

I looked around the apartment. I was out of things to do. I was out of tactics to delay my trip to the theater. I was out of details to distract myself.

It was time to head uptown for my opening night on Broadway.

* * *

As soon as I set foot in the theater, time sped up.

My leisurely sleeping in was immediately a thing of memory. My luxurious bath could have happened months ago. My calm, cool and collected stroll to Times Square might never have happened.

The house manager tracked me down first—he wanted to know how many tickets I needed. I told him that I was only expecting three guests—my sister, Justin and Timothy. He looked at me like I was speaking in tongues. "This is the first night of previews," he reminded me unnecessarily. "Everyone has a ton of guests first night of previews."

I smiled and said, "I didn't know that I'd be going on until yesterday. I'll hit you up for more tickets, later in the run."

Those words sounded so sweet on my lips—*later in the run*—that I didn't even see the house manager scurry away.

Ken grabbed me next. He was bouncing on the balls of his feet, so full of energy that I wanted to add a tether to keep him from launching into the catwalks. "Let's run through the first scene. I want to make sure you've got it—it was really rough yesterday."

Again, I found my serene smile. "I've got it, Ken," I said. He hollered for the other actors, and we ran the scene. I tried not to be offended by his amazement, by his pure and utter shock that I had the scene down cold. He had us continue through our paces, linking up spoken scene to spoken scene, skipping over the song and dance numbers in between.

I was warmed by the applause of my fellow actors as Tom delivered his final line. They all stared at me, obviously astonished by what we had accomplished. Yesterday's disastrous rehearsal was rapidly becoming a distant memory.

The choreographer grabbed me next. He led all of the dancers through a vigorous warm-up, starting out with stretching exercises, leading into some aggressive form of yoga. We finished by going through the show's most challenging combinations. Of course, with my Teel-backed abilities, I had no problem with that part of the show.

Nor with the singing that we did after that.

Acting, dancing, singing—I'd dashed through all of my onstage obligations. I had clearly surpassed everyone's expectations—the cast was virtually humming around me as we wandered back to the dressing rooms. Rumors started to percolate about reviewers in the house, about journalists waiting to write about our creation.

The stage manager announced, "Half hour," warning us that we only had thirty minutes before the show began. I called out, "Thank you!" automatically, falling back on the etiquette of years of doing plays.

I knew that I should take this last snippet of time to review the script, to walk through the blocking, to test myself one last time.

But I didn't need to.

I was ready to go onstage as Laura Wingfield. I was ready to star in *Menagerie!*

I left the dressing room and went backstage, savoring every minute of this incredible night. I stood in the shadows behind the set, listening to the growing hum of the audience filling the house.

"There you are!" I jumped at the voice, whirling around even before the exclamation had faded away.

"Shawn!" My fellow understudy stood in the shadows. A bouquet of long-stem roses sprayed across his arm, gigantic petals of pink and yellow and peach giving off a fragrance so powerful they might have been dipped in air freshener. "What are you doing here?"

He sashayed forward and kissed me on the cheek. "Mmm," he said. "Lavender." I probably blushed, but my cheeks were invisible in the dim light backstage. Shawn thrust his magnificent roses into my arms. "You know I wouldn't miss your debut, sweetie!"

Those tears that had plagued me earlier in the day were suddenly close to the surface again. "Shawn—" I said, but my voice broke.

"Now, stop it. The *last* thing you want is to ruin your makeup."

I attempted to smother my emotions by burying my face in the flowers. "These are amazing," I said. "You shouldn't have."

He tucked a rogue spray of baby's breath back into the arrangement. "I *shouldn't* have been such a bitch yesterday." He rolled his eyes in exaggerated condemnation of himself. "I just couldn't believe that *you* had done what we'd talked about so many times before. You had the courage to get rid of Martina, and I'm left standing in the wings!"

"Shawn, you know that I did nothing of the sort!"

His smile was wicked as he shook his head. "Of course not. My lips are sealed." He mimed turning a key in a lock.

"Shawn—" I started.

"Hush, sweetie. Congratulations. I know you're going to knock 'em dead."

I swallowed hard. "Thank you. Let me just go put these in water."

He took the roses back from me. "I'll take care of that for you. What else are we understudies good for, on opening night?"

"Shawn—" I began again.

"Hush," he said. He danced three steps toward the dressing room before he turned back. "And, Erin, sweetie? Break a leg!"

I started to protest, but he only laughed. The old theater good-luck mantra would never be the same for me. I settled for shaking my head and sighing as my partner in crime—or at least backstage gossip—disappeared around the corner of the set.

Before I was truly ready, the stage manager called all of us actors to our places. The house lights dimmed, and the audience grew quiet. The house lights went out completely, and we actors quick-walked to our spots, striking our poses for our opening scene.

And then the curtain rose.

My first lines were waiting for me, like old friends

who were thrilled to learn that I had finally come to visit. My body remembered where to move as I spoke. Instinctively, I mastered when to look back at my fellow actors, how to share the scene with them.

The audience was with me from the very beginning. I heard them gasp at one cutting line, laugh at a touch of comic relief. The applause after my first song shook me to my toenails—I'd never realized how powerful the ballad could be, how much empathy it could evoke from the crowd. I froze in the spotlight, accepting the adulation, preserving that long, perfect moment before the play moved on.

As the spotlight went out, freeing me to dart offstage, I sneaked a glance into the audience. Impossibly, I could see Amy and Justin sitting in the very front row. I was astonished to realize that Teel was beside them, fully decked out in his doctor persona. I wondered how the house manager had found him a seat, how the ticket had become available, but I didn't have long to dwell on the problem. I glanced to Teel's left, looking for Timothy, but he wasn't there. I looked to Amy's right. No Timothy there, either.

The edge of my elation frayed.

Before I could wonder what had happened, before I could worry that Timothy had somehow missed the show, the door opened at the back of the theater. Over the orchestra pit, across the audience, with the stage lights in my eyes, I couldn't begin to make out who slipped into the house. I only caught a glimpse of an usher's flashlight, of some late-arriving patron being whisked to the side.

There was someone else, though. Someone who didn't seek a seat in the crowded audience. Someone who stood just inside the door, perfectly still, silhouetted against the cool, blue light of the lobby, in the heartbeat before the door whispered closed.

I knew that shape. I'd seen it first, in the courtyard of Garden Variety. I could almost smell the Earl Grey tea that Timothy had drunk that night, the first time that I had entered his restaurant domain.

Timothy was in the theater. He stood at the back of the house, eschewing a seat, but he was there. To see me. To support me. To watch me play the role of my life.

The audience's applause had faded. The stagehands had changed the set; I was supposed to be offstage, in the wings, listening as Amanda and Tom fought another of their endless scorpion battles. Any instant now, the lights would come up, my mistake would be revealed. One of the stagehands hissed my name; she beckoned toward me from the shadows offstage.

I shook my head to clear it, casting off the sudden, choking joy that had rooted me to my spot. Timothy was there. And the play must go on. Tennessee Williams's tragic words flowed into another musical number.

The next two hours flew by. I wanted the play to last forever. I wanted to be on that stage, wanted to feel Laura's strangled emotions, wanted to convey her hopeless passion, forever and ever and ever.

But the finale came all too soon—the song, the dance, the cathartic liberation inside Laura's tortured mind. Before I'd fully absorbed the fact that the show was ending, I stepped forward for my bow during the curtain call. The entire cast was clapping behind me, breaking decorum to congratulate me for the job that I had done. The curtain came swooping down, and I was mobbed by my fellow performers. Ken joined the chaos, actually jumping up and down in his excitement. Everyone was quoting lines from the play, reciting stage directions, recounting every single second of the instant classic we had just performed.

"Erin!" Amy's voice cut through the clamor. I ran toward her, throwing my arms around her, laughing and crying as she told me how wonderful all of us had been.

Justin gave me a tight hug and said, "Aunt Erin, that was the best play I've ever seen." His eyes were huge as he made his pronouncement, and I didn't have the heart to point out that it was also the only play he'd ever seen.

Dr. Teel stepped forward, a grin lighting up his face, accenting his salt-and-pepper hair. It would have been the most natural thing in the world for me to let him hug me, to let him kiss me, to let him deliver another one of those soul-searing lip-locks that had confused me in the past.

I stepped back smoothly, though, settling a hand on his arm. To anyone else in the room, it would look like I was greeting a friend, a little overcome, perhaps, by the intensity of the acting experience I'd just completed. Only a flash in Teel's eyes let me know that he recognized something else, that he understood more about the gesture. He knew that I was making a statement. That I was declaring a path for myself.

I made myself laugh, and then I looked behind the three of them. "Where's Timothy?" I asked.

Amy's frown disappeared almost before it could place a divot between her eyebrows. "Timothy? We haven't seen him. Our bus was late getting to Port Authority. We only got to the theater about two minutes before the show started."

Two minutes. That must have been why the house manager gave my third ticket over to Teel. But I knew I'd seen Timothy at the back of the house. I was certain that he'd been there.

I glanced around, feeling helpless. I didn't have a chance to worry about Timothy for long, though. Actors swirled across the stage, crushing my family and Teel close. All of a sudden, someone announced that we were going to meet at the bar around the corner—everyone was going for a drink. Amy and Teel agreed to come along; Justin was excited at his chance to be with us grown-ups. I suspected that ninety-five percent of his enthusiasm stemmed from the fact that it was several hours after his bedtime. The other five percent grew out of anticipation for the inevitable maraschino cherry that would adorn his Roy Rogers drink.

I excused myself to wash my face, to change into street clothes. Every step I took toward the dressing room, I was stopped by another person associated with the show. Their giddiness was contagious—I was laughing like a starling by the time I grabbed my tote, by the time we all finally swarmed down the sidewalk.

Teel ordered a round of drinks for everyone. I saw him extract a billfold from the pocket of his impeccably tailored jacket. I suspected that the wallet was empty before he reached in, but he managed to manifest several large bills to underwrite his largesse.

I didn't waste time, though, worrying about the counterfeit nature of genie money. Instead, I raised a glass with my fellow actors. I laughed about our success. I toasted Ken, and the choreographer, and the ghost of Tennessee Williams.

And I almost convinced myself that I wasn't keeping an eye on the door, wasn't waiting, hoping, praying, that Timothy Brennan would come join in the celebration. He didn't, though. Not even after I phoned him again. Four times, before the night was through. Timothy Brennan was nowhere to be found.

Chapter 16

THE NEXT MORNING, I pulled myself out of bed just before sunrise, and I immediately fired up my computer. It took me about thirty seconds to scout out early reviews of the show. The big names—the *New York Times,* the *Washington Post*—they wouldn't get their notices up until the following week.

But there were plenty of other comments out there. My first stop was ShowTalk. I logged in automatically, just as I did every day, to check on gossip, to get ideas for new auditions. That morning, though, I was typing with my eyes closed. I was terrified to see what my fellow professionals had thought of *Menagerie!*

Fortifying myself with a deep breath, I forced myself to look at the computer screen. And there it was, in black-and-white, comment after comment after comment—they loved the show. They loved the show, they loved the concept, they loved the execution, and most of all, they loved *me.*

I caught a little shriek at the back of my throat. Obviously, I wasn't quiet enough, because Tabitha came galloping into the room to see what potential prey she had missed. I scooped her onto my lap and continued reading through the pages.

Several people mentioned that I'd been a last-minute fill-in, an understudy called up on the last possible day. A few folks said that they couldn't tell, that they'd never seen a blockbuster musical preview so strongly. One person, who was destined to become my best friend forever, said that I was the best thing onstage in New York the night before, in a straight play or a musical, on Broadway or off.

I blushed. And I kept on reading.

Other sites were complimentary, as well. The play had a way of reaching out and touching people, of raising up lifelong memories of being an outcast. Almost everyone who posted talked about a time when they'd been marginalized, when they'd been excluded from some group that had meant the world to them. People waxed eloquent about their own tangled family relationships, about challenges they'd faced with parents and siblings who just hadn't understood. They reminisced about their past loves, their failed romances.

Menagerie! was real. It worked. Even with Martina-inspired tweaks to dialog, *Menagerie!* grabbed its audience members, and refused to let them go. And I was part of the reason why.

I read until eight o'clock, until I could head out to Garden Variety, track Timothy down in person. I was worried about him, worried about how he had completely disappeared.

Once I had set aside the dreamy aftermath of Internet theatrical success, I barely had the patience to wait for the Bentley's elevator. Out on the street, people were stirring—the city was waking up for a hot summer Friday. I could already feel the heat rolling off the black asphalt of the street; it was going to be a scorcher before sunset.

Nevertheless, I walked toward Garden Variety as fast as I could, stopping just short of breaking into a run. I smiled when I got to the sign that pointed down the alley. It looked like an old friend, like a welcoming hand, beckoning me in the right direction.

The courtyard was quiet. Dusty. It felt empty, bare, and it took me a minute to realize that the outside tables were missing. Not pushed to the side. Not chained together to prevent theft. Missing.

As I moved closer, I saw a sign posted in the window. For Rent, it said, in stern letters. Restaurant Kitchen. A phone number shouted from the bottom of the placard.

I actually staggered backward.

I wanted to shake my head. I wanted to palm open the door, to pluck the sign from the window, argue that the restaurant couldn't be for rent—it was under lease to Timothy. But then I remembered the date.

August 1.

The days had flown by as I prepared for *Menagerie!*'s premiere. When had I last been here? Three weeks before? Timothy had been drowning in Amy's papers then, floundering in the business plan that she had drawn up just for him. I closed my eyes, recalling that conversation. He'd been tired. Frustrated.

But he'd had lots of ideas. Lots of possibilities. Lots of dreams. There'd been plenty of time for him to implement the new vision for his restaurant. Plenty of time for him to beat his landlord's ultimatum.

Even as I gibbered my protest, though, I corrected

myself. There *would have been* plenty of time. But Timothy had spent his days at the theater. He'd stuck around for our rehearsals. He'd brought us unparalleled food and drink, and then he'd hung out to watch the show. To watch me.

All of a sudden, I realized why he hadn't taken a seat in the audience the night before. He had lurked in the back of the house the way he had during rehearsal, day after day, so that he could hurry back to Garden Variety. The entire time that Teel was buying rounds after the show, the entire time that Amy and I were laughing, that Justin was curled up sleeping on the hard bench of a restaurant booth—Timothy had been here alone, working.

While we'd been singing show tunes, Timothy had been shutting down his restaurant, once and for all. He'd been burying his dream.

I flew across the courtyard and jiggled the doorknob, but it didn't give a millimeter. I pounded on the door, using the palm of my hand against the glass. "Timothy!" I shouted.

Of course he didn't answer. He wasn't inside. He didn't have any right to be inside anymore.

I put my face up against the window, cupping my hands around my eyes to cut out the glare behind me. All of the familiar tables were pushed against the walls, bare of their customary butcher paper. Chairs were stacked haphazardly. One had fallen to the ground, and it sprawled like a body in the middle of the room.

"Timothy!" I shouted again, knowing my cry was useless. I turned around and slumped against the door, sliding down until I was sitting on the flagstone step in front of the defunct restaurant.

For weeks, I'd been too focused on myself. I'd been too wrapped up in my own drama. I'd held the Master Plan between Timothy and me, manipulated it like a shield. I'd told myself not to think about him, not to dwell on anything he did, because I was all wrapped up in my miserable dating history, in my lousy track record with guys, in my stupid, selfish needs.

I didn't deserve Timothy.

As I stared at my knees, a glimmer of light caught my attention. For a second, I thought that it was the flash of an insect, an iridescent wing hovering at the edge of my sight. It wasn't, though.

My attention had been caught by my flame tattoo, by the feather light markings on my right forefinger and thumb.

I knew all the reasons why I should continue to keep a wish in abeyance. Justin was only five years old; there was no telling what danger he could get into. Derek was still overseas; who knew what horrors his military service might bring? Freeing Teel might bring back the demon child inside my nephew.

There were dozens of reasons to hold on to my fourth wish. But, suddenly, not one of them mattered.

I pressed my thumb and forefinger together and said, "Teel!"

The shimmer of light was immediate. The entire courtyard filled with jewels, with minute shards of ruby and silver, sapphire and gold. Without consciously thinking, I expected to see them coalesce into Dr. Teel. I wasn't disappointed.

"Erin," Teel said, almost before the thrumming energy had subsided. His baritone thrummed with vitality, with power. He glanced over my head, taking in the locked restaurant door, the sign in the window. "If Garden Variety's closed, there are plenty of other places to get breakfast. You don't need a genie to find a decent restaurant in this town."

"Ha, ha," I said.

He sauntered over to the step where I huddled disconsolately. He hitched up his trouser legs and slid down to take a seat beside me.

"So," he said. "Hunger isn't the diagnosis."

I grimaced at the medical word. "Not exactly."

"Let me guess, then." He held the back of his hand against my forehead, as if he were taking my temperature. He folded his lean fingers around my wrist, nodding as he pretended to count my pulse. When he tried to peer into my eyes, though, I squirmed away, sighing in exasperation. He merely shook his head, muttering, "Patient shows distinct dysphoria upon examination."

"I'm not your patient," I snapped. "And you're not a doctor."

He shrugged. "That hasn't really bothered you until now."

The words were heavily laden with suggestion. I blushed, immediately thinking of the narrow bed we'd shared in the hospital. Even now, I could feel the magic of his kiss, the purity of sensation that had coursed from my lips to my fingertips, to the very ends of my toes. Dr. Teel defined charisma. He emanated pure, unadulterated male power.

I caught myself leaning toward him. My breath stuttered in my throat as I thought about the fire of his lips against my own. I was swimming in pure temptation.

But Teel had used his magic to make himself alluring. He'd fashioned his guise of the doctor because he wanted to get his own way. He wanted entrance into the Garden, and he'd thought that he would get it sooner if he created a bond with me. An emotional attachment. An obligation.

And for far too long, I'd played along with his game. I'd fallen back on that idiotic Master Plan, told myself that whatever happened between Teel and me was outside the real world. Immaterial to my real life. To my real obligations.

Besides, it had been fun kissing him.

I swallowed hard, and when I looked at him again, whatever spell he'd been building between us was shattered. Sure, he was still gorgeous. Certainly, I could remember how his kisses had reached inside me, had turned me over, had seared me in ways no human man had ever done.

But that was it. He wasn't human—and he never would be. He didn't play by anyone's rules but his own. He didn't show up at my apartment, carrying eggs and cheese for a midnight omelet. He didn't sacrifice his own welfare for mine.

I sighed and asked, "Is Jaze still in the Garden?"

A bolt of energy shot through Teel. All of a sudden, he seemed to understand why I'd summoned him. What I was asking. He nodded an affirmative answer to my question, but he didn't speak. I hadn't realized that he could be overwhelmed by emotion, that he could be knocked speechless.

"Good," I said. I tested my next words inside my head. I needed to make them perfect. If I screwed up, I wouldn't have any chance to correct them, any chance to make them right. I'd have no more wishes in abeyance, no more options for straightening out the crazy chaos of my life.

I stared into Teel's astonishing blue eyes, and I said, "I wish that Garden Variety was a wildly successful restaurant, true to every one of Timothy's ideals and secure from any interference by his landlord."

"That's it?" Teel asked.

I wondered if I should add more. Should I force Timothy to include me in his vision of success? Should I make him love me, once he had all the professional satisfaction he'd ever dreamed of? Should I bind him to me, now and forever, before Teel disappeared for good?

I shook my head. Timothy had already proven himself to me. He'd already done what was right. Every step of the way, he'd been there with a steady goodwill, with a constant respect for my idiotic rules and restrictions. I realized that he'd believed in me, even when I'd been at my most insane. He'd trusted me to come to my senses. The least I could do was trust that he'd do the same.

"Yes," I said to Teel. "That's it."

He nodded and clambered to his feet. He held out a hand to me, and I felt like a medieval queen, being attended by a knight. "The lamp," he said, when I was standing in front of him. "If you pass it on while I'm in the Garden, the magic won't work."

"How long will you be there?"

"Measuring in your time? I can't say."

"But how will I know when you're out? When it's time to pass the lamp on to the next wisher?"

"If the brass is still polished, then I'm—" he interrupted himself, clearing his throat "—otherwise engaged. It will be tarnished when I'm available to grant wishes again."

"Fine," I said. I could picture the brass lamp, nestled in the box that Becca had given me so many months before. I had no idea what I was going to do with it, whom I would give it to. I suspected that, by the time I made up my mind, Teel and Jaze would both be back in the world at large.

Teel took a step back. He raised his hand to his ear.

"Wait!" I said. "Thank you. Thank you for everything you did. For me. For Amy."

"You're welcome," he said. His reply was serious, solemn even, but a jangling sense of urgency grew beneath his words. Teel's entire being yearned for the Garden, for the freedom he'd been so long denied.

Still, I couldn't let him go without finishing what I wanted—what I *needed*—to say. "Especially, thank you for Justin. He needed you more than any of us did."

"He's a good boy." Teel shrugged, as if he'd had nothing to do with Justin's behavioral turnaround. "He'll remember what we shared. He'll be strong until his father comes home."

Somehow, when I heard Teel say it, I believed him. "Well," I said, strangely reluctant to let him go. "Thank you. And good luck. I hope the Garden is everything you dream it will be."

For answer, Teel returned his hand to his ear. "As you wish," he said, and then he tugged twice.

The electric shock was stronger than I expected. I felt the jolt in the marrow of my bones. It shot through my heart, fired through my fingertips. I closed my eyes involuntarily, screening out the light, the noise, the sudden flaring power of Teel granting my last wish.

And when I opened my eyes, everything had changed.

Chapter 17

THE COURTYARD HAD turned into a movie set.

Folding canvas chairs were scattered in a loose semicircle on the flagstones. Metal stands held bright lights, and white umbrellas reflected the brilliance onto Garden Variety's front door. A half dozen people swarmed the flagstones; all of them wore headsets with rectangular electronics packages clipped to their belts.

I glanced at the restaurant window. The for-rent sign was gone, erased as if it had never existed.

Someone was calling for a sound check. Another person was ordering the lighting instruments to a different corner of the courtyard. Staff scrambled around like pieces of glass in a high-end kaleidoscope, falling in and out of endless patterns. No one seemed to notice me; I felt as if I were invisible.

I edged up to the restaurant door. When no one hollered at me to keep my distance, I tested the knob. It turned immediately; someone had unlocked the restaurant. I slipped in before anyone could order me not to.

The inside of Garden Variety was an island of calm after all the chaos in the courtyard. The tables were arrayed for dinner; each was covered with a sheet of butcher paper. Someone had taken care with the random dishes and pieces of silverware; absolutely nothing matched at any table, and yet the overall look was perfectly balanced, flawlessly ordered. Fresh flowers sat on each table—sprigs of lavender, I noted with a sudden breathless grab of my heart.

A headset-bound technician hurried past me, rushing from the kitchen out to the courtyard. She frowned at me as she jogged by, and I braced myself for her to challenge my presence. Instead, she pulled her mouthpiece closer to her lips and enunciated, "They'll be ready in fifteen minutes, tops." I leaped out of the way, lest I impede her passage. She pulled the door closed behind her with enough force that it slammed.

I realized that the woman's twin remained in the dining room. She was circling the tables, one by one, tweaking the already-perfect place settings. She swapped out one knife for another. She polished a water glass against a linen towel. She turned one spray of flowers slightly to the right, another to the left.

I was mesmerized as I watched her. Her job was clearly to create the illusion of perfection. And I could see that she was very, very good at her job.

In the eerie stillness, I could make out sounds from the kitchen. Timothy's voice flowed from the back room like maple syrup over waffles—smooth and even, despite an underlying sense of disruption. I glanced through the window in the galley door, and I could see two people, strangers, huddling by the stainless-steel center island, the same horizontal surface that I had last seen snowed under with the pages of Amy's unsuccessful business plan.

As I turned my head to catch a better angle, I realized that I knew both of the people in the kitchen. There was Lena, the homeless woman who had occupied the two-top on my very first visit to Garden Variety. She had pulled her hair back into a ragged ponytail; her face looked round and vulnerable. Her fingers plucked at the black apron that she wore over a plain white T-shirt and ragged jeans.

Having recognized Lena, it took me less time to identify Peter, the man who had sent Sam running from Garden Variety. He had shaved his scraggly beard—only that morning, by the bright pink rawness of his cheeks. He, too, sported a black apron.

Both Lena and Peter held large knives, the sort favored by Iron Chefs and serial killers. As I shuffled forward a half step, Timothy came into view. He held a matching knife. His fingers, though, were comfortable on the handle; he looked as if he'd been born with a blade in his grasp. I watched as he took a carrot out of a mesh shopping bag. He trimmed the ends with two clean chops, then reduced the vegetable to a perfect pile of orange coins. He narrated his action as he cut, as he changed angles, as he folded the fingers of his non-cutting hand, guiding the blade with his knuckles. Even with his steady patter, I was astonished by how quickly he worked.

"There," he said. "Now, you try it." He handed a carrot to each of his students. Not surprisingly, they moved more slowly than he had, and their resulting piles of carrot coins were far from the uniform jewels that Timothy had created. Nevertheless, he said, "Excellent! You've both come so far in the past few weeks! Now, take a few more. Practice. Think of this as a warm-up exercise for when the camera crew comes in."

A warm-up. Just like the exercises I completed at the theater before I went onstage. I must have made some sound at the familiar expression, some noise that made Timothy look up. The smile that bloomed across his face shook me to my toes. "Erin!"

He set down his knife, automatically taking care that the blade was safely settled on the countertop. He shoved the mesh bag of carrots toward Lena and Peter and hurried around the table. "And here we are! A Broadway star in our midst!"

I blushed. "I wouldn't say that, exactly."

"Isn't that what ShowTalk is saying?"

"How do you know about ShowTalk?" The site was private; only theater people joined up.

"Dani told me about it, when I stopped by for the carrots first thing this morning." He nodded toward the stainless-steel table. "She said something about using her son's access. She wanted to check up on you, to know if she was living across the hall from a celebrity."

Her son. That was Ryan, of course, the playwright who had gone to Africa with Becca months ago. Their trip had cleared the way for me to move into the Bentley. To get Teel's lamp.

I gestured toward Lena and Peter. "What is all this? Who are all those people in the courtyard?"

"It's *New York Eats*. The cable show. Don't you remember? They're featuring Garden Variety next month." I must have still looked confused, because Timothy stepped a little closer to me. "We're the focus of their 'Green Dining' month, because of the way we work with Dani and the Gray Guerillas? Because of the career mentoring, with Lena and Peter?"

I wanted to ask him when all of this had happened. I wanted to pin him down on specifics, to find out precisely when he'd been contacted by the producers. I wanted to know how far back Teel's magic had reached, how many memories my genie had manipulated to make Timothy's dream a reality.

And yet, I said nothing. There was no reason to question Timothy. No reason to test the strength of my genie's magic on real, human memory.

"Of course," I said. My voice was a little weaker than I wanted it to be. My words were simply washed out by surprise, by astonishment at how well Teel had done his job.

"Are you okay?" Before I could answer, Timothy glanced over his shoulder at Lena and Peter. "You guys are doing great! When you finish with those, why don't you get started on making the vinaigrette for the salad—the same recipe that we worked out last week. I'll be back in a minute."

As Peter nodded and Lena set down her chef's knife, Timothy edged his fingers under my arm. He guided me into the dining room, back to the corner where I'd sat with Amy and Teel, with Shawn and Justin, six weeks before. A lifetime before. It seemed like centuries since we'd gathered in the restaurant. So many things had changed in my life. In my life, and apparently in Timothy's, as well.

"Hey," he called to the black-clad technician, the woman who seemed to be taking yet another round to make sure that the tables were perfect from each and every possible angle. "Could we have a minute here?"

"Of course, Mr. Brennan," she said, but I heard her mutter something into her microphone as she slipped outside.

Timothy barely waited for the door to close behind her. "I'm sorry," he said to me. He reached toward my face, snagged a lock of hair that had slipped from behind my ear. He curled it around his fingers, and I could feel the tiny hairs between his knuckles as they brushed against my cheek. "I'm sorry that I couldn't be there after the show last night. They had me up until three in the morning, going over the menu for the shoot, working out who would wait tables, how we'd highlight Lena's story, and Peter's."

"It's okay," I said. I barely trusted my voice, though. I was remembering my devastation that very morning, when I'd stood in the deserted courtyard. I could still feel the resounding shock as I registered the date, as I realized that Timothy was lost to me, that Garden Variety had been destroyed.

Keeping that gaping loss in mind, it certainly felt petty to be upset that Timothy hadn't stuck around after the show. Especially since it seemed like he was prepping to be a major media star.

"No," he said, interrupting my thoughts. "It isn't okay. I know how much last night meant to you." His fingers moved from the single lock of hair to the back of my head. I could feel the warmth of his palm radiating through me, his calm power steadying me as he snared my gaze. "I knew that you could do it. I knew that you could play the part. But I should have been there to celebrate, all the same."

He *had* known it. He'd been certain, even when I'd been unsure. He'd been confident, even when I'd been a wreck.

"Timothy," I said, and there were so many things I

wanted to follow up with. Thank you for bringing me dinner. Thank you for running lines with me. Thank you for leaving me tea and breakfast, lavender, salt scrub. Thank you for waiting for me, when I'd spent the past two months finding ridiculous, immature ways to delay, to keep us apart, to drive you away forever.

I felt the balance between us, the quiet promise in his fingertips. I felt the power, the energy, the *strength,* that had drawn me to him every single day since I'd first crossed the threshold of Garden Variety.

Every single time that he'd moved toward me, I'd backed away. Every single time that he had offered something of himself—raspberries, hot meals, a fireworks display fit for the gods—I'd edged myself into a defensive corner. I'd left him dangling, left him vulnerable, ignored the potential, the possibility, the *rightness,* of life with him.

I'd told myself—I'd told *him*—that I was bound by the tenets of my Master Plan. But I'd been lying to both of us. I'd used the Plan because I was a coward. I'd used the Plan to keep from feeling emotion, from accepting the reckless, falling sensation of being committed. Of being in love.

"Timothy," I sighed again, and I closed the distance between us.

This kiss started as a gentle expression of friendship. After all, Timothy was the man who had restrained himself before, who had pulled back, acknowledging my boundaries, my rules and restrictions.

But then I tangled my fingers in his unruly curls. I pulled him closer to me. I opened my lips; I told him with the perfect absence of words that I was ready.

And he awakened, like a panther stirring to the hunt. His lips hardened against mine. He was driven, driving. His fingers arched into claws, pulling me closer, gathering me into the rock-hard lines of his body.

This kiss was completely different from the others. This kiss stripped away the boundaries between us. This kiss sparked from my lips to my belly; it weakened my knees until I was clutching at Timothy's shoulders, trembling against him, scarcely managing to keep my balance. We laughed as we kissed, and he said my name, murmuring it as he explored the pulse point in my throat.

"I'm so sorry," I whispered, regretting all the time that I'd kept us from getting together, all the steps I'd taken to drive him away.

He stopped the words before they fully formed, his fingers orchestrating a distraction against my spine, along the waistband of my pants. I tried again, but he growled me to silence.

I don't know how long we stood there, how much time passed as we explored all the things we could have said, should have said, in the preceding months. Both of us were startled, though, when the restaurant door crashed open. A wave of summer heat rolled in, shocking in its intensity. A gaunt man loomed in the doorway, glancing around as if he were the lord of the manor. Two assistants hovered behind him, jostling smartphones as they spoke into their headsets.

I knew a director when I saw one. After all, I was a trained theater professional.

Timothy sighed and loosened his grip on my hips. He leaned his forehead in to touch mine. Both of us worked to slow our breathing, to offer up some semblance of mature, sober normalcy. He caught my hand and interlaced my fingers with his own, before he raised my wrist to brush his lips across the heartbeat that pounded there.

"I've got to go," he whispered.

"I know."

"Come by later. After the show tonight? I'll make you dinner." His eyes promised a lot more than food.

"I'll be here," I said.

I could still feel his gaze searing my back as I edged past the director and headed out to the real world. With rehearsals over, with Teel gone, with everything perfect in my world, it was time to return to real life. It was time to go to the grocery store, to pay some bills, to catch up on a hundred and one ordinary duties that I'd completely overlooked in the panic of rehearsals.

I couldn't wait.

* * *

The show ran perfectly that night. I missed having special people in the audience, but that was going to be part of my life for a long time to come. I was able to concentrate on the energy that built with my fellow actors, on the magical theatrical spirit that we poured into one another.

Afterward, we all chatted companionably in the dressing room. We sponged off makeup. We changed into street clothes.

I thought about calling Amy as I walked toward home. We'd left messages for each other earlier in the day; there was nothing major for us to talk about, but I was accustomed to hearing her voice. It was late, though, almost midnight. I didn't want to take a chance on waking Justin.

As I turned into the alley that led back to Garden Variety, my heart started to beat faster. My fingertips grew numb with a sense of anticipation, and I resisted the urge to run my hands through my hair, to smooth down my blouse, to fiddle and fidget and fuss.

I paused in the ivy-covered passage, just before the courtyard came into view. I took a deep breath, held it for a moment, telling myself that I was being silly, acting like a schoolgirl, letting my anticipation run wild. I exhaled slowly, counting to ten.

And the world around me disappeared.

"Teel!" I screeched, throwing all semblance of calm to the winds. If there had been winds at the Garden. Which I was pretty sure there weren't. At least, I'd never sensed them there before, in that great, aching hole of nothingness. I glared down at the gray fog beneath my feet, the featureless blank that made me sway with sudden vertigo. I whirled to face my genie, furious that he still had this power over me, now, when I had made my fourth wish, when I had set him free.

I could see the Garden.

It was spread out before me, perfect and vivid and brilliant behind its ornate wrought-iron bars. A blue sky stretched into infinity, so painfully clear that my eyes vibrated with the brightness. Lush emerald grass came up to the very edge of the fence. I could make out each individual blade, impossibly detailed, as if the scene in front of me had been captured on a high-definition television with an infinitely large screen.

I staggered forward and caught myself against the iron bars of the fence. They were solid, warm to the touch, heated by the sun that was directly overhead. I pushed my face against the metal, breathing deeply, filling my lungs with the aroma of fresh-mown grass, of lilacs, of honeysuckle.

Birds warbled from a nearby tree, songbirds that I didn't recognize, that I didn't think we even had in New York. If I concentrated, I could hear the breeze whispering through the shrubs around me. A brook laughed somewhere to my right. I closed my eyes, the better to concentrate on sound.

"I thought you'd want to see everything here, but I was obviously mistaken."

The voice—a woman's—was new to me. I blinked hard to make her come into focus; she seemed to glow with the power of the Garden around her. She was tall, almost six feet, and lean. Her chestnut hair fell in soft waves almost to her waist. She wore a chain of purple clover like a crown, and a necklace of the same flowers dipped between her breasts.

I realized that she was naked, and I should have been surprised, but her bare flesh seemed appropriate, perfect, the only way that anyone should ever be, in the Garden. Her right wrist was covered in tattooed flames—the gold and red and orange leaping around each other with a vitality I'd never seen in any other genie guise. The tattoo wasn't any ordinary ink; it flowed, moved, changed with the woman's every heartbeat. My eyes were drawn to it, and my own fingers reached through the fence, desperate to touch the fire.

"Teel?" I whispered.

"Of course," she said, and her laughter freed me to look at her face once again.

"Is Jaze here?"

She pursed her lips into a perfect pout. "He's feeling shy."

As well he might, if he was as naked as Teel. I wasn't going to argue the point, in any case. Instead, I asked, "How am I seeing this? How am I seeing *you?* I thought that all the magic was over."

Teel shrugged, making the action a ballet of nonchalance. "I decided to grant you a wish."

"I didn't ask to be here."

Another little pout. "I figured that you *would* ask, though. If you knew you could." She stepped closer to the fence, bent her head toward me and whispered conspiratorially, "Besides, I had to let you see what you made possible." She laughed, as if the glory of the garden were more than she could process, more than she could believe, herself. "And I'll tell you something else," she whispered. "Something I didn't know until I got here. Until Jaze told me."

"What?" I asked, lowering my voice to match hers.

"We can grant unlimited wishes from inside the Garden."

"What?" I asked again. Her words didn't make sense. I couldn't process them, couldn't understand what Teel was telling me. My mind felt fuzzy, snagged by her dancing tattoo, overwhelmed by the scents and sounds and sights of the Garden around her.

"We genies can grant unlimited wishes from the Garden. No contract. No obligation. Whatever we want to do, helping whoever we want to help."

"But why would you do that?" I asked, utterly confused. "Isn't that like going on vacation, and then phoning in to the office?"

"That's just it. I don't have an office. I don't have an obligation, to anyone. But if I *want* to do anything, I can. Just for the sake of doing it."

I nodded. It had to be like Timothy, choosing to cook dinner for me, when he didn't have to. "So you wished me here?"

Teel smiled, and the curve of her lips lit up her entire face. She looked like a complacent harvest goddess, beaming with power. "I wished you here, so that I could see the expression on your face. I wished you here so that I could know what you'd say when I work my other wish."

"Your other wish?" I felt like I was being stupid. It seemed like Teel was infinitely older than I was, endlessly wiser. I imagined that I'd felt this way when I was a child, when my parents spelled words over my head to keep me from understanding whatever secrets they shared with each other.

Teel closed her eyes and took a deep breath through her perfect nose, exhaling through her flawless lips. She raised her fingers to her shell of an ear, once again snaring my attention with the endless wrap of flame around flame. She intoned, "I wish that Derek Carlson was home, safe and unharmed, from his duty overseas."

"Teel!" I shouted her name, awash in disbelief. I had never dared to make that wish. I wasn't sure that it would be a good one, that Derek would be happy at home. Sure, he loved Amy and Justin, that was never in doubt. But he was also proud of his career as a soldier, proud of his service to the country.

Teel merely smiled at me as if she were certain that Derek wanted to come home. And because she was so certain, I was, too. It couldn't be any other way. There couldn't be any other truth. Teel raised her fingers to her ear and tugged twice at the lobe.

I braced myself for the shock of electricity, for the

jangle that I expected to shake me from crown to toe. There was nothing, though. No sharp jolt. No lingering hum. "It didn't work," I said, and I was astonished to hear my voice shaking. I was on the verge of tears. How could I be so upset about losing something I hadn't known I could have, just one minute before?

"Of course it worked." Teel laughed. "You didn't feel anything, because it wasn't your wish. It was mine."

"Why?" I asked.

"Because I wanted to," she said simply. "Because I like Justin. I liked the time I spent with him. He's trying so hard to be good, which is more than I can say for most of you humans." She shrugged her impossibly delicate shoulders. "I made the wish because I wanted to," she repeated firmly.

"Thank you," I said. I could barely imagine how Derek's return would change things. Amy would be happy again—her old self, her strong self. She wouldn't judge her worth entirely by how she did in her classes. She might even drop some of her business school jargon. Justin would be happy, too. He'd follow through on the changes he'd begun under Teel's tutelage. He'd continue growing up, a good, healthy boy. And Derek... Well, I had to trust Teel. Everything else had worked out perfectly.

An owl hooted from behind a nearby bush. Teel rolled her eyes and laughed. "That's Jaze. She thinks she's being subtle. She thinks that you won't notice an owl during daytime. Jaze, dear!" she called. "I'll only be a minute more."

She. Jaze had been a "he" when I arrived. I'd never get used to genies' glib exchange of gender.

I wouldn't have an opportunity to try, anymore. I met Teel's eyes. "You shouldn't keep her waiting. Don't waste your time in the Garden."

Teel laughed, and the sound cascaded toward me like tiny silver bells caught in a breeze. "Thank you, Erin."

"For what?"

"For making your fourth wish. For freeing me. For letting me come here. I know you were reluctant. I know you were afraid."

All of that seemed so long ago. I shook my head. "No," I said. "Thank *you.*"

The owl hooted again, a little more impatiently. Teel glanced at the honeysuckle-shrouded bush before she raised her fingers to her ear. "Ready?" she asked.

"Ready," I confirmed.

She tugged twice. My eyes were swept closed. My chest was compressed with the enormous power of nothingness. I stumbled, missing the invisible floor, and then I opened my eyes to find myself back in the alley. The muggy heat of a summer night pressed down on me. I tapped my foot against the ground, reassuring myself that I was in New York, in the real world. The human world. *My* world.

My phone rang, deep in my tote bag. I recognized the ring tone—Amy. I didn't need to answer, though. I already knew what she was going to say. I knew that she'd just received word—from someone, from the base commander, from Derek himself—that her husband was heading home to New Brunswick. There'd be time enough for us to rejoice together, tomorrow.

I squared my shoulders and turned the corner into the Garden Variety courtyard. The canvas chairs had disappeared, along with the lighting instruments and all the scurrying technicians. The restaurant's four iron tables melted into the shadows. The light inside Garden Variety was dimmed, barely splashing onto the flagstones. I thought back to the first time I had visited. Then, as now, I felt as if I'd stepped into a fairy tale, a place as magical as Teel's Garden.

"It's warm for eating outside, isn't it?"

I realized that I'd been expecting Timothy to speak from the shadows. He'd startled me the first time I'd ever found the restaurant, but now I knew what to expect. He was robed in deep shadow beside the green-painted door. He stepped forward, utterly familiar in his dark jeans, his dark work shirt, his casually tied apron. I smiled at his unruly hair, at the waves that still refused to submit to any comb. I fought the urge to rub my fingertips across the rough stubble of his beard.

His hand was curled around a stoneware mug, and I caught a whiff of Earl Grey—the same hint of bergamot that he'd left for me the morning of my debut. Was it only the day before? He shrugged. "Sorry. I didn't mean to startle you."

He'd said that to me before, the first night that I'd come to Garden Variety. "No," I said. "You didn't." I felt like I was reading from a script. I strayed from the lines, though, when I closed the distance between us, when I clutched at his shirt, pulling him close, trying to melt his entire body into mine.

He buried his face in my hair, breathing deeply. "Hmm," he purred. "Honeysuckle."

I clutched him closer, relishing the feel of his palms against my back, the grip of his fingers on my hips. "It's late," he finally whispered, when we both came up for air. "You must be starving."

I smiled in the darkness and nodded toward the door. "I hope you have something to eat in there."

"As you wish," he said. I laughed as he drew back enough to usher me inside. Timothy would never know why those words were so funny. But that was all right. He didn't need to know. Teel was gone from my life forever.

Timothy locked the door behind us. "I think I might be able to come up with something for you," he said. As he took my hand and led me into the kitchen, I thought to myself, *One.*

From here on out, I was counting the good things that happened. And I was willing to bet there would be a lot more than three.

ACKNOWLEDGMENTS

No book appears out of a vacuum, and this one is no exception. I am deeply indebted to New York actress Kate Konigisor for sharing information about her never-boring career, particularly for walking me through the audition process that poor Erin must endure. Also, I thank Linda Lindsey, for her insight and advice regarding United States military spouses. Any inaccuracies about the real worlds of theater and the military are solely my responsibility.

My first reader, Bruce Sundrud, provided invaluable notes on this volume of the As You Wish series, meshing his review schedule to my writing calendar. My critique partner, Nancy Yeager, brought sharp eyes to later stages of the manuscript, finding flaws I didn't even suspect were there.

As always, I am grateful for the shrewd guidance of my agent, Richard Curtis, who remains a source of strength and stability in the crazed writing world. The folks at Harlequin/MIRA have outdone themselves in the creation of this book—my editor, Mary-Theresa Hussey, stands at the helm, with the always-able support of her assistant, Elizabeth Mazer, and the literally dozens of people who keep things moving smoothly behind the scenes.

My family remains my bedrock during the frequent tempests of writing. Many thanks to all of the Klaskys, Fallons, Maddreys, and Timminses, but a special, by-definition-inadequate thank-you to my husband, Mark, who always has to put up with everything, without even a single wish to help him out.

Most of all, though, I thank you, the reader of this

book. I look forward to corresponding with you through my website at www.mindyklasky.com.

ABOUT THE AUTHOR

MINDY KLASKY LEARNED to read when her parents shoved a book in her hands and told her that she could travel anywhere in the world through stories. She never forgot that advice.

Mindy's travels took her through multiple careers. After graduating from Princeton University, Mindy considered becoming a professional stage manager or a rabbi. Ultimately, though, she settled on being a lawyer, working as a litigator at a large Washington firm. When she realized that lawyering kept her from writing (and dating and sleeping and otherwise living a normal life), Mindy became a librarian, managing large law firm libraries. Mindy now writes full time.

For years, Mindy's dating life was a travel extravaganza as well. She balanced twenty-eight first dates in one year, selecting eligible gentlemen from sources as varied as Washingtonian magazine ads, Single Volunteers of D.C., and supposedly-certain recommendations from best friends. Ultimately, she swore off the dating scene entirely. After two years of carefully-enforced datelessness, she made one last foray onto Match.com, where she met her husband—on her first match.

Mindy's travels have also taken her through various literary genres. In addition to her Harlequin Special Editions, Mira, and Red Dress Ink books, Mindy has written six traditional fantasy novels for Roc (including the award-winning, best-selling The Glasswrights' Apprentice), short stories, and nonfiction essays.

In her spare time, Mindy quilts, knits, and tries to tame her endless to-be-read shelf. Her husband and cats do their best to fill the leftover minutes.

ABOUT BOOK VIEW CAFÉ

BOOK VIEW CAFÉ is a professional authors' publishing cooperative offering DRM-free ebooks in multiple formats to readers around the world. With authors in a variety of genres including fantasy, romance, mystery, and science fiction, Book View Café has something for everyone.

Book View Café is good for readers because you can enjoy high-quality DRM-free ebooks from your favorite authors at reasonable prices.

Book View Café is good for writers because 95% of the profits goes directly to the book's author.

Book View Café authors include New York Times and USA Today bestsellers; Nebula, Hugo, and Philip K. Dick Award winners; World Fantasy and Rita Award nominees; and winners and nominees of many other publishing awards.

www.bookviewcafe.com

Book View Café

18471623R00221

Printed in Great Britain
by Amazon